Aloha!

The Towers of Sand

Susan Weber Cyr

Susan Weber Cyr

PUBLISH AMERICA

PublishAmerica
Baltimore

ISBN: 1-60703-046-2
PUBLISHED BY PUBLISHAMERICA, LLLP
www.publishamerica.com
Baltimore

Printed in the United States of America

Acknowledgments

I am grateful for the assistance and support of so many people in the development of this book. The flying sequences were developed with significant input from Wesley Gibson. He and his wife Andy patiently pored over the manuscript poolside with us on a windy Maui afternoon. (Writing is hard work.) I still remember, "who has page 64?" followed by, "there it goes—it's blowing into the pool!"

Thanks also go to Helen Coleman and John Priestley who reviewed the early drafts and provided suggestions and corrections. Because of their input, I know I have a better book.

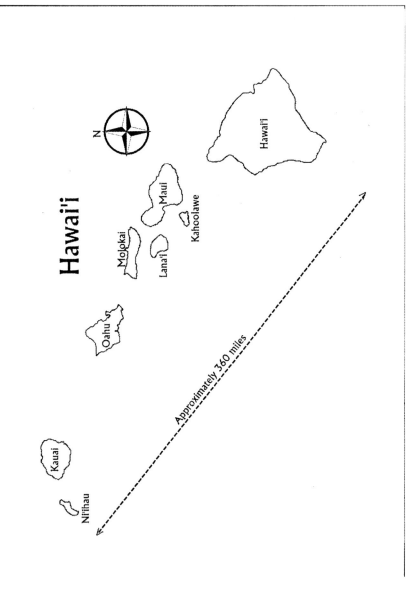

Hawai'i

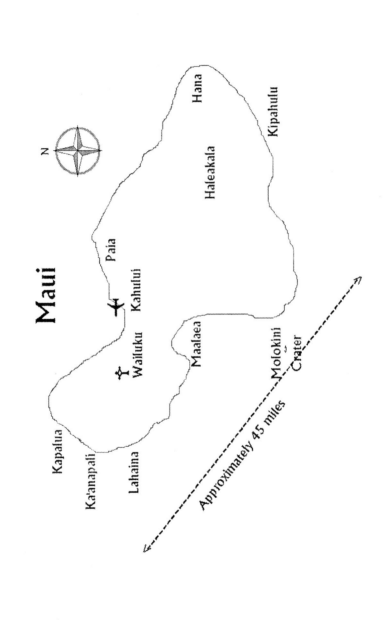

Maui

N

Kapalua
Ka'anapali
Lahaina
Kahului
Paia
Wailuku
Maalaea
Haleakala
Hana
Kipahulu
Molokini
Crater

Approximately 45 miles

Prologue

Stupid dream. Wake up. Don't open your eyes, go back to bed, go back to sleep. Dream about something else. Fishing. Dream about fishing.

Why can't this be a dream? Legs are lead, can't reach the place—where am I going anyway? Keep moving, can't get there. Can't see where I am. Familiar, distorted. Unconscious? Are my eyes open or closed? Pain…am I in pain or dreaming about being in pain? There's that smell; I recognize the smell. Can you smell things in a dream? I'm thirsty… I think.

Alone. Never sleep alone. Malia…wife…can't reach her. Someone's coming… Malia? Tell me this is a dream. Let's get back sleeping like spoons.

"Hey, HoHo, you don't look so good. Sorry about the accommodations, but it's gotta be this way. The Sheraton is full. Ha! I brought you some water. I should probably just pour it over you…you really need a bath, HoHo."

Know him, how? Doesn't belong here.

"I'm just gonna drop a line to your wife here, just so she thinks things are—you know—cool." A chair squeaked as the man sat down at the desk. The sound of fingers tapping at the keyboard…*my computer. Office. I'm in my office.* He absently started typing on his thigh.

"M a l i a i i a…w a t t e r…"

"Camping on Haleakala…that should keep her from wondering about you for a couple of days, hey HoHo?"

Is that where I am…camping? I don't remember this campground. I don't remember being in pain camping.

"Don't worry… I brought you lunch." The man got up from the desk and rustled about in a bag of some sort. *Am I hungry? I think so. Burger? Malia doesn't like me to have burgers. Don't tell her, OK?* "Here you go, HoHo. Sweet dreams!"

The needle's sting was startling, but only briefly until the dreamlike state resumed.

The man picked up the duffle bag and left, closing the office door behind him.

Wednesday, July 1

No wonder brides turn into monsters.

Sarah Jude Donovan was irritated with the seamstress. The woman had accidentally stuck her with pins one too many times. *She's used to working on mannequins that don't bleed or scream out in pain.* Yes, she had apologized, but "Oops, sorry about that" was getting old. Sarah steeled herself and vowed that she would neither gain nor lose any weight before the wedding that would require a refitting and alteration. *One torture session is enough. This woman doesn't realize what I'm capable of doing when I'm in pain.*

Making the final quarter turn back around in front of the full-length mirror, Sarah's irritation dissolved when she caught her reflection. She resisted the urge to swirl around to experience the rustling sound and the way the fabric seemed to dance in the sunlight, but she willed herself to be patient lest her movement coax any of the pins loose from their precarious moorings. From what she could tell, it was going to be perfect. A wedding in the tropics called for a simple design, without heavy layers of satin and netting that, along with the bride, would wilt in the moist climate. A shimmering ivory silk with sprigs of ivory flowers embroidered in an all-over pattern suited the climate and Sarah. Tiny gathers at the back let the fabric glide over her hips and fall into a gentle A-line. Tucks in the front just under the bodice softened the fitted style. Seed pearls on the spaghetti straps and along the scoop neckline completed the simple elegance of Sarah's wedding gown. The short veil complemented the dress with lengths of pearls and the palest of pink ribbons adorning it. She planned on wearing her light brown hair drawn up in loose curls; the natural curl would fall in waves down her back, with an upsweep held with ribbons of seed pearls. She might as well go with a style that let her naturally wavy light brown hair cascade as it wanted; it would end up doing it anyway. Her bouquet would repeat the pearl and ribbon theme with a loose cascade of pale pink roses. She had just the slightest regret that the sun had freckled her a bit more than she liked, but Dan assured her that he loved everyone one. She blushed at the remembrance of a whimsical afternoon they spent attempting to count them.

She admitted to herself that while the dress was not the most important thing about getting married, it was one of the fun parts. *I want a dress that suits me, not the other way around. I'm the one getting married, not the dress!* She closed her eyes imagining Dan standing next to her in his ivory shirt and slacks while they both promised to stand by one another for the rest of their lives. In their hearts they had already made the commitment; the wedding would be the public affirmation, a blessing and a celebration of their partnership with family and friends. She admonished herself not to be the stereotypical jittery bride. The marriage was the priority, not the thirty minute ceremony. *Let's maintain a little perspective here, girl. There's no reason to be demanding or bitchy; you are not the queen.* She paused in her thoughts before musing impishly, *maybe I am,* thinking about the Queen of Hearts pendant Dan had given her almost a year ago. *After the wedding I can have the dress dyed red. Then all I'll need is a crown.* She absently started to wave her hand in greeting to her royal subjects, but jerked her hand back down at her side when reality crashed in. Her lone "subject" was staring blankly at her from the floor below. Sarah blushed in embarrassment, but figured the seamstress was accustomed to bridal neuroses and fantasies.

As the seamstress completed a 360° inspection of her tailor's markings, Sarah felt the blood rush to her head and her temper about to explode when she observed a red spot near the hem. *Blood, from where she pricked me!* Just then the seamstress noticed the same thing and picked off the fuzz that had migrated there from the carpet. Sarah relaxed and again disciplined herself to maintain her cool. *OK, I won't scream,* "Off with her head!"

The fitting complete, Sarah gingerly slipped off the gown, ever mindful of the sharp edges that still had the potential to inflict pain and draw blood. She hoped it wasn't a metaphor or omen of things to come. *You're not being just the queen, but a* drama *queen.* She changed back into her capris and sandals, repacking the low white heels into their box, making a mental note to wear them for a few minutes every day to break them in.

Her cell phone rang, and she was relieved to hear her sister's voice. Diane laughed at Sarah's recap of the dress fitting debacle, which only served to bring Sarah back to the brink of her temper. "It's *not* funny. You don't know how close I was to getting married in a red polka-dotted gown!"

"Sorry, Sar."

Sarah could sense that Diane was having difficulty staying serious and sympathizing with what she had just endured. "I can tell you really feel for me."

"Remind me after the wedding to tell you how silly you are."

"I want to be there when she does *your* fitting."

"I was about to head over there to get my old maid's dress fitted. Wanna meet me for lunch before?"

"I'm not hungry."

"Have you eaten anything today?"

"I don't remember. Probably not."

"That explains it."

"That explains *what*?"

"You're like Jekyll—or is it Hyde—I forget which one, when you haven't eaten. Obviously Dan hasn't seen you that way, which is probably best."

"I love it when you get all literary on me. It's Hyde. Anyway, Dan makes me hungry, but I'll spare you the details. Let's meet over at Sugar Daddy's in about fifteen…? "

"Good choice. My treat, as old maid of honor to the bride. But, you start bitching, you buy."

"Ever the gracious hostess. Since you're treating, I *am* hungry." Diane had Sarah laughing again, and she looked forward to meeting her.

On the drive over to meet her sister, Sarah turned off the radio and let memories of the past year drift into her consciousness, the silence broken only by the white noise of muffled traffic sounds and the air conditioner.

A St. Louis native, Sarah met Dan Weatherby, her soon-to-be life partner on a Mississippi River cruise with her sister last summer. Dan was a pediatrician in Chicago who had joined the cruise with colleagues after enduring a medical conference in St. Louis. Throughout the fall the direction the relationship was taking became obvious to both her and Dan, and they became engaged at Christmas. A terrible misunderstanding exacerbated by a devious *femme fatale* acquaintance of Dan's conspired to destroy the relationship. And just when the emotional injury exploded in Sarah's face, a knee injury put her out of work from her job as a math teacher. Upon recovery, she made an escape as far away from Dan as possible. Maui. Five time zones, four thousand miles from her home in St. Louis. *It was decades ago…another life.*

A new teaching job, a new home, new friends, the potential of a new relationship with Gabe Callahan—all these were beginning to help Sarah heal, on the outside at least. Deep down, the wounds still refused to close. It took a family—a new one—that came to her rescue, and who in turn were rescued themselves. With their support and with the support she gave them, she found confidence, independence, and a realization of what mattered. And what was the truth. Her self-discovery was not without tragedy, and she knew she had played some part in causing the death of another person, however inadvertent it was. But her actions probably saved the lives of others as well. Her practical mathematical mind said it was better to lose one life than four. The emotional side told her it was still a high price. *A little of me died that day, too. My innocence, the pride of thinking that I could always be in control, and perhaps a few other deadly sins… Thanks for the lesson in humility, God. Was it worth it? And oh, I'd really like it if I didn't have to kill anyone else before the wedding, OK?*

It was her sister Diane that had been the catalyst in bringing Sarah and Dan back together. And in doing so, Diane herself embarked on a new relationship with Gabe. Diane imagined the whole story as a Rodgers and Hammerstein musical, with songs like, "Maybe he loved you first, but he loves me best," and "When I come up for air." Times were happy again, just like the happily-ever-after part in such stories.

I'm the luckiest girl in the world, but I'm still learning about trusting someone else, and trusting myself while I'm at it.

Sarah pulled into the parking lot at Sugar Daddy's and waved to her sister standing outside the front door. She was surprised and delighted to see Liliana Callahan, Gabe's aunt and a member of the family rescued by Sarah. She had recently recovered from the near-fatal assault that had also threatened Gabe, Diane, and Sarah as well. The three women greeted each other with hugs; the discussion at lunch would be about happy topics related to the wedding. Sarah had already forgotten about the torture session with the seamstress.

"Diane didn't tell me you were joining us, Liliana," said Sarah.

Diane said, "I called her on a whim, and she was glad to escape from the horde of teenagers that have taken over the church grounds." Liliana was the wife of an Episcopal priest. St. Nicholas Church was hosting a teenage leadership retreat for three days and would be the venue for Dan's and Sarah's wedding in just ten days. Tents were pitched around on the perimeter of the lawn, and bathrooms in their home were in great demand. Sarah herself had vacated the guest house at the church and was staying with Gabe and Diane in Wailuku. "You can always share the guest room with me at Gabe's, Liliana," offered Sarah.

Liliana laughed, and said, "Thanks for the offer, but it's only for three weeks—I mean three *days*." I'll never forgive George for abandoning me to go to that clergy conference in San Diego with Malia. I'm sure he offered to have Saint Nicholas host the retreat once he knew he and our deacon would be 2500 miles away. I'll have to think of some way to get even. I bet you two could come up with something! He owes me big time!"

Diane replied, "Actually, I specialize in revenge. Let's have lunch and figure it out. I got a paycheck, so it's my treat!"

Sarah replied, "Good, they have lobster salad as a special. I'm feeling very special today."

Diane snapped back playfully, "Just wait until I'm a bride, sis."

"I was just thinking the same thing," Sarah said. "Weren't you, Liliana?"

"Indeed," Liliana replied with a twinkle in her eye.

Conversation stalled for a minute while the women perused the menu and placed their orders. Then Sarah took the opportunity to quiz Liliana about George, their boys Micah and Thomas, George's son Alec, and their recent vacation on Oahu, home of Liliana's family.

"We had a great time in Honolulu. George got to play lots of golf and even started to teach Micah a little. I think the day will come when Micah will start teaching George a thing or two. Micah's got the brute strength from the male Hawaiian side of my family, although he's going to need a part-time job just to keep himself in golf balls. His swing is apparently a bit wild, and he spent a lot of time looking for balls that ended up two or three fairways over. George wore a hard hat the second day out, and Micah just about threw his clubs down and quit. 'Oh, Dad, you are embarrassing me.' It really became testy when Kimo—that's my brother—started calling him 'Mulligan Micah.'

"Then Thomas—well, he worships Alec. The two of them went out everyday in Kimo's outrigger and had a great time. I think Alec was glad to finally feel well enough to do something athletic. He's getting stronger, and isn't as pale as he was when he first got here. I think he's going to stay with us, and we may adopt him officially. We don't want to push it; the kid's had a lot to take in over the past several months, with losing his mother and learning about George being his father…he deserves the chance to choose his home and the family he wants to live with. He alternates between being a model big brother and a sullen kid who blames George and me for his mother's death."

And me, too, thought Sarah. She gently interrupted, "What about you, Liliana...how have *you* been?"

"I'm fine. My wounds are healed, just some faint scarring. I can still feel a lump on my head. I'm sleeping better now; the vacation really helped. Why are you looking at me like that?"

"I know you are an amazing woman, but the stress—and I'm not talking about the physical injuries—must be significant. George has lots of colleagues to work through his issues with; what about you? You know that martyr stuff won't work on us."

Liliana's face became flushed, and Sarah could see that tears were welling up in her deep brown eyes. "I know, but I just haven't had the time to think about it. I'll work through it, trust me. Oh, look, here's lunch. Enough about me, anyway, what have you two been up to?"

"Well, Sarah has been the typical impossible bride."

"I have not."

"What do you call humming *Jesu, Joy of Man's Desiring* in the shower every morning?"

"I do not."

"And that alternates with *Goin' to the chapel, and we're gonna get married.* And sometimes..."

"You're my maid of honor; this is not being very honorable."

Liliana laughed at the banter, saying, "You know, I think this reunion is just what I needed. OK, now it's time to pick on you, Diane. Think you and Gabe will ever wind up on dry land together?"

"Well, we hardly ever have to work nights," Diane said innocently. "And he certainly is an expert at heavy breathing." With that, everyone laughed until their sides ached.

Sarah admonished Liliana, "You had to ask."

"In the future I'll be more careful," she replied, still laughing.

Like Sarah, Diane's boyfriend Gabe Callahan was a teacher. When Sarah first arrived on Maui, she and Gabe became acquainted through his Uncle George and Aunt Liliana, as well as through their teaching jobs at the same middle school. She taught math; he taught science. They started to date, but the renewal of Sarah's and Dan's relationship brought that to an end. Gabe's interest turned to the younger sister who had arrived to "rescue Sarah from ruin," as Diane liked to say. Once the initial awkwardness had been dispelled, it was "win-win" for both girls—and their men.

In addition to having a job as a teacher, Gabe was a dive master and conducted dive tours as a side business that supported the tourist trade on Maui. During the school year, his diving was limited to weekends and holidays, but during the summer, he was out almost every day.

When Diane appeared on the scene, it was a wonder that she and Gabe ever got together. She was a pilot, and that meant she would probably never share Gabe's underwater passion. The human body was not designed to alternate between a life in the clouds and a life underwater. On this, there was no room for compromise.

They spent their first weeks together in a patient-caregiver relationship. He had been badly injured in the same attack from which Liliana was still recovering. A cast on his arm, together with the loss of most of the skin on his legs as the result of being pushed off a rocky lava cliff, meant a strict care regimen to prevent infection while he regained his mobility. Once they were on equal footing, it became clear that the relationship held promise for both of them. Like her sister Sarah, Diane moved out from the Midwest and became an island girl. Her caregiver role now obsolete, she began to look for her own job, and she and Gabe settled into a developing relationship. She found work with an air charter business, and was soon shuttling islanders from one end of Maui to the other, as well as to Lana'i, Moloka'i, and Hawai'i. Although the distances were not far, trips by land and sea would take hours that her clients preferred not to waste. Within a short time she had surpassed Sarah in her knowledge of Hawaiian geography. For once, Diane knew more about something than her academic sister did. That it was a subject as technical as geography was ironic.

Liliana said, "As good as it was to get away on vacation, I'm glad to be home." She paused before continuing, "Although I'm not sure I really will have my home back until Friday. Of course the boys love having all the kids around. But I admit I derive just the smallest bit of satisfaction from the birds waking them all up before dawn. Just a little revenge for their keeping me awake until all hours."

"Sarah and I have always said how truly wicked you are, Liliana."

"Yes, I'll have a lot to atone for come Lent. Diane, are you sure you don't want to split that check?"

"It's mine, so there. You all just remember how sweet I was when Sarah was the impossible bride."

Sarah said, "We'd better let her do it, Liliana; we may never see the likes of this graciousness ever again."

"All right; thank you, Diane. It's so good to see you two. Sarah, what's been happening with the wedding plans and that little detail about where you're going to live happily ever after?"

"Well, Dan and I agreed on one thing—it was a hard decision on whether to go back to Chicago or whether to start fresh here. We decided that home would be Chicago, for now anyway. But, we're buying a house with Gabe and Diane here on Maui. They're going to live in it, and we'll have a place to stay when we come out, which we plan to be as often as possible. I feel responsible for making sure Diane doesn't wear Gabe out."

Diane protested, "Hey—he's never been happier. Tired, yes, but never happier."

Liliana laughed and said, "Oh, you two! That's great news. So when are you looking?"

"Well, Dan arrives Thursday, and we're all going to look at houses this weekend. There's also the possibility that once we are reminded of the reality of the Chicago winter, we may immediately turn around and never look back. It wouldn't be that hard; Dan's young enough in his career that he could start over here. And Vice Principal Hoana did not want me to quit teaching at Maui Middle so soon after arriving. Neither did I. And while it's a long way from home for both of us, we thought it would attract relatives to come out to visit…often enough, but not too often!"

Diane added, "Except that they'll stay longer. Don't you dare stick me with Aunt Adeline all by myself!"

Liliana laughed and continued, "I don't know her, but I think every family has an 'Aunt Adeline;' for us it's George's brother. Well, I can tell you that Thomas is disappointed that you won't be his math teacher this fall. Micah, of course, is off to high school. I can't believe it. I'm glad that Alec will be there, too." She stopped herself before continuing, "That is, if Alec decides he wants to stay."

An awkward silence set in, so Sarah asked, "Are they all going to SCUBA school this summer?"

Liliana shook off her dreamlike trance, and responded, "Yes, later this month. We had to postpone it until Gabe was seaworthy. Diane, are you joining the class, too?"

"I'm afraid that our chosen careers are incompatible. If I dive, I can't fly for twenty-four hours. Having last-minute types for clients, I can't risk it. I'll join the snorkeling crowd, and I bet Gabe will have no trouble putting me to work topside. I like being there...oh, never mind about that. The four of us are going on an aerial tour of the island on Friday. It's a rare opportunity for Gabe to fly, since he's not diving that day or the next for that matter. I think his weariness has finally caught up with him. I'm going to keep him on land for a couple of days, except when he's in the clouds with me."

"Oh, good grief," said Sarah.

Liliana changed subjects. "Ladies, I have got to get back to the rectory to help with dinner preparations. I'd prefer that thirty teenagers didn't all invade my kitchen, so I need to be there to bar the door and keep the action outside. I'm not sure the bathrooms will ever be the same again. I'm not used to having teenage girls...boys are so much easier." She hugged both girls and dared them to come over. Sarah said she would help out after Diane's dress fitting.

With that they parted, and the sisters got in their cars to head over to the seamstress for Diane's fitting.

At the dressmaker's, Diane critically eyed the sage green tea-length dress that glided over her figure. Cut on the bias, it clung provocatively to her curves. It was definitely a "Diane dress." Sarah smiled, thinking about how her sister would certainly catch the attention of the men at the wedding, but anything more conservative would not be Diane. It really was perfect, and the pale pink lei would complement it and even offer a little more coverage. Sarah's other two bridesmaids had dresses out of the same fabric, but each in a style that they selected themselves.

"Look, Diane, it was your idea to have lunch before your fitting. No, you're not fat. It's a great dress; you don't look like a banyan tree. I'm surprised you even know what a banyan tree looks like. Hey, I thought it was the bride's privilege to be crabby."

"I'm just practicing so I can be as good at it as you. Ouch!"

"Oops, sorry about that," said the seamstress.

George Callahan and Malia Hoana, the priest and the deacon respectively of Saint Nicholas Episcopal Church of Maui, had settled into their rooms at the Sheraton in San Diego. This morning they were meeting their collared colleagues at a breakfast reception at the cathedral. It was a chance for both to reconnect with classmates from seminary as well as put faces to priests whose names they knew but whom they had never met. Technology facilitated the sharing of ideas, concerns, and information, but not surprisingly, face-to-face communication was this group's preferred style.

As they entered the cathedral, Malia asked George if he had talked to Liliana. "Yes, and this little boondoggle, as she calls it, is going to cost me plenty. The thirty teenagers have crash-landed at the church for a retreat, and the brunt of the logistics fell on her."

"She's an expert at it, but yes, you will owe her. I got an email from Owen; he's going camping for a couple of days at Haleakala. Wonder why he emailed instead of calling me. He didn't say with whom, only that his communications would be limited. He said he would try to message me just to let me know he's OK, but he wasn't sure if it'd work from there. He's lucky he reached me; I only grabbed the laptop at the last minute in case I had some time to work on the sermon."

"I'll tell Liliana in case she wants to join him in the wilderness."

"She'd have to be pretty desperate! Here we are—wow, it's been awhile since I've been around so many people in black."

Dan Weatherby, M.D., young pediatrician at Chicago Lakeside Hospital, was distracted. He was anticipating the upcoming holiday weekend like a kid with a new bicycle waiting for Dad to put it together. On Thursday he was flying to Maui to be with Sarah, his fiancée. Nothing was going to get in the way of their relationship again, and certainly nothing was going to happen to disrupt their wedding next weekend. They were both getting tired of the long-distance requirements of their relationship, but that would soon end. Of course it made sense for Sarah to stay in Maui until the wedding. But good sense did not necessarily mean he liked it.

To make the time go faster in the month since he had seen her, he had been working long six-day weeks in the office and on-call. His colleagues were also taking advantage of the summer to take vacations themselves, and it meant everyone covering for one another. Dan would have the next two weeks off, but he was exhausted. Children's ailments and injuries did not take vacations. There were fewer colds but more ear infections and allergies. Baseball replaced ice hockey as the cause of broken arms.

Dan entered Exam Room #3 to find a dirt- and tear-streaked Billy Addison holding his right arm. *Not again.* "Hey pal, is this *déja-vu?*"

"Huh? No, it's my arm. It really hurts."

"Baseball?"

"Uh-huh."

"Were you safe?"

"Uh-huh. And we won."

"I'll bet you did."

Billy's mother had obviously been interrupted in the middle of a haircut to rush him to the doctor. She had put on a baseball cap, but it wasn't enough to disguise the halfway job on her hair. Dan forced himself to keep from smiling, not so much at the mother's appearance—amusing that it was—but imagining Sarah doing the same thing, someday.

"I thought they taught you how to slide...?"

"Yeah, well the kid I ran into is in the next room. At least *we* won."

"Well, there's a limit of one broken arm per year. You're over your limit for the year, Billy. I don't know what to tell you."

"Can't I have my sister Julie's? She hasn't broken nothing this year."

"You going to be a salesman when you grow up, Billy. What do you think, Mom? Shall we use Julie's broken arm for Billy?"

The mother nodded, and added, "At this rate, he's going to need his brother Simon's as well."

"Can I have a red cast this time? It'll look like blood."

"I'm sure the technician will do his best to make it look as gory as possible. Let's get an X-ray just to see what you managed to do to yourself. So, you say your opponent's in the next room? Anyone else I'm likely to see today as a result of this game?"

"Nope. When can I play again? We're in the championships!"

"Six weeks, maybe eight, depending on where and how it's broken. Sorry, champ. Just remember, you got them there."

"Not fair. Mom? It's not fair."

"Come on, Billy, let's head down to Radiology. Thanks Dr. Weatherby. We'll probably see you again during soccer season."

The kid next door was a mirror image of Billy, holding his left arm and trying hard not to cry. Having lost the game, he was even more upset, and his father was not making things easier.

"Doc, can't you wrap it up? He's supposed to compete in a Tae Kwon Do match on Saturday. Jake, why couldn't you have fallen on your side, and not your arm?"

"Sorry, Dad."

"Jake, we're going to get an X-ray just as soon as Billy gets done in there. You two must have hit pretty hard."

"Yeah, well *I* know I tagged him. But there was so much dust, the ref couldn't see. It's not fair."

"I know. But if it's broken, we'll have to set it. Sorry, but I think your summer athletics may be over for this year."

"What about Billy?"

"Oh, he's pretty much done for the summer, too."

"Oh." Then Jake erupted with, "Say, Dad, can you see if me and Billy can go to that computer camp? Please?"

Dan endorsed this with, "There you go, Dad."

Caught by surprise, Jake's father was speechless, but soon recovered, saying, "Well, let's go see how bad your arm is first." Dan guessed that Dad was still hoping it was just bruised.

"OK. What color cast is Billy getting? I want black unless he's already…" Their voices drifted away as they rounded the corner to Radiology.

Exam Room #1 held a different story. Tiffany Ann Kincaid was slouching in the chair in the corner, her arms crossed in front of her chest. She would rather be anywhere else, and with anyone but her mother. At fifteen, Tiffany Ann was every parent's nightmare. The defiant, sullen demeanor, the pallor of her skin, the sunglasses, the restless body language, and the rat's nest that defined her hair style—Tiffany Ann was on drugs.

Dan's heart ached at the sight of someone who used to be a dream child. He remembered the pony-tailed little girl, tears streaming down her cheek from a cut on her leg suffered in a bike fall. He wished he could send her back in time to that day when all problems could simply be stitched up.

"Tiffany Ann, it's good to see you. Tell me what's going on."

Tiffany Ann shrugged her shoulders and responded, "It's Tiff, and it's nothing. I'm fine. Mom's just being dramatic." Her cell phone rang, and she reached for it, but Dan gently covered her hand and said, "Let's let that one go. They can leave a message. I'd really like to hear about what's going on, Tiff."

The mother interjected, "Tiffany has been doing drugs, Dr. Weatherby. I—we—need to figure out what to do."

Dan asked Tiffany, "What kind of drugs, Tiff?"

"It's nothing. Just some grass. Come on, everybody does it. Don't tell me you didn't get high in college, Dr. Weatherby."

Dan ignored the implied question and continued, "Tiff, grass is bad enough, but I think you know we're looking at something else." He reached for the sunglasses and removed them before Tiffany could protest. The dilated pupils spoke volumes—methamphetamines. "Tell me when you last took something."

"I don't know. Maybe last week; I'm clean, Dr. Weatherby. This is so lame; can we go, Mom?" Tiffany started to get up, but Dan put his hands out to indicate that the appointment was not over.

"Let's try this again, Tiff. Aren't you a little warm in that shirt? Please roll up your sleeves."

Tiffany rolled her eyes, but did as requested. "See, I'm not shooting up."

Thank God, thought Dan. "Now, let's check out your teeth. Say ahhhh."

"Ahhhh. My teeth are fine. You're not a dentist."

"Methamphetamines will destroy your teeth, and it doesn't take long. Battery acid has that effect on things. Surprised? That's one of the lovely ingredients that are used to make the stuff. And you should know that it will be extremely—I mean *extremely*—painful. And there's nothing a dentist or I can do. Tell me about school, Tiff."

"School's a drag. It's boring, and the teachers are total bitches. It's all I can do to stay awake while they are blathering on. So, I just needed a little help. You get in big trouble if you fall asleep in class."

"She's been bringing home D's, Dr. Weatherby. In summer school! She cut algebra twice last week. Tiff, where do you go when you're not in class?"

"Just around." The cell phone rang again, and Tiffany's mother took it from her. The girl lashed out, "That's mine! You can't take it from me! I hate you! I want to go live with Dad." Tiffany opened the door and walked out towards the waiting room.

The mother put her head in her hands and rubbed her face in exasperation. "I don't know what to do. I feel like I've lost my daughter. I can't do anything right, and all we ever do is fight. She knows just what buttons to push."

"Elizabeth, this is not your fault. I know that's easy for me to say, since it's not my daughter, but it's true. You did the right thing by bringing her in. I suspect that she is doing methamphetamines, maybe some Valium or other drug to calm her down after the uppers, and grass, as you heard her admit. I don't think she's shooting up. At the same time, this is serious. I wasn't exaggerating about her losing her teeth. We need to get her into an intervention program. Actually we need to get the both of you into an intervention program. Tiffany's father, too; this has the best chance of working if you and he are together on this. She must not think that Dad is going to bail her out. These programs do work, even when she's as uncooperative as she is right now. I want you to call Joe Caldwell; here's his card. He runs a well-respected and safe drug rehab center, specializing in teenagers. He's got the experience and the reputation. Call him today, OK? See, he's also got a web site, so you can get a little more information before you call him. But do call him today."

The mother nodded and let tears of relief spill. "If I lost her, I don't know what I would do."

"You won't lose her; she's smart and she—you—will both get through this. I referred two other patients to him. I'm going to call them to see if they would be willing to talk to you. OK if I give them your phone number?"

"Absolutely. Why is it some kids get through puberty just fine, and others make it a living hell for themselves and their parents?"

Dan had no answer, but gave the mother a hug and wished her good results. "Now I'm going to be gone for the next two weeks, but I want you to contact Dr. Dunlap if you have any questions. She's familiar with Joe Caldwell, so don't hesitate to call her."

"I hope you're going some place fun…can I come with you?" Dan was glad to see the mother getting back a little sense of humor.

"I'll check with my fiancée; I'm sure she wouldn't mind."

"You're getting married? How exciting! Congratulations! I hope this doesn't keep you from having kids. Although maybe it should. You know, I feel a little better having something to do that might help."

Gabe Callahan slathered sunscreen onto his pale left arm and down his scarred and sensitive legs. The injuries from the dangerous fall down the cliff were healing, but there was still evidence of trauma, particularly on the skin on his legs. The cast on his arm was gone, and he was trying to even out the skin tone on both sides. He was like a tourist again, fresh off the plane from winter's half light, and he had seen all too many of them fooled into thinking they could get that golden tan in one day.

His dive boat, the *Rain Dancer,* was back from a morning tour with a party of ten divers. He and his business partner Terry collected the gear and washed down the boat with fresh water before loading up their SUV's and heading back to their small combination office-warehouse in town. Gabe's young cousin Thomas was there as well, and Gabe was grateful for the help, even though the 12-year-old dropped half of whatever he happened to be carrying. Gabe was still wearier than usual after a morning indulging his underwater passion. Since the injury, Terry had taken on more of the heavy work. Gabe led the second, shallower dives, and even occasionally let Terry do both. He was frustrated at his slow progress, but diving was not a sport for the unfit.

"Hey, Gabe, I'll get those tanks," called Terry. "You're loaded up; go on over to the warehouse. You can check out the gear for tomorrow. Oh, Nico is coming along tomorrow, so all you have to do is play host to the divers and lead the second dive. We want you back, man, but all in one piece. And remember your promise that if you aren't up to a dive, you stay dry."

Gabe was relieved that Terry's son Nico was joining the party the next day. He was looking forward to a soak in the spa at the condo later on, maybe with Diane. But before that, there was still a lot of work to do. While Thomas hung up the soggy wet suits, Gabe checked the equipment for any damage and made minor repairs. He checked voice messages to see who was coming out the next day, and started to call the divers to get the details on height, weight, and level of experience. Four returnees…great! Four new ones, referred by delighted customers. Even better! He noted each diver's equipment needs on a spreadsheet. Nico would get it all ready, and the cycle would start all over again.

Terry pulled up with the rest of the gear and practically lifted Gabe into his SUV to get him to leave. "OK, 'Mom,' I'm going. I've got the cash and checks, and I'll deposit them in the bank. Then I'll be at home moaning and groaning."

"Spare me the details about your love life, dude. Although you still don't look very lovable."

Gabe laughed and added, "I must have other redeeming qualities. *Mañana*, Terr!" He waved good-bye as he drove away to drop Thomas off at a friend's house.

"Can I go out with you again tomorrow, Gabe?" a hopeful Thomas asked.

"As you heard, Nico is coming with us tomorrow. We'll get you out there next week, OK, champ?"

Thomas was obviously disappointed, but Gabe added, "You know Dan arrives tomorrow, although you probably won't see him until Friday or so. And it's only another couple of weeks before you guys start your certification class."

"Can we go out to see sharks?"

"Eventually, but you guys have all got to learn how to use the equipment before you go anywhere but the pool over at the high school. You and Nico are going to have a little bit of a head start from helping me out here. The rest of the kids won't even know what a regulator is." Gabe then changed the subject. "Which house is Matt's? And who's driving you home tonight?"

"He's on Waimanu Court. Matt's dad said he'd drive me home, but I'd rather stay at Matt's. Everyone's camping out except me and Mom. It's not fair. And there are girls everywhere. They're always running out of TP. How come girls use so much TP? Can I come stay at your place?"

"There are almost as many girls at my place, Thomas. I may come stay at your place!"

"That'd be good. Oh, wait, one of the counselors has Micah and Alec's room. I'll be glad when everyone goes home. I think Mom will be, too. She keeps saying stuff like, 'Your father will owe me.'"

Gabe laughed, and said, "OK, here you go, champ. Thanks for all your help today. I'm sure I'll see you over the weekend if not before."

When he finally arrived home, there was a note from Diane saying she would be back around seven. Sarah was up at the church helping Liliana with the retreat. He almost convinced himself to join them, but thought this was one time they could do without him.

That gave him several hours to clean up, check email, and rest up before Diane returned. Things were never quiet when she was around. *Quiet was highly over-rated,* he thought to himself, smiling. She had rescued him from a critical fall, but more important, she had rescued him from a rather mundane and predictable existence. She shared many characteristics with Sarah, to whom he had initially been attracted when she first arrived on Maui. Light brown hair, an infectious smile, and a bit rounder than her sister. A fierce independence. Why do many men prefer women who worship them? Life is much more interesting with a capable and confident woman. They fit together in so many ways. He no longer considered what might have happened with Sarah. The sudden reappearance of Dan had brought the budding relationship with her to a halt, but before Gabe knew what had hit him, Diane had found her way into his heart and to the top of his list of priorities. Life without her was unimaginable, and he envisioned his bachelor life becoming history. *No regrets*, he thought.

After showering, Gabe got on his computer. He ordered diving manuals and other materials he needed for the upcoming certification class he was teaching. Thomas' 14-year-old brother Micah, as well as the boys' 16-year-old half-brother Alec, were also joining the class. Gabe smiled thinking about how they were probably not going to be thrilled with the book learning and required written tests.

Emails from four other kids who also wanted to register brought the total to eight. On Tuesday he had emailed Owen Hoana, Vice Principal of Maui Middle School, to see if he could use the school's library, the Owl's Nest, for the classroom portion of the training. The response from Owen was puzzling.

Gabe, OK if you use the O.N., but they're going to be painting the bleachers that week. Love, HoHo

What bleachers? There are no bleachers in the library. And frankly, he was a little surprised there wasn't something like "hope you're feeling better" in the message. But the "Love, HoHo?" He started to compose a response, but deleted it. All that mattered was that he could use the library. And if Owen ever went back and read the message he sent, he would likely be embarrassed to learn that he had signed it "Love, HoHo." It was better to let it go. He signed off and stiffly rose to go get a beer. After settling into a chaise on the lanai with his latest *Dive Tropical* magazine, he soon dozed off and was awakened by a key turning in the lock.

"Gabe? Hello? It's Sarah. Oops, sorry to wake you! No, don't get up. I'll just get a beer myself and join you out there."

"How's Liliana doing with the invasion?"

"She is amazing, you know. She had this assembly line going building burgers, icing cupcakes, and mixing up lemonade. She solved the bathroom crisis by assigning the boys to the main house and the girls to the guest house. It's still chaos, but they're kids; they'll adapt." She paused before continuing, "Is Diane back yet?"

"Around seven, she said, so anytime now."

"Good. You two had to work today, so I'll make dinner. How do burgers and cupcakes sound?"

Gabe laughed and said, "As long as I can have beer instead of lemonade. Although I think I'm going to turn into a pumpkin early. I hope I can stay awake for a soak in the spa with Diane. You can join us, too."

"I learned long ago not to share a bath with Diane. She always made me sit at the end with the faucet, although that's probably not an issue in the spa. I'll let you two have your private bath time together. I appreciate your letting me stay here during the assault on St. Nicholas. And Dan arrives tomorrow, so we'll really be crowding you for awhile."

"Not a problem. Oh, I picked up some real estate info when I was out. It's over there."

"So, oceanfront, six bedrooms, six baths, a pool, and servants' quarters?"

"Sure…dream on. And when you wake up, you might start with an ocean *view*, a pool, and three, maybe four bedrooms."

"You know Diane will want her own bathroom."

"I can always rig up a shower outside."

"Who's taking a shower outside?" They both turned when they heard Diane come in at the end of the conversation. Gabe winced as he stiffly got to his feet to embrace the woman in his life. "We're just talking about the possibilities for the beach bungalow."

"I want my own bathroom."

"No, really?"

"Hey Duke, wake up, man."

"I'm awake; what do you want?"

"What are we going to do with HoHo?"

"Did you put him into dreamland?"

"Yeah, but he's going to start needing a bigger dose to keep him doped up. It's going to eat into the profits."

"Cost of doing business, Wally."

"Yeah, but we can't keep him there. I mean, someone's going to start looking for him, or someone's going to come to work, or…"

"You worry too much, Wally. That's when you start making mistakes. Me, I don't worry. That's why I've been so successful, you know."

"Why couldn't you have picked a smaller guy that don't need so much drugs? It's like trying to bring down an elephant, man."

"That's a good one, Wally. Anyway, I didn't pick him; he was in the wrong place at the wrong time, and you picked him. He's kind of like a casualty of war. It's his fault, really."

"I hadn't thought of it that way."

"That's OK; I'll do the thinking, and you won't have to."

"OK, Duke. Got any beer?"

"In the fridge. Did you think to look there?"

"You told me you would do the thinking."

"Now you know why."

"So, why don't we just drag HoHo over here and do him? We could hide him, and no one would find him until after we finished the job."

"Timing is everything, Wally. Bring me a beer while you're at it. So how is our elephant man?"

"I figure by Friday, he'll do just about anything we want him to do."

"Good. I want to put him to a little test, just to make sure. You're sure he'll be all softened up?"

"Nah, don't worry, Duke."

"I told you; I never do."

Micah and Alec settled into their tent on the south side of the lawn at the church. It would be awhile before things became quiet, particularly on the north side where the girls' tents were pitched. As teenagers, the half-brothers' conversations focused on sports, computers, cars, music, girls, and school, in more or less that order.

Even though they were half-brothers, Alec resembled Thomas more than Thomas' full brother Micah did. But at twelve, Thomas did not qualify for participation in the teenagers' retreat, and had been banished to the rectory—the family's home—with his mother for the night. His presence was limited to helping his mother prepare meals for the group. He would not be sad when the event was over, since his two older brothers had virtually ignored him since the beginning of the retreat the day before. He had jumped at the chance to escape with Gabe out on the *Rain Dancer*. But he was now back home for the night, stuck in the house with his mother, rather than outside with the fun the older kids were having camping out. This was the first time that Thomas had been treated any differently than Micah for as long as he could remember, and he didn't like it. He and Alec had a great time on vacation with his new family, but he was feeling left out of the older boys' activities since they had returned home.

Alec had realized that he was not the Callahan family's sole center of attention, as he had been with his mother, particularly when he had been so ill with failing kidneys. Now, as one of three kids living in a household of more modest means, his every wish was not someone's command. His mother had promised him a car when he got his license. The man, his father, George, had made it clear that he would need to earn the money to buy one himself. He wondered if his mother's sister, his Aunt Adrienne, still back in Seattle, would make him do the same, or whether she would buy him one. She was probably richer than George, but her children were all girls. He wasn't sure he wanted to live in a house full of women back there. It rained there a lot. It rained here a lot, but it wasn't the same.

Alec had recently learned the specifics of his conception. He was the result of a brief affair between his mother and George Callahan when they, along with George's now-wife Liliana, were in graduate school in Washington. Two years ago Alec had developed life-threatening kidney disease. A serious car accident eight years earlier had cost his mother a kidney, so Alec's best hope had to lie with other relatives. His mother went on an exhaustive and unsuccessful search with those on her side. With no compatible donors on his mother's side, Alec's next best hope was with his father. Thus his mother embarked on a frantic search for her long-lost lover with whom she had broken all ties even before she learned she was pregnant. George did not know about Alec, and she had been fine with that. That is, until Alec became gravely ill.

As a single mother making it on her own, Angela's mental as well as physical health had degraded over the years, and was made even worse after the car accident. When she finally discovered the whereabouts of the father of her son, she became obsessed with his agreeing to donate a kidney so that Alec would not die. At the same time, she imagined that George's wife Liliana would try to stop him, and Angela's mental state became even more deranged. In an attempt to kill Liliana along with Sarah, Diane, and Gabe, Angela herself was mortally injured in a fall. In dying she was able to donate the kidney for her son. George would always be a backup, but so far, Alec's prognosis appeared to be excellent. He was largely unaware that his mohter's mental state had driven her to the point of attempted murder in her desperate campaign to ensure her son's survival.

Once the crisis of his health had been resolved, Alec was able to focus attention on a future he apparently was going to have, as well as the more emotional components of his relationship with his father. George Callahan was a decent enough man, giving every indication that he cared about his newly discovered son. At the same time, he had given the boy the latitude to choose where he would live. When Alex was recovering from the transplant, George invited him to his home on Maui for the summer with the promise that it would be Alec who made the decision on where he would live when school started. He even told Alec that he could choose whether to call him 'Dad' or 'George.' George had told him he hoped it was the former, but the progress of the developing relationship would be the determining factor.

"Alec, we have many years to catch up on. I hope you'll give me, your half-brothers Micah and Thomas, and their mother Liliana a chance."

"Are you sure she—Liliana—wants me?"

"There's no question, Alec. She does. She was the first one to suggest it. The boys are anxious to meet you and are fighting over whose room you will share. I know it will be a lot different than living with one person and being an only child, and if you find that you really don't want to stay, that's fine. We will still welcome your visit anytime you want. But if you think you'd like to live near the ocean and have summer weather every day of the year, that's what we have. So, come for the summer, and then you can decide. What do you think?"

"I'll come for the summer, and then we'll see. I'm not sure about 'Dad' yet. What about Liliana? She's not my mother."

"True. Do you want to just try 'Liliana'?"

Alec nodded, and George extended his hand to seal the deal. "So, Alec, one more serious question…window or aisle seat?"

Alec smiled lightly, saying, "Window. Please. George."

Within days of his arrival in Maui, Alec decided that having two brothers had its plusses and minuses. He was never without company, but he had to share a lot of things—the computer, the bathroom, snacks and other food, and any available disposable income—with them. He missed his mother, particularly the part about being the most important person in the world to her. He was angry with her for leaving him, but he knew that he might not be alive come Christmas if he hadn't gotten her kidney. He also felt guilty that part of the reason for her death could be attributed to him, or at least his life-threatening condition that drove her to look for his father. He looked at the others to blame as well: George, Liliana, and Sarah. Probably Sarah the most. She was surely to blame for her mother's fall. Everytime he saw her, he associated her with the death of his mother. *She did not have to die; you could have stopped it.*

He liked his half-brothers, relating especially well with Micah, the older boy with whom he was sharing a tent on the lawn outside the church.

"Let's see if Gabe will take us out on the *Rain Dancer* this weekend, huh Alec?" Micah was still excited and unable to sleep in the strange environment, and the girls were still gabbing away in the night.

"OK, but I don't see why we have to go through all the school stuff before we go diving. What a drag. You just strap the tank on and start breathing. When you can't breathe anymore, you come up. How hard is that?"

"I don't know, but Gabe won't let us. He's pretty cool, and doesn't worry about stuff too much. I bet he lets us slide through the class stuff. He was a pretty cool teacher; he let us cut up worms and frogs and stuff."

"Think he'll let us cut up stuff we catch in the ocean?"

"Nah; he's always telling people not to hurt stuff."

"Well, once I get enough money for a car, we can go diving some place without him."

"What kind of car are you going to get?"

"A truck would be cool."

"Yeah, a truck would be cool. You can carry stuff. How much do they cost?"

"Dunno. I gotta get a job anyway. How much are we going to make painting the house and stuff?"

"Dad said he'd pay us each $200. Maybe you could work on the boat with Gabe. Nico gets paid for helping out, you know, doing stuff."

"Do they get girls on the boat?"

"Yeah, some. But Gabe said that once we all learn how to dive, the girls will want to learn, too."

"Cool."

"So, you gonna stay here when school starts?"

"Too soon to tell; I got some stuff to think about."

"Are you still mad at Sarah?"

Alec was startled at this question, since he had tried to hide his anger with Sarah. "She killed my mother; wouldn't you be mad?"

"Dunno. I like her. I don't think she would kill someone on purpose."

"Well, if she's not to blame, who is?"

"Why does someone have to get blamed? Didn't your mom fall?"

"I'm tired. Go to sleep."

Thursday, July 2

Sun hurts my eyes. Close the blinds, Malia. I have to pee. It can't be far to the bathroom. Malia, help me up. I need to pee. I want to feel better. I felt better earlier. I think I'm in the bathroom now. I can't find the toilet. She'll be mad at me if I can't make it to the toilet. I can't paint the bleachers until I pee.

"Hey HoHo, how'd you make it out here? You are one stinking mess, HoHo. Come on, get up, this way to the bathroom. Then I'll make you feel better. Yeah, doesn't that sound good? All you have to do is get up. Hold on, no, don't start peeing yet. There you go. That's a good boy. OK, now let's go back to your office, get comfortable, and I'll make you feel real good."

Wally let Owen settle back onto the sofa and decided he needed to test just how far Owen was on his little journey to dependence. "Tell you what, HoHo, I need you to do just one little thing for me; then I'll have you feeling good again. Here, take these scissors, and let's see you make just a little cut right here on your hand. That's all you have to do, and you're going to feel great, man. Good job! OK, here's your reward."

Owen gasped as euphoria set in, and settled back down on the sofa, watching Wally, but unable to care what was happening. Wally sat down at Owen's desk and checked his email to see if there were messages that needed responses from "Owen." He browsed messages that Owen had sent in his lucid times to capture the tone and wording he would use in his communications. It was Malia that called him HoHo privately, and those messages were pretty casual. She hadn't emailed him, so he didn't write to her. He thought he would text-message her tonight from Owen's imaginary campground, late enough that she wouldn't try to call him back. He was startled to see a message that Owen had sent sometime yesterday; how did he do that? Maybe it was during a short span of consciousness between the time that the drugs had worn off and withdrawal started to set in. The message was nonsense. To some gal named Gabe; the "Love, HoHo" brought a smile to Wally's face. *Oh, wifey, what you don't know!* Anyway, Wally had been around enough addicts to know that Owen wasn't likely to send anymore emails in his current state. He needed to keep the computer on and logged in, so that "Owen" could keep up his appearance.

Wally tossed a paper bag over to Owen, who ripped it open and ravenously wolfed down the two sandwiches inside. He was in his own world, and he couldn't have cared less about Wally.

Wally checked the corridors and doors to make sure everything was secure and the windows were covered. *Can't have some stupid cop discover a door left open, or go peeking in the window.* The place needed to look like what it was: a school closed for summer vacation.

"OK, HoHo, I'll see you later today. You try to behave, OK? You don't have nothing to worry about, just like Duke says. I'm going to take care of you."

Wally secured the office and locked the building with Owen's keys, careful to watch for any human activity before he walked nonchalantly out to his car in the back parking lot.

Duke had lied to Wally. He worried a lot. Meeting Cho was always cause for worry. If Cho didn't like something, he would not hesitate to let you know in such a way that you would never do that something again. Cho derived pleasure from these "little lessons." At their last meeting, Cho had been furious with Duke for showing up with bad breath. He gave Duke a wire brush and kitchen cleanser and had one of his associates brush his teeth.

Today, Duke dressed carefully and made sure his teeth and breath were clean. His gums were still raw and prone to bleeding, and simple brushing brought tears to his eyes. Clean clothes, deodorant, no dandruff, clean fingernails... Duke was pretty sure he was safe. Cho's "little lessons" were worth it, for the time being. He paid Duke a lot of money, out of which Duke paid Wally. He would need to keep Wally away from Cho; he didn't think Wally could handle one of Cho's "little lessons."

Duke was somewhat relieved that his meeting with Cho was to be at a restaurant. He hoped he would not be expected to eat; he was still only on soft and bland liquids. But it would be a public place, and Cho might have to restrain himself from imposing his "little lessons" on Duke.

Duke parked his car and made a final check of his physical appearance and breath before he entered the restaurant and looked around for his employer. Cho saw him from across the room and waved at him.

"Duke! It's so good to see you, my friend." Cho embraced Duke as a long-lost friend, and smilingly invited him to sit across from him at the outdoor restaurant overlooking the Maui Channel. Cho appeared to be alone, but Duke knew that appearances were deceiving. Discretion among his staff was the primary hiring criterion. *Minty breath, too.*

"I took the liberty of ordering lunch for you. You look very smart today. You must have a lady you're trying to impress. Lady Luck, maybe?

Ha ha! So, Duke, how have you been?"

"Just fine, Mr. Cho."

"Excellent. Oh, here comes our lunch. The special today was Cajun barbeque ribs. Don't those look good? Would you like something to wash it down…maybe a Bloody Mary? Good one, huh? Bloody Mary here, waiter!"

"No, thank you, Mr. Cho. Just a beer please, waiter."

"I hope you can manage those ribs, OK, Duke. How thoughtless of me to order them when you are wearing such smart duds."

"I'm fine, Mr. Cho. I'll just be very careful."

"I'm sure you will, Duke. Everything we do should be done with great care, don't you think? It's one of the secrets of my success."

"That's a good rule to live by."

"So, Duke, have you been exercising the right amount of care on our little project?"

"Absolutely, Mr. Cho. Plans are being executed to the smallest detail, and I'm sure you'll be pleased."

"Excellent. Duke, I'm sorry that your lunch doesn't appeal to you. Something else, perhaps? A steak?"

"No, Mr. Cho; I'm just not very hungry."

"I see. You should know that our timetable has been pushed back a few days. It's now next Friday. Ah, here's my wife. I must excuse myself, Duke. I hope you will forgive me. Waiter, could you come take this, please?"

"Not at all, Mr. Cho. And next Friday will be fine. Thank you for lunch."

"Take care of yourself, Duke. You're looking a little pale." Then Cho turned his attention to the matronly Asian woman approaching him, and

Duke took his cue to disappear. He was sweating profusely and wanted to avoid giving Cho any reason to admonish him further. Although the public place was not conducive to one of Cho's "little lessons," Duke was sure that the man could come up with something creative. Sick, yes, but creative.

Back at his apartment, Duke found Wally out on the lanai smoking a joint. "How's our guest doing?"

"He's cool. We got him. He's ours."

"Good. We need to keep him under control a little longer, until next Friday."

"Oh, no, that's too long. Where are we going to keep him? And guess what? HoHo's got a girlfriend. Hard to imagine he's got a wife, much less a little nookie on the side. She's going to start looking for him, too."

"Just keep them all away. That's your job, Wally. Did you drink all the beer?"

"Did you check the fridge?"

"Don't start with me."

I need to remind myself never to bring a medical journal on an airplane flight again. Dan was sitting next to a woman who was taking advantage of his captivity to discuss every ailment she had in hopes of getting free advice. It was clear that many of them could be relieved with the loss of fifty pounds. *Make that seventy-five.* He was not afraid to discuss such matters, but patients usually weren't sitting next to him for nine hours after he had given them his advice. *No wonder people drink themselves into a coma on airplanes.* It was tempting, but Dan wanted to arrive lucid. The five-hour time difference would already put him at a disadvantage, and he wanted to save as much of his energy and faculties as he could. He finally told the woman that he had to get some sleep so he'd be able to stay awake for an important engagement. It was not a lie, he reminded himself, smiling inwardly. At that point, he closed his eyes and simply ignored her. He could hold off on dispensing his advice until they were closer to landing.

"Have you heard from Owen on his wilderness excursion?" George asked Malia.

"No, but it's not surprising," she responded. "I text-messaged him this morning before we went into the meetings, but I really didn't expect him to reply right away. I know reception out there is dubious, so I'm trying to tell myself not to worry. He knows what he's doing. I just wish I knew who he was with; I'm sure he wouldn't go camping by himself."

"Later on, why don't you call a couple of his buddies to see if they know."

"Good idea. Like I said, I'm sure he's fine. Oh, I see a couple of people I went to seminary with. Come over, I'll introduce you. They're the two people over there dressed in black."

"Malia, almost everyone's dressed in black," George teased, and Malia laughed.

Sarah had looked everywhere for her lunch cooler: the box of belongings she had brought over from the guest house at the church, the guest house itself last night, her car… Diane hadn't borrowed it; neither had Gabe. Had she left it somewhere when she had gone for a walk on the beach? She didn't think so. It wasn't that important, but she was anxious about Dan's arrival later in the day, and decided the search would give her something to focus on. They might want it for a day at the beach. *You're being silly. Why don't you just go buy another one?* There was one more place to look—her classroom. She had already turned in her keys, so she'd have to rely on someone being there to let her in. She knew the school was open some days during the summer, but the administrative staff took their vacations at this time as well. *I'll call over there first.* She promised herself that if the cooler wasn't there, she'd just write it off as lost. The answering machine was all there was. She started to leave a message, but decided she'd just drop in sometime late morning, on the chance that someone was there.

Twenty-four hours. Liliana looked at the kitchen clock and gave a sigh of relief that the teenage leadership retreat was in its final countdown. Sarah and Diane were both coming over to help with lunch as well as the setup for dinner, but she would be on her own this evening. Dan was arriving for Sarah, and from that point forward, the wedding would be their primary focus. *As it should be.* She would miss Sarah when she moved back to the mainland; she shuddered to think how different things might have been had Sarah not arrived when she did. Thoughts of Sarah's spunky sister Diane brought a smile to her face, and she hoped that Gabe would make an honest woman of her. *I like weddings. They renew my faith in people and remind me how blessed I am. Why am I crying?*

"Mrs. Callahan? Mrs. Callahan, I'm sorry to bother you, but the guest cottage is out of TP. You know girls."

Liliana regained her composure, and forced a laugh, "Oh, yes. Check the storage closet out by the laundry, Sandy. I think there's some there."

"OK, thanks! You know, this is such a nice place for this retreat. You are so sweet to open up your home to this circus. I know you'll be glad to have it all to yourself in—say twenty-four hours?"

"Twenty-three and a half, but who's counting? We love doing this, Sandy. The kids have been great. Maybe next time, though, I'll let George do it, and I'll go to San Diego!"

"Seems only fair."

Sarah parked out front of West Maui Middle School and tried the main door first. Locked. She peaked in the windows of the office, but the window coverings had been completely drawn across the glass. She tapped on the glass and called out in case someone was in there anyway. She heard rustling, but it soon stopped, and she guessed it was just a ceiling fan blowing papers around. She walked around the side in case a maintenance worker or another teacher happened to be there. The place looked deserted, but she continued her search around to the windows in her former classroom. *I'll probably just see the stupid cooler sitting on my desk, and I can stop worrying about such a little thing. I'll just get it another day.* She heard a motor and noticed someone cutting the grass out on the football field. Another guy was using hedge clippers on the shrubs. Neither was likely to have access to the inside. She waved to the latter, and he looked up, a bit startled, but waved back before returning to his task.

Sarah didn't think she had ever looked into her classroom from this vantage point. It was easy to find it from inside, third door on the right. From outside, she had to look in each window to figure out where one classroom stopped and the next one began. The blinds were pulled down, and she had to peer through narrow openings between the slats. She tried not to look as if she was trying to break in. Eventually she found a window into her classroom that had just enough of a view of the cooler sitting on the floor next to the door. *Mystery solved. I'll just leave a message on the answering machine asking whoever is around to call me when they are there.* Then she thought,

I'm going to miss this place. She knew that she and Dan were making the right decision about their immediate future, but she had just started to feel part of a community again. Time to start over again, *again. He's worth it,* she thought with a smile, closing her eyes and taking a deep, satisfying breath.

She tried the front door one more time, but the place was locked up tight. A different sound startled her when she tapped on the office windows again, almost like a chair scraping on the floor. She tapped again, but there was no subsequent sound. She listened for another minute before deciding it was nothing, walked back out to her car, and drove off.

Owen jerked his head up when he heard the sounds. "Come in," he said hoarsely, but no one came in. A few minutes later, the tapping resumed. He groaned and noticed that his right leg had fallen asleep. He shifted his large body into a different position on the sofa and in doing so caused the coffee table to scoot away from him. He almost lost his balance, but managed to prop himself up to a sitting position. His leg was starting to hurt as pins and needles replaced the numbness. He had a terrible taste in his mouth and looked around for something to drink. There was an open water bottle sitting on the floor next to the sofa. It took several tries, but he eventually was able to take hold of it.

He felt terrible. He was starting to be more aware of his surroundings, but it came at the cost of a dizzying headache and other pains that seemed to be everywhere, but no place specific. He wanted the pain to go away and to feel good again.

That man. That man would come back and make me feel good again. I'll do anything to feel good again. Please come back.

He picked up the scissors and started to make a cut on his hand again. *That will make the man come back and make me feel good again.*

Wally continued to watch the woman as she made her way over to the windows outside the classrooms. She put her face up to each window as if she was looking for something. Apparently she saw what she was looking for, and started to walk back around to the front. Wally wanted to follow her, but he needed to keep busy at his job of trimming the bushes. His supervisor on the tractor was always watching to make sure he wasn't slacking off. He did not want to have to tell Duke that he had been fired. Finally he heard the woman's car start up, and Wally realized he had been holding his breath until then.

Gabe let Terry lead both dives. With only eight divers, there was plenty of room for Nico to help out on the boat and earn his keep. Nico was a good kid, seventeen, and also enrolled in the upcoming dive certification class with Gabe. Already an expert with the equipment, Nico was going to be a big help to Gabe in the class. Childhood ear problems had prevented him from handling water pressure before now, but he had largely outgrown them. Gabe hoped that Nico would not be disappointed again this summer. Another summer hauling equipment around that he would never use would devastate the boy, and would likely sour his desire to ever indulge in the pastime, whatever his role. Gabe was torn between wanting to instill enthusiasm in Nico for the sport, and downplaying it in case he couldn't do it.

Rain clouds were building in the southwest. An afternoon shower was brewing, not uncommon for a summer day anywhere in Hawai'i. He thought about the teenagers camping out at the church, and knew that if it did rain, preparing meals would get a lot more complicated. He had promised to show up the next morning as the group broke camp, but if there was rain later this afternoon, he'd also lend a hand with getting them resettled in the parish hall for the night. The spa bubbles and a massage from Diane last night had done wonders, but he was looking forward to a day off tomorrow. Not so much mentally, but physically.

Liliana brightened when she saw Sarah drive up. "Sarah, you didn't have to come up; don't you need to pick up Dan?"

"Not until later this afternoon. I thought you could use a hand, and *I* need to keep myself occupied until then or I'll go crazy. Besides, Diane can't come; she got called in to work."

"Well, I do appreciate it. I can certainly use the help, although I think the kids could manage pretty much on their own. With the weather threatening, I'm afraid things may have to move indoors this afternoon. I'd rather do it in daylight than the middle of the night. The kids may think it sounds like fun to sleep in a tent in the rain, but after a couple of hours, they will be dashing for cover."

Sarah giggled, adding, "And wet kids will be cold kids. I'll bring some wood over to the parish hall in case they want to build a fire. So, what's the menu for lunch?"

"Taco fixings. I've already cooked the meat, so maybe you could help me carry everything over to the parish hall. While we're setting things out, you have to tell me who all is coming out for the wedding. I meant to ask you yesterday, but time got away from us. I do love weddings, and talking about them is half the fun!"

"As you know, Dan arrives today. Things will get pretty hectic after that, because before our families arrive next Wednesday, we—that's Diane, Gabe, Dan, and I—want to find a house. So Sunday afternoon and Monday have been set aside to do that. We may be dreaming to think that we can find our little love nest getaway in two days, but isn't that what weddings are all about?"

"I hope that before things get too crazy, we can all get together. This could be the last time before you two come back here on vacation, whenever that is."

"Sounds good; just let us know which evening works for you all. And *we* will do the cooking."

"I am too tired to argue! So what about all the other guests?"

"Our parents arrive next Wednesday. Funny, they live just a couple of hundred miles apart, but the first time they will meet it will be in Hawai'i. Then Dan's two brothers, their wives, his sister, her husband, and other assorted sisters, cousins, and aunts, they arrive on Thursday. On Friday, Dan's boss and some of his other colleagues arrive. On Friday, we have the rehearsal and dinner—a beach party at the hotel. You *are* coming, by the way. The boys, too. Then Saturday is the wedding, reception…and Diane's boss is flying us over to Lana'i for three nights before we fly back to Chicago. Then the next weekend, we're going down to St. Louis for a second reception with family and friends who just couldn't do the Hawai'i trip. I get to wear my dress a second time. If we're not married by then, I don't know what!"

"Does anyone need to use the guest house?"

"If it's OK, Diane and I will stay here next Friday night. Gabe and Dan's brother Brian might be planning the bachelor's party at Gabe's place, and we'd just as soon be somewhere else."

"I'll send George down to make sure they stay in line."

"Isn't that a little like having the fox guard the henhouse?"

"You're probably right." Sarah and Liliana laughed while they completed the lunch preparation.

"How is Alec settling in?" asked Sarah.

"He really is a good kid, but this has not been easy for him. His mother is dead, and some of the blame lies with a variety of people here, including me, you, George, Gabe, and Diane. I guess that's all," she said wryly. "We still have to be careful of infection after the kidney transplant, but as a teenager, he wants to be independent, finally—not that I blame him. As the only son of a financially independent woman, he was used to a somewhat material life. That's not our lifestyle, as you know."

Sarah offered no comment to this last, but thought to herself, *these people have it all. They lack for nothing of importance, and are richer than many so-called wealthy folks.*

Liliana added, "You know, this little retreat has been good for Alec as well as the other two boys. Two of the campers have diabetes, and another is in remission from leukemia. Good health is not a guarantee for the young, and it may be that he's feeling a little less sorry for himself after seeing that he's not alone in having medical problems." Liliana smiled at Sarah and continued, "It also helps that there are a couple of really cute girls in the group." Her smile faded, and she continued, "Although we could petition to adopt him legally, he's old enough that we think it needs to be his choice. If Micah and Thomas had their way, it would be a done deal! In their minds, he's already their big brother. I think if he decides to go back to Seattle, it will break their hearts."

Sarah took a chance and asked the ultimate question, "So how are you and George doing with this sudden change in your family structure."

Liliana heaved a heavy sigh. "To be frank, it stung at first. I can't undo the past, and it's like I need to forgive George all over again. I was shocked at how much he looks like George, and Thomas, too, for that matter. Jealousy…it's pretty ugly and even embarrassing. I don't particularly like this about myself, but it's real, and I—and George—have to deal with it. We'll survive it. George is walking a little on eggshells around me, and that adds to the stress. I keep telling myself, 'get over it. It's done, and you can't keep beating George up about it.' I'm sure Alec thinks I'm less than thrilled about his existence, but of course I don't blame him." She sighed and then added, "He really is a good kid."

Sarah offered, "I think you're reaction is very normal, and I also believe that you are strong enough to get through it. You are amazing, but I think you need to let yourself work through all the feelings—both good and bad—that you're having. They're real, and you can't ignore them. Give yourself—and George—a chance. I know you will do more than just survive."

Liliana gave Sarah a hug and tried to avert tears that were close to the surface. Sarah stroked Liliana's glossy dark hair, her own tears threatening to join Liliana's.

"Damn," Liliana whispered, looking upwards as if to keep tears from having a chance to roll down her cheek. "My sister always says I cry too much. Happy, sad, it doesn't matter." She changed the subject to a less emotional topic. "The boys are staying busy this summer. Gabe's putting them all through diving certification, and they all have a summer job painting the rectory and the guest house. This way they can buy some of their own dive gear, so this is what we came up with for them to earn some money. Don't worry; they're not starting until after the wedding." Then she changed subjects again, "I think we're ready; let's call the thundering herd in for lunch." Further discussion would have to wait, but Sarah sensed that Liliana was glad to have the chance to vent. She had never heard Liliana curse.

Thomas rushed up to hug Sarah when he saw her. The older boys held back, conscious of appearances in front of their peers. She got a somewhat more reserved hug from Micah as well, but Alec merely nodded his head and waved at her from a distance. *I see what Liliana means. I'm the wicked witch who was responsible for his mother's death.* She wondered if they would ever be able to reconcile. Her heart ached for him, and she hoped he would someday find peace and emotional healing for the pain she had inadvertently caused.

Sarah stayed as long as she could to help with the dinner setup and likely resettling of the campers inside the parish hall. She felt like she was saying good-bye to a phase in her life that had been the catalyst for her own emotional healing. In three short months with this family, she had grown up—become stronger and more independent. It surprised her that this was actually making her more ready for marriage. She hoped—no, she *knew*—that Dan would want her this way. He did not want an appendage, but an equal partner.

The emotional turmoil she had endured was really the result of another person's conspiracy. It had been a waste of a perfectly good storehouse of tears. *I was not totally innocent, either. My own pride nearly cost me everything.* Dan had nearly died, and she herself would have a constant reminder in a knee still healing from a crippling fall. The death of Alec's mother Angela still brought twinges of guilt for the high price she, Angela, had paid in the name of lust, pride, greed, wrath…just a few deadly sins.

George told Sarah that it was important she forgive herself. *Learn from it, yes, but don't beat yourself up forever.* Together they prayed, and she found herself talking to God more often. *Did you just show up, God, or have you always been there?*

Sarah felt tears welling up, and she wasn't sure why, although it seemed to happen more often lately. Diane had told her it was typical bridal histrionics, and she had "better snap out of it." Sarah smiled at her sister's tough love approach, and she tucked the phrase away for a time when she could use it on her.

Dan patiently repeated the information to the large woman sitting next to him. "Yes, it's Dr. Al Simpson, Albert or Alfred, I can't remember. He's in the Chicago phone book. His specialty is weight management. I recommend you give his office a call. Good luck with it!" Dan was finally able to spring himself free of his fellow passenger. *Next time I'm bringing* National Geographic. The New England Journal of Medicine *is like a magnet for people wanting nine hours of free medical advice.*

He glanced out the window into the downpour and was glad the plane was parking at the covered jet way. Tourists grumbled about wanting their money back because of the poor weather. They wanted to get their luggage and rental cars, and go quickly in search of the sunny side of the island. Dan smiled inwardly, knowing that he would be exactly where he wanted to be in five minutes. Luggage in hand, he let the desperate vacationers brush past him. As far as he was concerned, a rainy afternoon on Maui was not going to be a problem.

Their eyes met just past the security checkpoint. Hearts skipped a beat as the crowd of humanity disappeared in the eager embrace from which neither Dan nor Sarah wanted to ever break free.

"I've missed you so," they both said simultaneously, and then giggled before resuming their intimate greeting.

Sarah said softly, "You can't imagine how much I missed this."

Dan said, "Oh, yes I can. Think we can find a less public place?"

Sarah said, laughing, "We do have to drive home."

"You're torturing me."

"Down, boy. The car's just out here."

"Hmmm… You smell wonderful. What is that…lilacs, tacos…?"

Sarah continued laughing as they walked awkwardly out to the car, arms around each other while toting Dan's luggage.

"We have to behave ourselves for awhile; Gabe's probably at home, maybe Diane, too. Wait 'til you see the places they found for us to tour this weekend. In my wildest dreams, I never thought I'd own property in Hawai'i. We may not want to leave."

"I'm this close to saying, 'let's don't.' The condo is a cavern without you."

"As it should be…no more night visitors?"

"Only in my dreams."

Owen heard the crowd cheering. "Go, Owls, go. Go, Owls, go," he absently sang the school cheer with what little voice he had. Anything to fill the time until the man came back to make him feel good again. He liked hearing students cheering on their athletes. His water bottle was empty, and his stomach was growling continuously. He slowly got to his feet and walked out of his office, staying close to the walls and stopping every few feet to get his bearings and steeling himself against the headache that had returned with a vengeance. *It must be lunchtime. Everyone else is at lunch. I think lunch will make me feel better. The man brings lunch.*

Owen left bloody handprints along the walls from where he had cut himself. His goal was the back door, out to the lunch patio where everyone would be. He tried the windowed door, but it would not open.

The heavy chains around the handles rattled with metallic scraping that drove arrows of pain into his brain. He pressed his hands against the window, leaving bloody handprints as he attempted to find a way to open the door. He sank to the floor, the exertion making him dizzy and amplifying his headache. The pounding eventually subsided, and Owen slowly got to his feet again. He was still dizzy and sought stability from any protrusion he could take hold of to navigate the darkened corridors. The cafeteria was not far; he should be there by now. He tried each door he passed along the way, but none would give way. He came to a bank of metal lockers, and one-by-one grasped the handles as he felt his way along the wall. The sounds of the doors crashing off of one another caused his head to explode, and he finally submitted to the pain and slid down the wall to rest. Grimy sweat rolled down his forehead and stung his eyes, forcing tears to stream down his face and onto his bloody shirt. He was shaking uncontrollably and started to call out, "Help me. Man, where are you? You promised you'd be back." His hoarse pleas degenerated into sobs, and he collapsed in a fetal position outside Room 306.

"Malia, have you reached Owen yet?" George tried to sound light, but he sensed worry in Malia's demeanor.

"Just cryptic text messages that arrive at odd hours. He never replies directly to my questions like, 'Where are you? Who are you with? When are you coming home?' I know he's a big boy, but it's still odd. Late at night when I'm lying awake, all kinds of theories emerge. They're all ridiculous, but you know how your imagination can run wild when you're sleep-deprived."

"I'm just as worried about you as about Owen. Let's make some calls. I'll start with Gabe; he can check out the house, the school, neighbors…"

"I know I'm just being silly; there's nothing specific I can point to that tells me something is wrong. When this is resolved, he is going to tease me something fierce about being a mother hen. I should probably just kill him."

"You know I offer marriage counseling as an intervention to spousal whacking."

Malia laughed wearily, and said, "OK, I'll keep that in mind. Good idea about calling Gabe. I'd prefer that as few people as possible are aware of my paranoia."

George asked, "What time is it… 6:30…so 3:30 at home… I'll try Gabe at home or just leave a message for him to call me. He's usually at home late afternoons."

"If you can't reach him, don't worry about it. We'll be home tomorrow, and by then I'll have figured out what I'm going to use as a murder weapon."

George laughed, adding, "Let me buy you a glass of wine. At least they're serving a decent California vintage at the dinners. That's at least some reward for sitting through all the discussions. Not like the meeting I attended in Utah three years ago; no wonder no one drinks in that state."

"You don't have to twist my arm. Now what's that song you like to sing…"

"You mean, 'Let's get a rock…'" George continued his mostly on-key rendition of the song from *The Full Monty.*

"That's it."

Gabe's condo was empty when Sarah and Dan arrived. Diane had left a note, saying, "We're helping Liliana with dinner…be back around 8:00. Call us if we need to stay away longer—Ha Ha! Love you both, D&G"

There was a message on the answering machine from George for Gabe to call him. Sarah jotted down the phone number and left the message on the kitchen table.

"Too bad it's still raining," said Sarah.

"Yeah, a real tragedy on my first day here. Whatever shall we do? I know; I want to get back to counting your freckles; let's see, where did I last leave off…?"

Wally was growing impatient with the messages that Owen's wife kept leaving for him on his cell phone. He never answered the phone, but he listened to every message in case a response of some kind was needed. He had sent a few text messages at hours that he thought the wife would not be able to answer right away. She was starting to probe deeper into Owen's whereabouts. Wally needed to keep her at bay for another week; after that, he didn't care. *And neither will HoHo,* he chuckled to himself. Duke was going to have to find another place to keep him, some place where he would stay alive, quiet, and under control, and where no one would look for him. Or for Wally either. In a week, he could buy that big TV and enough grass to last him awhile. Life would be good then.

He drove up to the school before sunset and parked against some bushes that would conceal his van. He grabbed the bucket of chicken, oranges, and bottles of water that would keep Owen quiet until morning. He thought that Owen had looked a little weak this morning, and figured he needed to invest a little more into his charge's care and feeding. Wally did not want to have to tell Duke that they had let their "associate" die; it would be a waste of valuable merchandise that had already come directly off their bottom line.

Wally unlocked the solid metal door by the garbage bins and entered the school. He left the dead bolt protruding to keep the door from closing completely. He let his eyes adjust to the darkened corridor. Duke had told him not to turn on any lights. As always, he first listened for any sounds, and then carefully peered around corners as he headed to the main office. As he passed a long corridor, his heart skipped a beat as he saw a mass lying on the floor against the wall about halfway down the hall on the right. He slowly and silently set the food down and pulled out his gun from the waistband of his jeans. He observed the mass and eventually determined that it was Owen, collapsed on the floor. Wally tentatively approached him and hoped he wasn't dead; he did not like dead bodies. They were creepy and smelly, and they attracted bugs and rats. Duke hadn't told him what to do if Owen died.

Dead men don't snore. Wally realized he had been holding his breath and he exhaled in relief. He knew he could not move Owen himself, so he knelt down and shook the man to awaken him. Owen groaned and tentatively opened his eyes into a squint.

"Let's get you up here, HoHo. I brought you some food. Yeah, I thought you'd like that."

Owen showed the man his hand, and Wally knew that was his way of saying he wanted something else as well. He decided that Owen would be a lot easier to manage if he first got his "medication" then and there. Afterwards he helped Owen to the bathroom and got him resettled back in his office. Wally made a mental note that he had better survey the halls and clean up any blood stains that could attract vermin, and that included nosy school or security personnel. So far, no one had come into the building, and he guessed that the upcoming holiday weekend would continue to keep everyone away.

Wally used some of the bottled water to clean Owen's scissor cuts. Owen watched him weakly but perked up when Wally brought out the bucket of chicken. Wally opened all the water bottles and placed them within Owen's reach. He did not want Owen to feel compelled to leave the sanctuary of the office again. He didn't think Owen had tried to escape, for that would mean cutting off his drug supply. No, it was probably hunger or thirst, and Wally made note that he needed to keep Owen better supplied with food and drink. Now was not the time to start nickel-and-diming their "associate." *You have to spend a little to make a lot,* Wally thought to himself, envisioning the forthcoming improvements to his lifestyle.

Owen was soon focused on the fried chicken, and Wally took the opportunity to read email and listen to the answering machine. He judged none of the emails in dire need of a response, but was startled at the message on the answering machine.

"Hi, this is Sarah Donovan. I left my cooler sitting on the floor of my classroom, and I'd like to come get it sometime. Could you call me when someone will be there so I can stop by? My number is 555-0925. Thanks. Bye."

She was the one who was poking around the school earlier. Why can't they all just go on summer vacation? Go get a new cooler at Wal-Mart! Hell, I'd get you one if I thought it would make you stay away.

Owen had stopped eating for the moment, so Wally took him to the bathroom one last time. It would be dark soon, and Wally wanted to be done with his evening chores before it became impossible to see anything. He had Owen remove his shirt so Wally could dispose of it: one less smelly thing. He still had to make a pass through the hallway to restore order to the chaos that Owen's little field trip had caused. Once re-settled,

Owen lay down on the sofa, his eyes glazed over to Wally's satisfaction. Wally left the office, and as quietly as possible closed the open lockers. He took a wet paper towel to the blood stains he could see in the faint light. He hoped that the morning would be soon enough to finish anything he had missed. As he let the metal door close noiselessly, Wally took one more glance around before getting in his van and driving away.

"Gabe, you look like day-old *poi*." Liliana brought her nephew some decaffeinated coffee as she joined him and Diane in the living room at the rectory. Diane reached around and worked on his shoulders, adding, "I think he's just spoiled with this kind of attention."

"Yeah, I wonder how long I can keep up the act," Gabe replied wearily. "I'm looking forward to a day off. Actually I have two days off. There are too many idiots out there on the Fourth of July."

It was still raining, and the sounds of the campers were somewhat muffled since they had moved into the parish hall for the night.

"Did Dan get in OK?" inquired Liliana.

"Sarah called; they were staying in for the night. The rain didn't seem to dampen her spirits."

Gabe laughed. "How long do you think we need to stay away?"

Diane said, "Finish your coffee; we need to let Liliana go to bed. George is coming home tomorrow, and she's got to get an early start tomorrow on her list of what he's going to owe her."

"This is a side of you I've never seen, Liliana."

"Oh, I think you may see it more often now. Anyway, thank you both so much for all your help. Sleep in tomorrow; don't bother coming up. They've already packed up the tents since they're sleeping indoors tonight."

"If you're sure; I could definitely use a morning with no alarm clock."

Gabe let Diane drive back to the condo; he was almost asleep by the time she pulled into the garage. Sarah was still up, but Dan had finally given in to jet lag. Gabe said, "Looks like you two have worn out us tough guys. Let's see, which room is mine? 'Night ladies. I'll save you a spot, Diane. Wake me for my sponge bath."

The sisters made some tea and decided to sit out on the covered lanai where they could talk without awakening the guys, as unlikely as that seemed.

Sarah said, "I'm going to miss this."

"Are you getting maudlin on me?"

"Maybe."

"How's Dan?"

"He's wonderful. OK, I'm not maudlin anymore. How long has that word been in your vocabulary anyway?"

Diane laughed, and asked, "So how was your greeting by Alec today?"

"He waved, but didn't say anything. I think he needs time. He may never forgive me, you know."

"But you weren't to blame. Are you still kicking yourself over it?"

"I think he needs to blame someone. I'm the easiest."

"I don't know how you deal with teenagers. They are positively the most self-absorbed creatures on earth."

"I've got my teenagers; you've got your rich and famous clients. Surely they are pretty demanding."

"Some, but most of them are pretty laid back. Mostly they want to escape the rat race. There is this one woman, tho'. She's the interior decorator for some guy that's building a beach villa on Lana'i. He keeps flying her back and forth from Honolulu with all these samples. He hasn't made up his mind on whether he wants to go with early American décor or fifties retro. Neither would be anything short of disastrous in this setting, so she's trying to nudge him into something better suited for out here. She's very frustrated, and more than once she's burst into tears trying to figure out what to do. She knows he's going to hate it if he gets his way, and she's going to get blamed for it. And to make things worse, the guy is starting to put the moves on her. No matter what happens, this is going to end badly. I feel like a bartender at times. But it's a lot more fun that flying big commercial planes."

"I'll keep my teenagers, thank you. Say, are you sure you'll be able to give us the grand tour tomorrow?"

"You bet. Gabe's got the day off, and I'm really looking forward to having him see what my passion is all about. We can't take off until around noon so that he's got a full twenty-four hours behind him since he went diving."

"Well, Dan is really excited about it, and so am I… I've been here three months and haven't seen much of the island yet."

Diane added, "My plan is to convince him to leave Chicago behind and start up a clinic specializing in treating disadvantaged offspring of the millionaires I fly around."

"It might just work. Does he know about this scheme?"

"I think we need to make him think it's his idea; what do you think? He'll just need us to tell him how smart he is to think of it."

"It wouldn't surprise me if he's coming up with a plan of his own to convince *me!*"

Friday, July 3

Wally drove slowly down the street in front of Owen's house to see if anyone was up. He figured 3:00 a.m. was late enough for even the night owls to be in bed, but too early for the early birds to be up. He wouldn't be there long anyway. He parked behind a truck on the street so it would not appear that he was at Owen's house. He waited a full minute to see if he had awakened anyone and to let his eyes adjust to the darkness. He put on a hat, grabbed a small duffle bag, and quietly emerged from his car, walking across the street to the side of Owen's house. He took one last look around and noiselessly opened the side door with Owen's keys. He instinctively pulled out his gun in case someone happened to be home. He had never had to shoot anyone, but the stakes were high in this job, and it might come to that. There was enough light coming from the streetlight to enable Wally to navigate through the small house and satisfy himself that there was no one there. Apparently they didn't even have a cat or a dog, which would have been just as worrisome since no one had been around to feed it anyway.

He found what apparently was Owen's bedroom and opened the closet door to pick out some clean clothes. *Two changes of clothes should be enough. If HoHo has to meet Mr. Cho, he had better be presentable. Golf shirts. That way, he won't call attention to himself on the golf course.*

Wally selected a white shirt with wide navy stripes, as well as a red shirt that said "Maui Middle School" embroidered around an owl. He also found two pairs of very large khaki slacks and assembled everything on the bed with underwear and socks. He heard a car drive by and decided that he had to go with what he had and get out of there before the rest of the neighborhood woke up. He pulled out Owen's dirty shirt from the duffle and tossed it in the laundry basket, glad to be rid of it. Wally did not want Owen's dirty clothes to be traced to him; it was better to leave Owen's clothes at Owen's house. He restuffed the duffle bag with the clean clothes and quietly left the house the way he came in, looking up and down the street before crossing the street and getting back in his car. As he rounded the corner, he took a final glance in the rearview mirror before turning on the lights.

Dan was the first one up at Gabe's condo. Only two or three lights were on at the neighbors, and even the birds were still asleep. He wished he could have slept longer, since he knew the day would be a long one. He made a pot of coffee and quietly made some phone calls back home to colleagues, as well as to patients whose ailments were not on holiday. He was pleased to hear that Tiffany's mother was making progress getting her daughter into a drug intervention program. As expected, Tiffany was not making it easy, and the two had a rough road ahead of them.

Browsing through the real estate brochures brought a smile to his face. Even a year ago, he had not imagined that he'd be looking at houses with *ocean* views. No fireplaces except at the higher elevations, no worries about whether the driveways would be navigable in winter. He wondered if the houses had central heat at all.

The two girls had folded corners down on the brochures and circled houses they liked. He continued smiling as he observed the features that each sister considered important. Sarah liked the ones that promised views from spacious lanais and "gourmet kitchens." Diane only earmarked houses with at least three bathrooms. She had put a giant smiley face by a mansion with six bedrooms and six bathrooms that was hopelessly out of reach for normal mortals. *What is it about women and bathrooms?* He didn't know what Gabe would like, but if he's like most guys, a large garage with a workshop and storage would be a plus. One bathroom would be enough. What about a pool? Gabe certainly had plenty of opportunity to get wet, but a pool would be nice for Dan and Sarah. But Gabe and Diane would be left with the bulk of the maintenance, so he and Sarah would have to be sensitive to what they'd be able to handle.

He heard the newspaper bounce against the front door. Somehow a newspaper seemed so everyday in a place that's supposed to be an escape from the ordinary.

A million miles from anywhere, Maui had the same issues as anywhere in the country. The developers *versus* the environmentalists. Affordable housing. Education. Dan wasn't sure what he was expecting, but the realization that people actually lived and earned a living here struck home. Traffic accidents. Boating accidents. Drug busts. A woman arrested for stealing jewelry from her employer. Local sports, but not much on professional sports. In Chicago, you were either a White Sox fan or a Cubs fan. There didn't appear to be any one professional team that received more billing than another. There was plenty on the local amateur and youth teams.

There was a whole section focused on island recreation. Cruise ship *Sun and Moon* cited for harassing sea life. Bikeathon Saturday to benefit diabetes research. *Haleakala* campground closed for maintenance after a fire.

The weather. High 85, low 75. The same for the foreseeable future. Chance of rain everyday, somewhere. Excellent chance of sun everyday, everywhere. On paper, it was not that different from a summer day at home, *but Chicago doesn't have those tropical breezes*, he thought to himself, *the kind that warm and cool you at the same time.*

Classifieds: Homes, autos, horses, puppies, boats, computers for sale. Help wanted—health care workers, SCUBA instructors, hotel reception, restaurant servers, hotel housekeeping, conductor for the Sugar Cane Train, boat crew, maintenance workers, winery workers (on Maui?), groundskeepers, window washers. It looked to Dan like everyone was either supporting the tourist industry or those who did.

Like Sarah, Dan wasn't completely convinced that Chicago was where they wanted to live. Sarah's crippling knee injury on the ice, his own life-threatening bout of pneumonia—was someone trying to tell them something? Was this the time to start fresh here?

A yawning and stretching Gabe soon joined Dan, welcoming him to Maui and his last week of bachelorhood. They compared notes on their women's house-hunting wishes. The pool issue had already been resolved: with Diane's airborne profession keeping her above sea level, the house had to have a pool. Dan had the impression that whatever Diane wanted turned out to be what Gabe wanted. He smiled, thinking that wasn't such a bad thing.

Having dated Sarah briefly before Dan and Diane appeared on the scene, Gabe had felt some initial awkwardness around Dan, but being guys, he figured they'd get through it. And they did. Before Diane, his life had consisted of three priorities, and he structured his time accordingly. If it wasn't school teaching, diving, or his Uncle George's family, it probably wasn't on his agenda. But Diane filled all the voids in his life he hadn't realized existed. He found himself thinking in terms of "we" and "someday," and wondered how he had survived without her. He hoped he wouldn't have to. Other women had told him he was self-absorbed and commitment-phobic. They were right. He wondered what they would think if they saw him now. No lingering regrets about Sarah remained; their relationship had barely gotten off the ground. She had become a sister to him, while Diane was, well, his woman. *My woman*, he thought playfully with a raised eyebrow, as the scent of her made his skin prickle with desire. Recollections of their intimacy the night before made him shiver and perspire. *Must be the coffee, right?*

Gabe noticed a note scrawled on the kitchen table: *Gabe—George called…weird—Malia can't find Owen. Any idea? Camping maybe, dunno. Call him—Sarah*

Was he supposed to call Owen or George? *Does it matter? Call them both, you idiot. Time to wake up.*

"More coffee, Dan?" Gabe asked from the kitchen.

"Thanks. Both girls still asleep?"

"Probably. They're resting up so they can wear us out again."

"That they do." Dan laughed at the double meaning in Gabe's statement.

Dan changed subjects. "So I hear we're all getting a bird's eye view of the islands today."

"You know, I haven't seen the islands from the air in probably three years. If I didn't have tomorrow off, I still couldn't do it."

"Better make sure you've got a parachute."

"Being with Diane is a lot like jumping out of a plane without one."

"That good, huh?"

"Oh, yeah."

"Coffee, knave!" called Diane from the master bedroom.

"I await your bidding, my bo…" Gabe stopped short of responding with his pet name for her. *Some things are not for sharing.*

A groggy Sarah emerged from the guest room and joined Dan out on the lanai. She leaned over him from the back of the chair and started to massage his shoulders.

"Hope you slept well," she said playfully.

"I may need a nap later."

"I guarantee you will."

Observing Gabe walking back into the bedroom with coffee for Diane, Dan stole an opportunity to reach inside Sarah's robe to refresh his memory of her. She leaned into him, and he whispered, "So, what have you got planned for us today? Stay here and do more of this?"

Sarah giggled, "What makes you think I've got plans?"

"Because I know you."

"Ummmm…yes, you do. Although I can be persuaded. OK, let's get practical…oh, that feels so good…you should probably stop. Where was I? You made me forget. Oh, right. We have to go get our marriage license. You realize that the only reason I wanted to get married here is that we don't need a blood test."

"Good, I hate needles."

"Really?"

"I'm OK administering them, but I really don't like being on the receiving end."

"Good to know. Oh, you did remember your birth certificate, didn't you?"

"Oh, no. I forgot to tell you; I'm not from this planet."

"Neither am I, so that's good." She continued, "Then we're going over to the hotel to see the reception place. They're giving us a choice of two locations, and it's your job to decide. I couldn't."

"Well, I guess the important criterion is: where will you look best naked?"

She roughed up his hair and replied, "Actually we have a family tradition that grooms always appear naked at the wedding."

"In that case I'll need an extra long *lei.*"

Sarah giggled and Dan continued. "Whatever we do today, tomorrow, and so on, as long as I don't have to live 4,000 miles away from you, I don't care what we do. Whose idea was it for you to stay here without me anyway? That guy was an idiot!"

"He certainly was."

At breakfast the discussion centered around the parents arriving on Wednesday. Gabe asked Dan, "Are you ready to meet the people that not only spawned the Queen of Hearts, but also 'Annie Get Your Gun?'"

"Hey, I stopped sleeping with a gun under my pillow weeks ago," Diane replied in retort.

"It's the spurs that we still have to talk about."

Dan added, "Sarah's more into leather. I think I got the better deal."

Sarah laughed and replied, "I think Mom's got some fetish about hand cuffs, and Dad keeps a whip under the bed. Diane, did you tell Gabe about your pet scorpion?"

Gabe choked, saying, "I think I'm going to join the Witness Protection Program."

Dan echoed, "I'll join you.'"

Diane brought the conversation back to reality. "They're actually pretty normal. Quirky, but mostly normal."

Gabe said, "Did you catch that, Dan? Somehow they went from 'pretty' normal to 'mostly' normal, all in one breath"

"Dad's got this thing about cameras and taking pictures," Sarah said.

Dan said with mock terror, "Say no more. The image of your parents—who I haven't even met yet—taking pictures with hand cuffs and whips…"

"Oh, stop. He's mostly normal."

"There's that 'mostly' word again."

Sarah pretended to ignore him and continued. "I hope you're prepared to have memories of every family gathering recorded for posterity with hundreds of pictures. Dad's got a room that is filled with boxes of pictures he took of us growing up."

"Any naked ones?" asked Gabe.

"Plenty of Diane."

"I'm not surprised."

"You shouldn't be."

Dan asked, "So what about your mother? Neither of you seem particularly obsessive, so you must be more like her."

Gabe jumped in, "You haven't seen Diane make a bed. I'm afraid to get it in for fear she'll make me up in it."

"Fear of the bed is not your problem."

"I guess you're right."

Sarah and Dan laughed at the lovers' banter and affectionately reached for one another's hand. Sarah said, "Well, Mom is great. I think she puts up with Dad's little hobby—OK, he's obsessive—so he can't complain about her Broadway music collection. She does push his buttons by putting ice in her beer, tho'."

Dan queried, "Somehow I can't imagine your mother—who I admit I've never met—relaxing with a glass of wine—or beer on ice, you say?—listening to, or much less, watching, *The Full Monty*."

"That's George's favorite. She's more into *The Sound of Music* and *The King and I*, although secretly I think she liked *Hair*."

Dan said, "Well, all I can say is your Dad must be a saint having survived in a household full of women."

Diane added, "We had a male dog and a bunch of male cousins, but you're right. He put up with a lot of female hormones."

Dan shivered and said, "And to think I almost went into gynecology."

Sarah was startled at this and stared at him in disbelief. "You did?"

Dan smiled, and queried, "Proctology—you'd like that better?" Sarah realized he was teasing her. She got up from the table and said, "You're just going to have to take pot luck with the rest of the family. After all, they're mostly normal, aren't they, Diane?"

"Mostly."

"Malia, you look exhausted." George was shocked at how bedraggled his colleague and friend looked.

"I didn't get any sleep. I'll be glad when we're on our way home. Maybe I can sleep on the plane. Did you hear from Gabe yet?"

"No, but I'm sure I will. They should be getting up about now."

"OK."

"Coffee…bourbon?"

"Yes."

Duke took the trash out on the pretext of checking out any suspicious activity around the apartment grounds. He knew what to look for: someone sitting in a car, a guy doing maintenance without making much progress, a van with some bogus company name on it—carpet cleaning, pool maintenance, or air-conditioning repair. He waved at the neighbor lady he made eye contact with when he walked back. He had the feeling that she timed her visits to the trash bin so she would run into him. She wasn't bad looking... *No, not now. Later. There would be time later. They could have a very good time. Some place nicer than this one.* He tried to appear encouraging in a way that still indicated he was in a hurry and couldn't stop to talk. He realized that if she was watching him from her window that he would have to be very discreet in what he carried in and out. Back at his apartment he noticed the old bag of golf clubs standing in the corner. Women like guys who play golf, he decided. The bag was a perfect container as well as an investment in sex appeal he could cash in on later.

A knock at the door startled him, and he did an instinctive survey of the room to make sure there was nothing in sight that might arouse suspicion. Another knock, and a voice, "It's your neighbor, Erin."

Duke answered the door, and found himself face to face with the woman from the trash. She grinned at him, saying, "I'm sorry to bother you, but I'm Erin North from the unit across the pool over there. I was wondering if you knew how to fix the garbage disposal; mine just stopped."

A damsel in distress. Maybe.

"Uh, sure, I can take a look."

"Great! I really appreciate it—uh..."

"Duke. It's Duke."

"Duke. I'm Erin."

"Erin. It's nice to meet you."

They walked across the lawn to Erin's apartment. "It's in here, Duke. Silly. You know where the kitchen is, of course."

"Yeah…let's take a look. Yup, it stopped. There should be a restart button under here. There. OK, give it a try."

"It works! Thank you so much, Duke! I feel so stupid."

"No problem."

"Would you like a cup of coffee, or a beer?"

"That would be great, but I'm late for a golf game. Can I take a rain check?"

Erin's face spoke disappointment but she shrugged it off, saying, "No problem."

Duke asked her, "Could I get your phone number?"

Erin's face lit up, and she said, "Sure." She handed him a business card that indicated she was a free-lance writer and worked out of her apartment. They shook hands warmly, and Duke made his exit.

Back at his apartment, Duke realized that he was sweating. Erin was a fox, but she would have to wait. In his profession, people screwed up when they let themselves get distracted from business. He'd have to come up with some legitimate job story, and there simply wasn't time right now. Business first.

He had to go play golf. Actually he had to look like he was playing golf, which meant that he had to leave for at least five or six hours. Wally would be here soon, so it could look like they were heading off to play golf. He hoped Wally didn't show up in a raggedy T-shirt and jeans.

Duke glanced out the window to make sure his neighbor wasn't making a return visit. He partially closed the window blinds, thinking that closing them completely would look unfriendly. He took the golf clubs into his bedroom and emptied the bag onto the bed. He rummaged around in his closet for the canvas golf bag cover. Carrying out a golf bag with no golf clubs in it would look suspicious. He made another quick check out the window to make sure he wasn't about to receive another knock on the door. He did not want to be interrupted while he assembled the package.

Most of Duke's cocaine supply was safely hidden in the void in his box spring. For what he had planned today, he only needed six packages. The golf bag would hold them easily. As he packed the golf bag, a knock at the door made him jump. He hoped it was Wally, and was relieved when he saw his partner through the peep hole.

"Hey, Duke, you playing golf today?"

"No, but Owen is."

"Huh? Oh, I see. Hey, that's good."

"I've got a nosy neighbor. Here, go in the bedroom and put on one of my polo shirts."

"Sure."

"How's our elephant today, Wally?"

"Wasted. I went to his house in the middle of the night to get him some clean clothes; he was pretty ripe. Don't worry! Nobody saw me. And over at the school I put him in the shower in the locker room to clean him up. He still needs a shave, but at least he's not going to call attention to himself. I'm just not sure how long we can keep him there. I mean, someone's gonna show up there sometime next week. Maybe even Monday. Can we move things up? This is taking too long."

"Let's see how he does today. Here, carry the bag out to the car. Think you can look like you're about to play golf?"

"No problem."

Owen was floating. He wondered why he had never thought about flying, since he was sure that he could now. *I have to tell Malia how wonderful it is to fly.*

He felt wonderful. He was having trouble keeping his pants up and kept stepping on the cuffs. *I'm so happy here in my office. I want to stay here and just be happy. I'm going to be happy forever. I'm happy when the man comes. He's a good man. He loves me. I love him. I think he's God. God makes me so happy. I hope he comes soon. There's my computer. I like my computer. I'll sit there and be happy. The screen looks funny…it's so funny! Everything is moving around. My chair spins around…whee! Malia, come spin with me!*

Kahealani Levine greeted Dan and Sarah at the hotel with leis and chilled glasses of champagne. Dan kept calling the wedding coordinator Kaliani, but the woman graciously ignored the mistake, and escorted the couple around the property so that they could get a feel for the ambience of their wedding reception venue. Kahealani first took them to the beach party site Sarah had selected for the rehearsal dinner. All Dan could say was, "wow," and Sarah breathed a sigh of relief that she had done well choosing the site for the dinner his parents would host. He knew his family would love the casual ocean front setting, and he imagined his young niece and nephews frolicking in the sand and dodging the waves. He put his arm around Sarah in approval and said, "Well done, lady." This would be a dinner his parents would love hosting, and it would long be remembered.

Sarah smiled at him and responded, "Glad you like it. Wait 'til you see the reception spot, or spots; I can't decide which one I like better. You have to choose, since I picked the rehearsal dinner location. Remember, *my* parents are hosting that one. Choose wisely. No pressure."

The trio followed the curving paved walkway as it meandered through the grounds, passing waterfalls, parrots perched on stands, activity shacks, and sculptures of Polynesian gods, birds, and fish. The path ended at an expansive grassy lawn surrounded by palms. A stone dance floor occupied the center of the lawn. One end of the lawn was open to the ocean, but the palms acted as a wind and noise break against the pounding of the surf that Sarah knew would be even stronger in the afternoon.

Mouth open in awe, Dan dryly stated the obvious, "This could work."

Sarah giggled, "Yeah, it's not bad, is it?"

Kahealani said that they also have weddings here, and in fact a Jewish couple was getting married there on Sunday. "They're going to have a canopy right in the center, and all the guests will be in chairs around it. Then it gets converted into the reception."

Sarah said, "OK, this is Plan A. Now let's see Plan B. I don't want to bias your opinion."

Kehealani escorted Dan and Sarah back to the main path and up to *Manu Punana.* "This is the Bird's Nest. I think you can see why."

Both Dan and Sarah realized they were holding their breaths. They were above it all: the waves, the noise of the beach and the pool, and the grounds of the hotel. A canopy of live greenery filtered the sun shining on the expansive lanai. The setting offered nearly 360° views of the ocean, the island of Lana'i, and the green Maui mountains shrouded in clouds.

Dan said, "I didn't notice the climb."

Kehealani said, "It's very gradual and off the beaten path, so we don't get too many people up here. It's a jewel, isn't it?"

Sarah said, "You see why I couldn't decide? OK, I have one question. You call it the Bird's Nest; are there birds?" Sarah had visions of birds adorning the wedding guests as only they could.

"The birds do have this place to themselves until about 8:00 in the morning. The noise is deafening, and then there are the droppings. Then they leave for the day and don't return until sunset. So, if you like this spot, you'll want to be gone by then, for obvious reasons. What time is your wedding?"

Dan said with mock concern, "Noon. Maybe we could make it later, say 4:00—that's one way to get people to leave the party! It keeps the bar bill manageable. I'm just thinking of your dad, Sarah. Don't look at me like that!"

Kehealani joined in the laughter, adding, "And don't worry, we give this place a thorough washing down before every event. I don't recall any complaints. We thought about removing the trees, but they really offer some nice shade. Anyway, we've got some photos of receptions at both locations, so you can see what it might be like for you. You can check the tops of people's heads for, well, you know. Anyway, you'll certainly be fine until at least 6:00, but if you think the festivities will go into the evening, it's probably better if you go with—what did you call it—Plan A?"

Back at Kehealani's office, Dan and Sarah browsed through a photo album of prior receptions. Dan said, "So, if I choose—what is it—Manu Poopoo, and even one person gets hit, it's *my* fault for choosing the spot for the reception. Now I know the *real* reason you're making me decide."

Sarah put her hands on her hips and said, "Look, I had to make all the other tough decisions, like how low-cut I'd let Diane have her dress, and whether we'd allow white zinfandel to be served—yes, I know your mother likes it, and, well, it's just been one thing after another." She dabbed her eyes with a tissue.

Dan just rolled his eyes, and Sarah looked at him innocently. Dan finally said, "OK, it *is* perfect. I guess if they've had other receptions there without any problems, we should be fine. We'll go with Manu, uh…"

"*Manu Punana*," offered Kehealani. "I'm so glad, you two. It will be unforgettable, and I mean that in a good way! Now, I've arranged for you to have lunch out on the terrace as our guests. I'm going to make sure all the arrangements get made for both dinners, so please just enjoy the beautiful day and each other. Dan, it was nice to meet you, and I hope you have a wonderful time here on the island. If you two want to come over to enjoy the beach and watch the fireworks tomorrow, here's my card in case anyone asks you what your room number is."

Beaming, Dan and Sarah walked hand-in-hand over to the open-air waterfront restaurant. Sarah said, "I'm getting so excited; it's really going to happen!"

Dan replied, "Nothing is going to stop us now." He paused briefly before asking, "Can we talk about that nap now?"

"Tee time, HoHo! Wally is here. Here, let's get you presentable. Yes, I brought you some lunch." Wally tended to his docile captive, satisfying both hungers: food and drugs. It was a fine line between keeping Owen lucid enough to walk and carry out basic tasks, while keeping his pain level down. The addict will always choose the latter.

"Let's go out for some fresh air and sunshine. This office is getting ripe."

"Golf? I can play golf?" queried Owen. He instinctively started to swing an imaginary golf club and nearly lost his balance before Wally propped him up against the wall.

"That's an impressive swing, HoHo. I bet the ladies are standing in line to swing with you. Wifey, Gabrielle...all the little sweet things. Whoa, buddy, let's wait until we get on the course to start swinging. Yeah, in you go. Good, yes, buckle yourself in. HoHo, this is Duke; he's going to play golf with us today."

"Hi, Duke! Wally is a nice man, don't you think? Is he God?"

"Yes, I do, HoHo. God...maybe, you think so?"

Wally made a final visual check of the surroundings before locking the door of the school. The three men then drove off.

"Three-putt. Three-putt, three-putt, three-putt. Putt, putt, putt. FORE! Oh, shit, it's in the lake. It's a gimme. Uh-oh, I just farted. Excuse me. Ha ha! Gotta pee behind the tree with Wall-ee on Mow-ee!"

Wally and Duke tried to keep from laughing at Owen's babbling, because they didn't want him any more excited than he already was. When the drug started to wear off, Owen would come crashing down. So as long as he was happy, things were manageable. This was Owen's dress rehearsal. It would be a controlled environment, a test, to see whether he would be up to the real performance. Wally's and Duke's reputations— and perhaps more—were on the line. It was no laughing matter.

Wally deliberately drove past the warehouse in Kahului without slowing down. He turned around in the industrial *cul de sac* and approached the warehouse more slowly before parking. Owen's gibberish was becoming annoying, and at this point a liability. They needed him to be quiet.

"You know, HoHo, we have to be quiet while people are teeing off."

"So, why are you talking so loud, Wally? We have to be quiet. Shhhhh!"

Wally whispered, "That's right, HoHo. Are you ready to play golf?"

"I thought we were going to play golf." Owen started to sound depressed.

"Would you like to play golf?" asked Wally.

Owen nodded.

Duke said to Wally, "We need to get moving. How much stuff did you give him?"

"That's what I've been trying to tell you. He's like an elephant. Except an elephant would smell better."

"OK, HoHo, let's go. Here, you can carry your clubs."

"I can carry my clubs. I can carry my cubs. I mean clubs. My cubs can carry my clubs. Ha ha!"

Duke walked into the warehouse and instructed Wally to stay behind until he gave an 'all clear' sign. It was a long three minutes before Duke came back out, waving to Wally to come in with Owen. Wally helped Owen sling the golf clubs onto his shoulder, and they joined Duke in the darkened warehouse.

Gradually the contents of the warehouse came into view after the trio's eyes adjusted to the sudden contrast of light and dark. Pallets stacked two stories high became visible and were labeled as golf equipment. Golf carts covered in plastic occupied a quarter of the floor space. Owen instinctively headed towards them, looking for a place to store his clubs. Wally gently guided him back to the central aisle. "You said you could carry your clubs, HoHo." Owen nodded absently.

A man driving a golf cart came from the back of the warehouse and stopped in front of Owen. "Is this our fourth?" he asked, with a raspy voice.

"Good one, Edgar," said Duke. "Yes, HoHo, you can put your clubs in the back of this cart. You're going to ride with Edgar." Duke and Wally then got into a second golf cart that had two golf bags already in it, and the "foursome" drove out the back door of the warehouse. Almost immediately they were on a golf cart path at a municipal golf course. Duke smiled at how perfect the disguise was: four guys out playing golf. The hard part was driving the cart path slowly to the golf cart garage where they would meet Benny, another of Mr. Cho's associates. If they went too fast, they would attract the attention of other golfers, and perhaps the course marshal, a guaranteed disaster. Duke had a gun and would use it if he had to, but the situation would have to be pretty desperate. No, staying under everyone's radar was best, even if it meant the operation took a little longer.

Owen was babbling and starting to become irritating to Edgar. But Edgar was a professional, and a certain level of discomfort was just part of the job. Sharing a golf cart with someone else his own size was a challenge. The cart moved more slowly and was harder to control. Also, their flesh hung out over the edges and got jabbed with branches and railings. He was tempted to pull out a joint to relax a little, but the chance of someone catching a whiff of grass on the golf course was not worth the risk. Anyway, the cart garage was in sight, and he signaled to Duke and Wally behind him that they were approaching the semi-camouflaged utility building. He slowed the cart so that another party of golfers could get significantly ahead of them. It was best if they saw no one up close, since it would require the exchange of polite golfer greetings. And no one wanted Owen to talk to anyone.

Edgar parked his cart in a small paved area that was almost completely enclosed by dense bushes, and motioned to Duke to park alongside him. Edgar jumped out and quickly surveyed the area around the garage, while Duke and Wally tended to Owen. Wally thought Owen was starting to crash, and he estimated he had at most a half hour before painful withdrawal symptoms would take over. He preferred to have Owen situated back in his office, but he would probably not have that luxury today. As glad as he was that Owen was quiet, it meant that the euphoria was wearing off.

Wally helped Owen get the golf bag off the cart, and took him around to the far side of the garage. Across the fairway was a limousine parked on the road. "Here's the game, HoHo. Think you can carry that bag across the fairway to that man standing over there by the black car? Yeah, just over there. That's right. Then just come on back here. OK? You said you can carry your clubs."

"Sure, Wally."

Owen hoisted the bag over his shoulders and walked erratically across the fairway. Wally hoped he wouldn't fall. It was important that Owen pass this practice test; otherwise he would fail the final exam.

Benny motioned for Owen to pick up the pace in the way a man would encourage a puppy to come. When Owen reached Benny, he shook his hand in greeting and took the golf bag, putting it in the trunk of the limousine. Owen was sweating and panting from the exertion. Benny pulled the clubs out of the bag and reached in to pull out the cache of cocaine. With a knife he made a small cut in one of the bags and sampled its contents. Satisfied, he stuffed the cocaine back into the golf bag and gingerly returned the clubs to the bag on top of the packets. He gave a high thumbs-up sign to Owen and then to Duke and Wally across the fairway. Owen mimicked the gesture smiling to Benny and the others. Benny then gave Owen an envelope and told Owen to go back over to Wally. Owen clumsily walked back across the fairway, this time into Edgar's waiting hand clasp.

"You did great today, HoHo. We're very proud of you." Owen was starting to weep, and Edgar put his arms around him.

"Thank you, Eggo. Gotta pee"

Wally interjected and said, "HoHo, come on. I'll take you to the bathroom. You are quite a golfer, big guy. You beat all of us." He pulled out a small pouch whose contents would take away HoHo's headache, and enable him to stay comfortable (and hopefully quiet) on the trip back to his office-prison.

"I did good? I don't remember."

"Oh, yeah. Real good."

"I carried my own bag."

"Yes, you did."

Gabe was starting to get worried. He didn't know Owen personally that well, but it was still a cause for concern that he seemed to be unreachable, not so much by him, but by Malia. He had tried his home number, the school office, and his cell phone. Diane sensed the distraction in Gabe's demeanor, particularly when he shook off her offer to make breakfast.

"Gabe? What's up?" she asked.

"Strange. I'm trying to find Owen, you know, Malia's husband, and my boss." He showed her the note Sarah had scribed, and Diane queried him on where he had tried to reach Owen.

"I'm halfway thinking I should drive over to the school and his house. I can at least see if his car is around. He's probably camping like he said, but still, Malia's not one to worry over nothing."

"Go find him, Gabe. The three of us can drive over to the air field, and you can meet us there."

Gabe nodded, saying, "Good plan. I'll see you over there." He kissed the top of Diane's head, grabbed his school keys, and was gone before he had finished his sentence, dialing his cell phone as he walked out to his car.

There was no answer on George's cell phone. *He's probably airborne about now.* The school was closer, so he checked over there first. He used his keys to get in the building, but he didn't have keys to the office. It was apparent that no one was there anyway. Not surprising, the place smelled stale, having been closed up for weeks. He went to his own classroom and found a notepad and some tape. He then left a note on the office door: "Mr. Hoana, please call me when you have a chance. Thanks—G. Callahan 555-2426. 11:00 a.m. July 3."

Gabe glanced down the corridor and was taken aback by the sight of a partial handprint smeared on the back door jam. Brownish…blood? A maintenance man probably cut himself. He didn't see any other blood evidence and dismissed it as inconsequential. "Where are you, Owen?" he asked himself. "Not here, obviously."

Wally felt adrenaline rush into every extremity. As he drove up to the school with Owen, he noticed a white SUV parked in front with some dive logo painted on it. "It's summer vacation. No one is supposed to be there. Leave," he said to no one in particular. He couldn't risk entering the parking lot, so he decided to go to a drive-through to get food for Owen. It would give him time to think.

Gabe's next stop was Owen's and Malia's house. He hadn't thought to get the address before he left, but he had been there a couple of times and thought he could find his way there. During the drive he called home to see if George had left any other messages, but he hadn't.

At Owen's house he parked out front so that the neighbors wouldn't think he was trying to break in. He noticed both cars parked in the carport. He wasn't sure what that meant. He knocked on the front door several times, and then went around back. The house was closed up, unusual considering the weather, if indeed anyone was home. He checked with neighbors on either side. No one had seen Owen or Malia. Once again, Gabe left Owen a note to call him, and slipped it in the mail slot where he could see several days of mail scattered on the floor. He counted three newspapers in the driveway, which he collected and placed on the front porch to make the emptiness of the house less obvious to passersby. *Makes sense if he's camping. That's probably it. I might have had a neighbor bring in the newspapers, but it's not really a big deal. I'm not sure what else I can do. I can tell George that he's not at work and not at home, and his car is here.* Owen's car was not one he would take camping in the high country, so he was probably with someone. Gabe didn't know who Owen's camping buddies might be. Malia surely did, and she could start on that list when she got home. He wished he had more than the absence of information, but the evidence was pointing to a camping trip, and there was nothing to suggest anything was wrong.

Gabe got back in the car, left George a voice mail message with a summary of his findings, leaving out the part about the bloody handprint. It wasn't relevant anyway. Then he made his way to the airfield to meet Diane, Sarah, and Dan.

Wally slammed his hands on the steering wheel. "Shit! Who is this guy?" The same white SUV was parked at Owen's house. Wally watched him from half a block away. The guy was looking in windows, searching around back, and even talking to the neighbors. Fortunately Owen was snoring, and Wally needed time to think. "I told Duke someone was going to start looking for him. Better call Duke. He'll know what to do. He never worries about anything."

"Did you find Owen?" Sarah asked as Gabe got out of his car at the airfield.

"No, and I'm not sure that's bad news. He's not at the school, and he's not at home. His car is there. It looks like he's away for the weekend camping with some buddies. Malia is going to kill him when he gets home."

"You don't think he might be—um, with someone?"

"I really can't imagine…"

"No, neither can I. We're going flying in that?" Gabe had a big grin on his face as he greeted Diane with a hug and a kiss.

"This is a man who plays with sharks for a living, and he's scared of a little flying?"

"Being with you is like flying."

Dan and Sarah stood by, smiling at the banter that was typical of the conversations between Diane and Gabe. They were clearly in love.

"OK, mount up!" called Diane to her friends.

"Wait, aren't you going to check the oil, put air in the tires, refill the windshield wipers…?"

"What do you think I've been doing while waiting for you? And I filed an FAA flight plan, got a weather briefing, went through a checklist, did a walkaround checking all the flight controls, fluid levels, reviewed the log book, and…"

"I love it when you talk pilot."

"I made sure there are two wings on the plane and glass in the windshield. Can you hand me that parachute over there?"

"Where's mine?"

"Think you'll need one? Actually I got you a life vest; I thought you'd be more comfortable with one."

"Just remember, you have yet to go diving with me. I'll be sure to give you a parachute."

"I still want my own bathroom."

"You'll have the entire ocean at your disposal."

"And today, you'll have the entire sky."

"Not a problem, huh, Dan?"

Dan held his hands up indicating he was pushing back on this point. "Gabe, I'm staying out of this; you're on your own. I think we just need to let Diane be in charge. It's not like we have any choice."

"Smart guy you've got there, Sarah," Diane acknowledged. "I kind of like being the one in charge for a change. You're in my town now."

They boarded the Cessna Citation, with Gabe in the front seat next to Diane, and Dan and Sarah behind them. Gabe started rummaging around and Diane finally asked, "What are you looking for?"

"The air sick bag."

"It's next to you, there. You're not going to get sick on me. Just remember that when I go diving. I'll keep it nice and smooth today. No turbulence, no lightning, no bird strikes, no acrobatics. Boring. Just how I like it. I prefer to keep all the excitement in my earthbound life. Now, that's good; you found your seat belts. In the unlikely event of a water landing, you'll find your life vests under your seat. Yes, those orange things you see. This is how they work…"

Diane continued with her pre-flight briefing aboard the twin-engine turbo-prop. She then handed out maps, outlining their flight path. "Today I thought we'd enjoy flying over Maui, of course, but also Kaho'olawe, Lana'i, and Moloka'i as well, in that order, like this. Sarah thinks Maui looks like a silhouette of a rather buxom lady facing south." She pointed out the clockwise route they would follow heading eastward out of Kahului airport situated on the back of Lady Maui's neckline. "We're going to travel down Lady Maui's back, then across her bosom, like this. Then we'll give Kaho'olawe a glancing blow before we give some attention to Lana'i, here. Then onto Moloka'i—a lot of people think it looks like a shark. Behave yourselves or I'll drop you over the leper colony. Oh, and your in-flight service consists of those water bottles you see there. Passengers in first class"—she batted her eyes at Gabe—"are entitled to a second bottle."

Gabe raised his hand. "Oh, Madam Navigator, I have a question."

"That would be Madam *Pilot*. Yes, what is your question?"

"How fast will we go?"

"We'll probably keep it around 160-180 knots. You don't want to stall, do you? And we'll be up around 4,000 feet, 10,000 when we head over the mountains and out to sea. Yes, Gabe, do you have another question?"

"What's a knot?"

"You're a sailor, and you don't know what a knot is?"

"I figured Dan and Sarah would be too shy to ask."

"Well, then, you tell them what a knot is."

"Madam Pilot, I have just one more question. Are you a member of the Mile High Club?"

"No, are you?"

"Oh no, Madam Pilot."

Sarah finally got a word in. "A knot is 1.15 miles. Now, would you two like some time alone in the luggage compartment? I'm sweating from all the heat you guys are giving off."

"One more request, Madam Pilot: tell me more about Lady Maui's bosom."

Diane ignored Gabe and turned to the front, saying, "Now you behave while I go through my checklists. They're cleverly referred to as the Before Starting Engine checklist, followed by the Start Engine Checklist." She was silent for a few minutes while she focused on her important tasks. Then she started the engines and checked her instruments, satisfied with the readings. She took hold of the radio, saying, "Kahului Ground, this is Cessna 1169. We're ready to taxi."

A voice responded, "Roger, Cessna 1169. Taxi Foxtrot to Alpha cross Runway 23 and take Runway 23 and hold. Monitor Tower on 118.7."

"Roger 118.7, Cessna 1169."

Diane released the brakes, advanced the throttles, and taxied as instructed. She handed Gabe the Before Takeoff Checklist to read to her.

"Think you can be my copilot for a few minutes?"

"Oh, yes, Madam Pilot."

Diane rolled her eyes and shook her head. "I just thought you'd like to be sure we have brakes, fuel, oil, and—you'll love this—suction."

"Indeed, Madam Pilot."

The Tower called, "Cessna 1169, winds calm, altimeter 29.94, cleared for takeoff."

"Roger, Kahului Tower."

Diane advanced the throttles, and in no time they were airborne. She retracted the landing gear and flaps and continued to climb. The passengers were silent when they realized that their lives were now in the hands of Diane and the small plane.

"I'd appreciate it if everyone would start breathing again. That take-off was a '10' if I do say so myself. Oh, no, I forgot to de-ice. Gabe, would you mind? There's an ice scraper over there. Just reach out and scrape the windshield. No? OK, we'll just have to get by." She paused, then spoke into the radio again, "Kahului Tower, this is Cessna 1169. I'm at 2000 feet and clear of your traffic area."

"Roger, Cessna 1169. Contact Maui Departure on 120.2 and squawk 1200."

"Roger, Tower, 120.2." She adjusted the dials on the radio as instructed, set 1200 on the transponder, and pushed the IDENT button. She called Maui Departure saying, "Cessna 1169 climbing through 2200 feet." Maui Departure replied calmly with, "Cessna 1169, radar contact three miles north of Kahului." Diane idled back to maintain her cruise altitude and accomplished her level-off check.

Sarah grabbed Dan's hand; both were smiling now that they were relaxed with confidence in Diane's ability.

Dan asked, "So what's the story on Kaluhula?"

Gabe answered, "Kahului...don't worry, lots of people get confused with the names. It's the main harbor, sprang up in support of all the plantations. Still the only deep water port on Maui. It's hard to tell where Kahului stops and Wailuku begins. Wailuku is the county seat."

"What county?" inquired Dan.

"Maui; it includes Lana'i, Moloka'i, and Kaho'olawe, although I don't think there are any registered voters on Kaho'olawe."

Diane added, "You know, Kahului wasn't the intended location for the main airport for Maui. The first one was down in Ma'alaea on the windiest spot on the island. Landing there was absolutely terrifying."

Dan said, "Look, there's a little town there."

Gabe answered, "That's Pa'ia. It's a little town that that was built on the sugar industry. Lots of artists, surfer dudes. And a few quirky folk. I heard, but never personally saw, that there's a naked lady who paints herself green when she does her Christmas shopping."

As Diane had said, they were soon rounding Lady Maui's slightly humped back. Sarah pointed to Ho'okipa Beach Park, the location where she had first seen Gabe's dive boat soon after her arrival on Maui. She said, "You can tell it's afternoon; see all the windsurfers down there? In the morning it belongs to the surfboards."

Gabe added, "The north shores of all the islands get the winds, and therefore the giant waves."

Diane interrupted, saying, "Quick, there's Maliko Gulch. One of my clients told me that when they built the bridge, the workers had to swing on ropes down into the gulch. It's 300 feet down, and they weren't willing to do it. Then one day the boss—Baldwin—as in the sugar mill Baldwins—did it himself, and he only had one arm! After that, no one ever refused to do it. I think that must have been when they invented bungee jumping."

Diane continued, "Pretty soon you'll start to see the famous Road to Hana. There—see the twisty road? There's something like 600 switchbacks. Believe it or not, it's an all-day trip there and back. You guys are getting off easy. There's an airport there, and I've flown some people here who really want to get away. I think there are some famous people who live there. They're pretty safe from just about any intrusion into their privacy. Personally I think I'd go mad."

The view of the winding road carved into the rugged coastline was amazing. There was a car every half mile or so, but it was clear that there was never a rush hour. The sand beaches and rocky shore were virtually devoid of humanity. It became easy to see why the area attracted people who wanted the peace and quiet of a place almost untouched by modern civilization. How long would it remain that way?

"See, there's the only authentic volcanic black sand beach on Maui. When the hot lava hits the ocean, it explodes. Presto: beach! Since volcanic activity hasn't been around much in the last couple of hundred years, most of the time the black sand beaches disappear pretty quickly. This one is sheltered enough tho'. The Big Island of Hawai'i has lots of these, but here on Maui, all the other black sand beaches are formed by erosion."

Misty white ribbons of waterfalls cascaded down the cliffs, leaving pools in the ledges of hardened lava as they made their journey. "Have you ever driven this road, Gabe?"

"Once. I dated some girl who thought it would be fun. She was terrified the whole time. When we finally got to Hana, she wanted to take a boat back."

"What happened?" asked Diane.

"I used my charm—you know all about that—and she finally agreed to come back with me, but only after I let her drive. Then it was my turn to be terrified." He shook his head, adding, "Give me sharks and jellyfish; I am never getting in a car with that woman again."

"Anyone I know?" queried Diane coyly.

"No, but Sarah does—Julia Ingleside—the P.E. teacher," Gabe said innocently, looking out the window.

"Oh, Julia. Yes, I know who she is. You went out with her?"

Diane jumped in, "Why, what about her—uh, Julia?"

"Nothing."

"Sarah!"

"Well, she's pretty cute. OK, she's a babe, right, Gabe?"

"Can I plead the fifth?"

Dan asked playfully, "Is she coming to the wedding?"

The other three answered together, "No!"

Gabe said, "Can we change the subject? Look, you can see Hawai'i over there: The Big Island. The tip of the island there is the almost ghost town of Hawi, the point closest to Maui."

"We'll have to do Hawai'i another time; I haven't seen much of it myself. But now we're about to head up to Haleakala."

"Holly who?" asked Dan.

"Not who, what," answered Diane. "'Hale' means house, and 'akala' means sun."

Gabe added, "Supposedly the Hawaiian god Maui captured hold of the sun and kept it tied up until it promised to move more slowly across the sky. That's why we have such long sunny days."

Diane teased, "Wow, you stayed awake during your history class."

Sarah teased dryly, "Most people do, Diane."

"That way I didn't have to. Anyway, I'll take you over the crater. It's 10,000 feet up, so we'll have to do a little climb."

"It looks like the moon!" exclaimed Dan when they approached the crater. "When did it last erupt?"

"1790, I think. Anyway, it never rains here," said Diane. "The clouds get wrung out before they get this high. So it's wet on the east side and dry on the west side. You saw the lush forests above Hana?"

"That looks like an observatory over there," observed Dan.

Gabe said, "That's Science City. They shoot lasers into the sky to measure distances." Changing the subject, he said, "You know, Haleakala is famous for its sunrises."

"So, who did you come here at sunrise with?" Diane asked accusingly.

"Micah and Thomas. You want to go? We'd have to get up 2:30 in the morning to go see it. And it's freezing cold and windy."

"Uh, maybe not. OK, quick take a look...that's Molokini Crater. Looks different than below the water line, huh, Gabe?"

"Someday you have to see it from my angle; it's equally amazing."

Sarah added, "That's where he took me snorkeling." Just the slightest awkward pause arose at the reminder that Gabe and Sarah once dated. Diane quickly changed the subject.

"OK, now we're going to get a rare look at Kaho'olawe. We can't fly directly over it unless we'd like to get a military escort back to Kahului, followed by arrest and dreadful orange jumpsuits. It used to be a military bombing range. They stopped in 1990, and now our taxes are paying to clear the island of all the unexploded bombs that our taxes paid for in the first place. I'm sure someday it will be a tropical paradise. But they'll have to convince the rain god to show a little mercy; there's no water on the island. Maui sucks it all up. In the early 1800's it was a penal colony. But it was too easy to escape, and some prisoners paddled and even swam over to Maui to get food, since the government was too stingy to provide enough. And—I love this—some even paddled over to Lana'i where they had a women's penal colony. Isn't that a romantic story?"

Gabe added, "You know, I think Owen Hoana is a descendant of one of those trysts. I've never asked him about it. Have you, Sarah?"

"Oh sure, that's something we talked about all the time. 'So Owen, tell us your sordid family history. Were they murderers or simply thieves and rapists?' Tell you what: ask Malia."

Diane flew south around Kaho'olawe and headed northwest to Lana'i. "Now we're going to see your honeymoon spot. I bring lots of people over here, mostly folks who are going to stay at either the lodge or the beach resort. You guys are staying at the beach, right? It's awesome, and so is the lodge. The only other hotel was built in the 20's, and some people actually prefer it as a more laid back and less expensive spot. Good restaurant there, I hear." She continued, "This place is almost as dry as Kaho'olawe, but the Dole Company apparently dug wells and got enough water to support some agriculture, particularly pineapple. But the plantation owners decided that serving *piña coladas* was more profitable than raising the pineapples that go in them, so now most of the people support the tourists instead of planting pineapples. Anyway, when you guys get tired of each other and the gorgeous resort, you can hop a ferry across the channel back to the town of Lahaina and the rest of us on Maui. The locals do it all the time to make their Costco runs."

"It's on my list of things to do on our honeymoon, how about you, Sarah," teased Dan.

"Isn't he romantic?" swooned Sarah, kissing her fiancé.

Gabe said, "Well, I've never been to Lana'i with anyone…yet."

Diane smiled and responded, "I doubt if you'll ever have as good a view as this."

He replied, "I don't know about that."

Diane blushed, and changed the subject. "OK, here's a view to remember. You can see all the islands from here."

Gabe said, "You know she's going to expect a tip after all this."

"Gladly," said Dan. "This is gorgeous. So tell me which island is which."

"Way out there on the left you can see Kauai, and if you look carefully you can see Ni'ihau just west of Kauai. We could go big game hunting there some day. Then closer we see Oahu. See Diamond Head? Turn around and you can see Hawai'i, particularly Mauna Kea and Mauna Loa. Mauna Loa is where the active volcanoes are."

"I think you've got the best job in the world," said Dan. He was clearly impressed and in awe with the wonder of the scenery.

"You've behaved yourselves, so let's head over to Moloka'i. Look, there's a shipwreck down there off of Lana'i. Ever dive there, Gabe?"

"You think I'm nuts? It's all rusty, and God knows what might be hiding in there. We dive close by; it's called Shipwreck Beach, for obvious reasons. But I make sure I've got lots of slower swimmers so I can outrun the sharks. Most people like diving at Cathedrals. Must be the religious experience."

Everyone groaned, and Diane continued.

"So, on to Moloka'i. Legend says it's where Maui's mother lived. You've probably heard about the leper colony founded by Father Damian. You may be surprised that there are still a few patients there. We'll swing over it on the northern side."

Dan said, "Diane, you are a natural tour guide. How did you learn all this?"

"Clients. I meet lots of interesting people. It's nothing like flying a commercial plane. As you can see, I'm kind of one with my passengers." She paused before continuing. "So Moloka'i is like two islands, part rain forest, part dessert. The underground water supplies have played out, so presto: you've got the topic *du jour* for all the local politics. It's probably why there are only about 7,000 people there and zero traffic lights. Oh, and check out those cliffs over there! And look down there; there's Kalaupapa, the leper colony. Uh-oh, I think I'm running out of gas."

"Is anyone still there?" asked Dan, realizing Diane was kidding.

"Supposedly a couple of hundred people or so, some of whom are still infected," Diane responded.

Sarah noticed that Dan became quiet, and she asked if he was OK.

"Fine. I get frustrated when people get diseases that are completely treatable, not to mention avoidable in the first place."

Diane asked Gabe, "Have you ever been to Moloka'i?"

Gabe shook his head. "No, but that would be fun…we could take a mule ride and see the sites. Then we can herd some cows, go backpacking, and climb some cliffs."

"Now isn't he romantic?" Diane asked rhetorically. "Hey, remember the 'Iao Needle? Well, Moloka'i has its own testament to manhood. Maybe you can see it down there. Apparently some childless woman slept at the base of it and soon became pregnant." She fanned herself, saying, "Is anyone else hot in here?" She continued, "We're going to swing back around to see West Maui. You'll be able to see Ka'anapali Beach and the other big resort areas."

Diane headed counterclockwise from the top of Lady Maui's head down her forehead. Countless beaches, some heavily populated, some almost empty, skirted the shore. Low-rise hotels and condos formed a barrier between the ancient lava flows and the sea. It was easy to see new development going higher and higher up the slopes. Red dirt—had it been brought in, or had it been dug up?—broke up the green and brown landscape. Gabe said, "Now you see the subject of most of the political wars these days: economic development versus ecological and cultural preservation. You know, at any given time, 30% of the people on Maui are tourists."

"Look at all the kites," announced Dan.

"Actually there's probably, hopefully, someone attached to each one…they're parasailing," corrected Gabe.

"Have you…?" started Diane.

"No. Do you want to?"

"Maybe," she said playfully. "OK, there's Lahaina. Gabe, you know more about it than I do," said Diane.

"Historically it was a big whaling port and Hawai'i's first capital. As a whaling port, it had its seedy side, and the missionaries tried to tame it. The natives, of course, got caught in the middle of it all. Now it's a big tourist spot, probably because it's always sunny. It's very dry here, something like only fourteen inches of rain a year. You saw the West Maui volcano just a minute ago; it gets four hundred inches. Well, I guess you really didn't see it; it was shrouded in clouds. But it ensures they can grow sugar cane and pineapple on this side of the island, as well as raise cattle. See the fields over there? I'm afraid it's just a matter of time before the developers take over, tho'."

Diane said, "We're going to continue along the lady's face…there's her nose…it's the town of Olawalu."

Gabe added, "This is where I bring a lot of beginning divers, particularly students. They can't really hurt themselves, and they get to see lots of colorful fish, eels, rays, and turtles. Actually when I'm teaching kids, the first person who can spell the state fish gets to dive first."

"H-u-m-u-h-u-m-u-oh, I can't remember," said Diane.

"Humuhumunukunukuapua'a," announced Gabe, spelling it out. "Gabe: One, Lady Pilot: Zero." He then continued, "The town itself is famous for its General Store, where everyone stops to get picnic supplies. Other than that, it's a nice sleepy little town, although there was a massacre a couple of hundred years ago. Some British sea captain took revenge on the death of one his sailors by ambushing and killing about 100 Hawaiians."

Diane interrupted the history lesson. "We're going to head north along the isthmus that connects Lady Maui's head to her torso."

Sarah teased, "Wow, I didn't know you knew what an isthmus was."

"Good thing you're the bride; otherwise I wouldn't let you get away with such insults." Then in a stage whisper to Gabe, "What's an isthmus, science teacher?"

"Humuhumunukunukuapua'a. That's my answer for everything."

"That's what I thought." Back to her travelogue, Diane continued. "In a minute you'll be able to see the 'Iao Needle. It's impressive from up here. Speaking from a woman's point of view, of course."

Once in view, the 2250-foot volcanic spire brought silence to the cabin. All were remembering tragedy and terror from a Sunday afternoon in April. So long ago. Only yesterday. Dan took Sarah's hand and brought her close to him. He had almost lost her again that day. Gabe put his hand on Diane's shoulder and gently rubbed her neck. He remembered the pain of his near-fatal fall down the rocks and said a silent prayer. Much had been lost that day: Alec's mother. So much more could have been lost.

Diane broke the silence as she got back on the radio to communicate with Kahului Tower. The tour was coming to an end. She reached for her checklist now that the serious business of landing the airplane was occupying all of her attention

Gabe said, "Remind me to tell you about the Swinging Bridges hike; it would be fun. Almost as much fun as herding cows on Moloka'i."

"I've got a message, Malia." George turned on his cell phone as soon as the flight attendant gave permission to the passengers who had just landed on Maui. He silently listened to the message from Gabe, nodding as if he was listening to him in person. He relayed Gabe's message to Malia, adding, "He's got to be camping, just like he said."

Malia allowed herself to breathe. She had a haggardness that George had never seen in her, and he knew that she was anxious to get home to try to reach him—before she killed him.

Liliana met them outside baggage claim, and she, too, observed Malia's distress. They quickly got into the car, and Liliana drove as quickly as possible while George calmly explained the situation. Upon arriving, both George and Liliana insisted on coming in, George first. Everything was in order, not that anyone expected otherwise.

"Let me see if his camping gear is gone," said Malia, trying to sound in control and relieved.

Liliana picked up the mail and brought in the newspapers. She opened up the windows and turned on the fans to get the air moving. She did a cursory check of the mail to see if there was anything unusual. George checked the answering machine, but the only messages were from Malia.

"Who is the lady principal, Malia? Let's call her to see if she's been in touch with him this week. Malia?"

Malia was standing in the kitchen doorway, shaking as she held Owen's sleeping bag clenched in her arms.

"No, Wally, don't bring him to my apartment. I've got too many neighbors. Even if they don't see him, they'll smell him. Did you ever put him in the shower? Man, I hate addicts. Stick him back in the warehouse. There's never anyone around, and there's an office that we can put him in." Duke rubbed his forehead in an unsuccessful attempt to rid himself of the stress. He did not like the fact that Owen was becoming the subject of a man hunt. He thought Wally would be able to keep him sequestered at the school until Monday anyway. But Wally could only handle so many changes in the plan before he mentally shut down. It was clear that he, Duke, would have to manage Wally on every detail, or the plan would collapse. "You need to get into Owen's office again to check his email. We don't know when his wife and the little side dish will start looking for him. Any messages on his cell phone? Well, just deal with them. They need to think he's camping, just like you said, and he'll be back…oh, why don't you say Monday? It's a holiday weekend; he's on holiday!"

Duke had a headache, and Wally's situation with Owen was not helping. He wasn't sure what he'd do come Monday, when Owen's disappearance would get an elevated level of attention. The wife might call the police, but they still will probably ignore it since "Owen" sent his wife a message saying he'd be gone until Monday. Maybe they would pay attention on Tuesday. That still left a week where they had to keep Owen alive and under their "care." After that, he could be found, and Duke didn't care how or where, as long as it didn't lead back to him. He planned to be off the island by then anyway. Owen might have to be eliminated. Well, maybe not. *No, he has to be. This is not the time to get chummy and concerned for your fellow man.* Owen was probably a nice guy when he didn't smell so bad, but he was a loose end. *Don't think about it.* Anyway, after this job, he could turn respectable, leaving his shady past behind him. He could start a relationship with what's her name…Erin. But he still had to come up with some legitimate job story.

You're delusional, Duke. You've got to get off this island and forget about everyone here. You won't miss what you never had.

He certainly wanted to get away from Cho. Would Oahu be far enough? He hoped so. The mainland had too much cold weather, and he hated the cold.

"Malia, when Owen goes camping, does he always take a sleeping bag? Doesn't he sometimes go with some guys that have an RV?"

"I don't know; I never paid any attention. No, he always takes his sleeping bag. Think, Malia. All right, I need to call some of these guys. I'm not sure I want them to answer or not. I know I'm being ridiculous. Owen is capable and not someone you trifle with. The sixth graders are usually scared speechless when they first see him. His independence—it's something I love about him, but it can make me feel unneeded at times."

"Oh, Malia, he's never been happier than with you," countered Liliana. Then anxious to be of help, she said, "I'll make us some iced tea."

Malia started to make phone calls, but she found herself more frustrated with each one. The two friends she knew had big RV's didn't answer; maybe that was good news. Owen's good friend Kip was at home for the weekend; his wife's parents were in town, and no, he hadn't been in touch with Owen. Principal Crockett was on vacation on the mainland. The office administrator hadn't been into the office since school closed, and no, she hadn't talked to Mr. Hoana. George looked around for shopping receipts, anything that might confirm that Owen had gone camping. Owen's cell phone was the only lifeline, but there was still no answer. Malia decided to leave a message letting him know that she was worried about him. He could chastise her for worrying about him later; she didn't care. He needed to get in touch with her now.

She had run out of phone calls to make. Liliana sensed that Malia wanted to be alone; she had put up a front as long as she could. Liliana rousted George from his investigation to head home to see their boys. As they were leaving she said, "Call us later, no matter what the hour, when you learn anything. If you need moral support, we'll be here. If nothing else, we all need to put our heads together on how we're going to kill him!"

Malia laughed through her tears as she embraced Liliana and George. "I was thinking about that song again—'Let's get a rock...'"

"Malia!" George exclaimed. "I've created a monster!" He walked out singing the rest of the song with Liliana shaking her head, nudging him along.

Gabe had almost given up when George picked up the phone. "Welcome home, Uncle. How's Malia?"

"We still don't know where Owen is, and Malia is alternating between death threats and calling the police. Have you learned anything new?"

"No, we're all just back from a flight over the islands with Diane. I called you as soon as I could. What do you think we should do? I just don't know Owen well enough to say what he might be doing."

"Camping is still the most logical. I think we should call the police tomorrow anyway. You've been through the school, you said."

"I can't get into the office, but the place looked pretty closed up. Any clues in the house?"

"Not really. Malia found his sleeping bag, which is a little worrisome if he did go camping. So, how was the flight? Was Diane the pilot?"

"Yes. It was amazing. We had a great time. We're getting cleaned up to go out to dinner, but if there is anything we can do to help find Owen, just say the word."

"Let's talk in the morning."

"Sounds good. By the way, you owe Liliana. The retreat, you know."

"Oh, I know."

Wally got Owen settled in for the night. He was tempted to stay there with him, since he wasn't sure what Owen might try to do in a strange place. The warehouse was in a remote area on the edge of the golf course, but there must be roving security guards that patrolled the area. He figured that as long as Owen stayed quiet he wouldn't attract attention. Wally was starting to worry about the timing and was pretty sure someone was already starting to look for Owen. Duke didn't seem to be worrying about that, and Duke always told Wally not to worry.

Nevertheless, staying in the warehouse was probably the wisest course of action. But the office where Owen was being kept was too small for a second person to sleep there, and frankly, Owen was pretty smelly. Wally wished he could go back to Owen's house to get some clean clothes, but that was out of the question. He thought he ought to drive by the house in the morning to see if the wife had returned. According to Owen's calendar, the wife was due back today. He hoped she stayed away and didn't start looking for him, not that she was likely to think about looking for him at the warehouse. He cursed himself for leaving the trash in Owen's school office, thinking he should go back to restore the place to the way he had found it.

Wally remembered that Owen had another woman on the side, "Gabe," probably Gabrielle or Gabriella. He looked at his captive and wondered what one woman saw in him, much less two. On the other hand, he hadn't seen too many good looking drug addicts, and he had forgotten what Owen looked like when he was straight.

With Owen comfortably secured for the night, Wally made a final check of the environment. He left the bathroom door partially open with the light on. Too many lights would call attention to the supposedly empty warehouse. He showed Owen the small refrigerator where Wally had stored water and pineapple juice, as well as two sandwiches, apples, and cookies, all open, unwrapped, and accessible. Everything had to be immediately and totally consumable without requiring Owen to open

THE TOWERS OF SAND

packages or start looking for a knife. Leaving food out was not an option; Wally did not want to come upon rats when he returned. Warehouses have rats.

Wally decided that if Owen was to venture out into public without attracting attention, he'd have to be more presentable. Since returning to the house was not an option, he would tell Duke they would have to get Owen some new clothes, as well as some toiletries—toothbrush, razor, deodorant, soap. Lots of deodorant. The warehouse didn't have a shower. But at least if Owen had a change of clothes, Wally could wash the ones Owen wasn't wearing. This whole thing would be over in a matter of days—days that seemed like weeks now that Owen's disappearance had been noticed.

I don't know where this is, Owen thought to himself. *This must be another dream.* Except for the light, the surroundings were devoid of anything familiar. He stood up slowly and awkwardly and went over to the light. *Too bright.* He turned out the light and was immediately plunged into total darkness. *Not good. Too dark. Need lights.* He switched the lights back on and partially covered his eyes. Someone had left sunglasses on the desk, and Owen put them on. *Good. Now I can see. Now I can pee.* He laughed at the rhyme. *I wonder where is Wall-ee. Ha ha!*

"What's in the fridge?" Owen asked out loud. "Sandwiches! Cookies!" He grabbed both sandwiches and the pineapple juice and consumed them ravenously. He wiped his mouth on his shirt sleeve and went for the cookies. "I'll eat the apples later; I like cookies better," he told himself. "Don't tell Malia," he said to no one in particular.

Satisfied, Owen decided he was now bored. He looked around the darkened office and found three golf clubs standing in the corner. He took the driver and started to practice his golf swing. He screamed in pain from the deafening sound of the club crashing through the flimsy wall. "Uh-oh, Principal will be so mad. She'll put me in detention."

He found the door and opened it out into the darkened warehouse. As his eyes adjusted to the expansive space dimly lit by the bathroom light, he began to see shapes. "Golf carts! Malia got me a golf cart! She got me lots of golf carts." He picked one out of the row of identical units that were parallel-parked and backed it out. The backup beeps hurt his ears, so he stopped. He looked around and found the cart at the front of the line that wouldn't need backing up. He found the walk to be endless, and he had to stop frequently to catch his balance. When he reached the cart, he practically fell into it, but managed to get into the driver's seat, instinctively releasing the brake and engaging the accelerator. He started going in circles, driving recklessly down the aisles and around corners, screeching the tires on the smooth concrete floor. The cart fishtailed around a shelving unit precariously stacked with golf bags, striking the edge of the unit, causing the bags to tumble off the shelves and onto the floor all around him.

Owen was in a canyon amidst a mountain of golf bags. He couldn't back up or go forward. "Malia, why did you get me so many golf bags?"

A bright light shone painfully in his eyes. It started talking to him.

"Keep your hands where I can see them, and get out of the vehicle— er, golf cart." Then the light started talking to someone else. "Police? Yes, this is Jack Likio of Island Securities. I'm over at the Palm District Warehouses, and there's a break-in. One guy, so far. A big one, stoned out of his mind. No, not a kid. More like a Sumo wrestler. More than I can handle if he ain't so stoned… Building 6… OK, see you in a few minutes."

Jack tucked the cell phone back into his pocket, keeping the light shining on the big man. The light seemed to bother the man enough that additional restraints weren't needed, but Jack needed to find out if the man had companions.

"Hey buddy, are you here by yourself?"

"Where's Wally? The light hurts. Turn off the light."

"Ok, buddy, let's go find Wally. You just follow the light, and we'll go find Wally."

Jack retrieved his revolver, now that he knew that the big guy was not alone. He kept the man in front of him as protection from the second burglar, shining his flashlight on the floor, so both of them could navigate around the piles of golf bags."

"So, where do you think Wally is?"

Owen was confused and started to move towards the office.

"Over there, huh, big guy?"

Distant sirens reassured Jack as he sought protection behind Owen's massive frame and the shelves of golf merchandise.

"Yeah, sit there, big guy." It was clear that no one else was in the office, and Jack decided he would wait there as well until the police arrived.

"What's your name, big guy?"

"HoHo. I played golf."

"HoHo? Do you have any identification?"

Owen reached into his pocket, but did not have his wallet to show Jack. He looked blankly at the guard, and then started to get up.

"What do you want, HoHo? OK, you can get something from the fridge. Then just sit down, OK? What are you on? You and Wally out on a party?"

"Wally? Where's Wally?"

"I don't know; we'll go look for him later, OK?"

Owen nodded and focused on the bottle of water he got out of the refrigerator. He removed his sunglasses and rubbed his face, which made the oil and dirt on his face sting his eyes, bringing on tears.

"You are a mess, big guy. Go in and wash your face. Oh, good, the cavalry is here."

Two police cars arrived, and the four officers emerged, guns drawn as they entered the warehouse. Jack stepped out of the office his hands up holding his identification and gun. The police approached cautiously, guns aimed in Jack's direction. One of the officers took the gun, another, his i.d.

"Mr. Likio, have you secured the suspect?"

"Yes, but he's pretty docile. He keeps talking about Wally, but I haven't gone looking for him."

"We'll do that. What's the big guy's name?"

"Says it's HoHo. Looks like he's downed a few of them in his day. He doesn't have any i.d. He's really out of it. I have a feeling that when he comes off of whatever he's on, he's going to be a handful."

"I'll call for an ambulance, a big one." Then into his walkie-talkie, "Any sign of the other guy? No? Maybe he left when he heard us coming. We might need help with this fellow. I'd hate to think we could have two this size."

The two officers approached Owen cautiously. "Wally?" Owen asked.

"No, this is Officer Rubio, and I'm Officer Makai. Where's Wally? Is he your partner?"

"Wally? Wally is God."

"So, what are you on—uh, HoHo? Cocaine, grass?"

"Huh? Where's Wally?"

Officer Rubio pointed to Owen's arms. "Heroin?"

Owen shook his head. "Please find Wally. My head…"

"I'll bet," commented Officer Makai. "Sorry, big guy, you're going to go through a lot worse before you get better. Let's get him out of here, Chuck. Give me a hand getting him up. Come on HoHo, we're going to get you some help."

"Wally?"

"Something like that. Whoa, steady, big guy."

The ambulance arrived, and Officer Rubio rode in it with Owen while Officer Makai and Jack processed the warehouse scene.

"Who owns this place, Jack?"

"Some Asian corporation, I think. Some guy named Chen…no, Cho."

Saturday, July 4

Dan woke Sarah early on Saturday.

"One week and counting, my dear! I've got a marriage license, and I know how to use it. You've got seven days to change your mind, and I don't intend to give you any reason to do so."

"You just have…what time is it? The sun's not even up!" Sarah groaned and rolled over, but Dan waved steaming coffee vapor around her face.

"I'm very persuasive."

"That you are. I'll remember this when I want to stay up late, and you want to sleep. I'm not sure we're compatible…you're the early bird, and I'm the night owl."

"We can discuss it with George during pre-marital counseling. He'll be on my side, of course."

"I'm not sure that's the point of the counseling."

"Come on, let's go have coffee out in the spa before it gets too warm outside. No one else is using it, and we can watch the world wake up."

"Of course no one else is using it…it's only…what? 5:30! You're waking me up at 5:30 on Saturday…on the Fourth of July? Is this your way of getting back at me for missing your nap yesterday?"

"Still love me?"

"Yes, but you will owe me."

"I can live with that. Here's your bathing suit. Remind me that our house has to have a private spa, so we can enjoy it *au naturel*."

"I'm not sure it matters at this time of day."

"I'm game if you are."

"Hand me my suit."

Alec was the first to wake up at the Callahan house and tried to persuade his brothers to follow him. He wanted to go to Ho'okipa Beach with them to try surfing. He knew that Micah and Thomas had two old boards, and he was sure they would be willing to share.

Micah rolled over and said, "Sure, but how do we get there?" He wasn't going to open his eyes unless he knew there was a reason to get up so early on a Saturday.

Alec hadn't thought of that. "When do your folks get up? Maybe one of them can drive us down there. This is why I need a car...or a truck."

"Hmmm... I don't know. Maybe 6:30 or 7:00. What time is it?"

"It's about 6:15."

"Ask Dad when he wakes up. If he says he will, then come get me up."

"OK."

Alec wasn't sure he wanted to ask George by himself. On the other hand, it might convince him that he needed to get his own set of wheels. At least he needed to get a driver's license. Then he could start by borrowing one of their cars. He would go crazy if he couldn't get away from time to time.

He heard movement in the other side of the house and hoped it was George. He decided to wait until George was out on the lanai and well into his coffee before approaching him about driving them to the beach.

"Good morning, Alec," said George, when the teenager came out the door. "There's some juice in there. Come join me."

"Good morning, uh, thanks." Alec still wasn't sure how to address George. Dad? Father? "How was San Diego?"

"Good. How familiar are you with the Episcopal Church, Alec?"

"Not very."

"That's OK. I think if you ask five different Episcopalians what the Episcopal Church is like, you'll get five different answers. Say, how was the retreat?"

"It was good. We got to camp out, which was fun, except the girls talked all night."

George laughed. "Thank God I've got three boys." Alec was startled at the inclusion of himself in the count, and the reaction was not lost on George. "What have you guys got planned for today?"

This might be easier than I thought. "Micah and Thomas and I were talking about going surfing. There's supposed to be a beach nearby...? How do you get there? Can we walk to it?"

"You won't find many better spots to surf... It's pretty far to walk. I'll drop you off on my way down to Malia's house, probably around 8...? Is that OK?"

Alec was disappointed that he would have to wait so long, but decided he had better show gratitude rather than disappointment.

"That would be great...thanks, uh, Dad."

"You're very welcome, son."

It's working.

Harry Cho was furious. He hoped the police assumed his anger was directed at the break-in and damage at the warehouse. That didn't even scratch the surface of his rage.

"Mr. Cho, does it look like anything is missing?" asked Officer Rubio. "All we saw was the wrecked golf cart."

"I don't keep any money here, and there's no safe." *That's sort of true,* he said to himself.

"We've checked the perimeter and the interior. The pile of golf clubs around the golf cart seems to be the focus of the damage. Have you informed your insurance company?"

"Not yet," responded Cho.

"You'll probably want to beef up your security. We didn't see any evidence of a break-in. Who has access to this building?"

Cho wanted them to stop asking questions and leave.

"Just my immediate business associates. I think what probably happened is that someone left the door unlocked, and some drug addict wandered in to find a place to sleep for the night. I hope he gets the help he needs. Why do people do that to themselves?" Cho shook his head. "You know, it might have even been me that forgot to lock the door. I'm not sure this is worth mentioning to the insurance company. They'll just increase my rates, and I can probably donate the damaged golf cart to the high school, and write it off on my taxes."

"Whatever you want to do, Mr. Cho. Here's my card, and feel free to call me if you want to press charges, or if it looks like there was a robbery."

"Thank you, Officer, uh, Rubio. As long as you get HoHo off the streets, you're doing me and the rest of decent society a big favor. Say, be sure to contact me for a donation when you do the Widows and Orphans Fundraising Drive."

"Thank you, Mr. Cho. We sure will."

He waved at them as they drove away. *Idiots.* He turned to his chauffer, "Where's Duke? Get me Duke."

"Right away, Mr. Cho."

Wally suddenly felt sick to his stomach when he approached the warehouse. There was a large Mercedes parked out front, along with a police car. The doors of the warehouse were open; where was Owen? In any case, it was not a place he wanted to be. He had to talk to Duke. Duke would know what happened, what to do. Wally drove past the warehouse as if his destination was a different building. He parked out of sight and pulled out his cell phone.

"Duke, it's Wally… I don't know, probably 7:00 or so… I know it's early, but this is important. Duke, Owen is gone. I'm over at the warehouse, and there's a cop car and a huge Mercedes."

Duke was awake now. "What do you mean, Owen is gone? You should have stayed with him."

Wally agreed. "I know, but what do you want me to do now? I've gotta get out of here man; they can't see me."

"Did you wear gloves when you were there?"

"No. Oh, shit, Duke. Do you think they've got my fingerprints?"

"I don't know, Wally." Duke was quiet for a few seconds.

"Duke?"

"I need to think about what to do. Don't go home, in case they do find your fingerprints. Go stay some place out of sight. I'll call you when I figure this out."

"Whose Mercedes is it?"

"Cho's. It's his warehouse."

"Oh, man, I'm sorry. I should have stayed with HoHo. You don't think he's dead, do you?"

"I don't know. It seems like there'd be a lot more activity than one cop car if he was." Duke was silent again. Then he said, "Just get away from there, and don't go anyplace familiar, OK, Wally?"

"Yeah, man. Call me, OK?"

"Yeah. Bye."

The sight of breakfast made Owen sick all over again. It's just that there wasn't anything more for him to throw up. He was shivering and sweating. His head felt like it would explode. *This is the worst case of the flu I've ever had. Wally, God, please come and make me feel better.*

Even he thought he smelled bad. His body was declaring war on itself. He had scratched at all the places where ants were crawling on him, but they still wouldn't go away. The muscles in his back ached, and nothing he did seemed to help—sitting up, lying down, standing—not that this last was possible.

The white-coated attendants watched him from the two-way mirror.

"Who is he?" asked a stocky nurse's aide.

"Don't know, the cops brought him in during the night." The doctor observed Owen's misery, adding, "At least he's not an overdose. He's dressed better than most of them they bring in, although we'll probably have to burn the clothes he's in."

"What do you think he's on? LSD?"

"Heroin, I'd bet. Classic symptoms."

"Think he'll come out of it?"

"That's up to him as much as us. We need to find out who he is."

"Think he's a tourist?"

"Good guess; he's dressed like one, like he's going to play golf. Did he have any identification?"

"Don't know; I wasn't here when he was admitted. How long will he be like this?"

"Two days, maybe three, maybe more. Actually he's going to get worse before he gets better. If we can get him into a shower and some clean clothes, at least we won't have to treat infections from where he's scratched himself. Spiders, I guess."

"Huh, what spiders?"

"The ones he imagines are crawling all over him."

"This would make a good drug abuse film. I'll get Zack to help me handle him. Anything else you want us to do?"

"Whatever you can do to find out who he is, Jésus. The police said his name is HoHo."

"Well, they say you are what you eat."

Although he was physically up, Gabe was taking longer to wake up than the rest of the household, even though Diane had let him sleep. He was worried about Owen, and it took him hours to drift off the night before. While Sarah and Diane got showers, he and Dan sat out on the Lanai reading the paper.

"Rough night, huh, Gabe? Shall I have Sarah have a talk with Diane?"

"What? Oh, no, you don't want to do that!" Gabe smiled, and then continued. "I'm trying to figure out where Owen might be. He said he went camping, but it's surprising that he wouldn't be back, now that Malia has come home."

"I guess I don't think about camping in Hawai'i, but that's because I prefer more the lap of luxury when I'm on vacation."

"Thomas and Micah enjoy it, so I've taken them a few times, particularly when they were younger. We stay closer to sea level, since high altitude camping isn't an option for me. Owen, I think, likes Haleakala."

"Not this week, he doesn't."

"What do you mean?"

"Yesterday's paper… I think it said Haleakala. Anyway the campground is closed for maintenance. I think there was a fire. I would have mentioned it yesterday, but I didn't know it was important."

"What? Are you sure? Owen sent Malia a text message that he was camping in Haleakala."

"Maybe I was wrong about the place. Is yesterday's paper still here? There it is…uh, Section B. Here's the article."

Gabe turned pale as he read the article, simultaneously picking up the phone to call George.

Duke started to pack his bags. He needed to get away from Cho. As soon as Cho figured out what had happened, Duke would be the subject of another one of Cho's lessons. This time there would be no forgiveness, only punishment. He thought about letting Wally take the fall, but realized that it would only mean Wally would suffer as well. No, Cho would be after Duke. It was ultimately Duke's responsibility, Duke's fault.

A knock at the door made Duke drop his bag. Instinctively he reached for his gun under the mattress. Glancing out the window through the cracks in the window blinds, he saw the woman, his neighbor, and realized he had been holding his breath. He tucked the gun away and made sure his heart was beating again before answering the door.

"Hi, uh Duke, I'm not sure you remember me… Erin…from across the way there."

"Oh, Erin, absolutely, I have been meaning to call you." Duke came out and shut the door behind him. "How are you?"

"Great. Say, I was wondering if you'd like to go into town later today for the Lahaina Fourth of July festival. Or even up to Ka'anapali; they've got lots going on."

Duke's mind was racing. *No way. Stay focused on business.* But then he thought that a public place might be even better than going into hiding. He wasn't sure what he would do after the festival; coming back here was probably not an option. But it would give him time to think.

Erin kept talking. "Or, up to the Rodeo, no wait, that might be tomorrow, and the women's rodeo is next weekend…" Was she nervous about something? Asking a man for a date, something she probably didn't need to do very often.

Duke let her keep talking while he half listened and half contrived his escape plan, if only for the day.

"Or, we could catch a boat at sunset to watch the fireworks…"

"You could be a tour guide, Erin! I didn't know all those things were going on. They sound great. Tell you what, I've got a golf game this morning, so how about I meet you around 2:00 up at Whaler's Village? A sunset cruise to watch the fireworks sounds great; can you reserve that for us? And I know a great place for dinner."

"That all sounds like fun," said Erin, apparently relieved that her invitation hadn't been rejected. "I'll see you about 2:00. Good luck with your golf game!"

"Huh? Oh yeah, thanks!" Duke squeezed her hand and waved good-bye before quickly moving back inside and closing the door.

Are you nuts, man? This is only going to complicate things. What if Wally calls?

Duke's packing switched from suitcases to golf bags. And a duffle that could pass as a change of clothes.

This is what happens when you start thinking with your...

A knock on the door startled him again. He figured it was Erin again, but it was Wally. He quickly let him in. Instant golf buddy.

"Duke, I had to come. I'm really scared. Where are you going? You're playing golf? Are you nuts? We've got to get out of here."

"Calm down, Wally. My neighbor thinks I'm playing golf, so I—we—are going to play golf."

"Good thinking, Duke. Got any beer? Say, what are we going to do after we play golf?"

Malia had no luck reaching Owen, not that she expected it. The charge on Owen's cell phone had likely run out. Campgrounds don't have electricity for recharging cell phones. She was scared and angry. He had been in an accident and was lying injured—or worse—some place. He had been mugged. By a platoon of marines. That's what it would take. There was another woman. Isabel? Vicki? Impossible? She used to think it was. There was no indication that he had packed a bag, not even his toiletries. It wouldn't be much of a fling without eventual access to his razor, toothbrush, and deodorant. She wished the car wasn't still in the carport. Its presence deepened the mystery. It would be something the police could be on the lookout for. Down a cliff, parked at a hotel, at the campground.

The police. It's time to call the police.

A knock on the door startled her. Owen! But Owen wouldn't knock. George. She let him in and collapsed into tears all over again. He led her into the kitchen and got her settled with some water and tissues.

"Have you learned anything, Malia?"

"Everything he would take with him is still here. I think if he went camping, he would at least take his toothbrush."

George nodded. "I think we need to call the police."

Malia nodded in return, almost in relief. Action, finally. It was something to do. She was beyond embarrassment if it turned out to be another woman he had shacked up with.

George took charge and made the call. After hanging up, he said, "They're on their way over. Let's make a list of everyone Owen knows and who you've talked to. Also, every place he goes."

Malia was glad to have something constructive to do, and George prompted her when she ran out of names. "His doctor, where he gets gas, his favorite bar, friends with boats, teachers, colleagues, women…sorry."

"No, it's OK."

"Do you have his keys?"

"I haven't seen them. Do you think that's important?"

"Maybe."

The surf was lighter than Alec and his half-brothers were hoping for, but still typical of summer conditions on the north shore. They borrowed a third board and a wet suit from a friend, so the three of them stayed close to one another, dangling their feet over the boards, waiting for something that passed for a wave worthy of their efforts. Alec proved to be nimble enough to get the hang of the sport, and the gentle conditions were probably better for the novice anyway.

"Hey, you're surfing goofy-foot!" exclaimed Thomas. "You've got your right foot out front."

"Does it matter?"

"Dunno; everybody surfs the other way."

"I thought this was supposed to be such a hot spot for surfing," he grumbled, after a particularly long stretch of disappointing surf.

"Winter's best, 'cuz it's when we have the storms that bring the waves," answered Micah. "Unless there's a typhoon some place—that's what we call hurricanes out here. Then there's lots of surf, even in the summer. But all the big competitions are in the winter. There are still waves on the west side, but it's a long way to go. When you get your license and a truck, then we can go there."

"I can't wait."

"Me neither. Anyway, it gets windy in the afternoon, but we're not allowed out here after eleven."

"Who says?" protested Alec.

"It's the law or something. You have to be windsurfing after eleven. Say, maybe with some of the money we earn we could get a board."

"How much do they cost?"

"I dunno...we can ask some of those guys on the beach."

"I've gotta get a job."

"What kind of job?"

"Maybe I could work down here where all the surf shops are."

"That would be cool," added Micah. "Better talk to Dad, tho'."

"Yeah, I still have to figure out how to get to work."

"You can borrow my bike," said Micah.

"Cool. Thanks."

Thomas asked, "Are you gonna stay here all summer?"

"I guess so."

"How about when school starts?"

"Maybe. We'll see. Can you really come out here in the winter?"

"Yup! The waves are huge, and the water is almost as warm."

"Cool. What about school?"

"We gotta go to school, but lots of kids come out after school. Especially girls."

"You're gonna learn to dive, aren't you?" asked Micah.

"Is it really going to be free?"

"Yeah, 'cuz it's Gabe. I think you should get a job with Gabe. Hey, I think we have to quit; the windsurfers are heading out. Mom's probably waiting for us."

"Hey, look, there's a guy over there selling fireworks. Can we get some?"

"Yeah, let's get some," approved Thomas.

Micah cautioned, "Just don't tell Mom, OK?"

"Mrs. Hoana, do you have a photo of your husband?" Officer Jan Taylor questioned Malia as sensitively as she could, but it was beginning to look like the guy was off on a fling somewhere. But this was a decent woman who deserved the benefit of the doubt without jumping to conclusions.

Malia handed the officer several photos that she and George had collected from albums and framed pictures around the house. She added, "These are all very recent, within the past few months."

"He's a big man, isn't he?"

Malia smiled through her fatigue. "Yes, but he's a big pussycat. His size does help him in his job. He's Vice Principal at West Maui Middle School."

Officer Taylor returned the smile, adding, "I wouldn't want to get on his bad side."

Malia had exhausted her smile quota for awhile and became silent.

"You don't have children, Mrs. Hoana?"

Malia shook her head. "We joked about me not wanting to give birth to his children, but really, it just never happened for us."

Summertime, no school commitments. Wife is away. No children to take care of.

"Do you have pets? A dog?"

"No, we're both gone a lot."

"Can you think of anyone, even a student, who might want to harm your husband?"

"I'm not aware of any. George, do you think Gabe would know?"

"Maybe. I'll call him."

"Gabe?" questioned Officer Taylor.

"My nephew," responded George. "A science teacher at the school."

"Science? As in chemistry?"

George wasn't sure he liked the direction of the inquiry, but he knew she was just doing her job. The officer did not know these people, so she had to ask the questions that no one else would. He had detected her skepticism early on about the platonic nature of their relationship. He could imagine the officer's mind thinking he and Malia had off'd Owen so they could be together. Now Malia was acting the part of the grieving wife. George felt the hairs on his neck prickle when the officer started to question him about Gabe and his knowledge of dangerous chemicals.

"Not much chemistry. More like magnets and earthworms."

"Is there anything missing from the house?"

"No, quite the contrary. If he had left on his own, he would probably have taken something…clothes, his toothbrush. There's only one shirt in the hamper. It's what he was wearing on Tuesday, the day I left."

"Could I take it me?"

"I suppose. I was going to wash it. It's odd; there's no socks or underwear, just the shirt."

"I'll take it just like it is."

Malia went in to retrieve the dirty shirt and brought out, handing it to the officer, who had put on latex gloves in the meantime. As she turned it over, she noticed what looked like drops of blood on the shirt. Malia and George noticed it as well. Malia began to get very pale, and George had her sit down. She put her head in her hands and began to weep. "Owen, where are you?"

"Mrs. Hoana, is it OK if I look through the house and the cars?"

Malia looked at George, responding, "Of course. Anything. Here is my set of keys. I haven't seen Owen's keys."

"Interesting."

"If we're going to own property here, there are two things I need: a tan and some cool Hawaiian shirts," Dan said to Sarah as they packed for a day at the beach. "I look like a tourist."

Sarah said, "You and tens of thousands of other people. You're the doctor; have you seen the burns people get here after their first—and only—day at the beach? Just how much do you like my freckles, because you haven't seen anything yet? I'm sure my dad will be happy to show you hundreds of pictures of me freckled out in the summer. Shall I call him and have him bring some to show you?"

"Have you noticed how pale I am? People are going to think we spent every day in Hawai'i in bed."

"OK, you have a point. It's your fault you signed up to be blond and blue-eyed. Come on, *haole*, I'll let you have 30 minutes in the sun. You'll thank me for not letting you have more. I don't want you using sunburn as an excuse on our honeymoon."

"An excuse for what?"

"For separate beds." She threw his swim trunks at him, and he deftly caught them in one hand, using the other to wrestle her onto the bed.

"Aha! I knew this was all about you!" He buried his face in her neck and kissed her neck, shoulders, and finally her lips. "You know where my favorite freckle is?" Sarah giggled at the playful outburst, and they rolled over and over until they were on the opposite side of the bed, landing on the floor on their bottoms. Diane heard them from the living room and called out, "Need some help in there?"

"No!" they responded simultaneously, before starting their laughter again.

"I'm ready to go, whenever you are. Maybe I should find something to do for awhile, like reading *War and Peace.*"

"We're coming," said Sarah, as she and Dan got up and collected their gear for the day.

"Is it OK if I come with you guys? Gabe felt like he needed to go over to Malia's. He said the lady cop was starting to grill George about his relationship with Malia, and he was starting in on Gabe. Something about using his classroom chemicals to get rid of the body."

"What body? They still don't know where Owen is?" queried Dan.

"Nope."

"This is getting really weird."

"Yes, it is."

"Is there anything we can do?"

"I don't think so. Gabe said he'll meet us later; he'll call me on my cell phone to find out where we are. So where are we, anyway?"

Sarah said, "The wedding coordinator invited us over to the hotel to hang out there. They've got changing rooms, places to eat, and a great spot on the beach. We can find some place to watch the fireworks."

"Sounds great, as long as you two don't decide to go get a room and leave me alone at the bar. On second thought…"

"We'll try to restrain ourselves," said Dan, as he swept Sarah into his arms dipping her backwards in a passionate embrace and kiss.

"Where's that copy of *War and Peace?*"

"Hey, it's my turn! I've felt like a nun since I moved in here, watching you two… Anyone else hungry? I'm starving."

Duke and Wally carried the golf bags out to their vehicles. They agreed to meet at the Wal-Mart parking lot so all the bags could be transferred to Duke's car. They needed to separate. Duke wasn't sure what their next steps should be, but he needed Wally to go away. He couldn't think clearly with Wally bugging him. Wally suggested they get some lunch at a fast-food place and offered to treat Duke. Duke decided that Wally needed some reassurance so he wouldn't do something stupid like go home, go back to the school, or worse, try to contact Cho.

"Hana," suggested Duke. "Drive over to Hana and get lost there."

"Man, that road makes me sick. I don't know anyone there. Where are you going to go? Can't we just hide out together? Even catch a boat over to Moloka'i?"

"Wally, I just need to be alone to think. Understand?"

Wally nodded in acceptance, not in agreement. "I could hide out at the school."

Duke could feel his patience stretched to the breaking point. "Hello, Wally! The cops have got HoHo; they're going to go everywhere he goes to find out where he got the drugs. And that includes the school."

"Oh, right."

"Do you have any money?"

"Yeah."

"Just get lost, Wally. For a day or so. I'll call you. I promise."

"I just figured it out. I know a guy…"

"No, don't tell me."

"OK, man. Call me." Wally got up and left. Duke watched while he drove away, heading south.

Wally was desperate. *Rocky*. Rocky had a boat, but Wally wasn't sure Rocky would be thrilled to hear from him. The last time they had talked, they had fought over a woman. It was stupid. She ended up leaving both of them, but it had soured the relationship between them. He hoped that enough time had passed so that they could go back to being buddies. Rocky had always admired Wally's Rolex watch that he had won in a poker game. Maybe, if he gave Rocky the Rolex, that would patch things up between them. It seemed like a lot to give him just to be able to stay on Rocky's boat.

I'll just win it back from him again in a poker game someday.

Wally swung his van around and headed back to his apartment to get the watch and a few things that would tide him over on the boat for awhile.

Gabe had never been questioned by the police before except when it concerned a student that had gotten in trouble. This time it was personal. He found himself retreating into the teacher persona he used when he first met his students in the fall—formal, serious, unflappable. He was shocked to see how weary Malia looked; there was no way her behavior could be an act.

"The last time I heard from Owen was Wednesday or Thursday; I don't remember which. He sent me an email about my using the library for a diving class I'm teaching later this month. He sounded distracted, and his message was a bit, well, out of character."

"In what way?" queried Officer Taylor.

He looked at Malia, hesitating, saying, "Well, for one, he signed it 'Love HoHo.' Isn't that your pet name for him, Malia?"

She nodded, blushing, and added, "I got a few text messages from him when I was in San Diego. Do you want to see them? I'm not sure they're still on the phone, but you can look. He said he was going camping in Haleakala. And I know that cell coverage is really bad up there, so I wasn't totally surprised that he never answered my calls. The thing is, he would never go by himself, and I've called everyone I can think of who has ever gone camping with him. Even if he did go by himself, how did he get there? His car is here. And everyone knows you can only stay there for three nights."

The officer jumped on this, saying, "So, it's possible he'll be home today."

"Yes, it's possible. This is just strange behavior for him."

Gabe handed the officer the newspaper section reporting on the campground closure. "And he obviously wasn't camping when he emailed me. And this makes things even stranger. The campground up there is closed."

A long silence ensued while the officer and then Malia read the article. The officer appeared to mentally review all the possible scenarios in her mind. Gabe's sixth sense told him that she had concluded Owen was out on a fling, and he imagined that she resented having to go through the motions of filing a missing person's report—an almost certain waste of police resources.

"Mrs. Hoana, here is my card. I will be in touch as soon as I've found out anything. If you can think of any other place your husband could be, don't hesitate to call me."

"Thank you, I will."

Officer Taylor gathered the bag of Owen's dirty and blood-stained shirt and left.

"George, go home. There's nothing you can do here. I need to get some food and get settled back in. If—when—Owen does come home, he'll be hungry. It's the Fourth of July; you need to be with your family."

"All right. But *I'm* preaching tomorrow; I'll use your notes, but I don't think you're heart will be in it this week."

"I know better than to argue with you, Father Superior. Right now I'm thinking that I should have been a nun."

George laughed softly and bid Malia good-bye after she promised to call him often.

Duke drove by the house twice while the police car was at Owen's house. It was the first time he had been in Owen's house since he had followed Wally there to get rid of Owen's car. There was no ambulance, and it appeared to be a single female officer. The other car was unfamiliar. Duke wasn't sure if that meant they knew about Owen or not. It's possible the police hadn't made the connection yet between the junkie they'd arrested the night before and the middle school vice principal and husband of a church deacon. He assumed Owen was not there, but he needed to be sure.

The third time he drove by the house, the police car, the other car, and one of Owen's cars were gone. He parked on a side street and walked deliberately to the Hoana house and through the back gate. This time the blinds were ii open and he could see into nearly every room. No one was there. Duke cursed under his breath for having missed seeing everyone leave.

His cell phone had three messages on it from Cho's "associates." He had no intention of answering them until he had something that would ensure his own personal safety, something that would make him more valuable to Cho in a healthy state than in a damaged one. In his line of work, the potential rewards were high only because the risks were even higher. Assuming he could survive this deal, he vowed to embark on a safe and boring life well under the radar of Cho and his "associates."

He needed to disappear, to clear his mind, to let his unconsciousness work things out. Golf would do that, but there wasn't time before he had to meet Erin. In the meantime, he needed to come up with a life story and a job that would pass for conversation. Something other than "drug lord employee." True but unacceptable. "Investment banker?" Acceptable but untrue. Unrealistic. It had to be something he could talk about, but not encourage too many questions. And he had an hour in which to concoct the story.

"OK, medicine man, that's your thirty minutes. Come get under the cabana and we can order some drinks." Sarah laid a towel down on the lounge for Dan.

"Yes, ma'am. I'm going to jump in the pool to cool off, but I'll be right back. Get me something tropical, a Mai Tai, Margarita…"

"As you wish. Would you like a foot massage with that?"

"You can start there. And then…"

Diane interrupted, "You two! I'm hungry! Let's order something for lunch. I'll call Gabe and see where he is and if he wants something."

Dan said, "Nah, don't call him. Every guy around has been looking at me, envious of my good fortune."

Sarah flicked a few ice crystals at him from her melting slush. "We need to cool you down."

"What did you have in mind?"

Diane jumped in again. "I am definitely calling Gabe. Shall I roll down the sides on the cabana so you two can be alone?"

"Oh, would you do that for us?" asked Dan, as Diane glared at him, reaching for her cell phone. "Sarah, honey, you do have a terrific sister."

"Hello, Gabe. Where are you?…Good. You'd better get here fast; the lovebirds are driving me nuts. Are you hungry? We're ordering food… OK. How's Malia? Did they find Owen?…Oh… OK, see you in a bit."

"What?" asked Sarah.

"They haven't found Owen; Gabe said he'd fill us in when he got here. He's about ten minutes out."

Dan picked up the binoculars and scanned the channel for a few minutes, announcing his findings. "Sailboats, and there are people parasailing, and look way out there: it's a cruise ship. No whales."

Diane replied, "This time of year you're more likely to see pigs fly."

"What do you think about just buying this cabana, sister-in-law? It would probably be the same price as a three-bedroom house on the other side of the road."

"There's no bathroom."

"What do you mean?" Dan responded in mock disbelief, extending his hand towards the sea.

"I see why you needed rescuing," Gabe said as he approached the cabana.

"Gabe!" exclaimed Diane, reaching up to receive a kiss from him. "Do you believe this? Look at this view! Here—there's enough room to bring in another lounge."

Dan teased, "You know she's going to expect this kind of view at the house."

Gabe asked, "So, do you want a view or a bathroom?"

"Both, of course."

"Of course."

"And my own closet."

"You can have mine; you'll end up with it anyway. Just give me a cardboard box in the garage, and I'll be fine."

Dan interrupted the banter, saying, "Gabe, could you just pretend you're the waiter? I'm the envy of every guy here."

"Not anymore. But I will go get drinks, just to show my appreciation for being included in this outing. Too bad we can't see the big fireworks from here. So, who's going to show me around?"

Diane got up, putting on her hot pink cover-up and straw hat with the pink Aloha band. She said, "I'll show you the changing room. Later I'll show you the spots for the rehearsal dinner and the wedding reception."

"When do I get to see the honeymoon suite?"

"I think we've been sitting in it. I'm not sure they're going to make it to Lana'i!"

"Let's give them a breather; there's a sand castle exhibit at Whaler's Village."

"Uh, OK."

"No, these are amazing; it's not a couple of little kids filling buckets with sand. You'll thank me later. In fact, you'll owe me. I like that."

"Yeah, but you're easy to pay off."

"I know."

Wally parked behind the dumpster at the marina. He retrieved a cold six-pack of beer from the cooler in his trunk and walked across the pier to where Rocky had his boat moored.

"Hey Rocky! You home? It's Wally. Hey, buddy, where are you?"

The hatch opened, and a man emerged zipping up his pants.

"Wally? What are you doing here?"

"Hey, I brought beer."

"Beer is good."

"Yeah. So how have you been? Long time no see."

"Can't complain. What are you doing here?"

"Can I come aboard?"

"I guess. What are you doing here?"

"It's been awhile, and I was hoping we could, you know, patch things up."

"I'm not sure it's been long enough. What happened to…?"

"Gone, man, she's gone."

"Oh."

Rocky approved of the local brew Wally handed him as a peace offering.

"Been fishing?" asked Wally, as they relaxed on deck chairs under the awning.

"Some. Yesterday. Say, you want some fish?"

"Oh, yeah. Thanks, man. Say, I was wondering if I could maybe help you out on the boat, in exchange for staying here, just for awhile."

"You in trouble, man?"

"A little, just for awhile."

"Cops looking for you?"

"Nah, nothing like that."

"A woman?"

"I wish."

"What's wrong with your place?"

"I just need to disappear for a while. Is it OK?"

"I guess."

Wally was relieved. He didn't have to part with his Rolex. Sometimes beer worked just as well.

"Hey, thanks, man. I'll keep this baby looking good for you. And I brought some food. And lots more beer. How about I cook?"

"You don't like my cooking?"

"Only if there's enough catsup to cover it up."

"Hey, man, that hurts," said Rocky, pretending to be mortally wounded.

"Sometimes the truth hurts." Wally was happy to see his friend joking with him.

"OK, man, you can stay. There's lots that needs doing on *Da Big Kahuna*. Hey, no parties, OK?"

"I just want to stay low for awhile."

"OK. You say you've got more beer?"

"Oh, yeah. Want to help me bring it on board?"

"Duke! Over here! Hi, how are you? How was golf?" Erin called and waved to Duke.

"Oh, it was great. You know what they say about a bad day at golf." Duke was surprised how glad he was to see her. He needed an escape, and she was it. He added, "You look fantastic."

"Thanks! Say, I booked us for a sunset cruise so we can watch the fireworks. We have a few hours to kill…"

"Good. How about going into some spot for a drink?"

"Lead on."

Duke did not want to remain quite so visible, so he looked for a bar with a table away from the front door. It would be easier to talk anyway. He was ready for the inquisition.

"Mai Tai? Piña colada? Beer?"

"A Mai Tai would be great."

"I'll be back in a minute." Duke went to the bar to place the order, taking advantage of the opportunity to check for messages on his cell phone. One more from Cho. *Give it a rest, old man. It's a holiday. An American holiday, you jerk, not that you would care.*

He kept the phone turned off so that he wouldn't be tempted to answer it.

"Oh, this looks delicious," said Erin when the server brought the drinks over.

"Hungry? What are we supposed to get on the cruise?"

"Snacks and an open bar."

"Well, I promised you dinner, so how about a late lunch instead?"

"I think they're famous for their fish and chips."

"You're letting me off easy."

"There are lobster tacos, too," Erin added coyly.

"It's a holiday...go for it."

They ordered lunch and sat back, and Duke knew he was in for the questions. He decided to be the first.

"So tell me about your work."

"I do free-lance writing, mostly about Hawai'i for all kinds of magazines. The job forces me to explore all the nooks and crannies of the islands. I still feel like I've just scratched the surface. I'll show you some of my articles later, if you like."

"I'd like to see them. How long have you been on Maui?"

"About five years," she said.

"Do you have family here?"

"I have a cousin on Oahu, but most of my family is in California... San Francisco area. What about you?"

"I've been here fifteen years," said Duke. "I moved here about the time I lost three toes to frostbite in Montana."

"Really?" Erin's eyes were wide, until she realized he had been teasing her.

"Nah, but I really hate cold weather."

"So what do you do?"

Let the games begin.

"Well, golf isn't just my recreation, it's also my job."

"You're a pro?"

"I wish. I'm good, but not that good. No, I've got a golf equipment wholesale business, and it's been pretty successful."

"No kidding?"

"What, you don't think I am successful?"

"No! I mean, yes!" Duke was teasing her again. They laughed and changed the subject as their lunch arrived. *It's working. Probably because I wish it was this way. That makes it easy to talk about it.*

"Do you do a lot of traveling in your work?" he asked.

"Mostly inter-island. I'm going to Moloka'i next weekend. Have you been there?"

"Not for years."

Duke suspected she wanted to invite him to come along. At this point, he didn't want to commit to anything, although that might be a good escape if and when he needed it. He decided that he could probably invite himself later, but for the time being, it was best to keep her at arm's length. She'd be safer that way.

Erin couldn't read Duke, but she decided she wouldn't push what she was thinking…yet. "I'm also doing an article on the Kapalua Wine and Food Festival." Again, Duke sensed she wanted to invite him to come along.

Duke paid the check and suggested they walk around the shops and out on the beach where live music was playing. He didn't plan to hole up in a bar the rest of the day. It was just as easy to be invisible in a crowd. Eventually they had to drive down to Lahaina to catch their boat for the cruise, but he preferred the ambience of Ka'anapali for awhile. Somehow it seemed safer.

They bought two water bottles and walked out hand-in-hand. They stopped to admire the sand sculptures on display while sipping water. A gangly teenager on roller blades bumped Erin, forcing her to spill water on a woman nearby in a hot pink dress. The woman was startled, and Erin apologized, but realizing that the accident had been caused by the careless teenager, the woman just thanked her for cooling her off. She then overhead her tell her boyfriend, "I wonder how many bathrooms there are in that sand castle."

The boyfriend responded, "Think of it as one big litter box."

Erin commented to Duke, "I think it takes a special personality to build something like that, only to tear it down again the next day and start over. Although I guess people do it all the time with one another. It's a throw-away society."

Duke was taken aback at the unexpected analysis of failed human relationships, perhaps a reflection from personal experience? He wasn't sure where to take the conversation; he had little experience with deep, intimate discussions with educated women. His line of work had excluded him from relationships with them. He mentally continued

Erin's metaphor by comparing it with his own life. He had sculpted a life that may not be possible to sweep away and forget, however hopeful he might be of starting afresh. The sand would always be stuck under his fingernails, in his hair, in his shorts. When you start playing in the sand, all you think about is how much fun it is. But when you try to wash it off, it sticks to your wet feet. If you wipe your face with a towel, you get sand in your eyes. There's no escape. You must either stay on the beach forever, where you don't care how much sand there is on you, or you must painstakingly remove every grain from your body and your clothes. It was impossible; some of the sand always sticks. It gets in your car, your food, your bed. But you can't stay on the beach forever. You will end up hungry, alone, and burned.

Duke shook himself free of his metaphorical self-psychoanalysis, as if he was brushing himself free of sand. He noticed Erin, expecting—hoping—for some response to her comment.

"Sorry I drifted off. Guess I was lost in thought."

Erin smiled tenderly, deciding not to push him into some deep discussion about feelings. *Just accept the fact that men are from Mars.*

"It's OK. Say, we should probably make our way down to Lahaina. It may take us awhile to find parking."

"Good idea. How about I meet you at Moose's?"

"Good choice.

Duke took her head in his hands and kissed her. He smiled and said, "See you in something between thirty minutes and three hours."

Erin laughed and said, "Here's my cell phone number in case you need to reach me."

Duke hesitated, but returned the offer with his own number. He hadn't wanted to leave his cell phone on, but now it was a requirement, at least until they connected in Lahaina. He told himself that he had to make things right with Cho, or he would always be running scared. After that, he would tear down the sand castle and build a new one. On a different beach. He hoped he would get the chance. Maybe it was time to use something other than sand.

Don. I could get used to being Don again.

As expected, the catamaran was fully booked for the sunset excursion in the channel to watch the fireworks. Sarah and Diane scoped out a place for the four of them, while Dan and Gabe went to get refreshments. Diane saw the woman who had provided the surprise drenching earlier that afternoon, and she waved at her. The woman waved back and approached Diane to introduce herself.

"I see you've dried off," said Erin, smiling. "I'm so sorry…"

"You wouldn't have any more of that water, would you? It felt great!"

"Sorry, after I drenched you, other people came up and asked if I would splash them, too."

Diane giggled. "Join us if you would like. I'm Diane, and this is my sister Sarah."

"Hi… Erin, and my, uh, friend, is Duke. He's gone to get drinks."

"Same here. I think we can squeeze in two more over here."

"Thanks, that sounds great. Are you all on vacation?"

"Yes and no." Diane filled Erin in on their situation, and Erin responded with hers. The two were becoming fast friends.

"Congratulations, Sarah. Wow, a wedding on Maui. That's so romantic."

"Thanks. So, your 'friend'…?"

"It's our first date, but I hope it's not the last. He's really cute. And funny. A little mysterious, too."

"As in dangerous?"

"Oh, no. More like he's got some worries in his life. Oh, look there are three guys headed in our direction with drinks. I guess we should hang out with them tonight and not look elsewhere."

Diane responded, "At least until we want another drink."

Each of the men handed his lady her drink and was greeted by a kiss, followed by introductions all around. Dan said, "There's food down below, too, if anyone is hungry."

The catamaran started to pull away from the dock, and the cruise director immediately came onto the loudspeaker to instruct the passengers on logistics and safety.

Gabe said to Diane, "Two."

"Two what?"

"Bathrooms, of course. I assumed you'd want to know."

"Not including the ocean?"

"Not including the ocean."

Sarah interrupted, "Look, there's the fireworks barge. Hey, who keeps drinking my Mai Tai?"

Dan laughed, "They're going down way too quickly. Want another?"

"Yes—and no."

When the fireworks show was over and the catamaran had docked back in Lahaina, everyone went their separate ways home. With all the holiday traffic merging onto the highway at the same time, it was going to be slow-going. Duke and Erin stopped at a bar for a last drink to let the bulk of the traffic to get a head start. It had been a wonderful evening for both of them, and neither wanted it to end. Erin enjoyed an iced coffee while Duke had a beer.

"I had a great time today, Duke."

"Me, too. A Fourth of July to remember, huh?"

"Oh, yeah."

"I've got some work to do on the Fifth of July, but I'll give you a call during the week, if that's OK."

"Sounds good. Say, let me know if you'd like to come along on my Moloka'i trip, or even Kapalua next weekend."

"Will do. Well, it looks like the town has cleared out, so I'd better head back. Where did you park? I walk you back to your car."

"Thanks, it's about a block away."

Duke and Erin embraced and fell into a long, private kiss. Duke pulled away first, and Erin got in her car and drove off, waving.

You're an idiot, you know.

He walked back to his car parked in a lot that was nearly deserted by now. As he approached the car, two men emerged from a van, calling out to him.

"Hey, Duke? Don't you answer your phone, man?" The two looked like bouncers, but Duke didn't think he would bounce very well if they decided to make things uncomfortable for him."

"Huh? Who are you?" Duke felt the hair on the back of his neck stand up. He felt an uncontrollable shiver. *I should have parked some place else out of sight.*

"We work for Mr. Cho, you know, your employer."

"Oh, Benny, Edgar! It's you guys. How is Mr. Cho? I didn't realize Mr. Cho was trying to reach me. I was on a date, and didn't want to keep answering my phone."

"Yeah, that must be it. So, where is she?"

"Gone. Home."

"You must be irresistible, Duke. Can't get laid on the Fourth of July? How about that, Edgar?"

"Some women just don't appreciate perfection when they see it." Duke hoped that a little humor would gain himself a little empathy.

Benny ignored him, and said, "Mr. Cho would like to see you."

"Sounds good. Tomorrow would be good…" Benny cut him off.

"Now."

"Now's fine." *Shit.* "How about I follow you?"

Benny looked at Edgar, unsure whether to accept the proposal. Edgar said, "How about I ride with you so you don't get lost?"

"Whatever."

Duke was trying to decide whether to breathe or not. Every intake of air was painful. Somehow he managed to drive himself to the hospital emergency room before losing consciousness just outside the lobby. The beefy nurse's aides picked him up and laid him on a gurney. He awoke when the stabs of pain brought him back to semi-consciousness.

"Mugged."

"Where does it hurt?" asked one of the aides.

"Ribs. Hurts to breathe." With that he passed out again.

When he awoke, he was in a hospital bed, surrounded by a curtain. Something was dripping into an IV in his hand. He tried to get up, but he was in a body cast, and movement was impossible.

"Nurse," he called weakly.

"Mr. Garrity, my name is Violet, your nurse. How are you feeling?"

"I can't move. Cast."

"It's just a brace, but it probably feels like a cast. You've got a couple of broken ribs, and the doctor wants to make sure you don't puncture a lung. Do you need something for the pain?"

"Yes."

"When you're up to it, the police want to talk to you. You said you were mugged?"

"Mugged. Yes."

"How awful. I'll go get your pain medication."

"Thanks."

The morphine helped him think. He needed to have a story to tell the police. Once the pain had lessened, he chastised himself for coming to the hospital. But he had been in too much pain to think straight. But there would be too many questions, and he would need a story that would get the police out of the way. He certainly didn't want them poking around in his car, eventually discovering the cache of cocaine stuffed into the bottom of his golf bags along with his gun.

Once again, you're a real idiot. You keep shooting yourself in the foot.

The sand squished between his toes as he walked along the beach. Erin was swinging at golf balls, but they all ended up in the ocean. He tried to tell her to keep her arm straight; she was swinging like Wally. He tried to retrieve the balls in the water, but there were two big whales watching him. He couldn't move because every step was painful, and he couldn't breathe. Wally kept kicking up sand, and he wouldn't stop. He hated playing golf with Wally. You were more likely to get hit by Wally's ball if you stood behind him than you were standing in front of him.

The whales came up onto the beach heading for Duke. Duke pointed at Wally, saying, "He's the one you want. Get him. Erin, I can't reach you; get away from the whales." Erin just kept hitting balls into the water. That was OK; Duke could get the balls now that the whales were concentrating on Wally. "Let's go get them, Erin, OK?"

"Right, let's get them," she responded. But it wasn't Erin. It wasn't even a 'she.' It was a man in a tan shirt. Now it was two men in tan shirts.

"Mr. Garrity? How are you, Mr. Garrity? I'm Officer Chan, and this is Officer Riata."

Duke couldn't respond. Whales? The whales were gone.

"Mr. Garrity, we're investigating your assault, and we need your help to figure out what happened to you."

"Whales."

The two officers looked at one another, mouthing "whales?" to one another. The nurse came in, saying, "He's probably not very coherent right now. He's got two broken ribs, and he's on morphine for the time being. We need to keep him still."

"He said something about whales."

"I couldn't tell you. Maybe whales sat on him."

"When do you think he'll be more lucid?"

"Probably about the time the morphine wears off, just before he's due for another shot…in about three hours. Did this happen to anyone else?"

"Not that we know about."

"How did he get here?"

"Believe it or not, he drove here."

"With two broken ribs?"

"He's a fighter."

"So his car is here?"

"I guess; I don't know. There's his stuff; maybe his keys are there. They said he had about $500 on him. The ER folks put it in the hospital safe."

"That's a lot for a local to be carrying around."

"Pocket change for me," the nurse said wryly.

"Of course, us, too. Here are his keys; we'll go check out his car. We just have to figure out which one it is."

"At this hour, there shouldn't be that many, although it's anyone's guess where he actually parked it."

The car was easy to find in the relatively empty lot, occupying three spaces. It was amazing he hadn't hit anything when he was parking, much less driving.

"Nothing interesting here. A couple of bags of clubs, a change of clothes, looks like a guy out for the Fourth of July. Someone probably beat him up for just being in the wrong place at the wrong time. I'm surprised no one saw anything. Strange that he wasn't robbed. Let's go check out his house."

"Can we do that? He hasn't given his consent, and he's not really in a coma."

"Good point. We don't know what this guy's been up to. Looks innocent enough. Let's wait until he comes around. I'm going to move the car so it's parked properly. Then we can at least drive by his house. His address looks like an apartment, so it's not that private. Maybe someone saw something."

"Alec, where did you put the firecrackers?" Micah asked half-brother Alec.

"Outside, behind the washing machine."

"Let's shoot them off tomorrow, OK?"

"Yeah, in the morning."

"Maybe after church."

"Oh, yeah, I forgot. Do you go every week?"

"Sure."

"Why?"

"It's what we do. Dad's the priest."

"I thought priests had to be unmarried and not have kids."

"It's OK in our church. They can be women, too. Did you go to church in Seattle?"

"Nope."

Micah was quiet for a minute before inquiring further. "So what do you know about God and Jesus and stuff?"

"Jesus was born on Christmas and died on Easter. Isn't that it?"

"Sort of. Not exactly. He died on Good Friday."

"Doesn't sound so good. I'd hate to think what Bad Friday was like."

"Then on Easter he rose from the dead. It showed people that he really was God's son and he loved us."

"I don't think everyone believes that."

"Yeah, I know. Do you?"

"Never thought about it. Probably not. He let my mother die. He lets lots of people die. You don't see them rise from the dead."

"I don't think God said people wouldn't die, like, get sick and die because they're old. Just that—that's not the whole story. Maybe I'll think about it more when I get old."

"Your dad should have all the answers, since he's a priest."

"Well, he doesn't."

"Maybe he's not a very good priest."

"People think he's really good, and I think they like it that he doesn't have all the answers any more than they do."

"I'm going to sleep now. Night."

"G'night, Alec. Hey, you know, God let you live."

Sunday, July 5

It can't be possible. I feel worse today. Please, God, help me feel better. If this is cancer, let me die before it gets worse. I remember when I felt good. God—Wally. I felt good playing golf with Wally.

Attendants Jésus and Zack tried to get Owen cleaned up for the day. They sat him in the shower and cleaned off his scratches. "Spiders, maybe ants." said Jésus.

"Where?" asked Zack.

"In his mind."

"Is he nuts?"

"The drugs did it, so, yeah, he's nuts."

"Can he keep anything down yet?"

"Not much. Fortunately he's carrying some reserve."

"Do they know who he is yet?"

"I don't know, just something like 'HoHo.'"

"Think he's an illegal?"

"Wouldn't surprise me, except that he was pretty well dressed when they brought him in. Dirty, like he hadn't showered in awhile…a long while."

"Where did they find him?"

"In a golf equipment warehouse, driving a golf cart like he was in the Indy 500, stoned out of his mind."

"Bet he wishes he was still stoned."

"Oh, yeah."

Between the morphine wearing off and the nurses coming in every thirty minutes, Duke did not get much sleep. The pains were in different places today. With his ribs immobilized, Duke now became aware of his badly scraped knee and biceps. Both were bandaged, but they were starting to throb. Maybe they had been throbbing all along, but his brain could only process so much pain at a time.

His Fourth of July escape from the reality of the sand castle he had built for himself was a distant memory. *It's probably just as well. No one's going to let me just walk away from it. I have to deal with it. Time to come up with another story.*

"Mr. Garrity?"

"Come in."

"Mr. Garrity, I'm officer Chan, and this is Officer Riata. We came by last night, but you were in pretty bad shape. How are you now?"

"Oh, pretty much how I look, I imagine. I'm angry with myself for parking in such a remote location. I guess I looked like a big punching bag. Was I robbed?"

"It doesn't appear like it. The nurse said your valuables are locked up. We did move your car."

Duke shivered at the mention of the police getting into his car. Had they checked the trunk? He needed to know.

"You still have two sets of golf clubs in the trunk; does that sound right?"

Duke nodded, tentatively allowing himself to breathe a sigh of relief. Then he added, "You know, I didn't see anything. They punched my lights out, and I don't remember anything after that until I woke up next to my car. Any idea who they were?"

"No, we were hoping you could remember something."

"I barely remember the drive here. I guess I didn't do the best job parking."

"No, but understandable. We're glad you made it. Where were you parked?"

"In Lahaina…to see the fireworks."

"Were you with anyone?"

"A lady…a neighbor. We arranged to meet in town, since I was playing golf in the afternoon. She wasn't even parked near me. I'm so glad."

"Yeah, most women are smarter than men on where they park."

"We waited for the traffic to ease up before we headed home. I walked her to her car before I went to mine. It was stupid."

"Well, Mr. Garrity, if you remember anything else, please give us a call. Here's my card. Take care of yourself."

"Thanks very much."

I wonder how many more lies I will have to tell before I don't have to tell any more.

Officer Rubio sipped hot coffee while recalling the break-in at Cho's warehouse. Something odd, out of place, something most people wouldn't give a second thought about.

What was it?

The guy was effusive in his concern over the drug addict getting help, while being quite indifferent over the damage to his property.

I don't buy it. What was it?

"He called the guy by his name," he said out loud. "HoHo. How did he know the guy's name? He never even saw him." Pausing in his thought, he then said, "I never told him the guy's name, and I'm the only one who talked to him. Jerk. You're involved in this somehow. We *will* get you."

George's sermon began with a common point of reference. "I know a lot of you have big families, right?" Many in the congregation nodded. "Lots of brothers, sisters, cousins, yes? You go to school with them, you spend holidays with them, maybe you sometimes get into arguments with them."

A few sheepish grins.

"Sometimes it's their fault, sometimes it's your fault, right? OK, mostly it's their fault. But mostly you get along, and everyone is more or less about equal. Oh, maybe some are smarter, some are better athletes, some are better looking. But overall most of us are pretty average most of the time, would you say?"

Lots of nods, with people looking at one another, smiling.

"Yes, yes, except for you, Thomas." Thomas and his brothers laughed at the playful dig.

"What happens when one of your family members decides that he's somehow more special than everyone else and starts acting like it? That really bothers us, doesn't it? We like to think of that person as just another scrawny kid that does stupid stuff like the rest of us. It somehow makes it easier for the rest of us to accept the fact that we do stupid stuff, too. We don't like people who brag about how special they are.

"But what if, what if, he really was special? Let's say Jesus was your cousin, and he came home for the weekend to visit. Now you have to imagine that this is before Jesus died. He's just another one of the cousins as far as you know. But, he comes home and starts doing special things and tries to get you to believe he is special. What would be your reaction?

Come on, be honest. I would expect that you would get together with all of your other cousins and agree that he was just blowing smoke. Maybe some of you would believe Jesus had some special abilities, even just a little bit. But when you got together with the rest of your average friends and relatives, you would talk yourselves out of it, or you would at least keep your opinions to yourself. Because if you didn't, everyone would laugh at you. And you'd be just as alone as Jesus. Let me re-read a little of the sixth chapter of Mark's gospel.

"Jesus left that place and came to his hometown, and his disciples followed him. On the Sabbath he began to teach in the synagogue, and many who heard him were astounded. They said, 'Where did this man get all this? What is this wisdom that has been given to him? What deeds of power are being done by his hands? Is not this the carpenter, the son of Mary and brother of James and Joseph, and Judas and Simon, and are not his sisters here with us?' And they took offense at him. Then Jesus said to them, 'Prophets are not without honor, except in their hometown, and among their own kin, and in their own house.' And he could do no deed of power there, except that he laid his hands on a few sick people and cured them. And he was amazed at their unbelief.

"Now, imagine that you're Jesus, and you've come home to see your family—your mother, your brothers, maybe your father, although he might have already been dead at the time of this story in Mark's gospel. These are simple people, scratching out a living, no richer, no poorer than most people of the time. Everyone is working, and you show up. In some places you might have a little prestige as a rabbi, but at home you don't act like the other rabbis your family knows. You really don't have a job. You're probably scruffier than most of them. Don't we just love relatives like that?

"Your mother's on your side, as well as your father, but that's where the loyalty and the belief end. What do you do? Do you stick around? Why *would* you?

"It may sound surprising that Jesus left his family rather than trying to turn them around. But Jesus knew a little bit about human nature. *'Only in his hometown, among his relatives and in his own house is a prophet without honor.'* I'm sure he was disappointed. I mean, really: the Son of God. That's pretty special isn't it? But they weren't buying it yet.

"We've got it lucky. Most of us are in some level of agreement that Jesus was and is the son of God. As Christians, we question lots of things, but maybe not that. We have heard the stories, and we believe them to be at least relevant on some level, if not absolute fact. As Episcopalians, we are expected to study the stories and relate them to our own lives. That's hard sometimes, isn't it? It's a journey, a lifelong journey. It's hard enough to get through life without trying to figure out how some old guy living inside a smelly old whale is relevant, or whether a grimy nomad who eats bugs is totally off his rocker. When you see folks like that, you walk on the other side of the street.

"I want you to imagine one more thing. The person who checked your groceries this week is the son (or daughter) of God. The kid who tossed the paper on top of the sprinkler head this morning is the son of God. And the woman driving in front of you talking on the cell phone and putting on makeup is the daughter of God. The parent who did something that made you angry is the son or daughter of God. And this: *You* are a child of God. Remember your baptismal vow? Silly question; of course you do. 'I will seek Christ in all persons, with God's help.' Did you mean it? I looked for the fine print, you know the fine print that says, 'except for my own obnoxious little brother, or my mother who grounded me, the teacher who kept me for detention, or the paper boy who ruined my Sunday paper, and of course, not me.' I couldn't find the fine print. There isn't any fine print.

"Do you believe Christ is in all persons? If so, that includes the most common of folk. Jesus didn't come into the world with a trumpet fanfare and adorned in finery. That only happens at Wal-Mart, starting about the week before Halloween. Maybe if he did, things might have been easier for him.

"But Christ is alive in all of us. How about that for fanfare? Can we see it? I don't know why not. I see him in each of you, *each* of you. We sometimes forget to look…to seek. Jesus' family and friends from his youth couldn't see, or wouldn't see. When you're under the scrutiny of your entire community, you can't risk being viewed as different. You want to fit in; your security, your sense of belonging, and maybe even your life depend on it.

"I want to give each of you a homework lesson. When you are out and about with your family and friends, as well as with strangers, see if you can recognize the Christ in each of them. And then start looking for Christ in yourself.

"Then let's talk about it."

Alec was stunned. Had George—his father—been talking to him? They occasionally made eye contact during the speech—the sermon, and it made him squirm a little. He was a lot more comfortable keeping a simmering resentment of his father just under the surface. This church stuff was uncomfortable. Who was George that people should listen to him? Did Alec care whether his father saw anything or anyone in him? Alec certainly hadn't vowed to do it himself. Surely he was off the hook. He didn't have to think about it.

Fireworks. I want to go shoot off my fireworks.

After church, Sarah, Dan, Diane, and Gabe went out to lunch to discuss their house-hunting plans for the day.

"Three," announced Diane.

"Three what?" asked Gabe.

"Bathrooms, not including the ocean, the pool, the spa, the bushes, the Port-a-Potty, or the litter box. I think we need three bathrooms in the house."

Gabe rolled his eyes and shook his head. "So if there are only two, I suppose that means I get to use the ocean, the pool, the bushes..."

"Not the pool!" said Diane and Sarah together.

"There sure are a lot of rules I didn't know about," teased Gabe.

Dan agreed, "Me neither. So, how big a pool table do you think we need, Gabe?"

"Regulation, of course. We can probably use the living room. Or the dining room. Maybe both."

Dan nodded in agreement. "And we can replace the chandelier with one of those lights you see over pool tables."

"What pool table?" asked Sarah. "I didn't know you played pool. Nobody said anything about a pool table."

"No? I thought I had mentioned it. I've always had this vision of you and me..."

"No kidding? Now that you mention it..."

Diane interrupted, "Gabe, I think they need to be alone for awhile."

"I just lost interest in the pool table."

Sarah presented the list of six houses that they had expressed varying degrees of interest in seeing that afternoon. Not all of them had three bathrooms, but Diane agreed to see them anyway. They mapped out the locations and planned the route.

The first stop was to be Diane thought would be a dream house, a smaller version of the mansion with six bedrooms and six bathrooms.

The other three let her take the lead as they meandered through the small rooms. At just over 2000 square feet, the many rooms felt more like closets.

Gabe said, "Well, we could each have our own bathroom *and* own bedroom."

Diane said, "And there wouldn't be room to share any of them. OK, this isn't the one. Thank you for indulging in my fantasy."

Dan said, "No problem. Gabe did you see the pool table in the family room?"

"Never mind the pool table," said Sarah. "The kitchen is a mess. And I'm not sure I would claim this has an ocean view. I think it means you have to climb a ladder up to the roof."

House #2 was a condominium. For the price of a house, they could get a newer condominium with two master suites and an ocean view. They were tempted. Each of the master suites had a spacious bathroom, and Diane couldn't decide which one she liked better. "Gabe, I'd make the sacrifice of sharing the bathroom with you. Check out the closet; see there's my side, and there's yours."

"How come my side only has shelves?"

"Do you mean to tell me you intend to hang up your shorts and T-shirts?"

"Hey, I wear long pants and real shirts, sometimes."

"Nice kitchen!" Sarah called out from downstairs.

"This is nice," said Dan. "But if our parents came out when we were all here, it would be pretty tight."

"You really don't want to share a bedroom or a bathroom with our Dad," said Diane.

"What makes you think that we be the ones to share?" teased Dan.

The third house had a small pool and spa, but only two small bathrooms. The fourth house was on a busy street that could have been anywhere in the U.S.

"I'm getting depressed," said Diane.

"Well, those were at the low end of our price range. The next one is more expensive. Dare we?"

Their hearts skipped a beat when they drove up to the house on Kona Wind Court, and they looked at one another without saying anything, smiling cautiously.

"Check out the view from that lanai," said Dan, finally breaking the silence.

"I love it when you talk Hawaiian," giggled Sarah. An infusion of euphoria settled on the house hunters.

Another family was emerging from the house on Kona Wind Court as they went in. The realtor inquired about who the potential buyers were, and was not surprised that it was all of them. This was an area where many people had second homes. It was close to the north shore beaches and the practical aspects of living on Maui. The house boasted four bedrooms and three baths. The master suite had a huge bath, that, once again, Diane offered to share with Gabe. A second, smaller master bedroom had a good-sized bath, and the other two bedrooms shared another large bath.

"I love these people," said Diane.

Sarah's reaction to the kitchen was nonplussed. "Needs updating. But that might be fun to do. And I love the great room. Comfortable, big, and casual."

Dan added, "The pool table can go right there...lots of room to maneuver with my, what do they call the pole thingy?"

"Cue stick," laughed Sarah. "Oh yeah, you are *such* a pool shark."

Gabe called out to Dan, "Hey, come see our bathroom. It's got a diving board."

The pool was in good shape, and the spa was private enough for what each of them was thinking. There was little left of the yard after the pool, but enough for a surrounding garden and an attractive lanai.

The excitement of finding a home that had many of the features they were looking for made them less interested in the drive to the final house on Hale Luau Avenue. But they agreed they needed to see what another $50,000 would get them besides a larger mortgage payment.

"I don't know; we might be better off not being led into temptation," said Sarah.

The view was also impressive from the Hale Luau house, the pool exquisite with a waterfall beside the spa. The nearly quarter-acre lot gave the home more privacy than the others.

"There's your 50K," said Dan.

"All it needs is a few of those plastic flamingos stuck in the ground," joked Diane.

The interior was comparable to Kona Wind house, but about 10% larger.

Gabe said, "I need to cool off and clear my head. Shall we head back? Pool—the wet kind—anyone?"

"Sounds good," said the others.

Refreshed from a long dip in the pool at Gabe's condo, Dan brought up the practical questions. "So, would you rather be spending your free time doing this or doing yard work? That last house has a lot of maintenance. Unless we can get the womenfolk to do it."

"Seems like the least they could do, since we're letting them have our billiards room. And as long as they have dinner ready by seven."

"Absolutely."

"Sure, as long as you don't expect us to have time for *anything else*," retorted Diane.

Sarah added, "Yes, where are your priorities, gentlemen?"

Gabe said to Dan, "You think they're bluffing?"

"Hmmm. We *could* take a chance."

"You know, Dan is right," said Sarah. Both houses are very nice, but the maintenance on the Hale Luau one is largely going to fall on you two. Between you, you're working three jobs most of the year. And I know Diane; you do not want to rely on her yard upkeep. The issue just hasn't come up at the condo!"

Diane said, "Tell you what, I'll do all the snow shoveling."

"Don't count on that either, Gabe," said Sarah.

"Mrs. Hoana, this is Teresa Crockett, *Principal* Crockett. I'm still on the mainland, but I got your message on my home phone."

"Principal Crockett, thank you for calling me back. I can't remember what I told you on the message, but essentially: Owen is missing."

"Missing? Since when?"

Malia explained the situation to Owen's boss, then added, "I was hoping you could help fill in the blanks on where else he might be that I haven't thought of."

"Was he at the school last week?"

"We're not really sure. Gabe Callahan checked out the hallways, but he can't get into the office. The school really looked empty, he said."

"But Owen has keys…oh, never mind. Owen probably has his keys."

She paused before continuing. "I'll be in the office on Monday, so do you want to stop by? We can look in his office to see if there's something that will tell us something."

"I'll be there. Thank you Principal Crockett."

"Alec, what kind of fireworks did you get?" asked Thomas.

"Something called a 'crackling thunder string.' Let's go over to the park and set them off."

"OK, but don't tell Mom."

"No way. Where is she? Go see if you can find some matches."

Thomas said, "She's still over at the church. I know where the matches are."

Micah said, "I'll go tell her we're going over to the park. I know a good place to do stuff so no one will see."

The subterfuge laid out, the three boys found a horizontal bar that was high enough for the thunder strings to dangle freely. Thomas handed Alec the matches, and Alec untangled the long red paper tape fitted with the explosives, and attached it to the bar. He looked around one last time to make sure there was no one else in sight, and then struck the match and lit the fuse. The loud popping sent the three boys into laughter as they rushed behind the picnic table.

"Scared, Alec?"

"Nah, I was just protecting Thomas."

"I don't need no protection."

"Sure you didn't pee in your pants."

"I did *not*! But I think Micah farted."

"That was the thunder string."

"Wow, it was loud. Light another one."

They were prepared for the second one and dared one another to stand closer to it. But their reflexes took over and they jumped back instinctively.

"Cool!" exclaimed Micah. "Let's do two at once."

"Good idea; it's going to be really loud, I bet," said Alec.

"Yeah, cool," agreed Thomas.

"Make sure no one is around, 'cause this is going to be really loud," ordered Alec.

"Coast is clear," announced Micah.

They hung the two side by side on the bar, and Alec struck the match, lighting the first string, followed by the second. The second string had a slightly shorter fuse, so it started to pop as soon as it was lit. Alec dropped the lighted match and jumped back. It stuck to his arm, burning him, before he flicked it onto the ground.

"Ouch!" he cried, but the other two didn't hear him over the popping. Nor did they notice the dry brush under the picnic table starting to smoke.

"That was so cool!" shouted Thomas. "Let's do three."

Alec didn't want to let on that he had been burned, but his eyes were watering from the pain on his arm."

"You OK?" asked Micah.

"Fine, just the smoke. Let's save the rest for…hey, stomp your foot on that smoke there."

"No way, I'm barefoot. You do it."

"Get a rock or something to put on it."

"I don't see one."

The smoking debris started to flame up a little, and the boys backed up. "Do something! Put some water on it, Alec!" shouted Thomas. The three backed up further when the bottom of the rickety old table started to smoke as well and flames started to emerge.

"I don't have any water. Get away, it's starting to catch more."

"Let's get out of here," suggested Alec, picking up the duffle with the remaining thunder strings. The other two were happy to follow the suggestion of the oldest boy. "We'll run home and call 911."

As they ran to the park exit, they looked back and noticed smoke rising above the bushes. Thomas noticed his father coming out the church and called, "Dad, there's a fire in the park. Call 911!"

"What?" He looked over Thomas' head and noticed the smoke. He quickly ran around back to the house to call the fire department. A few others ran out from the park and stood watching the smoke from the other side of the street. It was getting thicker and bigger.

"Did you see where it was?" George asked Thomas.

"Over on the other side," Thomas cried.

"How did it start?"

"Dunno. When will the fire department be here?"

Alec had run inside to cool off his burn under some water and find a bandage to cover it. The boys always had bandages somewhere their bodies, so hopefully his would just blend in with the crowd. He actually needed three bandages, and he figured he had better come up with a story. He wished they were skin-colored; the bright dinosaur pattern was embarrassing for the sixteen year old, not to mention impossible to miss. The sirens beckoned him to join the gawkers; his absence would be noticed otherwise.

"There you are, Alec," said Liliana. "Were you boys over there when this started?"

"Yeah, I guess so. But we came back. I just needed a bandage." *Better to be the first to bring it up.*

"I'll say you did. What did you do?"

"I fell, so I came home and cleaned it off."

"You know you have to be especially careful of infection."

"I know, I know. I'm fine. Where are Thomas and Micah?"

"Over with your—uh—father, there."

"I see them."

"Just stay on this side of the road."

"I will."

Liliana smiled inwardly, realizing that a significant milestone had passed in the lives of the boys. It was time to stop buying dinosaur bandages.

The three boys stood back in silence as they watched the firemen attend to the blaze. The smell of smoke filled the summer air, and Alec was thinking about what to say—and what to tell Thomas and Micah to say—should they be questioned about their role in causing the blaze. It was just an accident and they were not responsible. He was sure the other two would go along with him, since they looked up to him as the oldest.

Unlike the rest of the kids in the neighborhood, the brothers were strangely quiet around all the excitement. The behavior was not lost on George or Liliana, who thought it odd that the boys were so nonplussed about the fire—almost stoic in their demeanor.

The blaze was proving resistant, and another fire truck appeared on the scene to help contain it. The smoke was spreading, and bystanders who were showing adverse affects were urged to go home. George approached Liliana and gave her a subtle "we need to talk" look that she acknowledged with an equally subtle nod. They both noticed Micah and Thomas frequently looking up to Alec.

A police car arrived, and the two officers got out, approaching the familiar priest and his wife. Alec was petrified, and the two younger brothers edged away into the crowd, hoping to become invisible. Officer Riata shook hands with George and Liliana, and stood by discussing the fire with them. Alec couldn't hear what they were saying, but he knew one thing: he had to get away.

Alec considered all the places he could go. With little more than pocket change his options were limited. Transportation on the island would have to be on one of his brothers' bicycles or hitchhiking. He also thought about calling his Aunt Adrienne in Seattle to say he wanted to come back home. His father had always said that Alec could make the decision about where he wanted to live. He wondered how quickly his aunt could arrange for his return flight. In the meantime, he needed to get away and think. He blamed his father for making it so difficult for him to have a life. His brothers were OK, but they were kids, not grown-up like he was. Even after school started in September, he wouldn't be any better off. Without a car, he was still at the mercy of his father or Liliana to take him where he needed to go. Surely everyone at the high school that was his age would have at least a driver's license if not a car as well. Well, it was too late now to discuss it with his father.

He grabbed some food and his medications, stuffing everything into a small duffle that he could sling over his shoulder. He quietly sneaked out the back door of the house and picked out one of the bicycles. He walked the bike through a neighbor's yard and out onto a side street, unseen by anyone of consequence. When confident that the coast was clear, he hopped on the bike and sped off.

"Looks like you won the bet." Dan handed Gabe the dollar from a wager on when the sisters would be ready to go up to the Callahans for dinner. "I thought Sarah's organization would trump Diane's spontaneity."

"There's no way I was going to lose! Either we would be leaving on time, or I'd be up a buck." Gabe looked at his watch while the two stood by the car waiting for Sarah and Diane to emerge from the condo.

With two picnic baskets and two grocery bags in tow, they eventually came out. Gabe called, "Hey, do you want Dan to help you carry those?"

Diane answered, "Oh, no, we're going to need him when we throw out our backs carrying all this."

"Well, hurry up; we're late," he teased. Diane tapped him with the loaf of sourdough, and he jumped back in mock pain. "You're my nurse; you're not supposed to beat me up."

"I think that arrangement has expired."

"Drat. I liked it. Particularly the sponge baths."

"No, really?"

The drive up to the Callahans was filled with conversation about their house-hunting. Dan said, "You know if you like that last house, I'll cover the cost of a gardener. But there's a lot more to it in other ways besides the yard."

Diane said, "While you guys were waiting for us, the realtor called and said he has a couple more for us to see tomorrow."

Gabe said, "Just what I need: more data! Maybe I'll feel more like looking at them tomorrow. No, tell you what: you guys look at them tomorrow while I'm diving. If you like them better, then I'll go see them."

"You trust me?" asked Diane.

"I have a choice?"

"Good point," she teased.

"Actually, I trust Dan and Sarah more," he countered, which

provoked laughter and nods from them, as well as another tap with the sourdough.

Sarah changed the subject. "It smells smoky up here. Someone must be burning sugar cane."

As they got closer to the church, the air got smokier. Conversation ceased and an urgency to get there increased. As they approached the church, many neighbors were assembled along the road, and two fire trucks were parked alongside. It appeared that the firemen were finished; some were putting away hoses and equipment while others inquired of the lingering crowd whether anyone had seen anything. George asked one of the firemen what damage there had been.

"The far picnic area is history. Way too much dry brush and an old picnic table on its last legs. But it looked like someone might have been shooting off fireworks. We were busy all day yesterday with fires like this, but some kids probably decided one day wasn't enough. We haven't had rain in a few days, so the park is very dry right now. If we hadn't contained the fire when we did, it could have spread throughout the entire park and to the houses around it. Maybe the church."

It was all Thomas could do to keep from crying. He wanted to run inside to his room and hide. Where did Alec go? He saw Gabe and the others pull into the driveway and park; he wasn't sure if he was glad to see them or not. His parents went to greet them and help unload the car. That gave him a chance to find Micah.

"Where's Alec?"

"Dunno; I saw him with Mom last."

"Think he told her?"

"Dunno."

"Did you know Gabe was coming over?"

"Yeah; they're cooking dinner for us."

"What do you think we should do?"

"Dunno. Stop asking me questions!" He paused before adding, "Let's go find Alec."

"Should we tell Dad?"

"No!"

After the groceries had been unpacked and stored, the adults gathered on the lanai for cold drinks and conversation. There was a lot of catching up to do—George's trip, Owen, the teenagers' retreat, wedding plans, house-hunting, and now the fire. The last was more urgent, but it was followed closely by the Owen mystery.

Gabe asked, "Are the boys still over at the fire?"

George replied, "Probably. It's just as well, since Liliana and I suspect they may know more than they're letting on."

Gabe smiled, "So which one do you want? I'll take one, too, and Liliana can take the other."

"Divide and conquer. I'd better take Alec. You take Micah, and Liliana can take Thomas."

"My money's on Liliana."

"I know better than to bet against her," agreed George.

"Should we call them home?"

"They'll be here; I think we should wait until they come home rather than chasing after them to conduct the interrogations in public. I also think I'm ready to switch to wine."

Gabe laughed and got up to open some wine.

Sarah then asked George, "What's the story with Owen? Is he still missing?"

"Well, as you know, we talked to the police yesterday, but frankly I think they suspect he's off with another woman."

Sarah choked on her wine. "Ridiculous."

"More ridiculous than my killing him so Malia and I could be together?"

"Oh, this is getting good. So what are they doing?"

"The usual, I guess…checking hospitals, hotels, airlines, alien abductions, the morgue. The last is pretty improbable, tho'."

"Of course." *It has to be.*

"Where could he be?" asked Thomas.

"Dunno; we've looked everywhere," said Micah.

"Maybe he went home."

"Yeah, maybe. Did you tell Mom where we were?"

"You said not to! Anyway, she probably still thinks we're with everyone at the park. I want to go home."

"OK. Then maybe we can get our bikes and go looking for him."

"You look for him. I want to go home."

Alec sat on a bench at the surfer's beach. With all the people around, he was essentially invisible. The burn on his arm was throbbing all the time now and turning red around the edges of the bandages. He thought about getting in the water to wash it off, but he didn't have anything to dry it with and re-bandage it. His clothes were dirty, as were his hands.

He absently started to collect sand in a mound with his bare feet. As soon as he shaped it on one side, the other side collapsed. He thought about getting some water to make it hold together better, but decided it wasn't worth the effort. Building things out of sand was a waste of time.

The sand always won, eventually, no matter how much you pounded it in place. Digging a hole in the sand was just as fruitless; the walls cave in on you as soon as it's just a few inches deep. You can't build it up; you can't dig down. You have to be pretty desperate to want to build anything out of sand.

Being invisible had an unexpected side effect—loneliness. He thought he had wanted to be alone, but he was starting to get scared. He thought he could sleep in one of the open-air shacks where the surfers sat to wax their boards, but he wasn't sure he wanted to be completely alone in the dark on the beach all night.

He kept an eye out for the police, half of him wanting to be found, half not. This had been one of the worst days of his life, and there was no one—*no one*—he could turn to. He weighed all of his options and found none of them better that the others. A group of scraggly guys smoking marijuana under the shelter of their boards motioned to him to join them, but he just shook his head. Another dead end.

He opened his duffle bag and pulled out some food. Nothing looked good, but his stomach was growling. He wished he had more time to think about what he was packing; the peanut butter crackers weren't going to last very long. Shadows were lengthening, and he needed to look for a roof over his head and a safe place to hide so he could think.

"George, better call the boys home. We're going to be eating soon." Liliana was trying to sound unconcerned, but the fact that she hadn't seen them in hours was worrisome.

Gabe responded, "We'll go get them. I know George wants to be alone with his bonfire. Tell you what, since you're recreating the inferno from across the street, I'll cook the steaks when I get back."

"Gabriel Callahan, I know what you're up to. You're just afraid I'll turn them into *pahoehoe*."

"It's not fear. Fear implies some doubt."

Dan laughed at the discussion and said, "I'll go with you, Gabe; the sooner we get back, the less time he'll have to do whatever it was you said. All I know is that it didn't sound good."

George said, "You see how he talks to me, Dan?"

Dan answered, "George, don't make me have to confiscate your meat fork."

"*Et tu, Bruté?* Just remember, I can make things very difficult for you on Saturday."

"Now *there's* a reason to be afraid," laughed Dan. "Wait, here are the boys, two of them anyway."

Thomas and Micah gave Gabe a hug, and ran over briefly to the others to say "Hello" before dashing inside. George called out, "Where's Alec?"

Thomas stopped mid-stride, responding, "Dunno…isn't he here?"

Liliana came out with Micah, who said, "Want us to go look for him? He's probably down the street or something." He started to go towards the outdoor shed to get his bicycle.

George responded, "Maybe. When did you last see him?"

Micah said, "Uh, not sure, maybe an hour or two ago. Have you got any snacks? I'm starving."

"Over on the table," responded Liliana. "We're going to eat soon."

"OK, we'll be back soon." Micah then called out, "Hey, Thomas, where's my bike?"

"Dunno; isn't it there?"

"No, who did you give it to?"

"Nobody." Thomas joined his brother to prove that the bike just had to be there. He whispered to Micah, "Maybe Alec took it."

Micah nodded and asked quietly, "Can I use yours?" Without waiting for an answer, he started off on the bike, grabbing a flashlight from the shelf in the shed. He called out to his mother, "I'll be back!"

"Half an hour, Micah. Dinner will be ready then."

If Micah was right about where Alec was, he was going to be late for dinner. He didn't think Alec knew that many places to go, but he figured he go some place where he could think. The beach? It would be dark soon, and Micah didn't think Alec realized how dark the beach was at night. There's a reason you never see pictures of the beach at night. It's because there's nothing to see. His mother used to tell him that they closed the beach at night, and as a child he wondered how they did that.

Please be there, Alec. If you're not there, I don't know where you are.

People were packing up to leave the beach. There were too many things to trip over in the dark, and there really wasn't any reason to stick around. Alec found a secluded shack and settled down out of sight. There wasn't any place to sleep; it was barely more than a glorified beach umbrella. He thought he would be able to think, but his mind was filled with visions—such that they were—of total darkness. He didn't know what creatures might inhabit the beach at night, but whatever they were, they probably weren't things he wanted to encounter. Rats probably. Bugs, biting ones. It was still so loud; it hadn't occurred to him that the waves continued crashing when it gets dark.

If I leave right now, I can see my way out to the road. I can just tell them I borrowed Micah's bike to go for a ride. I got lost but eventually found my way home. I wonder what they're having for dinner. What's that sound?

Alec hid behind an old wood desk that had been reincarnated as part of the structural foundation of the makeshift shack.

I hear someone. Don't make a sound. Can't the ocean be quiet for just a minute so I can hear it!

A flashlight was casting a narrow path on the darkening landscape. The voice was getting louder.

"Alec! Are you here Alec? It's Micah. Alec!"

"Micah! Over here! To your, uh, left. No, your other left!" Alec's voice sounded frantic to himself, but he didn't care.

"Where? Keep talking! Wave your arms. Man, it's getting dark out here."

"Keep coming…about thirty feet in front of you."

"Don't you have a flashlight?"

"No."

"That was stupid."

"I know. Hurry."

"You have my bike?"

"Yeah. Sorry. I just borrowed it."

"What is this place? Oh, it's a surfer's shack. I've never seen it at night."

"Can we get out of here?"

"I'm not sticking around. Get the bike, and let's get out to the street where there are lights. I need to find a phone and call Mom. She's going to be mad."

"I had to get away…to think. But I couldn't think. What do you think we should do?"

"Run away and join the Marines."

"Really?"

"No, you idiot. You're in trouble. We're in trouble." Micah then gave his attention to the voice on the other end of the phone. "Mom, I'm with Alec. We're down at the beach… I know… Can Gabe come get us? We've got the bikes, but Thomas' light doesn't work. Thanks, Mom. Yeah, I know."

"What?"

"Gabe's coming with his SUV."

"What else did she say?"

"Oh, they're going to give us a medal for the beautiful fire we set. What do you *think* she said? We're going to have to explain everything."

"It was an accident. I told Thomas to put the fire out."

"If I were you, I'd make that the last time you use that as an excuse. Because it doesn't mean we weren't responsible. Dad is going to be so mad."

"Think he'll tell the police?"

"Dunno. What happened to your arm?"

"I burned it. It hurts."

"Cool bandage."

"Yeah, it should impress the girls."

"Like Leeee-sa?"

"Who said anything about Lisa?"

"Well, she's not going to be impressed with a pyro. Her dad's a fireman."

"This day just keeps getting better and better."

"Have you eaten anything?"

"Just junk. You got anything?"

"No, I didn't exactly have time to think about it. There's dinner at home. I hope. But everyone else is there, too."

"Everyone, who?"

"Gabe, Sarah, Dan, and Diane."

"What are they doing there?"

"What do you mean? They're our friends; they're family. They're cooking dinner for us."

"That beach shack isn't looking so bad."

"Stay here if you want. Be a jerk."

"What do you mean?"

"You going to go around hating everyone for the rest of your life?"

"I don't hate you."

"You're trying to find ways to blame everyone for something bad that happened. You got a raw deal with your mom and your kidney and stuff. What do you want to do about it? You want to kill somebody? No one here has done anything to hurt you. *Your* mom tried to kill *my* mom. And Sarah. And Diane. And Gabe. You didn't know? Well, they probably didn't want you to know. But that's what happened. You need to know, so you'll stop being such a jerk around everyone."

"It didn't happen that way."

"Ask them yourself. That's what happened. Oh, look, here's Gabe. You can ask him. And next time you want to 'borrow' my bike, ask me, OK? And don't blame Mom and Dad for the fire, and don't blame Gabe and the others. And if you blame Thomas for the fire, *I* will hate you."

Gabe flashed his lights and pulled over to the curb so the boys could put their bikes in the back and then get in. "Say, guys, what have you been up to?" he asked.

"It's a long story, Gabe," said Micah.

"I'll bet. You both OK?"

"Alec has a burn."

"How'd you get that, Alec?"

"It's a long story."

"So I've heard. You guys have had quite a day."

"Can't we just forget about it?"

"Probably not."

Micah asked, "What do you think we should do, Gabe"

"What do you mean? What have you been up to?"

"So, you don't know?"

"Know what?"

"About the fire."

"The fire. What about the fire?"

"We, uh, sort of started it."

"How 'sort of?'"

Alec jumped in. "It was my fault. They were my firecrackers, and we were just shooting them off at the park, and somehow the match fell, and the fire started, and we couldn't put it out, and it just kept getting bigger and bigger…"

"Uh huh," said Gabe, trying very hard *not* to say, "Are you guys nuts? What were you thinking?"

"It got really bad," added Micah.

"Apparently," said Gabe.

"Does Dad know?" asked Micah.

"I'm not sure; what did you tell him?"

"Nothing."

"What do you want to tell him?"

"Nothing." With that both Alec and Micah laughed nervously.

"I'm not sure that's an option, guys. You're lucky you didn't get hurt."

"Alec burned himself."

"Where?"

"His arm. Show him, Alec."

"Alec, you know you have to be especially careful of infection. That doesn't look good."

"Yeah, it sorta hurts."

"You need to have your mom have a look. She may want to take you to the doctor tomorrow."

"Mom?" Alec said, instinctively. "Oh yeah. Mom."

"So, what's your plan now, guys?"

"What do you think we should do?"

"Well, let's weigh your options. First what are they?"

"Micah said we should join the Marines."

Gabe tried to make sure the discussion stayed serious. "OK, there's one option. What else?"

Micah said, "We could say nothing."

"There's number two. What else?"

Alec said, "Confess."

"Three. Anything else?"

"Blame it on some homeless dude."

"Four. Anything else?"

"Lightning. Yeah, it was lightning," suggested Micah, half kidding.

"Five. Any more, guys?" It was quiet. Then using his science teacher persona, he continued. "Five options. Let's narrow it down to two. What do you think?"

More silence. Then Alec said, "Confess. I guess we have to confess."

Micah agreed, "Yeah, we have to confess."

"So, one option?" queried Gabe, trying not to applaud the boys' choice of what he considered the right one.

"Yeah," they both said quietly.

"It has consequences, you know." said Gabe.

"Like what?"

"What do you think they should be?"

"We'll probably get grounded. Bummer."

"Maybe. Anything else?"

"We'll probably have to pay for it."

"Maybe. Anything else?"

"Dunno. What else could there be?"

"I think it depends on how forthright you are with what you're willing to take responsibility for."

Alec started to say, "It was an acc—Ow, stop it Micah!"

Gabe ignored the last, and waited in silence for one of them to talk.

Micah said, "What if we just tell the truth, and say we'll pay for it?"

"Uh-huh," said Gabe, still hoping for more, but wanting them to say it.

Alec added, "We have to clean it up and make it like it was."

Micah asked, "What do you think it will cost?"

Gabe said, "Depends on how much you are willing to do. It'll probably cost something, tho'."

Micah remembered, "Dad's going to pay us to paint the house."

Alec said, "My truck…" but then he stopped. "Yeah, we should be able to fix it up with the money we make painting the house."

"Can we still go to diving school?" asked a hopeful Micah.

"You'll have to ask your parents. I'm not sure I'd make that the first thing you bring up. OK, we're home. Ready, you guys?"

"Yeah," they both replied. They jumped out of the SUV and retrieved the bicycles out of the back, walking them over to the storage area.

"Is it too late to join the Marines?" Alec added rhetorically, as they approached the family gathering on the lanai.

Liliana saw them first. "Hi, boys! Everyone's starving, so get yourselves washed up. We're waiting for you."

"Mom…" started Micah.

"Later. We're going to have dinner first."

"What are we having?"

"Steaks. You might go see if your father needs any help."

Micah swallowed and responded, "OK."

George was taking the steaks off the grill when Micah approached him. "Dad…"

"Here, Micah, would you take this plate over? I'll bring over the rest."

"Sure."

"And Alec, could you close the lid on the grill so we don't get any sparks?"

"Sure." Alec wondered if George's request had the double meaning he thought it had.

The party of nine gathered around the large picnic table and sat down to say grace and enjoy the meal. Alex was surprised he was hungry; his stomach had been knotted up since Gabe had picked them up. The three boys were all quiet during dinner, which allowed the adults to carry on a greater part of the conversation.

Gabe said, "Diane, you'll have to tell Liliana about the house with six bathrooms."

"Only four usable ones, really, and even I didn't like it." She rustled his hair, and teased back, "At least I don't count the pool as a bathroom." Even the boys laughed at that. Thomas added, "It's just a little ocean, huh,

Gabe?"

Liliana changed the subject slightly to a more appropriate dinner conversation. "So, you're going to have a pool?"

"That's cool, Gabe," said Thomas. "How big?"

"Big enough when we have to take care of it."

"Can we come swim in it?"

"Sure. Just don't pee in it. Sorry, Liliana." Everyone giggled, including Liliana.

Dan said, "We found two we like, but Diane has threatened to make us look at more tomorrow."

"Hey, this is a big decision. I've never bought a house before. Neither has Sarah. You'll thank us for being so picky, right, Sar?"

"Unquestionably." Sarah leaned over to Liliana and said in a stage whisper, "And it's our strategy to get them to think they are making the decision."

"Gabe, we're being set up," laughed Dan.

"You're just now figuring that out?" teased Gabe.

George changed the subject. "So, have I redeemed myself with the steaks?"

Sarah answered, "They are wonderful. I think you've been getting a bad rap."

Gabe said, "You just want to make sure George is not going to give you a hard time on Saturday."

"Should we be worried?"

"Dessert! Who's ready for dessert?" inquired Liliana.

"I am!" shouted Thomas, raising his hand instinctively. "I saw; it's brownies. Mom makes the best brownies. Come on guys; let's take the dishes in." The generous gesture was not lost on the adults, and there was just the slightest smile among them.

"The least I could do after this wonderful meal. Thank you, all of you."

"Our pleasure," answered Sarah. "I wish Malia had come, too." She spoke softly while the boys busied themselves in the kitchen. "I bet you're worried sick about her and Owen."

"We are. She's going over to the school tomorrow to check out his office with Principal Crockett."

"Why are they waiting until tomorrow?"

"I don't know, but maybe Liliana didn't push it because she's not entirely sure she wants to know."

Gabe said, "I wish I could meet her there, too, but I have to work. I won't be back until early afternoon."

Sarah said, "I'll meet her there. I don't think she should go alone."

George said, "We would join you, but I think we need to stay around here tomorrow."

"Yes, you do. We're going to get out of here pretty soon, so you can have your discussion."

Gabe added, "I wish I could be a fly on the wall. We had a long talk on the drive back. I took the long way home—sorry, Liliana—but I think they came up with the best solution, and I wanted it to be their solution, not mine. In the long run, this might actually be a good thing…for everyone."

"Who wants ice cream?" called Thomas.

"I do," called George, followed by Dan.

"How come none of the girls wants ice cream?"

"Us *girls*," laughed Gabe, "are watching our figures for the wedding."

"I am *not* going in for another fitting," said Sarah. "My priority is chocolate, not ice cream."

Monday, July 6

Anxious to be back in the water, Gabe awoke early on Monday. He had missed the smell of neoprene and sunscreen, and especially the excitement of the divers out for the first time in perhaps a year. He'd even begun to miss his business partner Terry's jokes: "You know the best way to avoid shark attacks? Never leave Utah!" Gabe had his repertoire as well that he used for SCUBA school: "Welcome to the food chain, divers—you're no longer at the top!"

He stretched to see if anything was still sore, and pronounced himself healthy and fit. The few days off had been the trick to let his body completely heal.

Gabe quietly packed his gear and made coffee for everyone. Before leaving, he roused a groggy Diane for a kiss and an admonition to fly safe.

"Hmmmm…you, too." She drifted back to sleep, and Gabe left for the drive to the warehouse. He was glad that he had arrived before Terry for the first time in quite a while. His partner had borne the brunt of the operations since Gabe's injury in April. He hoped he could return the favor some day.

A young puppy greeted him outside the warehouse, and Gabe responded with, "Hello, girl…uh boy. Where did you come from?"

A voice called from around the corner, "Paco! Where are you, Paco?"

Gabe called back, laughing, "I'm over here!"

"Paco, when did you learn to speak?" called the voice.

Gabe said to the puppy, "Is that your name, Paco? What kind of dog are you?"

"That's what my wife keeps asking," said the voice from around the corner, now emerging with its body. "Paco, you are in so much trouble. Andrea is going to be furious."

Gabe said, "He must be quite an escape artist. By the way, Gabe Callahan." Gabe shook hands with the man approaching the puppy with a leash.

"Pete Chapman. Nice to meet you. You've already met Paco."

"You have a boat over here?"

"Yeah, we came over for the weekend from Honolulu."

"Must be a pretty big boat."

"Not big enough for my wife." He pointed to a luxurious craft docked at the end of the pier.

"Expensive wife."

"Oh, yeah."

"Beautiful—uh—*boat*!"

"Thanks, it gets us from here to there."

"And then some."

"Yeah," laughed Pete. "It's not the best place to keep a litter of pups, tho', but it was not planned that way. Sophia had a one-night stand with an Australian Shepherd, and Paco is one of six results from the illicit affair."

"And Sophia is a...?"

"Standard poodle. White."

"Interesting pairing," laughed Gabe. The little fellow was mostly curly white like his mother, with a few dark patches inherited from his vagabond father. He looked like a collie with a permanent wave.

"You know, some high class gals get attracted to burly working men. But my wife keeps saying that Reggie was not pleased."

"Reggie?"

"Sophia's betrothed. Another standard poodle that Andrea had plans for to give her grandpuppies."

"Of course. I see." Gabe knelt down and let the puppy snuggle up to him and give him a face washing.

"We are trying to find homes for the pups."

"He's pretty cute. He's one of six?"

"Yup. Say, you can see the other five, as well as the mother, on the boat. The puppies are seven weeks old. This one escaped and ran after me when I came ashore."

"I need to get ready for a dive. My partner and I own a dive boat, and we're heading out in a little bit. But, you know, Paco is quite a little guy. I'm about to move into a house, and a dog might be good way to warm it up. Can I call my girlfriend to see what she thinks and get back to you?"

"Sure, Gabe. Here's my cell phone number. We'll be here until tomorrow, so call anytime today."

"Thanks, Pete. So, Paco, what do you think?" Another face washing, followed by a roll over inviting a belly rub. "Maybe I'll see you later, Paco."

Malia forced herself to stay in bed until 6:00. She hadn't slept in nearly a week, and she knew it was taking a toll. *Lying down is the least I can do. I'm going to find you Owen, and I need my strength to do it. I don't care what you've been doing.*

"Yes, I do," she said out loud, tears staining her pillow. She pulled Owen's pillow into her arms and breathed deeply in it to bring out his smell. It calmed her and she drifted off to sleep for another twenty minutes until the sound of the newspaper hitting the screen door startled her awake. She got up and made coffee. Out of habit she made enough for two, and once she realized it, the tears resurfaced. *Where are you, Owen—HoHo?*

Malia wondered when Principal Crockett was likely to show up at the school. *Surely by 9:00; I'll get there about 9:00.*

She checked her phone and email for messages, disappointed but not surprised that there was nothing from Owen. She was pretty sure George was up, but it was too soon to call and wake up the rest of the household. Phone calls at 6:00 a.m. scare people; they're always bad news.

She showered and picked out clothes from the closet she shared with Owen. She noticed an empty space on Owen's side with four hangers and wondered why she hadn't seen them before. *What did you take with you? There's your yellow shirt…there's your blue one…where's the striped one and the red school one? And all your khaki pants are gone. Why would you take all that but no toothbrush or razor? And why would you take your good golf shirts camping? And your hiking boots are still here.*

She wondered whether she should call the police to let them know she had discovered some things missing. It would make it easier if they found him but couldn't be sure it was him. She admonished herself to stay positive…*get* positive. She was hopeful that Owen's office would reveal something about what Owen had been doing since she left for San Diego. Surely there had to be something, perhaps something only she would recognize as a clue.

Thomas and his brothers surveyed the park grounds charred by the fire. "Whoa," he said. "One little firecracker did all that?"

Micah added, "It really stinks, too. We have to clean up all this? It's not fair."

Alec disagreed. "Actually it probably is fair. But I don't like it anymore than you do. You heard Geo... Dad; how we fix this will determine whether we get to go to SCUBA school."

"It's not fair," said Micah absently.

"Stop saying that."

"Where do we begin?"

"What do you think? We've gotta rake all the dead stuff up. You got rakes?"

"I guess. When are the firemen coming by?"

"Dad said he was going to call them this morning. He said that they are going to give us just as hard a time if not harder. We may have to do community service."

"What do you call this?" asked Micah, rhetorically. "So after we rake everything up, what next?"

"We've got to replant...grass, bushes, and picnic table."

"Plant a picnic table?" asked Thomas.

"You know what I mean."

"But it was all broken down anyway."

"Why don't you just tell that to the firemen," suggested Alec, quickly losing patience with his brothers.

"No way. You tell them."

"I'm not that stupid."

"Then why did you want me to tell them?"

"Go get the rakes, Thomas."

"You go."

"Look, you guys. Dad said we have to do this together, or none of us goes diving or gets to do anything else this summer. You can blame me, him, God. I don't care. We still have to clean this up. Let's get it done and stop whining about 'it's not our fault' or 'it was just an accident.' Nobody's buying it, and nobody's going to do it for us."

Micah and Alec stared at one another, amazed to hear Alec's words. Alec was the first to break off the stare and started to walk off.

"Where are you going?" asked Micah.

"Thomas told me to get the rakes; I'm going to get the rakes."

"We'll all go."

Diane rubbed the sleep out of her eyes over coffee with Sarah and Dan. "I'm working today, so what are you two doing?"

Sarah said, "I'm going to meet Malia over at the school to go through Owen's office."

Dan said, "I've got a ton of phone calls to make to patients and doctors this morning. And I guess we're going to look at a couple of more places this afternoon?"

Diane said, "Unless either of the last two places we see is perfect. I actually would be pretty happy with the smaller one."

"A mere three bathrooms, not including the pool?" teased Dan.

"See, I can be reasonable." Just then the phone rang and she answered it.

"Yes, I'm up; we're all up. Did you call just to make sure?" Diane's laugh indicated she was obviously talking to Gabe. "A puppy? What kind of puppy? …Interesting… Sure we're ready to be parents? …No, he can't use my bathroom. No, I can't take him to work with me," she added playfully. "He sounds like a perfect dive dog. He'll herd all the divers into a group. Makes it easier for the sharks to pick out the slower moving ones. George? Want me to call him and ask? OK. You know, this means we're going to need the bigger house with the bigger yard." Diane looked at Sarah and Dan, who were both using the thumbs-up sign. "They're OK with that. I'll call you back after I talk to George and Liliana. I love you, too."

She hung up and looked at her breakfast companions. "Gabe met some guy with puppies. Get this: a cross between a standard poodle and an Australian Shepherd." She filled them in on the illicit love story, adding, "He also wanted me to check with George to see if he wants one."

"You mean, Liliana," corrected Sarah.

"Obviously. So, the bigger house is OK?"

"Obviously," laughed Sarah.

Malia's heart skipped a beat when she saw Principal Crockett's car in the parking lot. She said a prayer that there would be some answers that would lead her to Owen. She tried to calm herself so that she would be in control when she met Owen's boss. Parking near the Principal's car, she quickly emerged, setting her handbag on the other car's hood while she attended to locking her own car and pocketing her keys. She then briskly walked to the front door, which was unlocked as expected.

The hallway was dark and stuffy from being closed up. She made her way to the office, noticing Gabe's note stuck to the door from his own search for her husband last week. She called out, "Principal Crockett? It's Malia Hoana. Hello?"

Maybe she's somewhere else in the building or out back.

Malia continued her search for the Principal, calling her name frequently, so she wouldn't startle her. Peeking into the office, she called again, but there was no sound.

Strange that all the lights are out.

The door to Owen's office was open, so she rushed in, instinctively turning on the lights. She sat down in Owen's oversized chair, reaching for the lever to lower the seat so her feet would reach the floor, surprised that it was fine without any adjustment. She was also surprised to see Owen's computer on, displaying a backlog of unread emails. There was the strange message Gabe had described on Saturday. It was pretty much gibberish. *Love, HoHo? He must have been pretty distracted when he wrote it.* She hit the print button so she would have a copy of the message. His other sent messages were brief and indicated nothing about his being gone for a few days. She checked his online calendar, noticing he had a dental appointment last Friday. She called the dental office to confirm what she suspected; he was a no-show. There was nothing in his calendar about camping. Malia's trip was blocked off, as was his boss' vacation on the mainland. It seemed strange that Owen would leave while the principal was away as well. School was closed to the students and teachers, but the administrative staff had work to do year round.

A week-old coffee commuter mug contained a thriving science experiment. Malia dumped out the slimy contents and set the cup aside to take home to wash. She noticed water bottles and junk food containers in the trash. "You're so busted, Owen. I left you tons of healthy food."

Overall the office smelled damp and stale. Not like it hadn't been used, but more like it had been used without any fresh air flowing through it. The air was old. The sofa cushions were askew and the small coffee table sticky with food residue.

There are no answers here. Only more questions. Where is Principal Crockett?

Malia didn't particularly want to stay in the school building, but she felt like she needed to talk to the Principal in person. She walked the halls calling her name. She looked out the windows to see if she was somewhere on the grounds. She walked back out the front door puzzled that the woman was nowhere to be found.

Perhaps she went for coffee with someone, and they took the other car. I'll just have to leave her a note that I was here. Owen is not here, and I need to be at home if the police call.

She found a piece of paper and composed a short note. She then took some tape, intending to affix the note to her office door so she would see it and not wonder where she was.

She closed Owen's office door and walked over to tape the note to the Principal's door, but the door was already slightly ajar. Pressing the note pushed the door open further, revealing the body of Principal Crockett lying on the floor.

"Mrs. Hoana, this is Officer Jan Taylor. If you're home, please pick up. I guess you're not home. We have some news for you, and it's probably good news. We think we've found your husband. He's alive, but he's in the, uh, hospital. He's not hurt, but it looks like he's been on some drug binge. Call me as soon as you can. Good-bye."

Officer Taylor observed Owen through the glass. He was clearly in a lot of pain, but Officer Taylor had little sympathy for him. She was furious that a man in a position of trust with children had betrayed that trust by using drugs. She wondered if Mrs. Hoana would be happier that he was on drugs than if he had been having an affair. In either case, his life was ruined, and he had no one to blame but himself. She wondered if the wife knew or was involved herself. In any case, she had enough evidence for a search warrant of Owen's home, office, and car. This time the search would be more exhaustive, with little extended in the way of courtesy.

"Mr. Cho, how are you? I'm Diane Donovan, your pilot today."

"Fine, uh, you're a pilot?"

"Yes, sir. Shall we brief your flight for today?"

"Yes, of course." Harry Cho was expecting a man. In his line of work, questions were annoying, and women asked too many questions.

"We're heading to the Kona Coast, right?"

"Yes, there's a small airfield that is convenient for my business."

"That will be fine. What line of business are you in, Mr. Cho?"

Here they come. Why do they always have to ask so many questions?

"I'm a golf equipment supplier."

"What a coincidence. I met another man in that business on Saturday. Maybe you know him… Duke… I can't remember his last name."

Cho caught himself in a gasp, nearly choking on his words. "Maybe, I'm not sure."

"Well, it's a big business out here. You probably meet a lot of people."

"Yes. What does he look like? Maybe I'll remember him."

"Tall, blond hair, scar on his neck."

Duke. You idiot. You don't have time for a girlfriend.

"That's a lot of folks around here."

"I'm sure. So, I assume you're not carrying any cargo this trip?"

"No, I'm just meeting some of my associates."

"Will you want return transportation?"

"I'm not sure yet."

"Fine; just call us if you need us."

"I will." *Can we just go now and stop the idle chit-chat?*

Diane conducted her preflight planning, followed by her aircraft walkaround, before starting the passenger safety briefing.

Cho nodded occasionally but paid no attention to what she was saying. His mind was spinning, wondering how Duke could be so stupid as to risk getting mixed up with a woman while he was in such a critical stage of a deal. Cho demanded discretion and low-profile behavior in his employees; violation of that condition of employment had severe consequences. Cho smiled inwardly thinking that some of those severe consequences had already been meted out; he was pretty sure his men had redirected Duke's attention back to his job. This woman didn't seem to know anything about Duke's current situation; it was evident that his men had been very persuasive. Still, taking chances that she was ignorant of Duke's employment situation was risky. It was better to be careful than sorry, and Cho made sure he was never sorry.

Diane completed her weather briefing and filed her FAA flight plan advising them of her route. She had never been to the specific airfield Cho had requested, and it seemed a strange place for a man in his business to want to go. She detected some mystery about the man, but didn't think there was enough concern to refuse to take him to his location. It wasn't like he could hijack the plane and make her fly to China. He may have lied about his business, but that was his choice and had nothing to do with her. His destination of North Kohala on the Kona Coast was more famous—or non-famous—for its historical fishing villages and ancient temples that attracted few tourists compared to the volcanoes, golf, and ocean activities elsewhere on the largest island in Hawai'i.

She decided to skip the tour guide narration. Her client was probably more familiar with the sites than she was, and didn't seem very interested in making conversation. She felt a chill around him and was glad that it would be a short flight. *Just do your job. Not everyone wants a chatty pilot to help pass the time.*

With a minimum of conversation, Diane flew Mr. Cho to a small airfield in the ranch country in the North Kohala District. His ride was waiting, and he quickly deplaned with little acknowledgment of the pilot that brought him there. He was initially nonplussed in receiving Diane's business card, but then suddenly seemed eager to get it. He thanked her in a way that reminded him of a child being told by his mother to say "thank you—" practiced and perfunctory, but hardly sincere.

Diane received a call from her boss, who asked her to pick up a couple in Kona to take to Kapalua. "Perfect," she replied. "I need something to replenish the soul Mr. Cho just sucked out of me."

"What?" he asked. "Everything OK?"

"Fine. Just a strange passenger. Flight was fine. I'll see you later."

"Principal Crockett!" shouted Malia. "What happened?" Malia knelt down to attend to the woman lying unconscious on the floor. She rose to go to the phone, but was stopped by an arm that jerked her violently away, pushing her onto a chair. She cried out in pain and shuddered uncontrollably from the surprise. "Who...?" She didn't finish her question, since the man slapped her hard across the face.

"Stay still, lady."

Malia started to speak, but sensed another threat to slap her across the face.

"I said, *stay still.*"

Malia nodded. She was still shaking, a reflex not lost on the man, who was pleased that he had managed to make his point clear. She didn't see

193

a gun or a knife, but knew she was in no shape to try to challenge the man.

Why would anyone attack Principal Crockett? This guy is not a student, at least not now.

A keen observer of people and their behavior, Malia studied her captor. Washed out clothes, probably a local, five-six, maybe seven, slightly built. Not too bright, survival-driven, not a professional. Desperate. This had not been planned. He was making it up as he went along. She hoped he would realize that he had lost control of the situation and would simply leave. Her arm and face were throbbing, causing a flood of tears she could not control. He may have dislocated her shoulder when he jerked her away from the phone. She hoped he would not see her as a threat and just simply back away, take whatever he came for, and leave. Quickly, so she could call for help for the Principal. The woman had not moved or made a sound. Malia was worried that precious seconds were slipping away, if it wasn't too late already.

"Who are you, lady? A teacher?"

Malia shook her head. "I'm Owen Hoana's wife, the assistant principal here. I came to look for him, and…"

"You're HoHo's wife?"

Malia sat up and said with excitement, "You know him? Have you seen him?"

"We're old friends, HoHo and me. So you're his wife. He's been a bad boy, you know."

"Do you know where he is?"

"Not sure, exactly."

"When did you see him?"

The man ignored her and appeared to be thinking. Then he said, "How about I take you to him?"

"I thought you said you didn't know where he was."

"I said 'not exactly.' Let's go."

"What about her?"

"I *said*, let's go."

Instinctively Malia reached for her purse, but it wasn't in sight. The man wasn't going to give her a chance to look for it; he just dragged her to her feet and directed her towards the back door.

Where is Sarah? She was going to meet me here. I hope he didn't find her first. Be safe, Sarah. Please, God, keep Sarah safe. And Owen. And, me too, Lord.

"Malia? Principal Crockett? It's Sarah Donovan. Hello? I'm sorry I'm late. My parents called, and I couldn't get away as soon as I wanted." Sarah held the purse she found sitting on the principal's car in the parking lot. Malia's car was parked next to it. She checked the driver's license—Malia. So Malia is here. Sarah felt a pang of sympathy for her. She wasn't surprised that Malia had left her purse on the hood of the car; it was probably the least of her concerns when she arrived. She picked it up, intending to hand it to Malia when she saw her.

Sarah continued calling out as she went into the school office, walking over to the Principal's office, and tapping softly. She tried the door, somewhat surprised that it was unlocked. She gradually opened it further, continuing to call softly to Principal Crockett. As her eyes adjusted to the darkened space, she noticed disarray over the normal order the Principal usually maintained. As she looked to the left, the dark form on the floor became apparent as the body of Principal Crockett. Sarah put her hand to her mouth in horror and bent down to tend to the woman. Some bleeding on the side of her head. *Not again.*

She quickly rose and went to the phone to call emergency. They kept her on the line, asking her to report on the condition of the woman and any vital statistics Sarah knew about the woman. She wanted to call Dan, but they wouldn't let her off the phone until they got there. Common sense told her that was best, of course.

"Malia!" she screamed. "Where are you?" She wanted to search for her, hoping not to find a similar scene elsewhere, say in Owen's office. Since Malia was obviously here, why wasn't she answering?

She welcomed the sound of sirens approaching and ran out of the office to signal the paramedics to the principal's office. A police car arrived seconds later, and a woman emerged, heading straight for Sarah, hand on hip to be ready to retrieve a stick or a gun. Sarah realized she was hugging herself, trying to become as small as possible.

Dan, I wish I had let you come with me.

"Officer Taylor, ma'am. Who are you?"

"Sarah Donovan. I am—was—a teacher here. I came over to meet Malia Hoana here…"

"Hoana?" The officer was startled at the familiar name.

"Yes, I'm not sure whether you know, but Owen Hoana has been missing, so Malia and I were meeting here to see if there was anything in his office that would tell us something."

"Can you take me there?"

"Yes, in here."

"Where is Mrs. Hoana?"

"That's just it; I don't know. She's here, I mean. I found her purse sitting on the hood of the principal's car out there, next to her car."

"Let me go first."

Sarah nodded and pointed to Owen's office. The officer reached for her gun and opened the door, staying to the side of the doorway.

"It's clear. Please stay outside the doorway."

Sarah nodded and realized she had been holding her breath. Malia wasn't in the same situation as Principal Crockett, at least as far as anyone could tell. But where was she? Like Owen, she seemed to have vanished without a trace.

"Is there a place we can talk, Miss/Mrs. Donovan?"

"Miss…out here. Can I check on Principal Crockett?"

"In a minute. It's pretty crowded in there right now."

Sarah nodded again, and composed herself to tell what she knew. She kept her arms folded so she could keep herself from shaking.

Officer Taylor began to question her about her involvement with the Hoana couple. Many possibilities were emerging in the officer's mind, some had them as victims, some had them as criminals as she had suspected earlier.

"Can you think of any reason why someone would want to hurt Principal Crockett?"

"No. You don't think she just fell and hit her head?"

"I can't say."

"Well, I can assure you that neither Malia nor Owen would hurt anyone. Now both of them are missing."

"We think we have found Owen."

"Owen! Is he OK?"

"Mostly. He's been on a drug binge."

"What? That's ridiculous. Are you sure it's him?"

"He's been in detox all weekend, and when I heard they had someone there matching Owen's description, I called Mrs. Hoana to let her know. But she never called me back."

"And now she's missing. Doesn't this look just a little suspicious to you?"

"Why, yes, it does."

"I see what you're thinking. If I know anything, it's that they are the victims here. You need to stop wasting time seeing them as drug whatevers, and start looking for them as victims. You don't know these people; if you did, you'd know I'm right."

The officer was startled at the woman's outburst in defending Owen and Malia, as well as in her boldness ordering her on how to conduct her investigation. As a trained police officer, she was skilled at defusing angry situations and keeping her own temper in check. It was time to redirect the woman's emotions to something more constructive.

"Do you know how to reach Principal's Crockett's family?"

"She probably has speed dials on her phone, but I also have her home number programmed into my cell phone, if you'll let me get it in her office."

"In your purse? I'll get it for you. You also said you found Mrs. Hoana's purse. Is it with yours?"

Sarah nodded, her temper assuaged for the moment, as the officer appeared to be less focused on attacking the integrity of the Owen and Malia, and more on the concerns of the school principal and her family.

The paramedics came out with the unconscious form of Principal Crockett hooked up to an IV and secured upon the gurney. Sarah asked them, "How is she?"

"Stable, but she's still unconscious."

"Do you think she might have fallen?"

"Something got her on the side of the head, and we didn't see any blood on the edge of the desk or anywhere."

"Are you taking her to Maui Memorial?"

"Yes."

The officer called Sarah away from the ambulance. "Miss Donovan, which of these purses is yours?"

Sarah reached for hers, and said, "That's Malia's. I checked the wallet and found her driver's license."

"Apparently she was inside; we found a note stuck on Principal Crockett's door saying she had been there. Would you be able to recognize her writing?"

"No, but George Callahan would."

"You know them?"

"Yes." Sarah filled the officer in on her relationship with the Callahans.

"And the nephew, uh, Gabriel Callahan?"

"My sister's boyfriend. My fiancé and I are staying with them until we get married on Saturday."

"Oh. Congratulations," the officer said blandly.

"Thank you."

"Do you know where Gabriel is?"

"Diving, since early this morning. He owns a dive boat out of Ma'alaea. He usually gets back mid-afternoon."

"And your sister?"

"Diane. She's a pilot and flies for Ali'i Aviation. She's working now, but she'll probably be home around 5:00." Sarah was growing tired of the questioning, but knew that being anything less than fully cooperative would call even more attention to herself. Right now the questions were interfering with the investigation into where Malia was, but the officer was not in the mood to be reminded of that again. The sooner she gave the officer what she wanted the sooner Sarah could call George and Dan.

She needed them both; this was too big for her to handle alone.

"Did you see Mrs. Hoana's car keys?"

"I didn't notice them."

"So, all you did was pull out the wallet?"

"Yes." The officer was holding Malia's purse by the straps using latex gloves. She looked inside and rummaged around looking for the car keys. All she found was the cell phone and made note of the recent call log. She also made note of the cash and credit cards. Then she looked under both cars to see if the keys had dropped.

"Here's Principal Crockett's home number," said Sarah, holding her cell phone so the officer could read the number. "I've never met her husband, and I'm not really sure where they live."

"Uh-huh."

While the officer took notes on their conversation, Sarah retrieved her cell phone and silently asked permission to make her phone calls. The officer nodded, and Sarah went outside. She wanted to call Dan immediately, but knew that she had to call George first.

Liliana answered the phone, and was astonished to hear the news. Sarah sensed that Liliana was crying, and she wondered why she herself hadn't collapsed into tears. *Later.* Liliana made Sarah wait while she fetched George, and Sarah relayed the story again. Sarah paused briefly, and then asked, "Do you think there's any way that they could be involved in drugs?"

"You know the answer to that, I hope," responded George.

"Yes, but how did Owen get on this so-called drug binge?"

"I don't know. We need to get him out of there. Any idea what condition he's in?"

"No, but I definitely want Dan to see him."

"Absolutely. Is Gabe working?"

"Yes. So is Diane."

"Have you talked to Dan?"

"He's next."

"All right. Liliana and I will meet you at the hospital."

"How are the boys doing?"

"In a few years, we'll have a good story to tell, but right now, they're learning a good lesson."

"Fill me in later."

It was the call to Dan that finally broke down Sarah's emotional control. He asked if she was OK to drive to pick him up. She nodded, not thinking he couldn't see her. "Sarah?"

"I'm OK. Yes, I can drive. I'll pick you up in fifteen minutes. Assuming the cops let me go."

She checked in with Officer Taylor, saying she was going to see Owen. "You can reach me on my cell phone. I'm not going anywhere. I'm getting married on Saturday."

Without waiting for permission, Sarah walked out to her car, not looking back, and drove away. When out of shouting distance of the officer, she allowed herself to breathe a sigh of relief.

"Why am I here?" asked Malia. "Who are you? Where is my husband?"

"Lady, you ask too many questions. It's Wally."

"Wally?"

Wally wondered if he would regret telling the woman his name. Too late.

"You said you knew where my husband is."

"I think he's in jail."

"Jail!"

"He was helping us out on a little job, and well, your husband isn't so bright, you know."

"Right. What job?"

"Don't worry; we were going to cut him in on the profits."

"What job, uh, Wally?"

"We do a little business in party supplies."

"What kind of party supplies?"

"The kind that are worth a lot of money."

Drugs. "I see. And my husband was going to help you with your party supplies."

"Oh, yeah. He was more than happy to help. We gave him a little encouragement. However, the encouragement was coming out of his share."

"You gave my husband drugs?"

"You just shut up and be quiet. Sit down over there and don't say anything."

No! You haven't answered any of my questions, you jerk. Malia huddled down in the cabin of the boat. She didn't know where she was, other than some shabby marina on Maui about two hours away from the school. Wally had made her lie face down on the back of his van when he brought her here. She tried to guess where she was going, but lost track after he headed up the West Maui coast. *Somewhere north of Kapalua maybe. Honolua? Honokohau? Not as far as Kahakuloa. That road would have made me sick.* It was hard to pay attention when she was trying to get comfortable with her injured arm. Her pain seemed to have relaxed a little, and she was relieved that she probably hadn't suffered anything worse than a sprain, although that hurt plenty. She had tried to open the back door, but Wally had engaged the child locks. She thought about sitting up and screaming until someone paid attention, but she was still hoping that he was taking her to see Owen.

Would he kill her? Rape her? He didn't seem the type. She hoped. But he had hurt Principal Crockett, maybe killed her. She prayed silently for strength, for wisdom, for peace. Would she kill him if she had to? *God, what would you have me do?*

The sight of Owen through the glass saddened the four friends watching him in his suffering. Dan asked, "When did they bring him in?"

"Early Saturday, right after midnight," said George.

Dan did the math out loud, "So, it's been 48, 60 plus hours. Unfortunately, he's got a ways to go. He's at the worst stage of withdrawal, and it typically lasts several days."

"So it is drugs! I can't believe it! What's he doing? He's thrashing about, kicking at something."

"Now you see where the term 'kicking the habit' came from. That's what he's doing, although right now he would do anything for a fix. I'm going to talk to the doctor."

Liliana asked, "Can they give him something for it?"

"I'll find out."

"Someone did this to him," she cried. "This is not his fault. And now Malia is missing."

Sarah added, "I'm coming with you Dan. The doctor needs to know about Malia, too. I think she's caught up in this, too, somehow. Now that I see what someone did to Owen, I'm even more worried about her."

George said, "Before I saw him, I was determined to get him out of here. But there's no way any of us could handle him right now. This is probably the best place for him."

Liliana nodded in resignation, and called out to an unhearing Owen through the glass, "Owen, who did this to you?"

"This is Dr. Ahki," said Dan, introducing the young physician to everyone.

"Are any of you relatives?" asked the doctor.

"No, but I'm his priest, and we think you need to know what happened," said George, motioning to Sarah to relay the details.

After the doctor heard the story, he nodded, saying, "If he's only been on heroin for a few days, the prognosis is quite good for full recovery. We are monitoring all his vitals, and we will provide medication if necessary. In some cases, when someone is a long-time addict, going cold-turkey can be fatal. Fortunately that's not the case here, but he still has a few days of misery before he turns the corner. As you can see, he's in no condition to make rational choices of what's best for him. And even after he gets over the worst of it, recovery will take months or longer, depending on him. This is not a reflection on his character or integrity; heroin is a parasite."

The gathering back at the Callahans was quiet. George asked Sarah, "Have you talked to Diane or Gabe yet?"

"Not since this morning. Oh, that reminds me! The timing of this may not be the best, but Gabe came across a litter of puppies. They're the result of a brief encounter between a standard poodle and an Australian Shepherd. He's getting one, and he wanted to know if you wanted one."

"A puppy?" asked Liliana. "I'm not sure right now. It would be a good pal for Thomas especially, although it could be a mixed message in their current situation. What do you think, George?"

"I agree, but could we wait a few days?"

"Apparently not. The owners came in on their yacht for the holiday, and the puppies are on board, but only until tomorrow when they head back to Oahu."

George and Liliana looked at one another, waiting for the other to make the decision one way or the other. Sarah added, "Gabe said he'd keep the puppy for a couple of days for you, and we wouldn't say anything until you do."

Liliana nodded, and George said, "I guess we have a puppy."

"A female, please," added Liliana. "I'm grossly outnumbered here."

The phone rang, and George was relieved to hear Gabe's voice. After giving him a summary of the day, he added, "we understand that you and Diane are becoming parents. Do you think you could pick out a sister for us?"

"A girl? I didn't think you allowed girls!" Gabe laughed and added, "It will be my pleasure." He paused before returning to the more serious subject on everyone's mind. "I'm sorry I wasn't there when you went to see Owen, but at the same time, I'm glad he's in the right place. But we've traded one worry for another. I'll keep trying to reach Diane, and we'll both be up there this evening, once we get the puppy pen constructed."

The serious silence in the group was broken as the three boys noisily carried their tools back to the shed. George realized that none of them knew about Owen, but now that there was some progress in finding him, it was time they knew about him as well as Malia.

"Mom! Dad! We're starving." Micah rushed in at the head of the young laborers, all of them covered with soot and dirt. Liliana stopped them before they could walk past the kitchen, saying, "Off with your shoes. Then go get cleaned up. We'll have dinner as soon as you're presentable."

Sarah asked seriously, "How is your project coming?"

Thomas answered, "We've got it almost cleaned up."

Standing behind Thomas, Alec grimaced and held out his hand signaling that Thomas' assessment was a little premature.

George asked, "Did the fire department come over to talk to you?"

Alec said, "Yeah, two guys. They were pretty serious."

"I'll bet."

Liliana said, "How is the burn on your arm?"

"I think it's OK."

Dan's eyes perked up, and he said, "How about I take a look at it?"

"OK. Is it going to hurt?"

"Definitely."

Alec instinctively pulled his arm back, and then realized Dan was teasing him. It was the first time Dan had ever made a joke with him, and he wasn't expecting it. *It feels good to be teased; it makes me feel like I'm part of the family, not a guest.*

"Did you bring your lollipops?"

"I'm more into broccoli."

"I bet they love you back in Chicago."

While the boys were cleaning up, George readied the grill for burgers, while Sarah and Liliana prepared the accompaniments. Thomas came out first saying, "After we do the cleanup we have to put all the grass and plants back."

"How many bushes and how much grass seed will that be?" asked Sarah.

"I don't know. Dad will know."

"Well, you have to know how much to buy, and I think you guys can figure it out."

Micah joined them, saying, "Are you going to make us do math? It's summer!"

Sarah laughed, "I know. But just this once. I'm sure you'll never have to do math in the summer again. Come on; this won't take long. It's just a little word problem."

Alec came out and joined the groans.

"Go get a piece of paper, Thomas, please. Good. Thank you. So, Alec, could you give us a rough sketch of what the area is shaped like."

"I guess. It's kind of like this."

"Good. Hey guys, you know how to do this, especially you Micah and Alec. Thomas, we'll have a little math problem for you, too. But let's start with the area. It sort of looks like a thumb. How do you figure out the area of a thumb?"

"We never had to figure out the area of a thumb," protested Micah.

"No, well, I bet you can do it. Let's break the area into three shapes, kind of like this. No jokes about my drawing, now."

"Oh, I see," said Alec. We just figure out the three sections and add them together."

"Yup. So big kid, how do you do that?"

"First, I'm going to get rid of half the circle; then I have a rectangle."

Micah interrupted, "I remember! That's x times y. I don't remember the others."

Alec teased, "Stand aside. Let the master handle this. The triangle is x times y, divided by two." He signaled his victory with upraised arms.

"And the half circle, my young apprentice?" challenged Sarah.

"Uh, Pi something."

"Yes, Pi something."

"Two-Pi-R?"

"No, but we'll need that one later."

"Pi-R-squared," said Thomas. "It's Pi-R-squared, isn't it?"

"Very good, Thomas."

Alec let out a mock protest, "Beaten by the kid!"

Sarah added, "And since it's only half a circle…"

"Divide it by two!" exclaimed Micah.

"Good! So then what?" continued Sarah.

Micah answered, "We add them together. But how does that help?"

Sarah said, "I bet the grass seed bags say they'll cover so many square feet."

Alec said, "Oh yeah, then we just divide the whole area by how many square feet each bag will cover."

"If you say so," said Thomas.

"Yes, I say so."

Sarah added, "Don't forget the B-factor."

"We didn't learn about the B-factor; that's not until next year," complained Micah.

"Oh, I think you can figure it out," Sarah continued in mock seriousness. "How much of your grass seed do you think the birds will get?"

"The birds!" exclaimed Thomas. "Are the birds going to eat the grass seed? I'm just going to chase them away."

Alec said, "Good, so we won't have to worry about it. Thomas is just going to camp out there for two weeks, chasing the birds away. Thanks, baby brother!"

They all laughed at the teasing, and it was a good release for everyone. Sarah said, "I think dinner is ready. Afterwards, I'll let you guys figure out how big the perimeter is so you can determine how many bushes you'll need."

"At least the birds won't eat the bushes," said Thomas.

"My head hurts from all this," complained Micah.

"You'll feel better after a burger," teased Sarah. Her retreat into the unemotional and harmless subject of math had calmed her, as did explaining things to children.

I needed this, even more than they did.

"Catch him; he's starting to pee!" shouted Diane at Gabe. "I've got my hands full with Lucy."

"On the paper, Paco!" Gabe called to the puppy, picking him up and taking him to the newspaper.

"Don't look at me like that; it's not my fault that Lucy knows where the paper is. I guess we know who the smart one will be in this pair."

"Can you imagine what my life would be like if I picked out the dumbest dog for Liliana? Besides, Paco picked me! Come on, boy. You'll get it. Good boy. Don't worry; I'll teach you everything you need to know. Wait till you see the ocean!"

"But not my pool!" Diane laughed at the bonding taking place between the two. "You think they'll be OK on the lanai while we're gone?"

"I'm not sure what else I can do. They're surrounded on all sides with fencing. I bet they fall asleep after they eat."

"They are awfully cute. I may not want to give up Lucy."

"Only if you can take her flying with you. I can only handle one dog on the boat. The guy said that these pups are likely to be pretty social and will get into trouble if they are left alone for long. Like me." Gabe took Diane and both puppies in his arms for a gentle tumble on the floor. High-pitched yips and giggles filled the room until Lucy decided she needed to pee again. "Get her," Gabe, stunned that the puppy headed straight for the paper. "Not a word," Gabe admonished.

"Who, me?" giggled Diane. "Say, where's your digital camera? We should take one of Lucy to show Liliana."

"In my desk. I predict Lucy will be there by Wednesday, once they see how cute she is. You take the pictures, and I'll get their kibble. Then we need to head up to see George. I want to find out what the situation is with Owen and Malia. And they promised to have leftovers for us. The boys are probably eating early these days, as you would expect. I think we'll be lucky to see them before they fall asleep in their ketchup."

"Uncle Gabe! Diane! *Aunt* Diane!" called Thomas when he saw the SUV drive up. He slowly got to his feet, calling out to his cousin and his girlfriend with their traditional greeting.

"Uncle Thomas, how are you?"

"Good. Tired."

"Really? What have you guys been up to today?"

"Come on; you know. We've got to fix the park."

"Uh-huh. How is it going?"

"OK, except Sarah made us do math. And I beat Alec."

"Great! Where's everyone else?"

"Almost asleep. Everyone's inside. Do you want a hamburger?"

"Sounds good."

"Say, you smell like cereal. What's that dirt spot on your shirt? Looks like a paw print."

"Oh, you know. We've got a lot of dogs around. One of them wanted to say hello."

"Gabriel! It's good to see you. Diane, you make him look good." George descended the steps to greet Gabe and Diane.

"It's hard to believe he got this far without me. Good to see you, George."

George said to Thomas, "I'm amazed you made it this late. Why don't you call it a night?"

"'K. 'Night everyone."

"Good night, Thomas," said everyone.

"Do they know?" asked Gabe softly.

George shook his head. "There just wasn't the opportunity. We'll do it tomorrow. They're all exhausted and barely made it through dinner."

"I'll bet," agreed Gabe. "Can you fill us in?"

"Sure. Grab some food, and we'll all join you out here. We're still running on adrenaline."

"Hey, Duke, how come you don't answer your phone?" Wally was tired of leaving messages on Duke's cell phone. He needed for Duke to tell him what to do with the woman. It wasn't Wally's fault, but he had no choice but to make her come with him. She interrupted him when he was trying to remove evidence that he had ever been in Owen's office. The other woman—the Principal—she had to be stopped. She was getting ready to call the police. If she had stayed away for just another half hour, she wouldn't have been hurt. It was her own fault. School's closed in the summer; what was she going to do there anyway? He hadn't decided whether he cared if she was dead or not. He had hit her pretty hard, but again, it was her own fault. Why can't people use common sense?

Duke listened to his cell phone messages one last time before he drifted off. He could probably go home in the morning, but in some ways, his medically imposed vacation gave him an escape from everything and everyone. He wondered if Erin had tried to reach him; perhaps she was more old-fashioned and expected him to make the next move. After all, she had initiated the first date. When he got home, he could use the mugging story. After all, that's what it was. He also didn't want to risk getting her involved in the sordid side of his life that he wanted to put behind him as soon as possible. Like a sand castle, the more he tried to build it up, the more it caved in on him.

Have I told you lately that you are an idiot?

Another message from Wally. He had ignored all of them until just now, when he thought he had better listen to them in case his flaky partner had managed to mess things up even worse. As he listened, he first thought that what he was hearing was a hallucination caused by the morphine. Then he remembered he was off morphine, a requirement before he could be released.

"Hey, Duke. Where are you? I drove by your apartment, but you weren't there. Did you leave Maui? I need to know, man, 'cause I got a situation. I got worrying about my fingerprints at the school, and well, man, I went back this morning to wipe things down, you know. So this old lady shows up and wants to call the police, and of course I couldn't let her.

Then, you wouldn't believe who else shows up: HoHo's stupid wife! She starts poking around, see, and well, I didn't know if she might figure something out. Anyway, she's with me on Rocky's boat, and I need to know what to do…"

"What have you done, Wally?" Duke cried out to himself.

"Should I get her hooked, you know? Lock her up some place? Maybe the warehouse? How about your apartment? She's behaving now, 'cause she thinks I know where HoHo is…"

"No, you idiot!" Duke was appalled at Wally. He needed to call him, but he also needed to figure out what to tell him when he did.

The air in the cabin was stuffy, and Malia groped around in the dark, feeling for a vent or a porthole. Wally had locked her in and threatened to give her drugs if she didn't stay quiet. *Either way I'm locked up. It's better to be lucid and locked up. Escape from this hell had to be easier. Owen, are you OK? What did they do to you?*

She found a porthole that opened part way. The marina appeared to be deserted; the boats she could see were too small to have sleeping quarters.

A cell phone rang, and she reached for her purse, but remembered she had left it at the school. She felt the keys in her pocket and decided to leave them there until she needed them; how or when she didn't know. She couldn't understand the phone conversation taking place outside, but Wally's tone of voice sounded desperate.

I wasn't part of the plan. What was the plan?

Tuesday, July 7

George and Liliana bolted upright from bed when the phone rang. Sunrise was imminent, but the dim light confirmed what the clock read: 6:00.

"Hello, George Callahan," said George, with Liliana leaning over to hear what could likely be bad news at this hour. She couldn't make out the voice, but soon learned that it was not about Owen or Malia. She lay back down to let the day awaken her more gradually while George continued the conversation.

"Yes, Sister…where is she now? That's good. I am so very sorry…of course, we can arrange everything. Are you OK? I can be there very shortly…later is fine, Sister. We will both be there."

Sister, thought Liliana. *That can only mean one thing: Mama Lani.*

George hung up, and Liliana said softly, "Mama Lani?"

George nodded, saying, "About an hour ago. That was Sister, as you could tell."

"It's the end of a dynasty."

"Yes. At least this was peaceful and not unexpected. This week has suddenly gotten busier."

"It's the way it has to be."

They both lay down and embraced for a little while, sharing their sadness, and thinking about the grand lady the congregation had called

"Mama Lani" as long as they had been there.

Hardly grand in any way, Mama Lani was a feisty matriarch dedicated to her church and her family. She had fallen ill at Easter and continued to decline. A tiny woman in her mid-nineties, Mama Lani raised a family and had seen grandchildren married with children of their own. She stood for simplicity, dignity, and grace. There wasn't a member of the church who didn't know and love her.

Liliana said, "I bet she's smiling right now, knowing that she chose a Tuesday to go, and not a Saturday or Sunday, or worse: a holiday."

George smiled and said, "You win, Mama Lani. I always knew you would. Be at peace."

"Do you need to go see Sister?"

"Later. The hospital just called her, and she's just waking up herself. I was hoping we could both go."

"Absolutely. Oh, I hear our laborers up. Looks we're all getting an early start."

Dan was pleased to hear the teenager's voice. "Tiffany, this is Dr. Weatherby. How are you?" He paused and let her talk. "Tell me about the program and what you're doing… Uh-huh… No, I don't guess it is much fun. But it sounds like you're making it work. Say, is your mother around? I'd like to talk to her… No, I don't imagine she is ever far away these days. Good luck to you Tiffany. I know you're going to make it."

Dan waited for Tiffany's mother to get on the line, making notes to himself on the conversation. "Elizabeth… Hi… Dr. Weatherby."

"Dr. Weatherby, it's awfully nice of you to call while you're on vacation. How's Hawai'i?"

"Great, thanks! Say, Tiffany sounds a lot better."

"She is. Plus, she's staying in summer school. I told her she could have her cell phone back if she passes summer school. It's only been a few days, but it's a start."

"Good thinking."

"Plus, her father and I are in total agreement on what she has to do. It's the first time we've agreed on anything in two years."

"Good. I've been thinking about you all, and I'm glad to hear the program is working, and that you're seeing progress."

"So far, but she—we all—have a way to go."

"Just keep thinking about where she was just a week ago. She's smart, and my money's on Tiffany and you."

"Thank you. Now get back to your fiancée and have a great time. We're doing fine, and we appreciate your help. What do they say: Aloha?"

Dan laughed, "That's right! I'll see you in a couple of weeks. Aloha!"

Dan finished up his calls to the Broken Arm Twins. They had managed to find solace and summer companionship with one another at a computer camp. With continued healing, they would still have a couple of weeks before school started to enjoy some sports activities.

Gabe poured coffee and joined Dan at the table. As usual, the sisters were still sleeping, which gave the men a chance steel themselves for the lively antics of the Donovan girls.

"Diving, Gabe?"

"Yes, pretty much every day except this Saturday. It's typical for summer. I'll be glad when we can get one or two of the older kids certified to help out once in awhile."

"Alec?"

"Maybe. We'll see. Micah, eventually. During the school year, I do Saturdays and some Sundays so Terry can have some time off."

"And Diane's a lost cause, of course."

"Indeed."

"Why am I a lost cause?" queried a sleepy Diane, yawning and stretching on her way to get a cup of coffee.

"So many ways, my dear, so many ways."

"Hmmmm... How are the puppies?"

"Sleeping. I just fed them. They'll be up again soon, no doubt. I'm glad Liliana said they would be ready to take Lucy tomorrow. In fact, she said she wanted to stop by today to see her and get some of the food we've been feeding them. The boys did good work yesterday. I think they've got one more day of really dirty work to clear out all the debris. After that, it's restoration, and that will be less drudgery."

Diane said, "I'm flying this morning, but I should be back mid-afternoon. We all have to meet the realtor at 3:00 to do the contract on the Hale Luau house. Is everyone still agreed on it?"

"Works for us if it works for you," said Dan. "Count on us to cover the gardener."

"Thanks, big brother," said Diane, giving him a hug.

"Yes, thanks, big brother," echoed Gabe, leaning his head on Dan's shoulder.

"Would you three like to be alone?" asked Sarah, smiling at the playful scene as she joined the morning gathering.

"We're just bonding. After all, we're buying a house together."

"Hale Luau, right?"

"Is that OK?"

"Of course. It's beautiful, and perfect for Paco, and Lucy, too, when she comes over. Did Dan say we'd pay for the gardener?"

"Yes, but we were thinking we could save some money by getting a goat. He could give us cheese, too."

Dan covered his face with his hands, shaking his head, "Sister, I hate to tell you, but *he* won't give you cheese. Gabe, please tell her."

"I've got to go," said Gabe, laughing. "See you all later."

"You can't leave," protested Diane. "The puppies are peeing again."

"Have fun," said Gabe, kissing Diane through his laughter.

Duke got out of his hospital bed and tested his flexibility and maneuverability. He still felt light-headed, but he figured he just needed some breakfast. He showered and put his Saturday clothes back on.

Clean enough to get me back home.

The shower refreshed him, and he convinced the nurse that he was fit to drive home. His vitals were satisfactory, and he could walk unaided. He assured her that he had someone to look after him. *I wish.*

He hoped he could sneak back home without anyone noticing him. Erin would likely see that his car was there and knock on his door, unless she was waiting for him to call first. He had better call her so she wouldn't come over and surprise him. He needed for her to stay away; there was no telling when the brute squad might come back. He promised himself that he would not let her become involved in this. It was something he had to do by himself and make a clean break. He needed an honorable discharge from Cho's army. If the man felt that Duke still owed him—financially or bodily—Duke might never be free.

He resisted the urge to wince as he put his shoes on. All he wanted to do was get home and rest, to let himself heal for one more day. Wally—stupid Wally—needed an answer, though.

The doctor came in and reluctantly agreed to release him, as long as Duke had home care and promised to make an appointment to see him on Friday. The nurse came in with his take-home medication—pain killers and topical antibiotics.

As soon as he got to his car, he sat in it for a few minutes to let the pain spasms subside. Then he drove home.

"Hey, lady—Malia—make us some coffee, would you? There's a pot over in the corner of the galley."

This has got to be the strangest captivity anyone's ever had. Other than pushing me down and slapping me across the face, he hasn't hurt me any more, only threatened to do so. But he did hurt—or kill—Principal Crockett. He just doesn't know what to do with me.

Malia decided that a calm Wally was better than a desperate Wally. Maybe she could lull him into a false sense of control over a weak and docile prisoner. He was sure to slip up, and she could make her escape. "OK," she said. "It looks like there's other food here, too. Do you want something?"

"Sure. I'm glad you're being so reasonable."

"Will we go see my husband today?"

"Maybe."

"How do you know he's OK?"

"Just make the coffee."

Malia made the coffee and put together a food assortment from what was on hand. She called out to Wally when she was done. He opened the cabin door and took her offering, shutting and locking the door almost immediately. In the brief moment she had to scan the marina, she was able to see that there were people starting to arrive at the marina. *He can't keep me here much longer. There's too much risk I'll scream for help. Maybe he plans to kill me and dump me at sea. Maybe that's what he did to Owen.*

She thought more about who this man was and decided that he wasn't acting on his own. Keeping her here made no sense, but Wally had to wait for someone to tell him what to do. She thought about how she could take advantage of his desperation in order to effect an escape.

"Do you want more coffee, Wally?"

"Yes, uh, thanks." He handed her his mug through the porthole, and she refilled it.

"I didn't ask if you wanted sugar or milk."

"Black is fine."

"Is this your boat? It's nice."

"No, it belongs to a friend of mine. I'm taking care of it for him."

"Do you want to use the bathroom?"

"Maybe."

"It looks like you need a few more provisions in the galley. That was the end of the coffee."

"OK."

Time to be quiet now. Don't give him more than one thing to think about.

Dan and Sarah got comfortable in George's cozy office. Liliana brought everyone some iced tea and then left them for their final premarital counseling session with George.

"How are your feet, Dan?" asked George.

"Warm."

"Good, no cold feet this week?"

"Not even a chill."

"How are your nerves, Sarah?"

"Jittery."

"Good; sounds normal. You both pass. Well, we've covered all the important topics, I think. Now let's look at after the wedding, after the honeymoon, after you've washed all the new linens, after you've realized that the sterling silver and Waterford crystal won't get used everyday, and confessed that you really like sitting around—and maybe sleeping—in T-shirts and sweatpants. It's a Thursday night, and you've both been working all week, and it's not over yet. I'd like you to talk about what that evening will be like. And I'll know if you're not being honest!"

George seemed to hit all their potential hot buttons, where their personal stresses could be, as well as those they were likely to face as a couple. Some they had thought of and discussed already; some they had not. The discussion was hard work, but George kept it focused on how they could support each other.

"That was the warm-up. The main topic for today—our last session—is trust. Now because I've gotten to know you both pretty well in the last few months, I thought this might be a good topic. Let's talk about how your relationship got started and where there were some challenges related to trust."

Sarah started, "I suppose our first meeting was make-believe. It was a costume party on a riverboat cruise I was on with Diane…"

"And I was with some colleagues," finished Dan. "We were both dressed as riverboat gamblers, and Sarah had a Queen of Hearts protruding…"

"Yes, protruding," finished Sarah, giggling. "I remember our first date after that. I planned every last detail of what I wore, so as to appear willing but not eager."

George said, "What was wrong with eager?"

"I think—no, I *know*—I like to control things," confessed Sarah.

"Control is a big concern when you're teaching middle school, and it can spill over into my personal life. The lady gambler costume was a chance to give up a little control because I had the assurance that I'd never see any of those people again. Plus there weren't any seventh graders around! Meeting Dan under those circumstances, I risked losing control." Sarah paused and looked down.

Dan looked at her and took her hand in his. "I had no idea."

"Neither did I. It seems like such a long time ago; I was a different person."

George smiled, turning to Dan, "Dan, what is your recollection of that first meeting?"

"I was with some of my colleagues on the boat when I saw her. Even in the costume—which was amazing—did I mention the Queen...? I guess I did." Dan paused before getting serious again. "She had dignity and grace, along with the Queen of Hearts protruding..."

"Dan, I think George got the idea." Sarah blushed at the continued reference.

"And she was gorgeous, obviously," teased Dan.

"Obviously," agreed George.

"I remember not sleeping that night, wondering if she wanted to see me again, fearing that she might not."

Sarah interrupted, "I had no idea."

George nodded, "There seems to be a bit of that going around." He paused before moving the discussion forward in time. "There were one or two situations where you, Sarah, questioned Dan's devotion and even his character."

"I know. I was an idiot. It was about another woman."

"Vanessa," Dan said, and to which Sarah nodded.

"Tell me about her," challenged George.

"Dan knew Vanessa professionally; she had decorated his condo. But she apparently wanted to do more than decorate. She wanted Dan."

Dan jumped in. "But I didn't want her."

"I know," said Sarah softly. "Several times when I visited Dan in Chicago, it appeared that she had been in the apartment."

Dan nodded and added, "Sarah wasn't being paranoid; she *had* been in the apartment. And she wanted Sarah to know it. I was blind to how devious she was. It almost cost me everything."

"Each time she got bolder; one time she left a black negligee in the drawer, another time she left the patio door open in November just so we would know she could still get in. And one time she actually came into the apartment when I was there and Dan was at work."

"How did she get in?" inquired George.

"She had a key leftover from the redecorating," said Dan. "I did get it back, and that stopped her for awhile."

Sarah was quiet for awhile, building her courage to relay what happened the day after Christmas. Dan and George waited patiently, and Dan held her hand in both of his. Sarah continued the story.

"We got engaged Christmas night. The first time, anyway. The next morning when Dan had left for work, Vanessa knocked on the door and handed me a so-called Christmas present for Dan, and she opened it in front of me. It was a photograph of her with Dan and a child. She said the child was his, and that they were married. Looking back on it now, it was absurd, but at the time I couldn't deal with it. I couldn't control it. And I left, I think, because I couldn't control it."

"Are you OK, Sarah?" asked Dan, and Sarah nodded.

George said, "The issue of trust is important in any relationship, business or personal. And putting trust in the right place takes some work. Sarah, you were worried you couldn't trust Dan…"

Sarah interrupted, "It was really that I couldn't trust myself to make the right decision. It was me, not him."

Dan added, "For me, I was too trusting; I had put trust in the wrong place."

"Yes," agreed George. "Throughout your life together, there will be times when the trust you have with one another will be challenged, either because you, Sarah, worry that a Vanessa—whatever form that may be in—might tempt Dan away from you, and you can't control it. And, Dan, you may be tempted to put your trust in the wrong thing, not realizing the impact it has on Sarah as well as yourself. Fortunately, you won't be alone."

"Thank God," said Dan, followed by Sarah.

"That's the point," said George.

"Wally, how is your guest?" asked Duke, exhausted from the drive home and wanting nothing more than to rest. He was overdue for a dose of pain medication, but he needed to get back to Wally.

"She's behaving," said Wally, on the other end of the phone. "But I can't keep her here. There are too many people around. I think the only reason she hasn't screamed for help is she's hoping I'll take her to HoHo. Think he's still in jail?"

"Probably. I'm not going to ask, Wally."

"Can I bring her to your place?"

"No. Under no circumstances will you bring her here!"

"Should I let her go? Should she have an accident?"

"No and no."

"She's not worth nothing to us."

"She is to HoHo, and that might make her worth something to us."

"Maybe, but I've got to get her out of here. Today."

"Wally, you're in a boat. Just go out to sea."

"Rocky won't like it."

"Tell him you've got a woman, and you want to take her out on the boat. Make it worth his while. Tell him you'll give him $300."

"You got $300?"

"Yes. I'll call you later and I'll get it to you."

"I've got to get food."

"They deliver, man. Don't leave her alone. I've got to go. There's someone at the door."

Wally, sometimes I wonder whose side you are on.

There was no one at the door, but Duke knew that prolonging the conversation would not help the situation. Wally needed a few, simple, unambiguous instructions. He hoped that Wally would not find himself in a desperate situation and do something stupid. Again.

He called Erin to let her know what had happened to him. "I'm coming over," was all she said.

Good. Not good. Have I told you lately what an idiot you are, Duke?

He met her at the front door and gingerly embraced her.

"Shouldn't you still be in the hospital?" she asked.

"I couldn't get any sleep there. Right now that's really all I want to do. I should feel somewhat better tomorrow. Sorry to be a poor host."

"I might forgive you. Have you eaten anything?"

"Breakfast. I'm not very hungry. I need to lie down."

"Are you taking pain killers?"

"I'm due for a dose, but once I take it, I will just sleep."

"Good. I'll get out of here, but when you wake up, call me, and I'll bring dinner over. Is there anything else you need?"

"Yes." Duke tentatively took her in his arms and kissed her. "That."

"You didn't get that in the hospital?"

"There was this hallucination…"

Erin laughed and said, "Well, sweet dreams."

"They will be now."

Malia awoke to voices outside. *Should I call out?* She couldn't see who was with Wally, but before she knew it, the hatch opened and Wally shoved bags of groceries into her arms, closing and locking the door as quickly as possible. She heard the motor start up and decided she had better ask where they were going.

"Just for a ride. How about some lunch?"

Malia inventoried the groceries as she put them away. Fruit, cans of chicken, bread, raw vegetables, beer, juices, ice… *This is certainly a step above the chips and donuts. If he planned to kill me, he wouldn't buy food for me.*

She stored the provisions and organized things a little. *If I'm going to be here awhile, I may as well make the best of it.*

The ride became rough soon after the boat left the marina. She quickly fixed food and called to Wally that it was ready. He opened and shut the door quickly, but all Malia could see was water. After securing loose items, she hunkered down to avoid getting tossed about in the choppy conditions. *Eventually we have to dock some place. This boat is not built for much more than local recreation.*

She began to suspect that they were heading toward Moloka'i, or even Lana'i. *Is Owen on Moloka'i? Lana'i? If he doesn't take me to Owen immediately, I will escape. No, enough of this charade. He doesn't know where Owen is. And pretty soon Wally is going to get tired of keeping me imprisoned on this little boat. He can't be dumb enough to think I'm willing to stay locked up.*

The boat ride lasted two hours, during which Malia alternated between praying and planning her escape. Wally anchored the boat 100 yards off shore, thereby forcing Malia to revise her escape plan to accommodate having to get to shore. *I can swim that far. I think. I have to.*

She looked for a rope that she could use to tie her sandals to her waist. She could swim faster barefoot, but when she arrived on shore, she would need her shoes. She decided her rayon shirt and pants were seaworthy enough. She considered stripping to her underwear, but decided she would try the swim fully clothed. When she arrived on shore, she wanted to go straight to the police. A woman walking around in her underwear might raise questions of her credibility and sanity. She wished she had some identification, but all she had were her car keys. She pinned them inside her pants pocket so they wouldn't fall out during the swim. She found a rubber band and tied her long hair back securely.

She picked up a kitchen knife and made sure it was clean. She made a small cut in the fleshy part of her palm and encouraged blood to flow. When it did, she smeared it so that it looked like there was more and that she had seriously injured herself. Then she started to moan.

"Wally... Wally, I need help. I cut myself on the ride over. I cut myself bad."

"There are bandages in the bathroom, lady."

"I used them all. I can't make the bleeding stop. I'm feeling faint, and there's blood everywhere. Open the door; you can see."

"OK, sit over on the far side and don't move."

"Hurry."

The hatch opened, and Wally surveyed the darkened cabin. Malia hoped that she had drawn enough blood to make it look bad.

"I need more bandages. Please, Wally. Please go get some for me. I'll be quiet. I promise. Please help me. I'm so afraid. I don't want to bleed to death."

Wally shut the hatch again and told her, "I'll be back in ten, fifteen minutes. Stay quiet or you'll make it worse. There's no place you can go, and there's no one around. Do not do something stupid."

"Just hurry, Wally. I can't make it stop."

"Just shut up, will you? You're driving me crazy."

"OK," Malia said meekly. "Thank you. Please hurry."

Malia heard the sound of Wally lowering the small dinghy and starting its motor. She used the kitchen knife to pry the hatch open. When she finally succeeded she slowly opened the hatch, making sure he had reached the shore before she slipped out and over the edge of the boat.

The salt water stung her wound, but she said a silent prayer of thanks that she was alive and able to feel pain. She stayed as low in the water as she could, while swimming as fast as she could. The rope rubbed her torso raw, but she kept moving. Once on shore, she ran to a small hut where she could sit a minute and catch her breath while putting on her sandals.

That's Lana'i over there. This has to be Moloka'i. Owen, I will find you. Keep praying. I love you.

"Father George, Liliana, thank you for coming." Mama Lani's sister, known to everyone simply as 'Sister,' greeted her guests in a flowing *mu'umu'u* that engulfed the tiny woman within its folds.

"We both share in the sorrow at the loss of your sister," said Liliana softly, taking Sister's hands in hers.

"She told me yesterday that she was ready, and she didn't want to wait until Saturday or Sunday. She wanted to spend her own Easter Sunday with God."

"That she will," said George, inviting the frail woman to sit down. "I saw her on Saturday, and I was worried that she might not be with us for long. Is there anything you need? Do you need us to call anyone?"

"We have a big family, and they already know. You—we—need to plan the party. Lani wanted a big party."

George laughed softly and said, "That we will have. When would you like it?"

"Thursday OK?"

"It is indeed. We'll get the phone tree going so everyone will know today."

"Thank you. She loved you both so much. She wants everyone to come. And she don't want no one wearing black. Come happy for Lani. I'm happy for Lani. Sad for Sister, but happy for Lani."

"Absolutely. A special Easter in July for Mama Lani."

"Easter music, too."

"Certainly."

"Alleluia."

"Alleluia."

"Sarah, honey, are you OK?" Dan was concerned that Sarah had been quiet since the meeting with George.

"I am. I really am. George makes me think about things that I don't always want to think about, but need to."

"Me, too."

"But to be honest, I'm just not sure I'd want to face Vanessa right away if I had to."

"You won't have to, unless you invited her to the wedding!"

"Hmmm…let me think…didn't!"

Dan pulled her head to his chest and worked his hands through her hair. "She wouldn't come anyway, particularly since the most beautiful girl there will not be her!"

Sarah laughed and buried her face in her favorite spot under Dan's chin, taking in the scent she had loved from their first meeting on the dance floor. "I think I'm more at peace with what we have before us than ever before. What about you?"

"I feel like I'm the luckiest guy in the world."

"You are, of course."

They giggled and rolled around on the floor at Gabe's apartment, playing with the puppies, snuggling with them and each other.

"Get him! He's starting to pee! Lucy, show Paco where the paper is. Good girl."

"How come I'm in charge of Paco?"

"It's male bonding."

"I'm really more into bonding with females. One, anyway. I thought both breeds were supposed to be so smart. You know Gabe's not going to be happy when Paco pees all over his diving equipment."

"Who's peeing on my dive equipment?" Gabe said, entering the condo. Paco bounded into his arms. It was clear why Paco had been Gabe's choice. The two were mutually devoted to each other. "You're not going to pee on my dive equipment, are you, boy? Of course not. What time is it… 2:15. I've got just enough time to get cleaned up before we have to go to the Hale Luau house. Are you two ready? We're going to meet Diane there."

"You bet," said Dan.

"Oh, I got a call from the realtor. He's got someone interested in looking at this place tomorrow."

"We'd better make sure the pups stay on the lanai," said Sarah. "While you're cleaning up, we'll take them around the grounds to run around."

"Any news on Malia?"

"No. George called a little while ago. The police still have nothing, and Owen is still going through—well, you saw. He called Malia's family to let them know what's been going on. They haven't heard from either of them. Principal Crockett is stable, but she can't remember anything. Oh, and this is sad—Mama Lani died this morning..."

"Oh, no! It wasn't totally unexpected, tho'."

"True. They've been with Sister this afternoon and are planning the service for Thursday."

"She was a grand lady."

"Indeed. OK, the condo is yours for ten minutes. We'll be back soor."

The two couples went through the Hale Luau house again just to make sure it was the right decision. Gabe was particularly interested in the fence, now that he had a dog to worry about. He looked forward to having Paco on the boat with him, but the yard would provide the exercise for him. They agreed on the price they would offer and started talking about parties and relatives visiting from the mainland. The realtor wrote up the contract and promised to call the sellers that evening with the offer.

"How about a dip in the pool back at the condo?" asked Gabe.

"You didn't get waterlogged enough?" teased Diane.

"I'll make dinner while you all swim. Oh, cell phone...it's mine. Hi, George. Any news...?"

The other three stared at him and each other wondering what could cause him to be so speechless. He mouthed the word *Malia* with a thumbs-up sign. "Sure, I'll put her on. George wants to talk to you Diane."

"George, this is Diane."

"Diane, they found Malia. She's OK."

"Thank God. Where? How can I help?"

"She's on Moloka'i. It's a long story how she got there, but I was wondering if you could go get her."

"Of course. Gabe and I are on the way."

George provided the logistics for the rendezvous, adding, "The Maui police want to talk to her when she gets back, but I convinced them to do that at her house. She's been through quite an ordeal. She sounds fine, but she was in fragile condition before, and I'm sure she's running on what little adrenaline she has left. Please call us when you land, and we'll meet you at the house."

Diane hung up and joined Gabe who was filling in Dan and Sarah on Malia's whereabouts.

Sarah said, "Go. We'll see you at home. We'll just be in the way."

Dan said, "If she needs medical attention, call us. If she doesn't, call us anyway."

Gabe said, "She is going to want to see Owen. If you can find out his condition, that would be helpful. If there's any way he can come home…"

Dan nodded, saying, "We'll find out."

Now that Malia and Owen were accounted for, tears of relief filled everyone's eyes. Diane handed Gabe her car keys so he could drive while she contacted the airfield. Suddenly the new house seemed the farthest from anyone's mind.

Duke answered the phone without bothering to see who it was. He had finally gotten some sleep, and the jarring ring startled him.

"Duke! It's Wally."

Leave me alone, Wally.

"Wally, what's up?"

"She's gone."

"Who's gone?"

"The woman—Malia."

"Did you kill her?"

"No, but I should have. She got away. I went ashore to get some bandages. She said she cut herself bad on the way over to Moloka'i, but she was just faking it. I was stupid."

You got that right.

"What do I do?"

"Where are you now?"

"On my way back to Maui. If she goes to the cops, they'll find me."

"Don't let them find you, Wally. You hear? Go someplace new. Stay low."

"You got my money?"

"Yeah, you tell Rocky to come to my apartment. I'll give him his money, plus another couple of hundred so you can spend more time with your lady friend. You just got luckier."

"OK, I'm heading to…"

"No! Don't tell me. I've got to go, Wally. I'll call you later."

"Promise?"

"Of course. Now get lost. I mean it."

Duke hung up, but the phone rang again almost immediately. "What now?"

"Hey, Duke!" *Cho.*

"Hello, Mr. Cho."

"How are you, Duke? It sounds like you were expecting someone else to be calling?"

"Everything's fine, Mr. Cho. I wasn't expecting…"

"Glad to hear it. I just want to make sure you're still part of our team, Duke."

"Of course, Mr. Cho. Everything from this point forward will be perfect."

"What about your—uh—ward? HoHo?"

"He's still out of commission, but he's not going to remember anything, even when he gets over his little illness."

"I'm counting on you, Duke. Just like you count on me. Our relationship is built on knowing just what we can expect from each other, right?"

"Absolutely." Duke felt a spasm in his ribs that reminded him of what Cho meant by 'expect.'

"Be sure you keep your phone on. I will need to reach you very soon."

Malia leaned on the glass watching her husband moaning in pain, oblivious to anything and anyone else. "Why, Owen? How?" she spoke, her eyes filling with tears.

Dan said softly, "Believe it or not Malia, he's doing better. This initial crisis is coming to an end, but his treatment and recovery will take months."

"How long has he been like this?"

"Since they brought him in sometime after midnight Friday."

"Can they help him with the pain?"

"There are as many reasons to give him something as not, and if he can knock this on his own, that's better. They are monitoring him closely."

"I want him to come home, but I couldn't handle him, not like this."

"Malia, if anyone can kick this, it's Owen. He is not a lifelong addict, although right now, he would give anything for a fix."

"He's always been such a crusader against drugs."

"He will be again."

"I know he didn't choose to do this."

"No, but we won't have answers until he's kicked it. Oh, here comes the doctor and an orderly to escort you in. Doctor, this is Malia, Owen's wife."

"Malia, it's nice to meet you. I hear you had a close encounter with possibly the same perpetrator who—we suspect—forced Owen to take drugs. We're just starting to learn a little about what happened to your husband. Now when you see him, he is going to beg you with his very heart and soul for a fix. He needs to know that he's not going to get it from you or anyone else. He may say things that hurt you. Are you ready?"

Malia nodded and the three entered Owen's sparsely furnished room.

"Owen? Hi, Owen. It's Malia."

"Where's Wally? Please get Wally. Wally is God. I *know*. I pray to God all the time, but God doesn't answer. Wally answers."

"Where is Wally, Owen?"

"Everywhere. He's God. God is everywhere. You know I played golf with God? And I won."

"Good for you. Does it hurt?"

"Headache. Bad. Flu. So many ants. The ants are everywhere. See?"

"Owen, you will feel better, but right now I know it hurts."

"Promise me you'll find Wally."

"I promise I love you, and you will get through this."

"Please Mama, find Wally. I love you Mama."

"I'm going to go now, but I'll come see you tomorrow."

"Bring Wally, please. I love Wally."

"Good night."

Outside, Malia buried her head in Dan's chest and sobbed. "He doesn't even know me."

"He will, Malia."

The doctor said, "We take it day by day, and trust me when I say he's better than he was at first when the police brought him in. He's retreated back to a very primitive state where pain and its relief are his only concern."

"Is there anything I can bring him?"

"If this were a teenager, sometimes a favorite stuffed animal can bring some comfort. He doesn't seem like the teddy bear type, but I'll leave that up to you. He needs to realize that drugs are not an option. It's tough love, but it usually works, particularly when the addiction hasn't been lifelong."

"It couldn't have happened before Tuesday. That's when I left town."

The doctor counted in his head, "Four days then. Most of the time we're treating people that have been addicted for years. Some of them never recover, but I have confidence that is not the case here. I could show you much worse cases, but I'm sure that this is the one that concerns you the most. He's getting the right care here, but that's not how he feels right now. He needs you, but he can't see it yet. Is there anything I can do for you? You look like you're about to crumble. You keep rubbing your arm, and I hate to tell you, but you look like you were in a fight."

"I just haven't been sleeping. Oh, and when Wally first attacked me, I first thought he had broken my arm or dislocated my shoulder. Then he slugged me. Other than that, I'm OK."

"That's all, huh? Doctor's orders: I want you to ice your arm and your face. Dan, please see to that she does. Malia, then I want you to take this sleeping pill. Don't fight it. You need rest as much as Owen does. When he comes home, your own strength and personal well-being will be just as important as Owen's. And last: you've got a fantastic support system here; use it!"

Malia nodded meekly and accepted the medication.

"Let's go see the others in the waiting room," said Dan gently, with his arm around Malia's shoulder.

"I have been worried about his being with another woman."

"In a way, he has been, but you'll win him back. I'm sure. You're much better looking."

Malia gave out a small laugh and let Dan escort her out to the waiting room to the gathering of friends offering support. She fell into Liliana's and George's embrace, and thanked Diane and Gabe for rescuing her. "I had no idea," she said, shaking her head, tears flowing steadily.

"All the questions have finally been answered," said George.

"All except who was the son of a bitch who did this to Owen, and why," said Malia angrily, with her voice shaking.

"We'll take you home, Malia," said Liliana. "The police said there would be a round-the-clock patrol outside. It's likely that the man who kidnapped you is somehow related to this."

"I know he is. His name is Wally, and Owen is in love with him."

Back at Gabe's condo, the four sat quietly at the dining room table. The message on Gabe's answering machine from the realtor announcing that their offer on the house was accepted seemed irrelevant. He was jovial and congratulatory, and no one cared.

Sarah asked Diane, "What happened on Moloka'i?"

"When we picked up Malia, I was shocked to see her. She said she swam from the boat in her clothes. She kept saying, 'the pain felt good.' I'm not sure what she meant, but her hand was bandaged when we got her. She was exhausted in every way possible, but all she could talk about was getting to Owen. When we took her home to meet the police, she yelled at the lady cop as if she was personally responsible for Owen's disappearance. Gabe jumped in and suggested that letting her see Owen sooner rather than later was the best thing to do, and I was so relieved when the officer agreed."

The puppies were released from captivity and allowed to run around the apartment. They brought much-needed smiles to everyone's faces.

"Liliana is coming tomorrow morning to get Lucy, so I'll take Paco with me on the boat," said Gabe. That way the realtor can show the place. Hurry! Get them, they're starting to pee. On the paper, Paco!"

"Good girl, Lucy," said Diane.

Wednesday, July 8

"Can I go home today?" asked Owen. "I want to go home. I want to see Malia."

"You are doing much better today," said the doctor. "What do you remember?"

"What day is it?"

"Wednesday."

"Malia comes home on Friday."

"She did. This is *next* Wednesday. She came to see you last night."

"Why am I here?"

"Do you remember taking drugs?"

"What drugs?"

"Heroin."

"Oh, no. I would never take heroin. I hate drugs."

"Someone gave it to you. Does the name 'Wally' sound familiar?"

"Yes. No. I'm not sure. I think I played golf. My arm hurts. What are these marks on my arms?"

"Needle tracks."

"They hurt. My head hurts."

"I'm not surprised."

"Why did someone give me heroin? I didn't mean to take it."

"We don't know exactly who or why. Do you know where you have been?"

"I think I'm in a hospital. I remember my office. And playing golf. I had a golf cart. I think I hit something. Oh, I've got a beard. Did I go camping?"

"Do you remember Malia coming in last night?"

"Malia came to see me?"

"Yes, last night."

"Don't tell her I had heroin."

"I think you should tell her everything. She cares about you a lot."

"I'm a school principal. I don't do drugs. My arm hurts."

"How is your head?"

"The lights are too bright. They hurt my eyes, my head. Oh, I smell bad, too."

"That's easy to fix. Tell you what. Let's get you showered, cleaned up. Have breakfast. Let you walk around for awhile. Then rest a bit and have lunch. You might be able to go home this afternoon."

"Home this afternoon."

Over coffee Dan asked Sarah, "How does it feel to own property on Maui?"

"A year ago, if you had told me that I'd be a homeowner in Hawai'i, I'd have laughed in your face. But a year ago we hadn't met."

"So, is the rumor true that your wedding dress is the outfit I first met you in?"

"Who told?" Sarah teased. "You know, Diane would love to wear hers again."

"Maybe we can go on that riverboat cruise again some day…with her and Gabe, of course. Think they have those lady gambler costumes?"

"Maybe. I still have my Queen of Hearts."

"So do I," Dan said, smiling. "Think you'd like me in a handlebar moustache?"

"I think you'd have babies pulling on it all day long. Anyway, are you sure you want to look like General Custer?"

"OK, you talked me out of it."

"No way, cowboy. You don't get to blame me for your facial hair decisions." Sarah got up to refill their coffee mugs and changed the subject before the topic shifted to facial hair she may have some day. "So who's coming in today?"

"Nice try…changing the subject. Don't worry. I'll still love you when you have a moustache."

"Like this?" Sarah had poured milk in her mug and displayed an impressive milk moustache.

"It's you. Uh-oh, get Lucy! She's drifting away from the paper."

"No, perfect aim. Good girl. Liliana is going to love you, Lucy. I wonder how Paco is doing on the boat. I bet he's got plenty of attention from the divers."

Diane came out of the bedroom, saying, "Particularly when he pees on their wet suits. Love your moustache, sis. Say, did I dream that we got the house?"

"If you did, so did we," replied Dan. "You sure there are enough bathrooms for you?"

"*Just.* I can't believe I'm going to own property in Hawai'i." Diane fixed her coffee and joined Sarah and Dan. "Refresh my memory: who's coming in today besides Mom and Dad?"

Sarah responded, "I wrote it down, since it's going to get pretty crazy starting today. Let's see... Mom and Dad this afternoon. Dan's folks, too. Same flight from L.A. Dan's sister Stephanie and his brothers are coming tomorrow afternoon with all the kids. Uncle Dick and Aunt Julie, too. College friends, Dan's colleagues, and other sordid types—some tomorrow, some on Friday. We're only responsible for picking up parents. Diane, can you drive, too, so we have room for everyone and their luggage?"

"I live to serve the Queen of Hearts."

"Of course you do. I'll have more coffee now."

"As you wish. However, you're on your own this morning. I have a flight, so I need to get myself moving. I'll meet you at the airport."

"See how quickly she takes advantage of my good nature," teased Sarah. "Very well. You may go."

"Some day, sis. Some day," said Diane, rolling her eyes.

"That's what we're hoping for," said Her Majesty.

George answered the phone and was delighted to hear Malia's voice.

"Malia, you sound like you finally got a good night's sleep."

"For the first time in a week. I want to apologize for being…"

"There's nothing to apologize for. We—Liliana and I—have been so worried about both of you. We're still concerned about Owen, but at least he's safe."

"I have one more favor to ask."

"It's not a favor, but a pleasure, Malia. What can we do?"

"I'm hoping to get Owen home this afternoon and…"

"That's wonderful!"

"Yes, it is. But I'm going to need help getting him home. He's still unsteady, but I know he'll recover faster in his own home."

"No doubt. We'll meet you whenever they release him. Gabe might be able to join us, too, depending on when he gets back."

"Even better. Familiar people, familiar surroundings…"

"That's the best thing."

"Eventually we'll have some answers, but I'm most concerned about getting Owen back on his feet."

"Any idea how long that will take?"

"We just take it one day at a time. He's better today…finally. He asked for me."

"That's great news. How is your hand? Your arm? Your…"

"They're nothing…fine. I'll tell you the whole story some day. I've got to go. Thank you so much."

"Who named this puppy?" asked Terry, Gabe's business partner. "I think they meant '*Paki.*' He's a little squirt."

Gabe responded, laughing, "I taught him everything he knows."

"That's what I was afraid of." Terry laughed in return. "You take the first dive, and I'll take the second. Don't worry; *Pak* and I will be just fine, won't we, boy?"

"Sounds good. I'll brief our divers. Paco, you stay with Terry, OK?"

Gabe's voice was already Paco's signal to pay attention, although he wasn't pleased to be enclosed in his crate while the divers prepared for their first dive.

"All right, folks. This site is known as 'Nahuna Point.' You all signed your last wills and testaments, leaving everything to me, right? Just in case you don't make it, we won't have to carry you far. This place is also known as 'Five Graves.' Everyone's feeling good today? Good. This is not a particularly deep dive, 40 or 50 feet, but we've got caves and a shark or two. White tip. Gavin, you said you wanted to see a shark. There's a good chance he'll be there. Sometimes we have to navigate into the caves to see them. If you don't want to go into the caves, let your buddy know now. It's OK, and we'll pair you up with a non-spelunking buddy. Come on now; be honest. There are plenty of fish and turtles to see, so you won't miss out. Much. Good—let's put you two together, Marilyn and David. Have you met? You're now best friends. Did your death-defying spouses leave their wills with you? They left you everything? Good. So, John and Janet, you're buddies now as we go into the jaws of…just kidding. These sharks are not interested in us, and we won't be doing anything to change that."

Gabe continued his briefing. "It can be tight quarters in there, and it's possible you'll bump into a shark. Anyone else want to join Marilyn and David? No? Well, if you get down there and decide you don't want to go in, just get my attention and signal that you are staying outside the caves. That means, buddies: you have to go along with him or her, right? You're a team. Now, here's how we enter the water…"

Excitement tempered by anxiety filled the group as everyone squeezed into their wet suits. They donned their backpacks with tanks and buoyancy control devices ("BC's" in dive language) attached, and prepared themselves physically and mentally for the adventure. They checked their regulators, made sure they could reach their alternate air source or "octopus," and familiarized themselves with the depth gauge, the air pressure gauge, and the inflator / deflator. They adjusted their weight belts to keep them from riding around on their hips and throwing off their balance. They also checked their buddies' equipment, untwisting belts and connections that couldn't easily be seen or felt by the divers themselves, but could be uncomfortable and difficult to adjust once under water. Many put on gloves, knowing that the cave walls were likely to be rough and unavoidable in the ocean swells. Snorkels were detached from their masks, since they could get stuck in the tight quarters, potentially pulling the masks off the divers. They defogged their masks and adjusted fins to be secure but not so tight that they cut off circulation. Some prayed silently waiting their turn to enter the water. One by one, each diver sat on the edge of the boat, inserted his mouthpiece, held his mask to his face, and entered the water feet first. They deflated their BC's and slowly descended to the rest of the diving party waiting below. Gabe was first to reach the bottom and asked each diver individually to indicate his or her readiness to proceed. Each responded with the 'OK' hand signal, and Gabe indicated the direction they were heading. Buddies verified their partners' presence and swam alongside one another, glad to be off the boat and into the environment they were dressed for.

Almost immediately a green sea turtle swam by overhead, and the group slowed their progress to observe the creature. They would see several more at the turtle "cleaning station," as well as one large eel that surprised everyone when it burst forth from its small crevasse, escaping into the distance.

Gabe rousted a reluctant spiny lobster from its den, letting it take refuge again once the divers had seen it. An eagle ray floated by leisurely, apparently accustomed to the funny looking, bubbling sea creatures, nonetheless giving them a wide berth.

As the party approached the ledges and caves, Gabe turned around to ask each diver for the reading on his air supply. Most signaled '12' with their hands, indicating 1200 psi of air remaining, an acceptable level.

Swimming into potentially hazardous areas often caused people to use up their air faster. All the divers approached the ledges and scanned the area for sleeping sharks. Janet pointed out the first one 20 feet away, and soon the natural camouflage of the reef revealed its secrets, allowing another shark to be seen. The divers adjusted their BC's to maintain neutral buoyancy in their current positions so they could observe but not disturb the sharks. After a few minutes, Gabe invited the divers into the caves. Buddies checked with one another, and all but the two most experienced divers elected to stay where they were. This dive had already proven to be unforgettable, and a venture into close quarters seemed unnecessary.

Gabe escorted Jim and Chris into the caves, frequently looking back to check their progress. Former U.S. Marines, they were strong and capable, and Gabe was cautiously confident in their abilities. They happened upon another sleeping shark and proceeded no further, simply admiring the lithe animal from a safe distance. Jim and Chris silently applauded Gabe, and he bowed formally, before advising them to turn around and swim back out to join the rest of the party, with Gabe behind them. As they neared the entrance of the cave, another shark came around the corner into the cave, roughly bumping into Chris, knocking his regulator out of his mouth and causing him to bump up against the wall of the cave. Jim immediately got hold of his buddy and replaced the regulator, making sure it was functioning. He grabbed hold of his Chris' BC and brought him out into an open area to assess his condition. Chris signaled 'OK,' but Jim kept hold of him. Chris' mask was ajar, with water was halfway up the glass, but he was alert and proceeded to clear his mask himself. Gabe joined the scene and verified all was well, saying a silent prayer that Chris was OK. He gathered up the rest of the party, checked pressure gauges, and headed back to where the boat was anchored. The cave divers ascended first, followed by the divers with the least air remaining. Gabe was last, making sure no one dropped weight belts or anything else. He then ascended, anxious to verify that the diver was indeed fine.

On board, everyone was discussing Chris' "close encounter with Jaws, Jr." Chris peeled back his wet suit to reveal red marks from being bounced against the cave. A cut on his forehead completed the injuries, but somehow Gabe didn't think the man cared.

"They don't call you 'leathernecks' for nothing," said Terry.

"I wouldn't have missed it for the world," said Chris. "Kind of like boot camp, huh Jim?"

"Just one more time I had to rescue you," said Jim, teasing his buddy and relieved that he was fine.

"That makes it twice for me and about eight times for you," said Chris in retort.

"I can't help it if the ladies like me better," countered Jim.

"It's your choice of, uh, *ladies,* that gets you in trouble," Chris protested shaking his head.

Gabe tended the cut and affixed a waterproof bandage. "We don't want you attracting the big ones, you know. You should know that I can swim a lot faster than you."

Gabe took over as boat captain while Terry described the second, shallower dive off Wailea. Paco was released from captivity but ordered to stay close to Gabe, out of the way of the divers and their gear. He was learning fast. Gabe was looking forward to 30 minutes alone with his puppy while everyone else was diving. Once they had moved into the house, swimming lessons would be mandatory. He wanted to make sure Paco was comfortable in and around the water.

Once all the divers had descended on their second dive, an amazing peace settled on the boat. With no voices to be heard, other sounds had their turn. Flags flapped in the breeze that was gradually building as the sun rose higher. The anchor line squeaked in protest of its captivity, waves splashed on the sides of the boat, and the ever-present sea birds added to the symphony that routinely played aboard a dive boat. Paco was keen on all the new smells and sounds, and especially a twist of rope that Gabe gave him to chew on. Gabe readied the space for the return of the divers and the conclusion of their day at sea. He made sure sunglasses weren't lying around for someone to sit on, and hats were weighted so they wouldn't fly away. He refreshed snacks for the thirsty and hungry divers. Air in the aluminum tanks was very dry to avoid oxidation of the metal and a buildup of water. As a result, the divers would be parched, ironic considering the environment they had just come from. He refilled and hung the solar heated black shower bag with fresh water so salt water would not drip into the divers' eyes. He stowed away anything the divers were likely to want to stay dry. The transition back to being landlubbers was clumsy and wet. Divers would be eager to unload tanks, weight belts, and fins that had allowed them the privilege of surviving more or less comfortably in the alien environment only moments earlier.

The first diver's head popped up and Gabe positioned himself above the ladder to accept the dripping fins handed to him so the diver could climb the steps. Once seated on the edge of the boat, the diver detached himself from his backpack and Gabe lifted it off, so the diver could reboard and get out of the way for the next person. Gabe knew that it would be awhile before his new class of young divers would develop such smooth reboarding procedures that seasoned divers practiced naturally. He smiled to himself, imagining having to haul Thomas up off the ladder, with one or more of his fins floating away, and his weight belt falling back into the ocean.

I was there once.

Tears of joy spilled down Liliana's face when she saw Lucy. "She is adorable! I don't know why I'm being so melodramatic. Maybe it's because she's so happy and carefree, and it's just what I needed after this past week. Lucy, come! Oh, she's peeing…on the paper! Good girl!"

Sarah said, "She *is* a good girl. Paco doesn't have quite as good an aim, but he and Gabe are joined at the hip. It will be good for the two dogs to play together once they've moved into the house."

"The house! I'd forgotten! Did you get it?"

Sarah nodded, saying, "There are some pictures over there. It's really nice, and it has enough bathrooms for Diane. I'll get Lucy's food together for you. Do the boys know yet?"

"No. They've done a really good job on the landscaping. They're very proud of what they've done and said they can't wait for everyone to see it. You should have seen Thomas figuring out how much grass seed they needed. Micah's not much of a math student, but he's so much better after being in your class. Lucy will be a nice surprise for all of them. But I'm selfishly looking forward to her being all mine when school starts again."

The two chatted about Owen, the imminent arrival of the parents, and plans for the rest of the week. Having completed a round of phone calls back home, Dan emerged from the bedroom and joined the conversation on the floor.

"So, what do you think, Liliana?"

"Which one? I love both the house and Lucy. No, Lucy, my toes are not for chewing."

"I will miss her," said Sarah. "She's very smart. Paco is, too. He's going to be a lot bigger than she will be."

Liliana added, "I can't wait to see him. I'm happy that I'll no longer be so vastly outnumbered by men!"

"The daughter you always wished you had," joked Dan. He bit his tongue realizing that he really didn't know Liliana well enough to assume that there were no other children in her history. He was used to knowing his patients' lives almost from their first breaths.

But Liliana was obviously happy. "Oh, I love *all* my boys. Still, we'll teach them a few things, won't we, Lucy? She's very dainty, isn't she?"

"Wally, it's Duke. Are you OK?"

"Man, this place is a dump. I'm out of the way, but it's pretty seedy over here."

"You're sure no one knows where you are?"

"Yeah, I'm over at…"

"Don't tell me. Is there anything you need?"

"I just got groceries yesterday on Moloka'i before that stupid bitch ran out on me."

She doesn't sound so stupid to me.

"Just keep low and see if you can throw a tarp over anything that identifies the boat."

"How long do I have to stay out of sight?"

"Not long." *Forever. Now you've got two people who can identify you, not counting the Principal.* "I'll call you later."

"Mom! Dad! Over here!" Sarah, Dan, and Diane all called out to their parents arriving from Los Angeles on the same flight. Understandably bedraggled after ten hours on multiple planes, the four parents all perked up when they saw their children.

"You figured out who one another was!" exclaimed Sarah, happy to see the parents arriving together.

Her mother said, "Dear, take a look at Carl and this picture of Dan. We now know what Dan will look like in 30 years!"

"He should be so lucky! I'm so much better-looking," teased Carl, hugging his intended daughter-in-law.

"Absolutely. We're so excited that you all are finally here!"

The parents were simultaneously relieved of their bulky hand luggage and adorned with leis.

"You're really here, and this makes it official!" Sarah said. "I hope the flights were OK. I'm sure you're exhausted, and we have just the cure. Wait 'til you see the hotel. Dad, I hope you brought your camera."

"You've got to be kidding," said her mother, rolling her eyes. "Where's the mysterious Gabriel?"

"He's finishing up a dive tour and will join us later." Diane looked briefly at Sarah, who approved her avoidance of the Owen subject for the time being. "Besides, there's more room for you and your luggage. Let's get out of here! How about the guys get the luggage and we head over to the beach?"

Sarah laughed, "See how my maid of honor takes charge, making sure I don't do anything that might break a nail?"

Owen was beginning to feel some measure of peace for the first time in over a week. He was home. Still exhausted, with a persistent headache and muscle aches, the familiar surroundings would be the catalyst for his recovery. George and Liliana left so that there would be fewer people for

Owen to interact with. Gabe stayed to help Malia and to verify Owen's trustworthiness. Temptation was one needle away. Although there was no heroin in the house, Owen could resort to an act of desperation that could result in harm to himself or Malia. Malia fixed lunch consisting of some of her husband's most familiar food, all the while keeping her eyes on him. Both she and Gabe were gauging his behavior to see what he might do. It was clear that he was still suffering from withdrawal, but he was fighting it.

"Thank you for bringing me home, Gabe."

"It was something we all looked forward to, Owen," said Gabe. "I can only imagine what you have been going through. Do you feel like talking about it?"

"I can't remember much, mostly the way I physically sensed things. Smells. I felt good and bad—at the same time. I was alone a lot. Hungry, too. They say I broke into a warehouse?"

"I think that theory is being revised. It's more likely someone put you there."

"I remember being on the golf course. I didn't imagine it. You know, it was the smell of the grass, and the weight of the golf clubs on my back. And I was in a golf cart. I remember the sound of the electric motor."

"No one doubts you were on a golf cart. You crashed one in the warehouse."

"I remember that now, just now that you bring it up. But I *was* on a golf course."

"Did you play golf?"

"I can't remember. Maybe. Why would I be on a golf course?"

"I have no idea. Do you remember being in your office?"

"I remember school, the hallways, feeling like I couldn't go where I wanted. Like in a dream, where you're trying to walk down a hallway, but your legs won't move. My head hurt a lot. The sound of lockers crashing. Someone would come in sometimes. A man. Wally. Why would I think his name was Wally? I don't think I know any Wally."

"A student?"

"No, older. I sat at my desk, but I didn't sit at my desk. That makes no sense. I remember something about camping. Did I go camping?"

"Probably not. So, a guy named Wally came by? Black, white, Asian?"

"White. Short."

"Everyone's short compared to you, Owen."

"Shorter than you. He was up to here." Owen pointed to his chest.

"About five-six," Gabe guessed.

"He helped me walk."

"Is that the guy that got you on heroin?"

"I don't remember getting on heroin. How would he do that anyway?"

"You'd have to be willing or incapacitated. Probably the latter. But how? Did somebody knock you out?"

"I don't remember."

"Maybe you saw something you shouldn't see."

"I don't remember."

"Any idea how long you were there?"

"No."

"What did you eat?"

"Fried chicken, sandwiches. I slept there. I just remembered! I slept there. On the Interrogation Sofa. You know the one."

Gabe smiled, recalling the piece of furniture the students called the Interrogation Sofa in the Vice Principal's office.

Malia said, "The police still think he might be in danger, so they are going to be outside a lot over the next few days, at least until they figure out what happened."

"I think you should go stay with your family, Malia," said Owen.

"No chance of that, husband. I think I can handle anything someone throws my way. Besides, the police are out there. We'll be fine."

Owen did not yet know of Malia's kidnap and escape. There would be time for that later. He was obviously tiring, and Gabe decided that this interrogation had reached a limit for the day. Malia came over and joined her husband, who welcomed her in his embrace. Owen said, "Thank you for believing in me, my love."

"I never doubted you. I was mad at you, yes. Not returning my calls and all. Very rude."

Both laughed softly. It felt good to be a little playful.

"How did you hurt your hand, Malia? Why is there a bruise on your face?" asked Owen, noticing them for the first time.

"That's another story for another time. It's nothing really. I think you should rest now. I'm not going to let you out of my sight for a long time."

"I am tired; I think I'll take a nap. Just don't let me sleep through supper."

Malia laughed. "I think I have my husband back, Gabe."

Duke had never killed anyone. He didn't want to start now. He knew people who had been killed, and he knew people who killed them. Somehow not being personally responsible for the murder—yes, that's what it was—absolved him of the blame...didn't it? He wondered if he could actually commit murder under any circumstances. Maybe if he was backed into a corner, as in self-defense. Wally. Wally had just about backed Duke into a corner. Wally knew too much: where Duke lived and how he made his living. Duke was sure that no one in Cho's employ would think twice about removing such a security breach. It was simply a cost of doing business. Stupidity was too costly in any business. All Duke had to do was find out where Wally was and suggest to Cho that there was a possible breach in security. Duke needn't know where, when, or who took care of the problem. That was someone else's job. He was on a need-to-know basis, and he did not need to know. Did not *want* to know.

The problem was he felt some responsibility, or at least pity, for Wally. Wally was a loser, but it wasn't totally his fault. Some people are born that way. They are a liability to themselves and are easily misled. How much responsibility should someone assume for those who by an unfortunate blip in their genetics can't rise above their innate stupidity? Natural selection in the rest of the animal kingdom would have weeded them out long ago.

Owen—and now his wife—could identify Wally. Wally would give up Duke the instant things became uncomfortable. No one would believe that Wally was in charge of anything. He was a little fish, krill, and the police would want the guy at the top of the food chain, as well as all the ones in the middle.

Duke considered turning himself in, pleading his own stupidity for the life he had chosen. He could ask for witness protection. With his luck, they'd relocate him to North Dakota. Erin would be history. Even if was able to contact her, she'd never leave Hawai'i for someone like him. Who was the loser then? If he turned in Wally as the kidnapper and whatever they call someone who forces someone to take drugs, Wally was as good as dead. He wouldn't last a day in prison.

The walls of Duke's sand castle were caving in. It was only a matter of time before the tides reduced the whole thing to an insignificant mound on the beach.

The pounding of the surf kept getting louder and louder. Duke covered his ears, but the waves called out to him by name. Then he realized that it wasn't the waves, but someone knocking on his door. He shuddered, remembering that his defenses were weakened, but rose to answer the door if for no other reason than to make the noise stop.

"Duke! It's Erin! Are you there? Are you OK?"

"Coming. Just a second." Duke rubbed his face with his hands to bring himself back to reality and consciousness. He opened the door to see Erin trying to balance food containers while knocking on the door.

"Let me help you with that. I'm sorry. I was sound asleep. Were you knocking on the door long?"

"I'm sorry I awakened you. I figured you might be hungry and I brought you some food and I'll just leave it here so you can go back to sleep and…"

"Wow, thank you! That looks great. What time is it?"

"About 4:00. How are you feeling?"

"Better, actually. It's good to see you. I'm awake now. Come, sit down."

"How about *you* sit down, and I'll bring you some food over to the table."

"You convinced me. Something smells really good."

"It's my homemade chicken pot pie. Comfort food. I don't make this for just anyone, just the lame and unlucky."

"I meet both criteria, although I am starting to feel luckier. Oh, this looks fantastic. What are those things in there?"

"Those are vegetables."

"Where's the cardboard?"

Erin giggled and said, "I knew I forgot one of the ingredients."

"This is so good. Thank you."

"You're welcome. It's good to see you not hunched over. I think there's enough for tomorrow. I have to go to Moloka'i tomorrow. Is there anything else you need?"

"Yes, come here, please."

Maybe she would come to North Dakota.

"Daughter, I raised you well," said Carolyn Donovan. "When you said we would have dinner for eight at the beach, I had no idea. This is gorgeous. Clearly these are my genes showing forth."

"You see why we love it here?" queried Sarah. "Diane, did you bring photos of the house?"

"Here," said Diane. "The four of us bought a house."

"The *four* of you? I hope it has enough bathrooms…"

"No more about the bathrooms!" protested Diane. "It has three."

"*Those* aren't my genes either," teased Will Donovan. "How about a photo of all the ladies?"

Carolyn said, "That will make a picture of the ladies from each of the dinner courses. Here's one of the ladies having cocktails. Here they are having salads. Notice Sarah has her dressing on the side. Oh, and there's a good one of Pru buttering her roll…"

"See what I've had to put up with in a house full of women all these years, Carl?" pleaded Will.

Carolyn continued, ignoring him. "Here they are going to the ladies room. Here they are coming back from the ladies room…"

Dan interrupted, saying, "How about a photo of the ladies on the beach?"

"You've got a very smart man here, Sarah," said Will to his daughter.

"What was that fish again?" asked Pru, changing the subject. "It was delicious."

"*Ono*," replied Gabe.

"Why not?" Pru asked, taken aback at Gabe's response.

"*Ono*, that's the name of the fish: *ono*."

Pru laughed at her own unintended joke. "Really?"

"Oh, yes," laughed Sarah. "Sorry, Pru, but someone had to be the brunt of the oldest joke on Maui. You now have permission to try it on the next unsuspecting soul. To the beach, ladies, so Dad can have his picture before the sun sets."

Dan said, "I'll take care of the check."

Will protested, "Just charge it to the room."

"What did you think I was going to do? You did say I was a smart guy," said Dan, teasing his intended father-in-law and pulling out his credit card.

"Mom, where is Lucy going to sleep?" asked Thomas. "Can she sleep with me?"

"How would you like to share your bed with Micah, because that's how big she is going to get."

"No kidding?"

"No kidding."

"I'd rather sleep with her than Micah."

"So would I, Thomas," teased Liliana.

"Can we take her to play with Paco?" asked Micah.

"Sure, when he moves into his new house."

"What new house?"

"Gabe bought a house in Wailuku. It has a pool."

"Neat! Can we go there tomorrow?"

"They don't move in for a month or so. Diane, Dan, and Sarah all bought the house together with him."

"Are Dan and Sarah staying here?" Micah asked hopefully.

"No, but when they come to visit, they'll have a place to stay."

"And we can visit, too?"

"Yes, with Lucy, too."

"We can teach her to swim."

"Good idea," agreed Liliana. "Tomorrow you can take her to the park to show her what you have done."

"There's no grass yet, but she can chase away the birds that keep eating the grass seed."

"She's more likely to herd them together. She's half Australian Shepherd. Don't be surprised if she starts trying to corral you into a clump like sheep. Now, let's try to calm her down so she'll go to sleep. Who's going to get up with her in the morning?"

"Alec," responded both Micah and Thomas.

"Does he know this?" asked Liliana innocently.

"I do now," called Alec from the bathroom.

Sarah, Dan, Diane, and Gabe relaxed at the oceanside bar over coffee before they headed home. Diane said, "I'm surprised Mom and Dad made it this late after the five hour time difference."

Gabe agreed, adding, "When they wake up at three a.m. they'll wish they'd stayed up even later than 8:30."

Sarah said, "We should have told them about the sunrise ride down Mount Haleakala."

Dan responded, "Somehow I can't quite visualize my mother on a bicycle atop a mountain in the middle of the night."

"Dan! Hi, Dan, we're here! Aloha, everyone!"

A startled Dan turned around to meet the last person he hoped or expected to see: Vanessa. Sarah was silent, not believing what she saw. The woman who had tried almost everything to break them up was standing before her, on Sarah's island, apparently here for Sarah's wedding.

"Vanessa, you're here, with…?" asked Dan, standing up to extend the expected hug for someone traveling so far for the wedding.

"Cal Blakely, of course," said Vanessa, who would accept nothing less than a full mouth kiss from Dan. "You invited him and his guest to the wedding. We're here. Cal is still checking in, and I was walking around the grounds when I thought I heard your voice. So, like I said: here we are. Hello, Sarah. Congratulations to you both."

"Thank you, Vanessa. This is my sister Diane and her boyfriend Gabe. Diane, Gabe, this is Vanessa, a friend of Dan's from Chicago. Vanessa, you just arrived?"

"Yes, after a long flight. What are you drinking?"

"Coffee," replied Sarah. "We had dinner with our parents, and we're just about to leave to head home for the night…"

"I don't want any coffee. Anyone up for a Mai Tai? Gabe? And, Diane, is it?"

Gabe answered, "Thank you, but I—we—both have to work tomorrow, and I have to be up very early."

"What do you do, Gabe, as in 'Gabriel?'"

"I'm a SCUBA diver."

"Really? That is so interesting. I would *love* to try that while I'm here. Do you think you could teach me?" She sat down in Dan's chair and talked across Diane to Gabe from a position that gave her cleavage its best view.

"I'm taking anyone who wants to go on Friday morning, snorkeling only, I'm afraid. You're welcome to join the group."

"Sounds like fun," she replied with thinly disguised disappointment at being grouped with what would likely be a bunch of kids and old people. "Sarah, I love your dress. I'm afraid I couldn't wear that color, but it works on you."

"Thanks."

Sarah and Diane cast knowing glances at one another. Gabe got up saying, "I need to get going. Vanessa, it was nice to meet you, and I'm sure I'll be seeing you again." He reached down to kiss Diane, adding, "I'll see you at home. Drive carefully."

"You, too. I won't be far behind you. Yes, I'll see you at home." Diane gave a slight emphasis to the word 'home' to remove any doubt in Vanessa's mind that they were a couple.

Cal Blakely joined the gathering, handing Vanessa her room key and greeting Dan and Sarah warmly.

"Cal, it's always good to see you," said Sarah. She kissed both his cheeks, saying, "Aloha."

"Dan, you don't have to greet me the same way," teased Cal.

"It's tradition over here, buddy," replied Dan, threatening to repeat Sarah's greeting, but extending his hand at the last second. "It's great to have you here. I didn't know you were bringing Vanessa."

"I didn't want to come by myself. Are you OK with it?"

"Of course we are," Sarah said. "We are delighted you are here." She didn't know whether Cal was aware of Vanessa's past antics, but she did know that he had always been attracted to her. It was understandable.

Vanessa was jaw-dropping gorgeous, and she knew it. Any man in her sights was fair game. The more unattainable the prey, the more daring she was in going after it. It was a game for her, and when she succeeded, she simply added a notch in her gun handle and moved on to another target. Now many notches back, Cal was merely a catalyst, an agent that could get her into places where she could ply her trade. Gabe was apparently her next target.

Over Diane's dead body.

With Gabe gone, Vanessa turned her attention back to Dan, although her behavior was slightly more reserved in the presence of her meal ticket for the trip.

"Cal, sweetie, could you get me a Mai Tai? Who else would like one? Dan, Sarah, Deanna?"

"I'm going to pass, since I need to drive home," said Diane, not fooled by Vanessa's obvious and intentional misstatement of her name. "But thank you anyway. It's awfully sweet of you."

"Same goes for me," added Sarah, desperate to be alone with Diane. Vanessa looked hopefully at Dan.

"We really have to go," said Dan.

Vanessa's disappointment was apparent when she put her hands on her hips and pouted, saying, "Well, this is a sorry crowd. Going to bed at 9:00? You're not staying here?"

Dan ignored the last, saying, "I'm surprised you're still awake. Don't give up on our account. I need to get the ladies home. Diane has to work tomorrow, don't you?"

Diane nodded, not because she had to work, but because she sensed Dan wanted a reason to escape. She was happy to oblige.

"We'll see you all tomorrow, I'm sure," said Dan. "Enjoy the evening."

Vanessa rose to embrace Dan, who responded stiffly, quickly extricating himself before he was subjected to another lip lock, putting his arms around Sarah and Diane to escort them out.

Out in the parking lot, Dan said, "Sarah, why don't you ride with Diane, and I'll follow you. I can only imagine what you two have to talk about." He laughed and saw the sisters safely to Diane's car before heading to Sarah's car to follow them home.

On the 40 minute drive home, Diane said, "She is a piece of work. She's the one that created all the trouble last year?"

"That's the one," said Sarah. "You know she has her hooks out for Gabe."

"Over my dead body. His, too, for that matter."

"Funny, I was thinking the same thing. Your maid-of-honor job just got harder. Never mind my finger nails; you're a body guard now. And it's not my body that needs guarding. It's every man at the wedding, pretty much regardless of marital status or age. Now you see how devious she is. I only wish I had known about her earlier."

"Did Dan ever…?"

"No. That's why she was desperate. He was—and is—immune to her wiles. It was incomprehensible to her. I obviously still don't trust her. But I'm not letting her ruin our wedding, even if I have to send her packing."

"If anyone has to do that, it will be me. I have just as much motivation. I also don't feel like I have to be as gracious to her as you do. I simply don't care what she thinks of me. Did you notice she called Gabe 'Gabriel?'"

"She called him Gabriel and you Deanna. Not too obvious, huh?"

"Oh, Gabriel, could you take me diving? Oh, Gabriel, I want a wet suit that has cleavage. I'll show you cleavage, Vanessa."

"You more than me," teased Sarah.

"It's war. She's declared war. She's getting war."

"So, you don't think she has a chance with Gabe?" Sarah asked innocently.

"Over my dead body."

Wally drove by Owen's house to try to see who was there. He wished the car he had borrowed from one of the other boat owners wasn't so noisy, like it needed a new muffler. All he needed was to be pulled over by the police for "failure to maintain his vehicle in good working order." It was a classic "Maui Cruiser," 20+ years old, held together by bird droppings, bumper stickers, and tree sap that kept a perpetual sticky residue on the surface. Tomorrow he would ask somebody to follow him over to the other marina to get his van.

Wally felt adrenaline rush through his system when he saw Malia at the window. He hoped she didn't recognize him since he wasn't driving the van. She closed the curtains and Wally lost his view into the house. He needed to know if Owen was there as well. He parked the car on the street behind Owen's house and walked over to side of the house, listening for voices. A police car drove by and parked out front.

Shit. I'm dead. She must have seen me and called the cops.

Wally waited, but no one got out of the police car. He heard the phone ring in the house. Malia's voice was muffled, but it sounded like she was talking to the police outside. The conversation was short, and at its conclusion the police car remained parked with no one emerging.

Are they going to stay there all night? I need to get out of here.

There was still too much neighborhood activity to risk venturing into someone else's back yard. He had come this far, and he was determined to find out if Owen was home. He wasn't sure if that was where he hoped Owen was, but, in any case, knowing was better than not knowing.

It started raining, and Wally cursed his bad luck until he realized that the sound of the rain would muffle the sound of his movements as he hugged the shadows, hoping for a view into an uncurtained window. The back yard was private enough that curtains would be an unnecessary impediment to air flow through the house. He hoped the Hoana's weren't paranoid about someone creeping around in their back yard at night looking in windows.

Deep in the shadows of the yard he found a lawn chair. He got comfortable while the neighborhood gradually declared an end to Wednesday and settled into the night. Eventually he heard the police car drive away and decided to risk looking into the master bedroom. It had windows on three sides, one facing the street. The room had a faint glow from the street light, and Wally's heart skipped a beat when he saw Owen's large silhouette lying on the bed, wrapped around the small form of his wife. Both slept facing the street, so Wally could observe them undetected. The rain's intensity increased, and Wally decided the noise would muffle his escape to his car on the back street.

I just have to figure out what to do now. I'll call Duke; he'll know what to do. No, Duke told me not to go anywhere. He'll be mad at me for coming here. That's easy for him to say; no one knows who he is. HoHo and now his stupid wife have seen me. This is my problem.

Thursday, July 9

"Do you want me to put Vanessa on a plane and send her home?" asked Dan.

"Yes! No. I don't know. I simply don't trust her." Sarah rubbed her forehead, trying to figure out what she wanted to do. "She will lie about anything to anyone. I used to be naïve enough to believe her myself."

"You're not the only one."

"Which means she's going to try it again. Is there any reason why we should not expect her to try it here?"

"None that I can think of."

They heard a key turn in the lock, and were surprised to see Diane coming home at such an early hour.

"I just dropped Gabe off at the warehouse so you two can have another car. See how thoughtful your Maid of Honor is?" She joined Dan and Sarah on the lanai, saying, "Are you guys still talking about Cat Woman? She's my problem this weekend. Mine and Dan's sister Stephanie's. It's in paragraph five of the bridesmaid job description. If you send her home, you'll just feel guilty for throwing someone out of the party. I *guarantee* that she won't be a problem. At worst, she'll be a source of amusement. But we're not going to let her take over the party."

"I'm sure this is just bridal neurosis," said Sarah, relieved that her sister as well as Dan's would keep Vanessa under control. "She's really devious, you know. It will take both of you to handle her."

"Hey—it's me!" laughed Diane.

"Good point," agreed Sarah. "Anyway, I'm tired of what she brings out in me. I need to just to face her and kick her butt back on the airplane."

"If anyone is going to send her home, it will be Stephanie and me," said Diane. "Consider this a non-problem. You have other problems—dealing with the relatives from hell showing up today, the ones you consciously did invite, although I don't know why. I'll trade you four Vanessa's for one Cousin Eddie." Changing the subject, Diane said, "I have a long day ahead of me so I can get the next two days off. I'll see you at the bachelorette party. It will be a good opportunity for us to define Vanessa's parameters to her."

"Now what are you thinking?" queried Sarah with a wicked look in her eye.

"Now don't you worry your pretty little head about it," teased Diane.

Dan said wistfully, "I think the bachelorette party sounds like more fun than the bachelor party. Maybe I'll…"

"No!" Sarah and Diane exclaimed together.

"Who's Cousin Eddie?" asked Dan. "I thought there was an Uncle Ed."

"I'm out of here," called Diane. "Sarah will explain. This ought to be good."

"Sarah?" asked Dan lyrically. "Who's Cousin Eddie? Is he on the mostly normal side of your family that I've already heard about?"

"You know what they say—'Normal is just a setting on the dryer.'"

"We're going to have to get genetic testing."

"He's really only a half-cousin. My Uncle Ed's son from a previous marriage. There's no blood relation, the fact of which I am immensely grateful."

"Can we fix him up with Vanessa? That would mean all the potential problems would be concentrated."

"I'm not sure I would wish Cousin Eddie on anyone, but I might make an exception in Vanessa's case." Sarah got quiet, and then started to giggle.

"What is it?" asked Dan.

"I think that could be an interesting pairing," she laughed.

"Malia, I need to get out." Owen sat at the kitchen table, drinking coffee, looking out the window. "Is there any reason I can't go some place—even my office?"

Malia looked at him, realizing that he didn't know anything about Principal Crockett or her own kidnapping. Was it too soon to tell him? She herself did not know how Principal Crockett was doing, but sooner or later Owen had to learn what had happened.

"How do you feel? Are you starting to remember things yet?"

"It's more like bits of a dream. I remember feeling really good, and then feeling like death."

"Do you remember Wally?"

"More and more, who was he?"

"Let me fill you in on what you don't know, and maybe you can help fill in some of the gaps in what I know."

"OK, but I really want to get out. I'm feeling fidgety, like I'm going stir-crazy. Let's go to the park, OK?"

"Good idea. It will do us both good to get out. I'll pack us a lunch. I should do the driving, but maybe you can find the picnic cooler."

Owen wrapped his arms around his wife and said, "Thank you."

"For what?"

He did not answer.

"Mom! Lucy just pooped."

"Outside?"

"Yes."

"Thomas, you don't need to report on every one of Lucy's bodily functions. Did you clean it up?"

"What? No way."

"You'd rather just wait and step in it when you're barefoot?" Then under her breath, "Just wait until you're a father some day."

"What?"

"Here...take the plastic bag. You can do this. Remember, you wanted a dog."

"Mom..." Thomas started to whine.

"I could have sworn that sounded like whining, Thomas."

"What about Alec and Micah?"

"Did they poop, too?"

"You know what I mean!"

"No one is excused from cleaning up after Lucy."

"You and Dad?"

"No, us neither. I've already cleaned up three times. Let's see that makes Mom: 3, Thomas: 0. Guess it's your turn. I'll be over in the church getting ready for Mama Lani's funeral."

"Are we going to the funeral?"

"Do you want to?"

"I guess. She was a nice lady."

"Yes, she was."

"It seemed like she was always old."

"Most of us didn't know her when she was young. They've got some photos of her on display when she was young. You might be surprised to see pictures of her at your age."

"I'll come with you."

"After you clean up Lucy's mess."

"Oh yeah, I forgot."

"Good thing I'm here to remind you."

The phone rang, and Duke knew he had to answer it.

"Good morning, Duke. How are you feeling today?"

"Just fine, Mr. Cho. How are you?"

"Well, frankly, Duke. I've been better. I hear that our jumbo associate has recovered enough to go home. And his wife is with him."

The icy calm in Cho's voice was unmistakable. Duke would prefer it if the guy just yelled at him. It was probably one of the secrets of Cho's success, however. From the tone of his voice, you might think he was just complaining about the newspaper arriving late.

Cho continued his indictment of Duke's inefficiency in the handling of the business affairs that had been entrusted to him.

"I was also surprised to learn that you now have a lady friend in your life. I am a little concerned that such a relationship might be a distraction whose timing is most unfortunate right now, particularly considering the added security risks that you have allowed to develop."

Duke felt the adrenaline rush to his head, nearly causing him to pass out. *You leave Erin alone, you son of a bitch.*

"I can assure you, Mr. Cho, that the lady is not a distraction. She's not even on the island anymore."

"Excellent timing, I must say. But coincidentally I was surprised to meet a lady pilot who also seems to have made your acquaintance. Duke, you have been getting around."

"I don't think I know any lady pilots."

"She knew you. Name is Diane Donovan. She knew all about you and your golf equipment business. That's a good one, Duke: golf equipment business."

"I'm not sure I know her..." *Oh shit, that's one of the girls we met on the fireworks cruise.*

"Duke, this is not the time to expand your social life. Surely you must know that."

"Yes, of course, Mr. Cho. I do apologize for any slight indiscretion, and I can assure you that none of the plans have been or will be compromised."

"Of course they won't, Duke. I know that you've already met Edgar. Well, he is going to keep you company for a couple of days. That should be enough social contact for you, particularly now that your lady friend has left."

"Oh, I'm fine, Mr. Cho. You really don't have to..."

But Cho had hung up.

Duke hung his head in his hands and wondered how long he would have before Edgar the Horrible showed up. A matter of minutes at most. He wondered if Edgar was coming to kill him or just to ensure that Duke had no more distractions in his life. He decided to make a quick call to Erin's cell phone; it might be the last opportunity he would have for awhile. There was no answer, which was a relief. He wasn't prepared to answer questions.

"Erin, it's Duke. I know you're probably on your way to Moloka'i, and well, I thought about your invitation to meet you there. I might be able to find someone to cover for me over the weekend, but I won't know for a couple of days. I'll give you another call one way or the other when I know. Have a safe trip, and I hope to see you soon. Bye."

He hoped he had sounded calm, upbeat, and unhurried. He was tired of being anything but honest with her. Cho was right: she was a distraction—from lying, selfishness, and greed.

There was a loud knock at the door that seemed to say, "You'd better answer it now; next I break it down."

An unsmiling Edgar walked in offering no greeting or even eye contact. Instead he went immediately over to the refrigerator to get a beer. Then he called Cho on his cell phone to report on his whereabouts and Duke's condition. Edgar was a model employee for Cho, ruthless, obedient, and friendless. No distractions in his life.

"Where's the stash?" Edgar asked Duke.

"In the box spring."

"How do we move it out?"

"Golf bags."

"Oh yeah, I heard about your golf equipment business."

"It will work."

"It had better. What do you have for food?"

"Not much. Just an old chicken pot pie. I haven't been feeling well, and I need to get groceries."

"Sounds disgusting. No wonder you're sick. Order a pizza. Large. Pineapple and anchovy."

"Sure." *Chicken pot pie sounds disgusting?*

"Hand me the remote. I'm going to watch TV. Hope you don't mind if I don't watch golf."

"Watch whatever you want."

"I will."

Carolyn and Will Donovan were pleased as they toured the new house with Dan, Sarah, Dan's parents, and the realtor.

"Will, honey, what do you think?" asked Carolyn. "Think we could handle a vacation here?"

"Hmmm...lots of photo opportunities."

"Of course that's important."

"Of course."

"What do you think, Pru?" asked Carolyn of Dan's mother. "Our children have done well, I think."

"Not bad for a motley band of Midwesterners. Dan, when do you think you'll be back again for a visit?"

"Thanksgiving, hopefully. We're both half way to deciding making it permanent. The next Chicago winter may put us over the edge, particularly when we think about last winter." Dan rubbed his chest, feeling the residual effects on his lungs from pneumonia. "Sarah's knee has healed but she has to be careful not to injure it again. But, hey, you can come anytime. Does everyone like dogs?"

"Of course," said Carolyn. "Just another photo opportunity for Will. Who has a dog?"

"Diane and Gabe. Paco: he's the product of night of passion between two star-crossed lovers."

"So were you, dear," teased Pru.

"Yeah, but I was easier to potty train."

"You think so?"

"Time to change the subject. Who's up for lunch?"

Carolyn and Pru caught one another's eye, and Carolyn said, "We thought we'd head back to the hotel with Sarah, and you men folk could explore the surroundings. She can meet some of the St. Louis and Chicago people coming in today. I know Cousin Eddie is dying to see you, Sarah."

Dan started to protest, but then he saw his mother's intense look that seemed to say, *Just go along with it.* The twinkle in her eye convinced him that he had better comply.

"Good idea," he said innocently. "Dad, Will, let's escape from the womenfolk for a bit. We can go beat drums or something. I'm sure we can find something to do on Maui. I was thinking about 'Iao Needle; what do you think, Sarah?"

"Really? I suppose you could take them there. It was such fun the last time we went," she added wryly.

"Yes, and I have an interesting tale to tell."

"That you do. OK, you boys have fun. We'll find something to do. And I can tell you about Diane's landscaping plans for the house; they're positively frightening. When did she start this thing with flamingos? Mom, you have to do something."

Carolyn laughed, "I'll see what I can do."

"Thanks, Mom," said Sarah. She changed the subject. "OK, I'm ready: bring on Cousin Eddie. Say, is he coming alone?"

"I believe so."

"Interesting."

Wally observed his prey undetected. Owen and Malia returned to their picnic area after a walk around the lush Heritage Gardens. Wally made sure they had no reason to suspect they were under surveillance. His van was hidden, as was he. Malia opened a container of cupcakes and offered them to Owen along with a refill of iced tea. He listened to their conversation.

"Can we go see Principal Crockett on the way home?"

"Good idea. Maybe she's starting to remember more details."

"Did Wally give her drugs, too?"

The sound of his name startled Wally, and he felt a rush of adrenaline pulse through his body.

"No, thank God, although I'm not sure which of the two of you was injured the worst. How far back do you remember things?"

"A little more each day. I now remember the day I first saw Wally, or at least the first day I became aware of him as someone more than just some guy who cut grass at school. He was out by his van, and I startled him when he was moving around—what do they call them?—bricks of probably cocaine in the back of his van. I thought he was the guy who was going to paint the bleachers at the football field. I didn't think twice about approaching him; he was on *my* turf."

"Owen, if this is someone you have seen before that worked at the school, someone can figure out who he was. Why didn't you say something?"

"I just remembered it! Must be the cupcakes."

"Have another."

"If you insist."

"He pulled a gun on me."

"Someone was stupid enough to pull a gun on you?"

"Like I said, I startled him. And likewise, the gun and the drugs startled me. I froze in disbelief, like I was someone else observing me from a distance. I thought he was going to shoot me, but maybe he figured the sound would be heard in the neighborhood. So he just closed the van behind him and forced me to go back into the school, into my office."

"So this is a guy that's been working at the school, around students?"

Owen nodded.

I am so busted, Wally screamed silently. *He's coming around too soon. I should have just O.D.'d him like I wanted.*

Wally crept silently back to his van and retrieved the gun he had under the seat. He returned to his observation post to ponder what he needed to do next.

I can't handle both of them. He's too big, and she's too smart. Which one would be the best hostage, and which one could be made to do the drug sale? I can't do nothing about how big Owen is, but maybe I can do something so she's not so smart. I won't make the same mistakes I did the first time. She can't be trusted, so I gotta immobilize her. Not killed. Not yet.

Once again he went back to the van to search for the immobilizer. *Valium. That will do it. Two should be about right. A third one later. I need her to be able to walk. This time she's going to be uncomfortable.*

Sarah entered the dining room ahead of the mothers. Something was not quite right. The other people...she knew them...

"Surprise!"

"What?"

"Surprise, honey!" said the mothers.

"This is for me?" laughed Sarah.

"Who else?"

The room was filled with women who had arrived for the wedding. She knew most of them, except for a few from Chicago that she hadn't met yet.

Pru said, "It's a virtual shower, Sarah."

"A virtual shower?"

"You'll see. Come have some champagne."

"I hope *it's* real. How did you plan this?"

Carolyn said, "You're not the only one who can do these things, you know. Your college sorority sisters set this up. Come, let's go say hi to everyone."

Off to the side was Kahealani Levine, smiling and waving coyly. She then disappeared so the party could proceed as she directed.

Sarah greeted relatives and friends and was escorted to a long private table that had been set up to accommodate all 30 of them on the lanai, in full view of the sweeping lawn that led to the beach. As head conspirator in the surprise shower, her college roommate and bridesmaid Jeannie sat next to her. Dan's sister Stephanie, Sarah's other bridesmaid, sat opposite.

Jeannie said, "I'd have thought you'd have a better tan by now, roommate. Have you been hiding indoors since you've been here? Although I can't say I blame you. I hear Dan is quite a..."

"Yes, he's quite a..." interrupted Sarah, lest Jeannie come out with something typically Jeannie-like. Someone had to protect the dignity of the sisterhood. Then she added, "Thank you for doing this, you rascal."

"I can't believe you didn't know. Or maybe I can believe it. You were always so naïve!"

"Who, me?"

"Yes, you!" echoed the rest of her sorority sisters.

The revelry continued over lunch accompanied by a crisp white wine until Jeannie announced, "OK, let the shower begin! Sarah, we wanted to do this, but we also figured you didn't want to haul back pots and pans and linens and barbeque pits any more than we wanted to stuff them in our luggage. So this is a virtual shower. Ladies?"

At the cue, lavishly decorated envelopes appeared and were passed down to Sarah, along with a few small boxes and a larger one that seemed out of place.

"OK, begin," ordered Jeannie.

"Yes, ma'am."

The first envelope was from Pru, and Sarah opened it to find a photograph of a gas grill framed with designs of hamburgers, steaks, and chicken.

"I get it! These are *pictures* of the gifts. Oh, this is beautiful, Pru. I love it, and so will Dan. You know I think the picture smells like barbeque sauce."

"I think Carl held it over the smoker."

"This is so clever! Thank you!"

"You're very welcome. By the way, it's pork chops?"

"What's pork chops?"

"Your future father-in-law's favorite barbeque dish."

"I think we can handle that."

"Open this one next," ordered Jeannie.

"Dare I?"

"Of course. Don't you trust me?"

"Let's just say, I know you."

Inside was a photograph of His and Hers bathrobes, Dan's tastefully embroidered with his name, Sarah's with a Queen of Hearts.

"How did you know?"

"Your sister."

"Diane! Is she coming?"

"She said she'd be here in awhile, as soon as she picked up Gabe and brought him here. Is he a...too?"

"You'll see," said Sarah, laughing.

"Open the big one next."

"Who's it from?"

"Is there a card?"

"I don't see one."

"Well, maybe it's inside. Open it!"

Sarah carefully undid the wrappings, opening a box stuffed with red tissue paper. Sarah parted the paper to find a black negligee inside. Her face flushed with anger as she recognized the gown that she had discovered in Dan's bureau last year, one that Vanessa had planted there to make Sarah think she was having an affair with him. And she had nearly succeeded.

Control yourself. This is between Vanessa and me. Do not let on.

She composed herself and unfolded the silky gown from the red tissue and held it up for everyone to see. She forced herself to laugh along with everyone else. She glanced down the table, but did not see Vanessa. Sarah wasn't even sure she had ever been there. But there was no other person it could have come from.

Jeannie said, "I bet Dan would like to see you barbeque in that! Oh, it already smells like perfume. Boy, it's really gorgeous. Who's it from? Come on; confess!"

"I know who it's from."

"Who?"

"Vanessa."

"Vanessa who? She's not here. Did I forget to invite someone?"

Carolyn said, "She gave it to me this morning. I had invited her last night, but she said she couldn't come. Is everything OK?"

"Of course."

"Well, it's beautiful. You'll have to be sure to thank her."

"I'll be sure to. Diane! I'm glad you made it!"

"I see you got the surprise," said Diane, greeting her sister with a kiss. Then she turned her head and whispered, "You OK?"

"Fine. Come join us. We'll pull up another chair. Everyone, this is my sister and maid of honor Diane. Diane, this is everyone."

Diane sat down and looked at Sarah doubtfully. Sarah quickly said, "Later." Then louder, "You're just in time to see all the wonderful gifts I'm getting at my virtual shower. Look at these!"

Sarah showed Diane the photos, and then the negligee. Diane started to comment on the gown, but Sarah interrupted, saying, "OK, I'm ready for the next one."

"Dan, so this is where Sarah brought you?" Carl Weatherby teased his son. "Was she bragging or complaining?"

The view of the 1200 foot 'Iao Needle from the lookout was impressive. Clouds danced around the top, but no one could mistake the obvious reference to a celebration of manhood.

Dan avoided answering the question by saying, "Will, I recall it was your other daughter who was ready to build a house here."

"Poor Gabe."

"People say that a lot."

"I'll bet."

"Sarah and Diane didn't tell you about this place?"

"No, why would they?"

"Thanks to both girls, people's lives were saved."

"What do you mean?"

"Come on, I'll show you."

Dan escorted the dads down to the ledge where Alec's mother Angela had tried to kill Liliana as well as Sarah while in a rage brought on by mental delusion. He told the story of how Sarah had kept Angela from carrying out her plan, and how Angela herself had fallen down the cliff. Though firmly standing on the rocky path, the men sought support from the rugged cliff walls while Dan continued the story of how Angela had pushed Gabe over the edge and how Diane had managed to rescue him.

"These are my daughters you're telling me about?" asked Will.

"Yes."

"Why didn't they tell us?"

"Sarah still feels responsible for Angela's death."

"That's ridiculous."

"It's a painful memory, but she also knows that more people got to live that day because of her and Diane's bravery, although she probably would not use that word. You can still see the scars on Gabe, and when he's tired, he walks a little stiffly. You can imagine what those lava rock walls will do to bare skin. I wanted—we both wanted—you to see the place first hand. As much as she would like to undo that day if she could, she thinks she grew up that day. She feels attached to this place—to Maui, and so do I."

The fathers were stunned and became silent looking out over the narrow valley and imagining for themselves what their children had been through that day.

After a few minutes Dan interrupted the silence. "Enough of this melodrama. You guys ready to see some more of Maui?"

"Lead the way."

Back out on the road, Dan was surprised to see Owen coming out of the nearby park alone in a car. He waved, but Owen did not respond, which Dan thought was odd. Owen seemed focused on his driving. He tried to get closer so he could honk the horn at him, but Owen had driven too far ahead.

Tears streamed down Owen's face, and he slammed his fist on the steering wheel. He ordered himself to calm down. He needed to get home safely. To think. And to wait for the phone call from Wally telling him what to do. He would do whatever Wally asked.

Sorry Dan, but I can't talk to you now. He's got Malia, and he'll kill her if I talk to anyone. Where are you Malia? Please be safe. Damn. I'm sorry I couldn't keep you safe.

Malia awoke to the sound of her own moans. She couldn't move, but yet she was moving.

What's making me move? I can't make it stop. Owen, make it stop.

Slowly she returned to consciousness, but everything was spinning. She tried to call out, but something was keeping her from doing so.

Owen, listen. Can you hear me? I'm trying to tell you—come get me.

A door opened and startled her, and she tried to call out to Owen.

Not Owen. Another man. I know him. I know this place. It moves a lot.

"I'm glad to see you're behaving," said Wally. "Don't worry, you won't be wanting to go swimming again. Not that you could. Keep in mind that I have almost no reason to keep you alive." He laughed and slammed the door behind him.

Sarah alternated between cries of anger and tears of frustration. "Diane, do you now see how devious she is? And once again, she got to me. I wasn't prepared."

"She's history. She's leaving. I will personally take care of it," said the Maid of Honor.

"Not till I talk to Dan. But I need to calm down first. Should I tell Mom? She has no clue."

"Maybe. She's pretty tough, you know. And she'll agree with me that we need to send Vanessa packing. And I don't think you need to calm down before you talk to Dan. This may be a side of you he rarely sees, but it's still you. If he can't deal with it, he needs to figure out how."

Sarah collapsed into tears and nodded. "You're right. But the only times he's ever seen me like this is when Vanessa wins her little mind games with me. I'm angry with myself for letting her win again."

Diane moved over to the lanai in their parents' hotel room and became quiet as she peered off into the distance, watching the world go by during an average day in paradise.

"What are you thinking?"

"Give me a minute."

"OK, I'm going to wash my face," said Sarah, but Diane gave no indication that she heard her.

Refreshed and starting to relax a little, Sarah joined Diane on the lanai and waited for her sister to speak.

"Something you said about mind games, it got me thinking. I think we need to go on the offensive," Diane said finally.

"What did you have in mind? No blood. On second thought, blood is OK."

"No, this is better than blood. I'll tell you later. Mom's back."

"Am I going to like it?"

"Oh, yeah."

"Edgar, is it OK if I just take a shower?" Duke asked of his "companion."

"Go ahead."

Duke went into his bedroom and closed the door. He turned on the shower and pulled his muted cell phone out of his pocket, so he could check voice mail. One from Erin, telling him where she was and hopeful that he could join her. He deleted the message and the call log so there would be no trace of it. Another from Wally.

Wally, what are you up to now?

"Hey Duke. It's Thursday afternoon. I'm still on the boat, and I have a lady friend with me. Malia's back. I guess she knew a good thing when she had it. Ha! Anyway, she's not going anywhere, and HoHo—well, I think HoHo will do just about anything we want him to do. He's not going to cause any trouble as long as his wife is with me and he thinks she's still alive. So, give me a call, so I know what the schedule is, and I can guarantee that HoHo will live up to his end of the bargain. How do you like that—'live up to?' Ha ha! Later."

Wally, you're an idiot. So are you, Duke, for that matter.

Duke deleted the message, put the phone back on mute and in his pocket, undressed and got into the shower to think.

Maybe this won't turn out so bad. I just need to figure out a way to not let Owen and his wife die. If they die, North Dakota won't be far enough. What if it's them or Wally? Shit! This was planned to be a simple, highly lucrative business deal. No one died in the plan.

"Hey man, you've been in there forever," Edgar called from outside the bathroom.

"The hot water feels good on my muscles."

"Poor Duke. He's got a little tummy ache. Hurry up. I gotta pee."

Duke turned off the shower, saying, "OK, I'll be out in two minutes. Did the pizza come?"

"Yeah, but it's all gone. Thanks for buying. I found your wallet."

"My pleasure. You might have to go get more beer. Or I could."

"Mr. Cho wants us to stay here until he calls."

"Did he say when that might be?"

"Why? You got a date?"

"No."

"He'll call when he calls."

"That's fine. OK, the bathroom is yours."

"About time. Oh, I've got your car keys in case you were thinking about going out to get beer or something."

"I wasn't planning on going anywhere."

"That's smart."

Duke no longer worried that Edgar had come to kill him, not yet anyway. He would have done so immediately. No, Cho probably thought he still needed him. There was still a good possibility that at some point Duke would be viewed as expendable or even a liability. He was pretty sure that Cho had already cut him out of the profits; this was now an exercise in survival. Realistically that was the best he could hope for. And it didn't depend on anyone but himself. If Duke were to go anywhere it would be the police. He still had a lot to lose, but with Cho he had everything to lose.

Duke heated up Erin's leftover chicken pot pie and ate it while quickly composing an exposé in case he needed it.

At least if he kills me, I'll take comfort in knowing this didn't go to waste. Comfort. I could get used to comfort food. Anything is better than pineapple and anchovy pizza.

Two limousines greeted the bridal party and their friends at the hotel, and everyone piled in for a ride to a cocktail and dinner cruise hosted by the Dan's brother and Best Man Brian, and the Maid of Honor. Sarah wished there had been a chance to talk to Dan about Vanessa, but that would have to wait. She had no idea what her sister was planning for Vanessa, but she no longer felt like she had to deal with her alone. She refused to let Vanessa spoil any more of the wedding even if she had to take matters into her own hand. This was her wedding, Dan's and hers, and nothing was going to stop it or even ruin it.

As Best Man, Brian had been conspiring with Diane on the logistics of the evening. Neither Dan nor Sarah had been able to coax information from either of them on their devious plans, but it was fun to try. And of course it was expected of them.

Brian said, "Don't worry; you're not going on a night dive, to a ballet, or anything else dangerous. Other than that, I think that's all you need to know. What do you think, Diane?"

"You've already told them more than I would have," teased Diane.

"No leper colonies," added Dan.

"We would never…"

"Or cliff diving," added Sarah.

"You guys are no fun," said Diane. "I think we're mostly staying on the island."

"Gabe, there's that 'mostly' word again," cautioned Dan. "Like: our parents are 'mostly' normal."

Diane giggled. "Well, now that you've met them…"

"OK, they're mostly normal. Gabe, help me out here."

"Humuhumunukunukuapua'a," replied Gabe. "I told you, that's my answer for everything."

"Remember: I know about drugs and how to use them. Vee haf vays of making you talk, comrade."

"Scared," said Gabe.

"I'll bet. That was probably not the best joke, but it reminded me that I saw Owen today."

"Did you stop by to see him?" asked Gabe.

"No, when we—the dads and I—were driving out of 'Iao Valley, we saw him pulling out of the park nearby, you know, where we went with George, Liliana, and the boys. I waved at him, and I'm sure he saw me. But he ignored me, and started to drive faster, like he wanted to get away."

"Was Malia with him?"

"I didn't see her. Maybe she was in another car."

"I'm not sure he's supposed to drive yet. Do you think he simply didn't recognize you?"

"It's possible; the first time he ever saw me was when we brought him home from the hospital."

"I'll go see him tomorrow."

Sarah added, "Good. Let him know we're all thinking about him."

"Will do. Now, let's see what they have for us to drink on this land yacht? I know why they tint the windows: so we aren't embarrassed when people see us in this thing."

Brian said, "There's some beer on ice in here."

Gabe said, "OK, I'll stay. This isn't so bad." He looked at Dan and together they said, "Mostly."

Sarah giggled and asked, "How was your afternoon with the dads?"

"Good. They were suitably awestruck by the ' ao Needle. We ritually cut our fingers and dripped blood onto the cliff walls in homage to the god of something—big, uh, rocks, I guess. Made us feel all vigorous and virile."

"V'really?" teased Sarah dryly, fanning herself.

"I heard you had a shower."

"Virtually! Here, I'll show you. Look at these." She handed Dan a decorated folder with photos of the shower gifts inside. "That grill is from your parents. And see the bathrobes."

"Neat! Everything was a picture, so nobody would have to pack it up!"

Diane said, "*Almost* everything."

Sarah gave her a disparaging look for bringing up the sensitive subject.

"What else did you get?" asked Dan innocently.

"Oh, look, we're here," said Sarah with relief. She squeezed Dan's hand, adding, "Tell you later. This is going to be fun! Look, there are George and Liliana. Let's introduce them to our mostly normal families. Come along, my mostly normal fiancé."

A colorful sunset graced the panoramic view the guests enjoyed over dinner. Vanessa was forgotten, and Sarah enjoyed the reunion of family, soon-to-be-family, and friends on both sides. She prepared herself for the inevitable meeting of Cousin Eddie.

He approached her during the salad course, at which point she brought Dan to his feet.

"Dan, I want you to meet my Cousin Eddie. Eddie, my fiancé Dan."

The men shook hands, but Eddie quickly returned to the object of his attention, Sarah's chest. She immediately brought her wine glass up across her chest to continue what she hoped would be a brief conversation. Without looking away from Sarah, he said, "Dan, you're a lucky guy. Sarah and I have known one another for 15 years. She has certainly grown up."

"It happens, Eddie," said Sarah. *If he starts drooling, I'm going to be sick.* "When did you arrive?"

"A few hours ago. I came by myself, but I knew there would be a lot of people to meet. I don't suppose we'll get to play one of our famous games of SCRABBLE."

"I learned long ago not to play SCRABBLE with you, Eddie. You have a way of turning my five-point C-A-T into a million point 'CATASTROPHE.' You're one of a kind."

"That would be UNIQUE—15 points."

"See what I mean?"

"I hope you'll save me a dance on Saturday."

"Only if you promise to give some of the other girls a chance, Eddie. Look around, it's a feast for the eyes." *Bad choice of words, Sarah.*

"Yes, it is," said Eddie, not taking his eyes off Sarah's bosom. "A PLETHORA—63 points, maybe more."

"You're good," said Sarah. "Well, have a good time, and I'm glad you're here."

"Wouldn't have missed it. Nice to meet you, Dan."

"You, too, Eddie."

Then Sarah said lightly, "Oh, Eddie, be sure you introduce yourself to Vanessa. She's over there."

"Right. Oh, RIGHT! I see her. Vanessa, you say? Vanessa, you're about to get very lucky."

Once the cousin was out of earshot Dan said, "There's nothing mostly normal about him."

"He's harmless—mostly. Diane, Stephanie, what are you two snickering about?"

"Nothing—mostly." With that the bridesmaids could no longer

control their laughter, and Sarah looked at Dan, saying, "They're up to something."

"No, you think so?" teased Dan.

After dessert, Sarah and Dan invited George and Liliana over to sit with their parents.

In the shifting of chairs to accommodate two more, Liliana quickly whispered to Sarah, "I met her." She rolled her eyes knowingly.

Sarah smiled and said sweetly, "Uh-huh."

"Lorelei, come sit down here," invited Will.

Sarah whispered, "Liliana, Dad."

"Liliana. Sorry, Liliana."

"No problem," said Liliana graciously.

George said, "Just as long as you don't call her 'Hortense.'"

Liliana glared at him in silent admonishment for revealing the dreaded family nickname George and the boys had concocted for her. She said, "Lorelei will be just fine, Will. I hope you both know what wonderful daughters you have. Sarah's been a joy to get to know, and we will miss her when Dan steals her back to Chicago. Our boys will miss her, too. We're so glad we will still have Diane."

Dan said, "We'll be back, Liliana, and maybe we'll decide to abandon Chicago after all."

Liliana said coyly, "I know it's wicked, but I'm praying for an especially cold winter for you!" Then changing the subject, she asked if this was everyone's first trip to Hawai'i. She advised them on activities for them during their time on the island.

Gabe interrupted, saying, "Snorkeling for anyone who's up for it tomorrow! I have to warn you in advance, the boat sails at 7:30 in the morning."

Stephanie's husband Andy said, "Not a problem! My body will have been up for hours. It will think it's lunchtime. Just when Steph and I have a few days when we don't have to get up at 2 a.m. for feedings, we get stuck in a five—or is it six?—hour jet lag."

"Who's taking care of my nephew and his baby sister?" asked Dan.

"Andy's parents," said Stephanie. "I think your other nephews are with their maternal grandparents. They were all going to have a play date sometime this weekend. That should wear everyone out!"

Gabe stole a look at George and said, "I'm going to go watch the boat dock." George said he would join him. Up on deck, Gabe said, "Dan said he saw Owen today driving out of the Heritage Gardens."

"Sounds like he was ready for some fresh air and a little time with Malia."

"That's just it; he was alone."

"What? Is Dan sure it was Owen?"

"Pretty sure. Malia wasn't with him. Dan tried to get his attention, but Owen ignored him and sped away."

"That is weird."

"I agree."

"I'll call them in the morning. I should probably go see them. I couldn't today. I was tied up with Mama Lani's funeral."

"How was it?"

"Very heartwarming. I think her entire family was there, which apparently is most of the permanent population of Maui. They stood around telling stories about her."

"Well, you always do a good celebration."

"I'm sure she was pleased, but probably upset that we were making such a fuss over her."

"Surely she would forgive you just this once. Say, are you joining us at the bachelor party?"

"Dan invited me, but I think I'll let you guys enjoy the revelry without the priest there to inhibit things. You are taking pictures, aren't you?"

Gabe laughed and said, "Absolutely."

"Any idea where you're going?"

"Brian's in charge; anything goes."

George laughed, adding, "Go in peace," and making the sign of the cross on Gabe's forehead. "Be sure you leave a list of your favorite funeral hymns with Diane."

Gabe laughed and met up with Diane and the rest of the bachelor partygoers out by the limos. She and Brian were directing everyone into one limousine or the other. Dan kept trying to get into Sarah's limo, but Brian made him go with the men. "Come on, baby brother. You belong to me tonight. You'll see Sarah again soon enough."

"George! Please come! You're the only one who can save me!"

George laughed, shouting back at the limo pulling away, "Then you're in worse shape than I thought!"

Diane asked Liliana if she was coming, but Liliana also begged off. "Go! Have fun! Take pictures!"

"No pictures!" shouted Sarah, laughing at her play kidnapping. "Where are you taking me?"

"To your wildest dreams. Actually my wildest dreams."

The limousines separated from one another, the women's heading north, the men's south. Sarah said, "Are we at least staying on the island?"

"Mostly," said both Diane and Stephanie, giggling.

After a short drive they wound up at a hotel near the end of civilization. Torches lit the way as the women walked to a beach location where a large grass canopy had been erected at the edge of the sand. They settled around a large table that had a tall floral centerpiece cleverly formed into the shape of a well—*very* well—endowed man.

"Sit here, Sarah," ordered Diane, "so you can see Bubba. See: he's excited to see you."

"Your dreams are starting to frighten me," giggled Sarah. "Poor Gabe."

"How come everybody keeps saying that? Gabe is fine."

Jeannie asked Diane, "So, who posed for the—uh—centerpiece?"

"Cousin Eddie," said Diane and Sarah together, laughing uncontrollably.

"Have I met him?"

"No, but you can't miss him. We never figured out what color his eyes were, because we never saw them." Diane focused on Sarah's bosom, saying, "Get the picture?"

"He's just near-sighted," giggled Sarah. "Stephanie, what's all that?"

"Just a few little gifts for the blushing bride. Come on, open them up. They're actual presents, not just pictures. And here comes a Mai Tai to loosen you up. See how your attendants take care of you?"

"I'm overwhelmed. All right, Bubba has inspired me: bring on the big one."

"That's my sister. You heard her; hand over the big one."

Sarah screamed with delight when she unwrapped a huge hat made of balloons, flowers, and greenery, obviously constructed by the same hands that built the centerpiece. An obvious celebration of womanhood, it was mostly a pair of giant breasts. Sarah put the hat on and said, "This is one way to get Cousin Eddie to look up!"

"Where's the camera?" called out Diane. "We need a picture with you, Bubba, and your hooters."

"Who keeps drinking my Mai Tai?" complained Sarah.

"Don't worry about it," assured Stephanie. "It's a bottomless glass."

"Speaking of bottomless, open that present there," pointed Diane.

"How come none of these presents have cards with them saying who they're from?"

"They're all from Bubba. Now open it."

Everyone hooted in high-pitched laughed when she held up the crotchless panties.

"Gee, how did you know my size?"

"Bubba knows all. And does it really matter? See, your Mai Tai is filled up again."

"I never drink more than one."

"Right. Next present. Oh, it'll have to wait. Here comes the entertainment."

"There's entertainment?"

"Hush. They're starting."

A slow drum beat started off in the distance, gradually getting louder. A parade of three women and three men marched gracefully into the light from opposite sizes of the makeshift stage and paired off. The women were topless except where their long hair occasionally covered their breasts. The men wore thin loin cloths. All were lavishly adorned with flowers and greenery. Hearts skipped beats when the drums became more intense, and the dancers began their sensuous fertility dance against a background of moonlit waves. The audience mopped their faces with wet napkins.

Jeannie commented hoarsely, "It's a little steamy out here, isn't it?"

After several dances, the lead male dancer came out to the audience and bid Sarah to join him. She shook her head, but soon realized that neither he nor especially the audience would take 'no' for an answer. She ritually handed off her symbolic headwear to Diane. The three female dancers adorned Sarah with leis and a grass skirt and took her to the front to teach her some basic hula moves. Several of her 'friends' urged her to get into the authentic costume theme, but she laughingly declined their suggestions. Sarah got into the rhythm of the drums, and gradually two of the male dancers got on either side of her and swayed in sync with her. Their moves became more daring and passionate as they played off of one another in mock rivalry, each hoping to be the one who would win her as his prize. Two of the female dancers and the other male dancer did the same in reverse. Cameras flashed, and the audience began swaying to the drums. The intensity of the drums increased to a deafening climax, and then quickly ceased. Everyone roared with delight, fanning themselves and one another.

Sarah said, "If this is the bachelorette party entertainment, I wonder what the guys are doing!"

"Kahealani wouldn't tell me," said Diane.

"*She* set this up?" asked a surprised Sarah.

"Nice job, huh?"

"It's fantastic. Thank you! So, what do you think those dancers are doing later?"

"Sarah!"

"I told you; one Mai Tai is my limit."

"I've created a monster," Diane giggled.

"Where are you taking me, Brian, Cal?" asked a curious Dan.

"No place you've ever been before," said Cal. "But, trust us, you need this."

"Need?" Dan laughed.

The limo took the men to a secluded beach where a campfire had been lit and mats set out around it. An exotic woman dressed only in a form-fitting pareo from the waist down greeted the men with their attire for the event: loin cloths. She invited them to go into the shadows to change into them.

"This is something I need, right?" queried Dan.

"Oh, yeah," said Brian. "Say, do these come in an XXL?"

"You'll probably need to tie it *below* your gut," Dan teased.

"Does this one make my butt look big?" asked Cal.

"Yes!" said everyone.

"Excuse me, can I get a 34 Long?" asked Andy.

"You'll just trip on it," said Brian.

"Gentlemen," said a female voice lyrically. "Please join us."

"You first, Dan," ordered Cal.

"You just want to get a good look at my ass."

"There's no such thing as a good look at your ass."

"There had better be no cameras out," said Dan.

The woman who had handed out loin cloths then said, "Gentlemen, please come sit on the mats by the fire. We have some refreshments for you. My name is Makelina, and the other ladies will introduce themselves to you."

The men followed Makelina's lead and settled down on the mats, carefully arranging their loin cloths as modestly as possible. Makelina then said, "Well, this is a much better looking group than we are used to, isn't that right, Aika?"

"Indeed, Makelina," responded Aika, also attired in a pareo that left her breasts uncovered. "I'm going to join this particularly fine group of specimens of manhood. Gentlemen, I will be taking care of you this evening. I am Aika. And you are…?"

"Uh…" started Gabe.

"It's not a hard question," teased Aika. "I could provide name tags, but where would we hang them?"

The others laughed at Gabe while he remembered his name.

The other ladies also settled themselves among small groups of men and introduced themselves. Drinks were passed around, and Cal conducted the first toast.

"Dan, I have no idea if any of us will be alive tomorrow, but we are certainly alive now. With luck, we'll all be alive, but we won't remember anything. So whether we forget everything and die, or remember everything and live, here's to you as you abandon your wanton ways for a woman who is crazy enough to love you, at least until she hears about tonight. Here, here!"

"Here, here!" responded the chorus.

"Now, we have some gifts for you to see your way through the years of marriage to the same woman for, oh, sixty, seventy, loooooong years. First, I think it was Brian that thought you needed this."

Dan unwrapped the blow-up sheep, pretending to sob, "Esmerelda, where have you been? She and I go way back. Look at those big brown eyes. Don't tell Sarah, OK?"

"Looks like you called it right, Brian. Here, we'll let Gabe blow it up. He's used to breathing heavily. OK, here's the next one."

"A magnifying glass?" shouted Dan.

"That's actually for Sarah. Objects in the glass appear larger than they are."

"How come it has Brian's initials on it?"

Makelina interrupted the suggestive banter, saying, "Gentlemen, the ladies and I are so impressed with your physical—uh, gifts, that we would like to show you how women in ancient times prepared their men for battle, whether it was for blood or for love. We'll just refresh everyone's drink, and we invite you to sit back and try to relax. No one's ticklish are they?"

Makelina brought out a jar of a substance resembling mud. She scooped some out and started to paint intricate designs on Dan's shoulders and back. As he started to relax, she continued the ritual on his chest and a modest distance below his loin cloth. She finished with a design on his face.

Dan stood up to model the body art the lithe woman had painted on him by the light of the fire.

Brian shouted, "There's more than one full moon out tonight. Be sure you don't let the enemy see your ass! It'll give away our position!" Laughing, the rest of the men accepted the offerings of the other artists who painted detailed although somewhat simpler designs, out of respect for their warrior chief *du jour*. When they were done, everyone was adorned from head to toe with symbols representing bravery, strength, and sexual prowess.

A drumbeat started softly and the ladies stood up and started to dance to the rhythm of the ancient sound. They dropped their pareos, leaving only the barest of G-strings. Makelina invited Dan to his feet, and he in turn dragged Cal and Brian to their feet. Soon everyone was up dancing to the irresistible beat. Then the women moved into a makeshift chorus line and performed a provocative dance that left everyone, especially the men, glistening with sweat. The pulse of the drums and the dance became intense until finally they abruptly ceased, leaving only the sounds of heavy breathing to accompany the crackling of the fire.

After a few seconds of silence, the warriors jumped to their feet in applause and moved to embrace the dancers.

Cal shouted, "We need pictures. Cameras?"

Dan questioned, "Will this get me divorced before I'm even married?"

"Maybe. Now stand over there with Esmerelda. Say baaaa!"

"All right," said Dan. "If there are pictures of me, there have to be pictures of everyone!"

"And the ladies, too!" shouted Brian. "If it's OK with them."

After the round of photographs, Makelina said, "You can jump in the waves to wash off the body paint before you get dressed if you want. Unless you want to stay in your loin cloths. Most of it should come off by Sunday."

"Sunday?" shouted Dan, until he saw the twinkle in her eye. Then sounding disappointed, he said, "I thought it would last longer than that!"

"That depends on what you rub up against," said Makelina.

"Hey, wake up. Come on, eat this." Wally roughly shook Malia awake and stuffed a cracker in her face. "Eat this."

Malia groaned, not wanting to wake up, but Wally had no patience for her. "Come on, wake up. Eat this, and I'll let you go back to sleep. I'll take off the gag. You're gotta stay tied up tho'. I trusted you to behave the first time, but you lost your privileges when you ran away. You probably thought you were pretty smart, but now you see it was a pretty stupid thing to do. Look where it got you."

Malia let Wally sit her up in the small cabin below deck. Relieved to be free of the gag, she wolfed down the cracker. He handed her a bottle of water, but realized she couldn't take it with her wrists tied up. He figured she was not going anywhere but back to sleep, so he loosened the ropes and let her take the bottle. Then he let her use the bathroom before she crawled back onto on the narrow bed. In a couple of hours he needed to give her another dose of Valium. It was better than hand cuffs anyway. She had broken the lock on the hatch during her first escape, so this time Wally secured it with bungee cords. There was nowhere for her to go. At dawn he would head out to sea and around the island so no one would hear her if she called out. There should be plenty of places to dump her off once she had no more value to him. As long as Owen believed she might still be alive, he would do whatever Duke told him to do. Feeling confident that he had full control of the situation, Wally settled in topside so he could drift off for a few hours sleep.

Friday, July 10

"How are you feeling, Dan?" asked Gabe, in the faint pre-dawn that whispered the onset of a new day.

"It's still night, isn't it?" said Dan hoarsely. Gabe handed him a cup of coffee as both of them tried to wake up. "Thanks, how are you?"

"I knew better than to mix my Lava Flows with my Piña Coladas. Didn't they teach you than in med school?"

Dan laughed, "Maybe they did and I missed that day." He paused before continuing, "This place is quiet without the girls. Even Paco looks forlorn."

"I think this is one time that it's better they stayed with their parents. Any idea what they were going to do last night?"

"With Diane in charge, the possibilities are frightening."

"That they are," agreed Gabe. "Here, more coffee. Are you joining us on the snorkel trip today?"

"You can't fool me; you don't want to be left alone with Vanessa. Not that I blame you."

"She's something. How did Sarah take it when Vanessa showed up?"

"Upset. Very upset. Primarily because she let Vanessa get to her. I told her I would send her home, but Diane apparently has something up her sleeve. I don't want to know. Or maybe I do. No, probably not."

"It's better that way. Plausible deniability."

"I can't believe you can say that this early."

"I'd say it was a successful bachelor party."

"I just have one question: why I am covered with mud?"

"It's really better that you don't know."

"Plaudible designability?"

"Something like that."

Edgar was tired of babysitting Duke. He was more accustomed to work that was more physical in nature, and although it could turn out that way, for the moment his captive was boring him to tears. He had been ordered not to hurt Duke for the time being unless it became absolutely necessary. Duke didn't seem like any of Cho's typical associates. He could fit in with upper class people, a good cover in some situations. There didn't seem to be a woman around on a regular basis, which seemed odd to Edgar. Maybe Duke was gay. It made him sick to think about it. It would make it easier to kill him later, tho'. It was just a job anyway.

Edgar had slept a few hours; Cho didn't say he had to stay awake all night. Duke didn't seem like the type to murder someone while he was sleeping. *He probably should have,* Edgar thought to himself. *I would have.*

As soon as daylight cast gray shadows in the apartment, Edgar got up to make coffee. He didn't care if it woke Duke. Anyway, he soon heard him in the bathroom and made sure his gun was handy. Docile captives were sometimes the most dangerous, since you never knew whether it was an act or not.

"Good morning, Edgar. Hope I didn't snore too much."

"Sounded like my old lady."

"You got a wife…a girlfriend?"

"Yes."

"Good for you." Duke decided he wouldn't ask the obvious next question of whether he had a wife, girlfriend, or both. "Thanks for making coffee."

"No problem. I'm a nice guy. Hey, where are you going?"

"I thought I'd just go out there for a swim. Is it OK? You want to come?"

"No."

"No, you don't want to come, or no, it's not OK?"

"I'll come out with you. Don't guess you got much else place to go. Hey, man, you look like crap. You got some disease or something?"

"Colorful, huh?" Duke dismissed the yellowing bruises on his chest from the mugging Edgar and Benny had administered almost a week earlier. Changing the subject, he said, "The newspaper should be on the porch. Take it with you to the pool if you want." *Although I'd be surprised if you can read.*

Duke swam laps to loosen up his stiff muscles. He had correctly judged Edgar's demeanor as cabin fever, and getting him out of the apartment was as much for Edgar's benefit as for Duke's. People do desperate things when they feel caged in.

It was an odd pairing of adversaries sitting by the pool in the early morning, drinking coffee and reading the newspaper, just like two friends might do. Duke hoped Edgar would relax, thinking Duke had no intention of fleeing, and was at least a willing host for his captor. Duke himself had no illusion of Edgar as anything but a hired thug who would kill him as soon as pour coffee for him. Could he kill Edgar if he had to? Civilization might be the better for it.

Duke hoped that it wasn't just a delusion that he could complete this one last job without anyone getting hurt or killed, so that he could walk away from this life forever. If not, how far was he willing to go to make sure he didn't get hurt?

He was surprised that the pool had sand in it. It was all over him, sticking to his legs, his hair, in his teeth. It did no good to brush it off, since he was sitting in it. The grit had migrated into his shorts, and he wanted to scratch at it, but the microscopic grit could not be scraped away without scratching something else. The more he tried to move in the sand, the deeper the hole became, and the walls kept caving in on him. The sand was cooler underneath, but wet and sticky. The sand on top was dry, but it burned him when he touched it.

Erin, could you help me up, please? The sand; I can't get the sand off me. "Erin?"

"Duke, you jerk! Wake up! Who's Aaron? Your boyfriend?"

"Huh?"

"Wake up! Mr. Cho wants to talk to you. Now. Here, take the phone. Then you can call your boyfriend, or lover, whatever you call him."

Shaking himself awake from the strange dream, Duke wiped his face with a towel as Edgar handed him his cell phone.

"Hello, Mr. Cho."

"Duke, is Edgar taking good care of you?"

"Of course, Mr. Cho. I have some good news." Duke tried to sound convincing, as much for his own benefit as Cho's.

"We've got HoHo back; he'll do anything and everything we ask, no problem."

"Good. You have a big day ahead of you. We need you to persuade him to complete the job."

"That won't be a problem. I can guarantee his cooperation."

"That's good. I'm sure I don't have to remind you how important it is that everyone does his job…"

"Absolutely."

"…completely. As businessmen, we must make sure we complete our jobs. No loose ends."

"Right."

"I expect you to take care of the loose ends. So let me make them very clear. The loose ends are HoHo and his wife. And the idiot who was supposed to control them."

You might as well say it: I'm a loose end, too.

"No loose ends. It's very clear, Mr. Cho." *If I live through this day, it will be a miracle.*

"Edgar will be with you to assist with any loose ends as well."

"Fine. Anything else, Mr. Cho?"

"No. I will contact you through Edgar later." And he hung up.

Duke lay back on the chaise lounge by the pool and closed his eyes for a minute. He imagined his obituary appearing in the Sunday newspaper.

Don "Duke" Garrity. Died July 10 of injuries due to massive trauma and stupidity. Beloved relative and friend of no one. Suffered from delusions.

"Duke, you going to sleep all day? Come on, I want to get something to eat."

Duke rose stiffly and walked back to the apartment with Edgar.

Hard to kill someone on an empty stomach, eh?

"Did you have fun last night?" teased Diane with a sing-song tone of voice.

Sarah moaned and rubbed her eyes. "Please tell me I kept my clothes on…and you'd better not say 'mostly'!"

"Yes, your dignity is intact. Looks like your hat is suffering, tho'. Maybe you should blow it up some more. Oh, look, Mom put a lei on your center piece. We should take it with us to the rehearsal dinner. Hopefully it will still look perky by then."

"Speaking of perky, how come you're so wide awake?"

"It was my job to take care of your needs. Besides, I may have to work today. I told my boss I could make a short flight this morning if he needed me. He probably won't, and anyway, don't worry; I'll be back in time for the rehearsal. I just had coffee with Stephanie; she's in great shape, too."

"I think I'll take a nap."

"Good idea, but first you'll have to get out of bed."

"What time is it?"

"8:30. I brought you some coffee. And some aspirin. There's a bagel over there, too."

"I guess I had a good time last night. Say, I don't remember seeing Vanessa there."

"That's my fault. I think there was some confusion about when the party would be; somehow she thought it was tonight instead of last night. Not sure how she got so confused."

"That's really too bad."

"I'll be sure to apologize to her."

Sarah glanced over at the other bed in the hotel room and asked, "Where are Mom and Dad?"

"Mom is down at breakfast with Pru. The dads are out with Gabe; so is Vanessa, I think. Wish I could be a fly on the wall. I think all three Callahan boys are out with them, too. That should make sure we get the *whole* story," she laughed.

"They're all cute enough that I wouldn't put it past her to flaunt her wares around them. Should we worry?"

"About her or them?"

"I suppose you're right. She should be afraid, very afraid."

"Malia, are you OK?" Owen desperately reached out to her as best he could over the phone.

"Sleepy. Boat."

"Are you on a boat?"

Wally grabbed the phone from Malia and said, "See, she's OK. She'll be OK long as you do what you're told."

"What do you want me to do?"

"Stay there and don't say nothing to nobody. Stay off the phone. I'll call you." Wally hung up, leaving Owen with a dial tone.

"Please, God. Keep her safe," he said into the phone, holding onto it until the loud off-the-hook tone blasted into his ears. As soon as he hung up, the phone rang again.

"'lo."

"Owen? It's George. You OK?"

"George." Owen allowed himself to breathe, and suddenly remembered Wally's warning. *Say nothing to nobody. Stay off the phone.*

"I'm fine. We're fine."

"Is Malia there?"

"Uh, she's at the store."

"Were you over at the park yesterday? Dan thought he saw you there?"

"Uh, yeah. We had a picnic."

"Good for you. It's one of my favorite spots. Funny, but Dan said he didn't see Malia with you."

"Uh, she was lying down in the back seat. Tired. Say, George, I've got to go. I'll have Malia call you later, OK?"

"Uh, sure, Owen. You sure you're OK?"

"I'm fine. Bye."

George held the phone for a few seconds before hanging up. He was puzzled at the terse reception he had received.

Liliana asked, "How are they?"

"Fine, I guess. Malia wasn't there, at the store, he said. He seemed awfully anxious to get me off the phone."

"Call Malia on her cell."

"I'm already dialing. Come on, Malia, answer."

But Malia didn't answer. Instead, he got the standard invitation to leave a message and she would call him back. He left a brief message and hung up.

"She's not answering."

"Maybe she's driving or with someone and can't talk."

"I suppose."

"She'll call you back as soon as she can, I'm sure."

"If she doesn't, I'm going over there."

"What do you think happened?"

"I don't know."

Owen made another pot of coffee. He hadn't slept all night, alternating between thoughts of calling the police and fears for what might happen to Malia if he did. There was always the possibility that he was being watched, and he wouldn't take a chance with Malia's safety. This was supposed to be over; why were they still being pulled into Wally's criminal underworld? For some reason, Wally needed both of them, for the time being anyway. For what? He had wanted to tell George everything, but now that he knew Malia was still alive, he decided to obey Wally's warning for now. If Wally hurt or killed Malia, the island wasn't big enough for him to escape Owen's vengeance.

The call on Malia's cell phone startled him, and he stopped himself at the last second from answering it. He recognized the name on the display. George. *I can't keep this from him for long. Malia would never refuse to talk to George.*

Vanessa peeled off her gauzy cover-up to reveal a high-cut black tank with little left to the imagination. Unspoken words and fleeting glances passed among Gabe, Will, and Carl. All turned their attention to the dolphins providing escort to the *Rain Dancer* and its party of snorkelers.

Thomas shrieked, "Hey Vanessa, your suit is stuck in your butt. You've got a wedgie!"

Will and Carl tried painfully to resist the urge to respond to Thomas' blatant outburst of what everyone else was merely thinking.

Thomas continued, "You should be careful what you sit on. You'll burn your…"

"Thomas!" called Gabe. "How about helping me with the anchor line?"

"Sure, Gabe."

The two older boys joined Gabe and Thomas to provide an overkill of assistance in lowering the anchor. Muffled by the sounds of flags flapping in the wind and waves splashing the sides of the boat, Gabe's voice was heard only by his crew.

"Leave it alone, guys."

"What?" asked Micah, with feigned innocence.

"You know what I mean."

"Yeah, but…"

"Yeah, but it's her butt." Gabe couldn't help but start to laugh, and that got the other three started as well.

Alec says, "I just want to reach over and pull it out." He reached behind to make sure his own swim trunks weren't stuck.

The laughter became uncontrolled, and Gabe reached over the side to splash water on the boys' faces, trying to appear like he was teasing them on an unrelated matter.

Micah asked, "Are you going to tell Diane?"

"She already knows."

Vanessa called out, "Gabe, could you reach my back to put some sunscreen on it?"

Jeannie said, "I'll do it for you, Vanessa. Gabe's busy with the anchor."

Surprised, Vanessa said, "Oh, thanks. Never mind, I think I can get it."

Jeannie said dryly, "You do have to be careful out here. The water reflects the sun and makes it even worse. You should probably wear something on your back while you're snorkeling."

"I'll be fine," Vanessa said sweetly, sitting on the edge of the boat. "Ahhh!" she screamed, jumping to her feet. "Oh, shit, that's hot! I just burned myself."

She revealed two red welts on her buttocks. All eyes turned on her, and Gabe said blandly, "Careful Vanessa. There's some first aid cream below. Do you need some help with it? Thomas, how about going over to help Vanessa?"

"I'm fine. Thanks anyway," she replied with forced cheerfulness.

Gabe called out, "OK, snorkelers, masks and fins! The waves are still calm this morning, so it should be easy to just float along. No sharks, today. I know, Micah, you're bummed. Sea turtles, tons of fish, maybe a ray, squid, octopus, piranha...just kidding. You'll be glad to know that your fins are microwave safe and excellent with a little tartar sauce. As for your masks, let me know if any of you have one of the older models that says, 'In case of emergency, break glass.' Now, I'll be below you SCUBA diving, so I can take some pictures. Whatever you do, do NOT say 'cheese' when I take your picture. And don't hog the picture. I can't change film underwater! Now, anyone using PoliGrip? No? Good. I still have nightmares about this poor lady who got stuck to her snorkel, and we had to chisel it off her face. Any questions?"

"How deep is it here?" asked Alec.

"About 30 feet. Visibility is terrific, so you'll see lots. Watch me; I'll point out things I see. Everyone ready? OK, one at a time, down the ladder, then just float off. I'm right behind you, or below you, as the case may be. Carl, you're staying topside?"

"Yeah, I'll help people back on board. Anything I can do for you?"

"Snacks. There are snacks below. And drinks."

"Will do."

After nearly an hour floating in the gentle waves, the snorkelers gradually reboarded the boat, wrapped themselves in towels, enjoyed refreshments, and exchanged stories of what they had seen. Everyone but Vanessa had found a place on the benches to settle in, out of the way of Gabe, who was stowing gear. She stood, propped up against the canopy. She turned to get another drink, and Thomas could not help but shout, "Vanessa, look at your butt! It's sunburned! You're not going to be able to sit down for days."

Jeannie called out, "You didn't put any sunscreen on your butt! Vanessa! I told you to cover up!"

"I was underwater!" she protested.

Will and Carl exchanged knowing looks, and Will said innocently, "I'd offer to put some on now, but I think it's too late."

Vanessa sneered at him and wrapped herself up in her towel, wincing when the rough terrycloth rubbed her back side.

Gabe said, "We're heading back now; the wind and waves are starting to pick up. Did you enjoy the snorkel trip?"

Jeannie said, "It was great!"

Micah said, "I can't wait to go SCUBA diving!"

She responded, "Are you going to learn how?"

"Yeah, next week. Gabe's going to teach us."

"Good for you! Has Diane learned yet?"

"No, 'cause she's always flying. You can't dive and fly," said Micah with authority.

Diane answered her cell phone, "This is Diane."

Her boss, Wayne, said, "You remember Mr. Cho?"

"I've been trying to forget. Thanks for reminding me. Please don't tell me I have to take him some place."

"He wants you."

"Why?"

"He specifically requested you. He's flying to Lana'i today."

"I'll pay you $20 to tell him I'm sick."

"Hey, I know it's your day off, but he's paying a premium for such short notice."

"Who gets the premium? You will owe me."

"Don't I always?"

"OK, how many?"

"Four."

"I can't believe there are three people who would willingly spend time with Mr. Cho."

"And two of them are sumo wrestlers."

"I'll strap them under the wings."

"They've got cargo, too. A lot of golf bags."

"We're going to need mid-air refueling."

"Just let the air out of the two big guys."

"You're scaring me."

"I didn't think that was possible," laughed Wayne.

"I just figured out how you can pay me back."

"Am I going to like it?"

Diane just giggled, adding, "I'll explain when I get there."

"Duke, it's Cho."

"Hello, Mr...."

"Get HoHo. Bring him to the airport with all the cargo. Look for a building with a sign for Ali'i Aviation. Make sure his wife is under control, and he believes that it's up to him whether she lives or dies. Now give me Edgar."

Duke handed the phone to Edgar, who nodded, saying very little in response to whatever Cho told him. He hung up, and then told Duke, "Let's go. We gotta get the bags out of my car."

Duke nodded and followed Edgar out to retrieve six golf bags from Edgar's car. Back inside, they stuffed the packages of cocaine into the bags before resealing them up in their large, protective plastic bags as if they were new golf bags for sale. Both of Duke's bags were needed as well. When they finished, Edgar glanced out the window before picking up two bags and signaling to Duke to do the same. They made two trips carrying bags to the car, before returning to the apartment to close it up and make sure they had not left anything behind. Duke decided that he had better not ask Edgar if he was supposed to bring his gun. Instead, he just slipped his cell phone into his pocket, hoping Edgar would not search him and take it away. In the end, it might prove to be more valuable than a gun anyway.

When they got into the car, Edgar said, "Call Owen. Tell him you'll be there in ten minutes, and be ready to go."

Duke nodded and made the call.

"Owen, I'm an associate of Wally…"

"Where's my wife, you son of a bitch?"

"She's fine, and I know you want to make sure she stays that way." *I hate this job.*

"What do you want?" asked Owen impatiently.

"I'm coming to get you," said Duke.

"When?"

"Now."

"The cops are parked out front."

That might not be bad news.

"OK, you need to head out the back door, through the neighbor's yard, and I'll pick you up on the street behind. Make sure no one sees you."

"I want to talk to my wife."

"Later." Duke hung up, feeling nauseous. Edgar nodded, and Duke directed him to the street behind the Hoana house. Edgar pulled over and asked, "Where is he?"

"He'll be here. There he is. Flash your headlights."

Duke got out of the car and opened the back door for Owen. Owen squeezed in; there was barely enough room for him and the golf bags that didn't fit in the trunk of the big sedan.

"Where are we going?" said Owen, fiercely. "Playing golf? Where are the clubs? Take me to my wife or I'm not going to help you."

"Calm down, Owen," said Duke. "After today, we'll be out of your life for good."

"Why do you need me at all?"

"My employer likes your company."

"Who is your employer? What are you guys up to? Drugs? I'm not helping you with drugs. What do you have in these bags? Drugs, huh?"

Tired of Owen's raving, Edgar shouted, "Just shut up. That's all you need to know. Just shut up. Got that?"

Owen glared at Edgar from the back seat, trying to judge whether his two captors were what he suspected, the criminal equivalent of good cop / bad cop. "What are your names?" he asked.

"Duke, and this is Edgar."

Edgar said angrily, "And I'm a Sagittarius, and he's a Pisces. Now, just shut up, both of you. Thank God. We're here."

More like 'thank Satan,' you son of a bitch, thought Owen.

Edgar parked the car while Duke went to get a cart to haul the luggage. Owen thought about raising a commotion to get the attention of authorities, but he thought better of it. *As long as they have Malia, I'll play along.* He figured he had an even chance against Edgar as long as someone didn't try to make it more difficult for him. Duke. Duke was a wild card. Duke knew something about Malia's whereabouts, so it was best not to assume that he had Malia's welfare in mind.

Cho soon arrived and exchanged curt greetings with everyone. He sized up Owen and gave him a sly smile, but said nothing to him. Owen decided to adopt a somewhat meek demeanor, resigned to the situation, and in no shape to argue with anyone. Cho ordered the others to take the cart out on the tarmac and wait for further instructions. Diane came out of the office and greeted Cho. She was surprised that he smiled at her and shook her hand.

"I'm so glad you were available on such short notice."

"My pleasure, Mr. Cho. So, Lana'i today?"

"Yes."

"I'll finish filing my flight plan and get a weather briefing. Are the other passengers here?"

"Yes, they're outside with our luggage. Golf bags actually."

"Yes, I remember. That's your business." *Maybe he was just having a bad day on Monday. He's quite civil today.*

"Can you fit us all in?"

"Sure, but we'll have to leave out the beverage cart."

"Ha ha! We'll survive somehow. I'll be outside with my associates, waiting for you."

"We'll be ready to leave in just a few minutes."

"Excellent."

He's still creepy. Slimy. I'm going to need another shower.

Her paperwork completed, she met her passengers outside. She smiled when she recognized Duke from the Fourth of July sunset cruise. Duke responded rather formally at the recollection, apparently caught off guard by her presence. She decided to let it go; this was an odd assortment of business colleagues, if that indeed was what they were. She shook hands with Edgar and then extended her hand out to the fourth man. *It can't be.*

Her heart skipped a beat when she met eyes with Owen. He caught her eye and faintly signaled her not to act as if she knew him. She nodded almost imperceptibly, wishing he could read her mind: *What's going on? Where's Malia? I need to talk to you. Are you in danger? Am I in danger?*

"Anyone need one last restroom stop? Facilities in the air are well— non-existent." She looked directly at Owen, willing him to signal his need to use the restroom. He told his companion (captor?) that he needed to go.

"I'll show you where," she offered, but it was apparent Owen couldn't go anywhere by himself.

Duke took his cue from the wordless stare from other two.

"Uh, me too."

The three walked in silence around to the restroom, and Diane decided to risk asking Duke a question.

"How's Erin?"

"Fine."

"Going to play golf on Lana'i?"

"Uh, maybe."

He went to the same charm school as Cho. What is going on?

Owen came out of the restroom, and Diane waited for Duke to go in, but he said, "I changed my mind."

She asked, "Is everyone OK?"

Duke said, "Fine." Owen nodded.

Diane said, "All right. Let's go then."

Duke directed Owen to walk in front of him, so there was no opportunity for Diane to even exchange looks with him.

At the plane, Edgar and Owen loaded the golf bags into the cargo compartment. Diane then invited her passengers up the ladder. "Edgar, would you please sit by the window on the right, Owen on the left behind me, Mr. Cho in the middle there, and Duke next to me?"

Cho apparently wasn't too pleased with his seat assignment, but Diane didn't care. She wanted them to know that she was in charge, and whatever she asked them to do was what they would do. Weight-wise, Cho could just as easily have been next to her, but it gave her a wicked sense of satisfaction to put him in his place, physically as well as metaphorically.

Diane conducted the safety briefing with her passengers. There was no joking around among the passengers, not even the pleasant business-related conversation one might expect from a group of colleagues squeezed into an aluminum can.

She handed Duke her checklists and proceeded to go through them. *Stay focused. It's just a short flight. I'll be back in an hour, and I can forget this creepy assortment of humanity. Except for Owen. Why are you here? How are you involved with these guys?* She contacted the tower and they exchanged standard communications indicating the flight was a go. Some 25% of her wanted to abort the takeoff, but there was the other 75% that chastised her silliness. If they hijacked her, where could they go? Cuba? Afghanistan? Ni'ihau? *See, you're being a drama queen. Leave that to Sarah this weekend.*

Once clear of the Kahului traffic area, Diane informed the tower and adjusted her radio dials as instructed. She relaxed a little, comfortable with the control she had of her domain. *My turf.*

Diane broke the silence, informing Owen that he had the best access to the plane's beverage service, a six pack of water bottles behind him. Owen looked at his fellow passengers to see if anyone wanted one, but everyone ignored him.

He's invisible. Almost a pariah. I'm worried about him.

With forced humility, Cho said, "Diane, I know this will be inconvenient, but I just remembered that I need to make a brief stop on the Big Island. You know, where we went last week. I'm terribly sorry, but it's very important. I'd appreciate it if you would change course."

Diane felt adrenaline rush to her extremities and the hair on her arms stand up. *He's the customer. I'm just a taxi driver.* She willed herself to respond calmly, "Let me clear it with Kahului Ground."

"Actually, I would prefer that you didn't."

She glanced behind, starting to say, "I have to…" but she stopped mid-sentence when she noticed Edgar holding a gun pointed in her direction.

Cho said, "As I said, I would prefer that you didn't. Just head to Hawai'i."

Silently Diane gripped the control wheel and changed course for the Big Island of Hawai'i. Within a minute, Kahului Departure Control came on the radio, saying, "Cessna 1169, radar contact 3 miles northwest of the airport, squawk 1200 and resume normal navigation."

"Say nothing," ordered Cho.

Diane nodded and became silent.

Kahului Departure Control repeated their communications, this time more insistent that she respond.

Diane said to Cho, "I need to say something, or they'll send out the authorities. They can't do anything up here, but they can still track us to where we'll land."

Cho was quiet for a few seconds, then nodded, saying, "Keep it short; tell them your passengers changed their minds. That's it."

Diane nodded and breathed a silent sigh of relief. *I can do this. God, help me.* She took the radio, saying, "This is Cessna 1169. Passengers have requested a change of course. Heading to Hawai'i to a private airfield at Kohala." Upon completion of the radio transmission she set the transponder to 7700 and pressed the IDENT button.

After a pause, the voice responded with what Diane hoped was an undetectable quiver, "Cessna 1169, please confirm your transponder setting: 7700. Acknowledge setting course heading for 170. Repeat course heading 170. Continue to monitor Kahului Departure Control on 119.5."

"Roger 119.5, Cessna 1169. Confirm transponder setting 7700."

Would they get there in time?

She checked her peripheral vision to see if anyone was aware of her attempt to communicate her emergency situation to the ground authorities with the universal transponder signal set to 7700. She throttled back to the slowest possible speed to keep from stalling so the authorities would have more time to get in place. "Low altitude whirlwinds," she said, trying to sound nonchalant. "Typical in the summer. Like mini-tornadoes. Could make it a little bumpy."

High altitude whirlwinds? Might as well say I need to regenerate the dilithium crystals and recharge the warp drive.

Owen and Duke just sat in their seats, looking out the windows.

What is their role in this? Together they could overcome Edgar and Cho, but both seem so nonplussed. Guns on airplanes are every pilot's nightmare, and I don't want to provoke Edgar and Cho. But why are Owen and Duke so blasé? Did they know this would happen? What's the deal with the golf bags?

Cho said, "Now head over to Laupahoehoe. There's a landing strip there. You'll see it in a few minutes. You probably haven't been there before. It's very private."

"I thought you said Kohala!" said Diane, suddenly realizing that her attempt to signal the crisis to the authorities with the universal 7700 transponder code for an emergency situation had failed. The police might arrive at Kohala, but she would not. The Cessna's transponder would give their location, for all the good it would do in an emergency where minutes, if not seconds, counted.

The landing strip at Laupahoehoe on Hawai'i's northwest coast was empty except for a few beat-up cars and vans parked near the small building that served as the terminal. Barely more than a shack, it had no regular contingent of personnel. Diane could not imagine why anyone would want to fly there; Kona, the Kohala Coast, and even Hilo were more convenient for everything. This was nowhere, nothing in the way of resorts or even population out here. At most, there were 500 people, and no golf courses. Still, with enough flat land, anyone could build a landing strip.

If I wanted to bring someone or something to a remote place and not be observed, this would be it.

All of a sudden she longed for the crowds at the Kahului airport.

The question remained in her mind: *why are we here?*

Cho indicated she should taxi over to the building, and she did as instructed, making sure the plane was situated so that it could take off. Diane hoped she'd have the chance and wanted nothing to get in the way of a speedy departure. One of the rickety old vans started to move over to the plane, parking as close as possible to the cargo hold.

Diane said, "If you just want to take your stuff and get out of here, I'll be on my way, and you can be on yours. That is, unless you still want to go to Lana'i."

"Out," ordered Edgar, and Diane reluctantly turned off the engine. Edgar looked away for an instant, allowing her to stuff the key under the floor mat. She left her radio and transponder on, hiding the lighted displays with her body as best she could while she deplaned. She wondered if she could outrun the bullets if she had an opportunity to make a run for the plane.

Not likely. Someone please find us…soon.

George parked outside the Hoanas' house, waved to the police car cruising by, and knocked on the front door.

"Owen? Malia? It's George. Hi, can I come in?"

There was no answer, and George tried the door. It was open. He went in and left the door ajar, although he wasn't sure why. He noticed Malia's cell phone on the table next to her purse. *She has to be home. Maybe out back.*

He continued to call their names as he carefully moved from room to room and out to the back yard. He had a strange sense of *déjà vu.* Both cars were still there, but no one was home. Out for a walk? Possibly. Unlikely.

He decided to see what calls had been logged on Malia's cell phone. Just the one from him. He set it back down and picked up her purse. Under it was a piece of paper, hastily scrawled with, "They've got Malia."

George ran out the front door and flagged down the police.

"Did you try Diane on her cell phone?" asked Sarah's mother.

"I left a message, but she can't always get to it right away," said Sarah. "I think we should just go to the apartment and wait for her. Gabe might be back, and it will give you a chance to spend some time with him. I have a feeling you'll be back out here for another wedding! You haven't met Paco anyway. Your new granddog."

"Please reassure me that my grandchildren will not all have four legs."

Sarah giggled, saying, "What about fins?"

Carolyn Donovan sighed and teased back with, "At least I have hope since you're marrying a pediatrician and not a veterinarian!"

"We'll try not to disappoint you," replied Sarah. Then she turned to the centerpiece from the night before and said, "Bubba, we'll be back later to take you to the rehearsal dinner. Nice touch with the lei, Mom."

"Your father wanted to put boxer shorts on it, but that sort of emphasized the, well, you know."

Malia sat up in the small boat cabin, trying to shake the Valium out of her system. She wasn't sure what she would do anyway. Wally had been going in circles off shore—from Maui, she suspected—for hours. She was imprisoned, weak, and out to sea. He was apparently waiting for someone to tell him what to do, since he did not seem to be heading towards a specific destination. When Wally suspected the Valium was wearing off, he would make sure she got another dose. She had at most a few minutes before he would come below to return her to her drug-induced fog.

Where does he keep it? If he's got it with him, he risks it falling out of his pocket into the water. Bathroom. Quiet. He needs to think you're still unconscious. Hurry. Oh my God, it's a pharmaceutical warehouse in here. It has to be near the front. Why can't I focus? Diazepam, 10 mg. Generic for Valium. *Bingo. Little white pills. What else looks like it?* Sudafed. *Good. I have a headache. Hurry.*

Malia quickly emptied the Valium bottle's contents into her pocket. Then she dumped approximately the same number of Sudafed tablets into the Valium bottle and returned the Valium bottle to exactly where she had found it. Then quietly she opened up one of Wally's water bottles. She crushed two Valium as quietly as and as completely as she could and poured the powder into the bottle. She closed it tightly and covered it with a towel so she could shake the bottle to dissolve the crystals. It wouldn't completely dissolve, but she hoped the bottle tinting would mask the sediment. She then put it in front of the other bottles so it would be the first one he took. She made sure her own bottle had enough water in it so Wally would not make her drink from his. Exhausted and dizzy, she crept back onto the narrow bed and closed her eyes. She didn't need to fake her symptoms; the nausea was real, as was the tremor in her hand. *Please, God. I can do this with your help. I don't want to kill anyone, and I don't want to be killed. I trust you with everything I am and everything I have. Keep Owen safe; with your help, he can survive, I know.*

She started to weep but soon heard the sound of Wally opening the hatch. She rubbed her tears into her hair and face so he would think she had just been perspiring heavily in the close quarters. When he reached her, he grabbed her by the hair and sat her up.

"Get in there and pee."

Malia grabbed hold of the edges of shelves and bulkheads for steadiness as she went into the bathroom. When she came out, she sat back on the bed and closed her eyes. Wally went in and grabbed the Valium bottle and pulled out two pills. He gave them to her, saying, "Be a good girl."

Malia nodded and reached for her water bottle. She obediently swallowed the pills and lay back down. Wally then grabbed the tainted water bottle and went back up the ladder, closing and strapping the hatch behind him.

Thank you, God. I can do this now.

Duke and Owen unloaded the golf clubs into the van. One of the large plastic covers encasing the golf bags slipped loose, and a small tightly wrapped white bag fell out, breaking open and releasing a puff of white powder.

Padding, Diane thought for a second.

Not padding! Her eyes widened as she realized what she had just seen, and she quickly turned away hoping she would appear not to have noticed it.

Cho smiled, saying, "I told you my business is golf equipment. It's a very lucrative business." He laughed, adding, "Isn't it, Duke?" He got into the van, continuing his victory celebration about the fact that the deal was about to be concluded with such minimal fuss.

Duke stared blankly into space. Diane was aghast in the realization that Duke was somehow involved in this. A willing participant. What about Owen? Had he lied to everyone including his wife? She felt her stomach turn in disgust, and instinctively grabbed it.

"I don't feel well," she said.

"Get in the car," ordered Edgar, brandishing the gun to indicate the subject was not up for discussion.

Diane moved towards the car as directed by the hoodlum, but turned to the side and leaned over to vomit.

Edgar instinctively jumped back and tripped over one of the railroad ties that defined the edge of the landing strip. He dropped his gun, and Duke pounced on it. Edgar reached it a split second ahead of him, and got a shot off, striking Duke in the thigh. Duke screamed in pain, and Edgar prepared a more deadly aim. Owen kicked him in the head and the gun went flying. The driver of the van sped off with Cho in the front seat, leaving behind an unconscious Edgar and a seriously wounded Duke.

Diane screamed, "Owen? Are you OK?"

Owen nodded, saying, "You?"

"Fine."

"Thank God."

Diane said fiercely to Duke, "Give me one good reason why I shouldn't just leave you here with Edgar."

"I know where Malia is. Other than that, I can't think of a reason."

"I'll call for help, and you tell Owen how to get to Malia."

Duke nodded, wincing at the excruciating pain, wanting to die, wanting to live.

"Kahului Departure Control, this is Cessna 1169."

"Roger Cessna 1169, what is your status?"

"On the ground. Stand down on Code 7700. Here's what I need." Diane rummaged around for a clean towel to tend to Duke's wound as well as some rope with which to tie up Edgar while she communicated with Kahului Departure Control.

"Roger Cessna 1169, a chopper is enroute, ETA 5 minutes. I had already diverted them to your transponder signal."

"Roger Kahului Departure Control. I had hoped you would. Please advise, chocolate chip or peanut butter?"

"Repeat, Cessna 1169."

"I owe you cookies. Chocolate chip or peanut butter?"

"Affirmative on the chocolate chip."

"Roger Kahului Departure Control. Chocolate chip it is. Over."

Diane took the rope over to Owen, who tied up the groggy Edgar. Then she turned to Duke, asking, "Where is she?"

"At sea."

"Where?"

"I'm not sure…"

"You son of a bitch. I'll shoot you myself if you don't tell me where."

"Here, take my cell phone. No, I had better talk to him."

"Who?"

"Wally," said Owen from the side. "Wally has her, doesn't he? Like the lady said, I'll shoot you if you don't tell us where my wife is. Hell, maybe we'll both shoot you."

"I tried to get out of this, but…"

"Frankly, Duke, I don't give a damn about your problems," said Owen.

"Let me call Wally. He needs to hear it from me. Otherwise, he'll…"

"He'll what?"

"He'll kill her."

"Why?"

"Because she can identify him."

"So can I," argued Owen.

"Don't worry; you were on Edgar's list, too. So was I. Diane, too."

Edgar groaned, and everyone turned their attention to making sure the oaf was well restrained. Owen let Duke place the call, and Diane tended to the gunshot wound in Duke's thigh. She didn't think his wound was fatal—yet—but it was serious.

Once the call connected, Duke held the phone in his hand, dumbstruck, and handed it to an anxious Owen.

While tending to Duke, Diane asked accusingly, "So, Duke, whose side are you on? Whoever has the money? Whoever has the gun? How do you sleep at night? Does Erin know about you? Erin! Where is she? You better not have hurt her."

Duke shook his head, wincing at the pain, "She's on Moloka'i. She doesn't know, but she will. I will square it with her. She'll probably spit in my face, and I wouldn't blame her. I left a note behind my dresser in case I didn't make it, with all the information about Cho and his empire. Actually, even if I did make it, I was going to turn myself in."

"Why the change of heart? Why should we believe you? You're just as much to blame for the drug trafficking and all the death it causes as the other guys. I may vomit again."

"I may join you. It's greed. Pure and simple. Oh, I made good money, but I hated myself. I hated everyone I knew. I loved the money, I won't deny it. But it couldn't buy anything I wanted. And it can't buy peace of mind."

"How awful for you. How could you let Wally do what he did to Owen and Malia?"

"The reasons don't matter anymore..."

"What do you mean: they don't matter...?"

Owen interrupted, saying, "Guess who I just talked to! Malia! She's taken over the boat and has Wally tied up."

"What?" exclaimed Diane. Duke nodded and looked up as if giving a silent prayer of thanks.

"Long story, she said. She called the police, and she's bringing the boat into Kahului. She couldn't talk anymore, because the Coast Guard was about to pull up beside her. Can you call George and have him meet her there?"

Duke hung his head, and started to weep silently.

"Boy, are you lucky, you dirt bag," said Diane, as she started dialing. Duke nodded.

"This is not over," she said loudly over the sound of the approaching helicopter. "Cho still has all the drugs. Plus he knows who we are and where we are. Everyone I know is now in danger. Then there's the little detail of ruining my sister's wedding. You had better tell everything, mister. The cops are here." She ceased her tirade when George answered. "George! It's Diane. We're all safe for now. Please just listen…"

There was nothing festive in the demeanor of the bridal party gathered at the church for the rehearsal. Sarah and Dan were locked in a desperate embrace in the front pew, flanked on both sides by their parents. Sarah alternated between uncontrollable tears and prayers. Liliana stood guard by the back door to alert everyone upon the arrival of George or Diane.

It was George who arrived first. The boys came running over from the park to join Liliana in a fierce embrace of their father.

George pulled himself free enough to say, "I'm OK. Everyone's OK. Diane is on her way. I have a feeling that the hot topic right now is getting everyone home safely and finding out what happened. Agreed?"

Everyone nodded and allowed themselves to breathe and even smile in the knowledge that everyone was safe. At that moment, Diane burst in, announcing, "Madam Organist, bring on 'Hail to the Chief,' or whatever it's called."

Sarah jumped to her feet and climbed over her parents to embrace her sister. All of Diane's iron will crumbled, and she allowed herself to fall into Gabe's arms in sobs. He teased her gently, "You always have to be rescuing someone, don't you?"

She nodded and pulled herself free to wipe her face. "I think I'm done for the day."

"What were you thinking?"

"Just that I was glad I wasn't going to die a virgin."

The group laughed in relief, a catharsis for their anxious vigil awaiting the return of Diane, Owen, and Malia.

George said, "Let's all sit down. I confess I only know about 10% of the story."

Diane said, "That's the 10% I don't know. Tell us about Malia."

George took a deep breath, bowed his head briefly, and then said, "She is amazing. As are you, Diane." He paused before continuing. He told the group of Malia's kidnapping and imprisonment—both physically and pharmaceutically, as well as her triumph in turning the tables on Wally, again.

"Once Wally had received a taste of his own medicine—sorry, bad joke—no, maybe it's a good joke—Malia broke down the door and called the police on the radio. They dispatched the Coast Guard and escorted her back to Kahului, subsequently relieving her of the gentleman of the criminal persuasion."

"Is she at home with Owen now?" asked Gabe.

George shook his head. "Not exactly. There's more to the story. Diane?"

Clinging to Gabe, Sarah, and her parents huddled in the pew, Diane relayed the story of her own experience with the drug underworld.

She continued wryly, "The police helicopter landed and took Edgar and Duke into custody. You'll all be glad to know—as was I, you can imagine—that Duke will be fine. He may have some redeeming qualities, but I'm not ready to forgive him yet. Owen proved to be Edgar's match physically, but he's on a somewhat higher plane mentally. So, now two more bad guys are off the streets.

"Unfortunately," she paused and restarted. "Unfortunately, Cho and the driver got off with the drugs. The drugs are bad enough—get this—eight golf bags stuffed with cocaine. But he's not one to leave loose ends lying around. That's the unfortunate part. The loose ends are Duke and

Wally, of course. But also Owen, Malia, and me…"

Diane's parents gasped in horror, and Gabe pulled her close into him.

"…which is why there will be some additional guests keeping us company for awhile." She turned around to call everyone's attention to two serious-looking men standing in the doorway.

"Frank and Jason, come on in and meet everyone."

Sarah asked, "What about Owen and Malia?"

"They're in protective custody somewhere. I don't want to know where. They're together; that's all they care about. I don't know if they'll be at the wedding."

Sarah nodded in understanding.

Diane continued, "And now, as maid of honor, I would like to request that we get back to the festivities. We are going to have a party, and we are going to have a wedding." She paused briefly before asking, "Any objections?"

Everyone clapped and the hugs resumed with joy until George was able to gain some control.

"I usually have to warn the bridal party about making sure the wedding is approached with solemnity. I have a feeling that Frank and Jason will make sure that happens. Thank you, guys. We welcome your presence and will do everything to make sure you are completely and utterly bored."

Everyone clapped, and Frank and Jason smiled slightly, waving in acknowledgment to the family and friends gathered in the small church. They walked out to resume their patrol of the property, and George regained everyone's attention.

"Now, let us pray."

Sarah and Diane absently rocked back and forth on the chairs outside the guest house at the church. Sarah asked, "Are you sure you wouldn't rather be with Gabe tonight?"

"And miss being with you on your last night as a virgin? Oh, I forgot, you're not."

Sarah giggled, saying, "Well, I'm glad you're here. It's so peaceful up here. I thought it would be a nice retreat after all the commotion."

Diane agreed. "That is until dawn when the birds wake up. Lucy hasn't chased them away?"

"I don't know. We'll see. With Paco here with her, who knows what they'll get into. I'm glad he could stay here rather than being kenneled."

"And it was best if the guys stayed at the hotel. It's too easy to figure out where I live."

Sarah said, "I can't believe what you've been through today, and you're still awake!"

"Adrenaline. I know I'm going to crash. Soon, I hope."

"Can you see Frank and Ernest?"

"Frank and *Jason*? They're around. Liliana just made a thermos of coffee for them."

Sarah became quiet in reflection, and then said, "It was fun to see Jeannie's kids playing on the beach at the rehearsal dinner."

"I think the adult kids had just as much fun as the little kids."

"You know Mom is already keen on becoming a grandmother."

"You first. I gave her Paco. OK, I'm tired. Snore all you want; I can sleep through anything."

"I love you."

"I love you, too."

Gabe and Dan sat at the oceanfront bar in silence. Everyone else had retired to their hotel rooms, jet lag and the stress of the day having finally taken their toll. Gabe and Dan wouldn't be far behind them, but each needed some time to sit quietly, where the only sound was the endless rhythm of the waves crashing on shore. The white caps caught the glow of the torches, and stars cast what little light there was out at sea. The moon had not risen yet, and even the silhouette of Lana'i off in the distance disappeared into the endless blackness.

Dan held up his drink, asking, "Another?"

Gabe shook his head. "Thanks. I'm fine."

"How do you feel about guns?"

"Hate them, unless they are equipped with a spear that has my dinner on the end of it. You?"

Dan nodded ambivalently. "I always thought I hated them."

"Anything about to change that?"

He shook his head. "I'm a lot more deadly with a hypodermic."

"I'll keep that in mind."

"You scared?"

Gabe shook his head, saying, "No. Yes. Shit. I'm this close to driving up to the church to be with Diane. If I lost her…" Gabe sniffed and turned away, gazing blankly into the infinite night.

Dan's cell phone rang, startling both of them. "Hi!" he said, smiling at the voice he hoped he would hear. "Are you OK?"

"I'm fine. I miss you."

"I miss you, too. Is Diane asleep?"

"She's out, finally. I'm on the lanai. Frank and Jason are around. They said two other guys would be here in the morning to relieve them, but they won't hand off until we've met them. I think these guys are all FBI."

"Is the FBI joining us on our honeymoon?"

"Would that be a problem?" Sarah giggled. "I think Diane is more their concern. But she wouldn't let them put her into protective custody."

"Somehow that doesn't surprise me. You think this Cho guy will be looking for her?"

"She's seen too much. There's too much at stake for him. We're also both afraid that it's too late and he's already handed off the drugs. With that out of the way, his only focus will be on protecting his business. He can't get to Malia, Owen, Duke, Edgar, or Wally right away, so he'll go for the low-hanging fruit."

"Are you sure you're OK up there?"

"Fine. But I miss you."

"Me, too. Oh, Gabe wants to talk to you."

Gabe accepted the phone from Dan and said, "Is she sleeping with a gun under her pillow?"

"Now that would be a reason to be scared. I think our two knights have all the guns I want to have around."

"I suppose. How's Paco doing?"

"He and Lucy got acquainted with Frank and Jason, and I think he's sleeping with—get this—Alec."

"Interesting."

"Isn't it? Anyway, when he comes home, he may expect similar privileges."

"Only in his dreams."

Sarah giggled, "We'll see."

Gabe echoed her laughter, saying, "OK, I'll see you tomorrow. Here's Dan. Good night."

"G'night, Uncle Gabe."

Dan said, "You sure you're OK?"

Sarah replied, "We're in good company. We're both glad you two are staying at the hotel. Oh, but stay away from Vanessa. "

"Oh, rats. You're no fun. Anyway, I haven't seen her all day. Maybe she flew home. OK, now, you sleep well. I'll see you around 4:00."

Sarah laughed, "You'd better see me before then. We're getting married at noon!"

"I meant *a.m.* And that's pushing it! You know I love you."

"Yes, I do. I love you, Doctor Dan. G'night."

"Thank you, FBI," Owen said to the view off the hotel lanai in Kihei.

"Yes, thank you, FBI," echoed Malia. "And Diane."

"Oh, yes, thank you, Diane. So, you know for a couple of years we've been talking about getting a boat..."

"How about we set that aside? I've had enough of boats for awhile."

"So, should we invite Wally for Thanksgiving?" teased Owen.

"Only if he's stuffed."

"He's probably a bit gamey."

"Lots of cranberry sauce."

"It's good to hear you joking."

"Must still be the Valium. What a buzz. I hated it."

"I know what you mean."

"You know this isn't over. We may be in hiding for a long time. What's that Cho guy like?"

"Cold. Pretty much a scumbag. Darth Vader in a polo shirt."

"He won't stop until he's found us."

"Or until he's dead."

"Could you kill him, Owen?"

"Yes. I'm sorry, but, yes. I could kill him."

"What about Wally?"

"I think Cho will take care of that. Poor Wally."

"Poor Wally!"

"He's a bottom-feeder. Soulless. I can't imagine what even God sees in him."

"I had the chance to kill him. I could have just dumped him over the side of the boat."

"Are you glad you didn't?"

"Yes."

"If he had killed you, I'd have killed him. I didn't think I had it in me, but he brought out a side of me I didn't know I had. Him and Cho."

"What about Principal Crockett?"

"No, I don't think I could kill her," replied Owen.

"You know what I mean, silly. How is she?"

"She's not out of the woods. Wally almost killed her, too. There's only so much turning the other cheek I have in me."

"What about Duke? Wally took his orders from Duke, didn't he?"

"To a point," said Owen. "But Wally took it upon himself to beat up Principal Crockett, kidnap you, and almost kill you. Don't get me wrong. Duke is no saint, but he did have something like a Saul/Paul blinding experience. He saved my life and Diane's. Cho is not going to let him off the hook. As long as Cho is alive, Duke will be running for the rest of his life. That might not be too long, tho'. In a way, he reminds me of a kid who makes D's in his math class all year, and then begs the teacher for extra credit so he can pass."

"How does one earn extra credit with you, Mr. Hoana?"

"Come here. I'll show you."

"Mr. Cho, that Diane woman. I know where she live."

"Where, Benny?"

"Wailuku. Here's address."

Cho sat quietly in thought drinking beer with Benny on the lanai at a decrepit rooming house on the northwestern side of the island of Hawai'i. It had a reputation for not asking questions of its boarders. The van was parked deep in the foliage; things were secure for the night. Because of the attention they were getting from the police, Cho couldn't risk concluding the deal tonight. It had to wait until tomorrow.

"You know, boss, Edgar and Duke, they gonna talk, you know."

Cho nodded. Benny was smarter than Edgar. He had much better instincts, and Cho had learned that when Benny had an opinion, it should be considered. Benny had wanted to kill Duke, Owen, and Diane at the airstrip, but Cho had ordered him to drive away. He wished he could retract that decision. Then there would have been three loose ends instead of seven. He had to include Edgar now. It was just a cost of doing business. Edgar had to know it and wouldn't take it personally.

But Duke was another matter. Duke had betrayed him. Traitors got special treatment. Wally was just stupid, but Duke knew what he was doing. *And he has a girlfriend, or was it a boyfriend?*

"Benny, see if you can find Duke's lover. It might be a man. I want to send a message to Duke."

"Sure, Mr. Cho. No problem. I make some phone calls."

Saturday, July 11

None of the golf bags had faces, but they had legs made of golf clubs. They marched towards him, stirring up a cloud of white powder that eventually landing on the ground as a fine dust. Two of the bags were larger than the others, and were pressing in on him, making it hard to breathe. One grabbed his arm and squeezed, saying, "Mr. Garrity, can you wake up?"

I am awake.

"Mr. Garrity, you're in the hospital. Let's try to wake up."

Oh, no, not again.

"I'm awake." Duke recognized his surroundings from just a few days earlier. *I've got to find a different way to spend my weekends.*

"Mr. Garrity, do you remember me? It's Violet. I was your nurse last weekend when you came in. We've got to stop meeting this way."

"My leg…?"

"Yes, you were shot in the leg. The surgeon removed the bullet, and you're going to be fine. How does it feel?"

"Aches. Throbbing."

"Do you need pain medication?"

Duke nodded, taking stock of his physical condition and surroundings.

"Bathroom," he said.

"I'll help you up. But I'm afraid the officer outside the room will need to unlock your handcuffs. I'll get him."

Duke looked down at his arms, one handcuffed to the bed, the other attached to an IV.

"What day is it? What time is it?"

"It's Saturday morning, about 7:00. I just came on duty." Violet let the officer on guard into the room. The officer was apprehensive about freeing Duke for any reason, but the nurse said, "He needs to try to stand up. Doctor's orders." It was not a subject for discussion, and she held out Duke's arm for the officer to unlock the handcuffs. She then disconnected the IV and handed Duke a crutch.

"Here, take this. Try not to put any weight on the leg just yet. There you go."

Duke winced at the sensation of his leg tearing, and needed the nurse to support him. He was glad he didn't have a cast. That probably meant nothing was broken. He wanted to know what had happened to Cho, Edgar, and Wally. He seemed to recall that Owen had been rescued, or was that just part of his dream? He started to feel faint, and the nurse had him sit on the chair while she made up his bed. She then helped him get his face washed and teeth brushed. He was feeling a little better, but still couldn't make the room stop spinning. The chair was his refuge and he gripped it tightly to help steady himself.

"I'm feeling sick."

"That's probably the anesthetic. It will take a few more hours to wear off. Do you want to stay in the chair or the bed."

"Bed."

"OK, let's get you back in. Then I'll get you your pain medication. I suppose Officer Rubio will insist on the handcuffs again."

"They're fine. I just want to sleep."

Officer Rubio asked, "I'd like to ask you some questions, Mr. Garrity. But first I'll read you your rights."

Duke nodded, wanting to go back to sleep, but he knew he had to make an effort if he was going to get any reprieve from the consequences of his role in Cho's business.

When Officer Rubio finished his monologue, Duke said, "I would like a lawyer."

"You need one."

Duke nodded, jerking at the muscle spasms that shot down his leg. "Look, I'm no angel, but I'll tell you what I know. Once Violet gives me my pain medication, I'm going to be out of it. So, if it's OK with you, can I just start?"

"That depends on what you have to say."

"Fair enough. First off, did you get Cho?"

"No, he is still at large, as well as whoever was with him."

"Shit. This isn't over then. Do you have Owen and Diane under protection?"

"Yes."

"Cho is not going to stop until he finds them, as well as Edgar and me. Wally, too. And even with Edgar in custody, he'll get to him. And the pilot, Diane…"

"He won't get to them. The FBI is in charge."

"The FBI?"

"Yes, and they're going to want to talk to you, too. So, what was it that made you decide to jump ship? A visit from an angel? The Ghost of Christmas Yet to Come?"

"It simply wasn't worth it."

"He didn't pay you enough?"

"It's the medical. And the dental."

"Huh?"

Duke pointed to his leg.

"Dental?"

"You don't want to know. Don't get me wrong. I'm a jerk."

"No argument there."

"I guess it was a girl."

"What girl? Diane?"

"No my girlfriend. I guess that's what she is. *Was*. My girlfriend. I didn't want her to know me as, well…"

"Who's your girlfriend?"

"Erin. She lives in the same apartment complex. Oh, no! They're going to go looking for her. They know I've got someone; actually they think it's a guy. Maybe that's good?"

"Where is she?"

"Moloka'i. Working. Thank God, she's on Moloka'i. I need to call her and tell her to stay there. She can't come back. Where's my cell phone?"

"Where on Moloka'i?"

"A hotel. I was going to meet her there once I got through with…well, that's not going to happen. She's doing research; she's a writer. Look, she needs to stay there. Where's my phone?"

"No phone calls."

"Don't I get one?"

"You need a lawyer."

"This is more important! Can't you see that?" Duke winced in pain, pleading, "You call her, then. Get my cell phone; the nurse must know where it is. It's got her cell number programmed into it. You've got to protect her; isn't that part of your motto—to protect and serve? She is not involved, and she doesn't know anything about this. I've only known her for about a week. But Cho is going to go after everyone I know. See, I betrayed him. That's a death sentence for me and everyone I know. He'll want to send a message."

There was a knock on the door, and Officer Rubio instinctively reached for his gun. But it was only Violet with Duke's pain medication.

"Do you still want this, Mr. Garrity?"

"Yes, please. Violet, can you find my cell phone?"

Violet looked at the officer waiting for him to approve. She injected the medication into Duke's IV, and the pain soon subsided. Duke became woozy, but reached out to Officer Rubio, saying, "Please call her. I know you'll have to tell her things. I've lost her anyway. Erin North is her name. Promise me you'll protect her."

"I'll do what I can. We'll talk later."

Dan and Gabe had been awake since 5:00, not that the five or so hours before that had been restful. Worried about the sisters, neither one had slept well. They met down at the early bird coffee setup by the bar and watched dawn break in the east.

Gabe said, "Think it's too early to call them? It's after seven."

"Let's give them until eight."

"I could kick myself for not insisting on being at the guest house last night."

"I've already kicked myself black and blue," agreed Dan. "I'll see if there's a newspaper around here; I want to see if anyone we know made the front page. Or the obituaries."

"I think I'll head back to the condo after I finish this cup of coffee."

"I'm with you. Oh wait, the parents are up. Here they come. I'd better stick around awhile."

"Yeah, so should I," said Gabe. "But once it's 7:30, I'm calling Diane."

"I'm surprised you want to wait that long." Dan rose to embrace his future in-laws and invited them to sit down. He took their coffee orders and served them, trying to gauge their state of mind. *They're very worried.*

"Have you heard from the girls?" asked Carolyn Donovan.

"We were going to give them until 7:30 before we called them," said Dan, and Carolyn nodded.

"How are you boys?"

"Fine," said Dan. "Worried."

Carolyn nodded again and rubbed her forehead. Her husband took her hand and squeezed it, leaning over to kiss her forehead. Dan reached for his cell phone and started dialing. "7:05; that's close enough." He allowed himself to breathe when Sarah answered.

"Good morning! How's everyone up there?"

"It's quiet, except for the pups. I don't think anything will get past them unnoticed. We just met Frank and Jason's replacements, Greg and Ken. They're patrolling the grounds and the approaching streets."

"Good," said Dan, trying to sound assured. "Your folks are down at the bar with us…"

"Have you all been there all night?" Sarah giggled.

"Yeah, just relishing my last night of freedom," said Dan lightly. "You want to talk to your mom?"

"Yeah, but I forgot to pack the ten extra wedding invitations that are on the dresser. Could you bring them with you? Mom wants them. Is she upset?"

"A little," said Dan, injecting a lilt in his response trying to sound casual. "Here she is."

Carolyn took the phone and spoke to her daughter. When she heard her voice, she started to weep. "I'm sorry; I didn't mean to start crying."

"We're fine, Mom. We really are. Nothing is going to ruin this day for any of us. We've got Greg and Ken to watch over us. Do you want to talk to Diane?"

Carolyn nodded, saying, "Yes. I love you, Sarah, we both do, your father and I. And we'll see you up there around 10:00."

"I love you, too. Here's Diane."

"Hi, Mom," said Diane.

"Good morning, sweetie. Diane, you do what the FBI agents tell you to do. Enough heroics!"

"Of course! I'm not going to do anything stupid. Nothing's going to happen, Mom."

"I'm sure you're right, honey. Well, we love you and we'll see you soon."

"I love you, too. Bye."

Cho was unaccustomed to waiting so long before he could close a deal. But transportation via anything other than car or private boat was too risky. On the road the black van was too easy to spot; he had to assume the woman had seen the license plate. The first thing they had to do was get a different vehicle.

He told himself that he had to be patient; the drug deal would be lucrative enough to allow him to buy a new identity. His wife and children would go along with anything he said, as long as they could escape the authorities who had certainly surrounded the family compound, and perhaps already had a search warrant that granted access. They would have to take a lower priority for the time being. He had no reason to think they were in any danger. They would just have to be patient, too.

"We need another car, Benny."

"I can get one pretty soon," Benny replied and started to make a phone call.

"Good. Thank you, Benny. Have you heard from your friend on Maui yet?"

"Luca think he found Duke's girlfriend. I thought Edgar say it was boyfriend, but it's girlfriend, name Erin."

"And…?"

"She not there."

"Where is she?"

"Luca asking around. He call back. He also try to find Diane woman. She not home. Nobody home. Owen gone, too."

Cho was quiet as he processed the news.

"When we go back to Maui, boss?"

"As soon as we can. We have to go to Hawi first."

"Hawi? I thought we go to Kona to 'play golf.'"

"Yes, but then we have to take a boat back to Maui. It's 100 miles—maybe more—from Kona to Ma'alaea. From Hawi, it's half that."

"Good thinking, Mr. Cho. Harder to find boat, but I'll try. What about drop off? You want we take golf bags back to Maui?"

"No, I want to be rid of them before we leave Hawai'i. I'll call Swan; we'll just have to modify the rendezvous point."

Cho retrieved his cell phone and made a call to his associate, Ricardo Swan. Although he heard only half of the conversation, Benny could tell that Swan was not pleased with the change of plans, and still wanted Cho to meet him in Kona for the drop off. Swan didn't care about Cho's problems with the authorities. The only way Swan would back down was when Cho appealed to Swan's greed for future business by suggesting a compromise.

"Mr. Swan, in the interest of our future business dealings, it is important that I return to Maui as quickly as possible. The current situation makes it impossible for me to fly there. My man and I are planning to take a boat from Hawi to Ma'alaea. Do you have associates in Ma'alaea who can make the exchange? We can meet them there."

Cho listened while Swan first yelled at him for the suggestion, but eventually gave in—for a price.

Swan said, "I believe the price has just come down a bit, Cho Cho? One point five million instead of two."

Cho gasped at the outrageous suggestion and the insulting nickname, but knew that he had little leverage at that point.

"Agreed," he choked, not believing the words coming out of his own mouth. "One point five."

"Then we conclude the deal in Ma'alaea. Keep your cell phone on; I will call you soon with new contact information. How long before you are able to leave Hawi?"

"Just a few hours, depending on when we can get a boat out."

"I'll call you within the hour. I don't need to tell you how disappointed I am with the sudden change of plans. I hope this is not an indication of the way you manage your business dealings. Our relationship depends on knowing exactly what we can expect from one another, wouldn't you agree?"

"Absolutely, Mr. Swan." Cho winced at the words he himself often used in dealings with his own employees. "I appreciate your flexibility; it's something that I've always admired in your style." *Save your scolding for your underlings, Swan,* thought Cho, regaining control.

"I'll wait for your call." Cho hung up, not wanting Swan to have the last word. The $500,000 forfeit was more than enough penance.

Cho turned to Benny and said with forced calm, "It looks like our cargo will be with us on our trip back to Maui."

Benny knew when to stay quiet, since it was clear that Cho was cursing the wasted trip over to Hawai'i, only to be stranded with two—no, 1.5— million dollars worth of cocaine.

"Benny, we'll get breakfast in Honoka'a." *Keep the staff well fed.*

"Sound good, boss. I have car for us, here in fifteen minutes."

"We'll go to Hawi, then we'll go home. Luca will need help."

"You want me call somebody help Luca?"

"No, I want to handle this myself." *If you want something done right, do it yourself. Time to clean house.*

Gabe walked up to his condo, opened the door, picking up the paper lying on the porch. He was startled by the sound of a person approaching close behind him, breathing a sigh of relief when the man continued to walk by. He waved as he saw the man turn into the walkway between the apartment buildings. The man gave a perfunctory nod. *A new neighbor; that's all it is. Relax. Breathe.*

"New neighbor," he forced himself to say casually to Dan, who arrived just after him. "A real charmer."

"At this hour, I'm no Miss Congeniality either."

"You've got a point. I didn't know anyone had sold their place. Maybe he's a renter."

"He looks like a bouncer," said Dan, observing the newcomer out the window. "Which unit is his?"

"Can't tell. He doesn't seem to be heading for any particular apartment."

"Should we be concerned?"

"Before yesterday, I wouldn't have given it a second thought."

"Me neither. We'll take turns keeping an eye out."

Luca was just as startled as Gabe was. He thought it was odd that the man whose apartment he was watching was returning home so early in the morning. Another man soon joined him. Having been seen by his quarry, he no longer had the luxury of observing the apartment from a bench or other exposed location. He needed to talk to Benny to find out what Cho wanted him to do. Cho had given him a big job to find so many people who were all over the island. He would suggest he bring in another man. Surely Cho wanted speedy service; it was just more than Luca could handle alone. He wondered if he should just call in the extra muscle and tell Cho about it later, after the job was done.

No, better just check with Benny.

He dialed Benny's cell phone.

"Benny, Luca here. Say, brah, I'm at the woman's apartment. She not here, just two haoles. Just came home. You want me get some help. It's two guys, good shape. I can probably take them, but…"

Benny interrupted, "Mr. Cho don't want nobody else involved. If you can take them, do it. Call me when it's done. Quiet-like."

"OK, brah."

"What's my new neighbor doing?" asked Gabe.

"He's walking back this way. He's looking around. What do you say we get out of here?"

"Back door, Dan. I'm right behind you."

As they quickly went out the back door, they heard the sound of the front door being kicked open.

"Good call, Gabe. Keep moving. Out to the street. You got your cell? Call 911. Let's head down to the corner. I have a sudden urge to be around a lot of people. Where are all the tourists when you need them?"

Luca cursed when he saw the men scampering down the street. He had perhaps only a couple of minutes before the police would arrive. He checked to make sure the woman wasn't there and noticed suitcases packed in one of the bedrooms. On the dresser was a stack of white envelopes. When he opened one, he started to smile. *Wedding invitation. Reception.*

"Got you. I got you *all*. You're mine!"

Officer Jan Taylor surveyed the destruction at Gabe's condo. The neighbors congregated outside, asking everyone if they knew what was going on.

"Did you get a good look at the perpetrator?" she asked Gabe and Dan.

"We both thought he looked like a bouncer," said Gabe. "Pacific Islander, maybe 30."

"Six foot plus," added Dan. "Probably 250 pounds. Black shirt, black pants."

"Have you ever seen him before?" Both men shook their heads.

Gabe then suddenly remembered, "You know, that Duke fellow that

Diane saw get shot yesterday may know him. He's the guy that one of your buddies is probably guarding at the hospital."

Officer Taylor got on her radio to reach Officer Rubio. After a brief conversation she returned to Dan and Gabe.

"Duke is unconscious. Officer Rubio will question him when he wakes up. In the meantime, I strongly suggest you leave. I'll patrol the grounds while you gather your things."

Dan and Gabe nodded and proceeded to collect their belongings for the day. Dan brought out all the suitcases he and Sarah had already packed, and Gabe brought enough clothes to get by for a few days.

Trying to sound casual, Dan said loudly, "Mom, Dad, I'm moving back in with you! And I'm bringing a roommate."

He grabbed the stack of invitations, dropping them in his rush to be out of there.

There are only nine, he noticed, as he gathered them up. Sarah said ten. Sarah is a math teacher. She knew how to count. She's also a bride. The question remained—was it exactly ten, or ten, plus or minus?

Dan made sure none had dropped behind or under the dresser. He quickly picked up his cell phone and called her.

"Quick question, honey…was it exactly ten invitations or just a stack of about ten?"

"It was exactly ten. Why?"

"I can only find nine."

"I had five for Mom and five for your mom. I'm pretty sure it was ten. But don't worry about it. Is that all? Is everything OK?"

"Are Greg and Ken still there?"

"Of course. Why?"

"Gabe had a break-in here."

"What? Are you OK?"

"We're fine. Officer Taylor is here. You remember her?"

"A real sweetheart. Did they get the guy? Was it Cho? Wait, Diane's hitting me. Hold on, Diane. Everyone's fine. Someone broke in at Gabe's."

Dan said, "Good, Diane is there. Maybe she has seen the guy."

"Here she is."

"Dan? Hi, who was it?"

Dan described the man, but Diane said, "The only guy that I've seen besides Cho and Edgar was the guy driving the van. He was bigger than that, more like 300-plus pounds. Why, do you think he's got something to do with all this?"

"That's what I'm afraid of. Be sure you tell Greg and Ken to be on the lookout for this fellow. I think he knows where you are."

"How?"

"He took one of the wedding invitations."

"Oh, no! Can I talk to Gabe?"

"Sure…here."

Diane yelled, "Get out of there, now, Gabe. These guys are nothing to fool around with. They don't care about anyone."

"We're leaving. Dan's going to the hotel, and I'm heading up to the church as soon as I board up the front door. The Hulk broke it down. Anything you need me to bring? Nail polish? Latest issue of *Soldier of Fortune?*"

"Get out of there!"

"No argument. See you soon. Tell your guards not to shoot the guy in the red shirt. By the way, we're either staying there or at the hotel tonight."

"No, really? Now, go!"

Erin sat on the bed in her Moloka'i hotel room in shock, her cell phone pressed against her chest. She wondered if the phone call from the police was real or if she had imagined it.

How could I have been so naive? Thank God I didn't sleep with him. He's put me in danger now, and I did nothing to deserve it.

The knock at the door startled her, and she froze in terror.

"Ms. North, it's Officer Ian Lawrence. Officer Rubio asked me to look after you. He said he described me to you, so please come to the window."

Erin rose cautiously and approached the window from the side. Five foot nine, medium build, white, balding, six-inch scar on his forearm, he looked like a decent person and not a thug. More importantly he looked like what Officer Rubio said he would look like. He held up his badge, although he was in civilian attire. She unlocked her door, leaving it open.

"Are you OK, Ms. North?"

"Erin."

"Erin, OK. I'm Ian. You don't have to let me in; we can talk from here."

"Ian. No, please come in."

"Officer Rubio suggested that I be in civilian clothes and in an unmarked car."

Erin nodded, still clutching her cell phone, realizing she was shaking. She tried to make a joke of it, saying, "Getting rescued wasn't on my itinerary for this trip."

"My job is to make sure you don't need rescuing. We don't think you are in any immediate danger, but this is not the time to take chances. I'd like us to get acquainted so together we can make this as safe and as comfortable for you as possible. Can I get you a glass of water or something?"

"No, thank you. Would you like some coffee? I just made some."

"Sounds great. Thanks. But before that, I'd ask that you do one thing."

Erin was again startled, but forced herself to reply, "Yes, what is that?"

"Call the local police just to verify that I'm really one of them. Use your phone book there to get the number."

Erin nodded and did as Ian requested. He sat patiently in full view on the chair until she hung up. Again she nodded, allowing herself to set her cell phone down, but still kept one arm wrapped around herself.

Ian broke the silence saying, "Coffee?"

"Coffee, yes! I'll get it. Black?"

"Fine. Erin, do you carry a gun?"

"No."

"Good, I just wanted to know. I do, although I don't plan to use it." He paused before continuing. "Feeling better now?"

"A little. Sorry, I'm still in shock."

"Understandable. I'd like to explore our options, and I want you to know that you have a lot of say in this. As long as you agree to stay on Moloka'i. Going home right now is too dangerous."

Erin nodded in understanding. "OK, shoot. Oh, bad joke. Yes, let's 'explore our options,' as you say."

Gabe drove up to the church slowly, waving at the man walking towards him. "I'm Gabe Callahan. You Greg or Ken?"

"Yes, sir," he said, not clarifying which one he was. "Do you have some identification?"

"Yes," Gabe said as he reached into his back pocket for his driver's license.

"Thank you, Mr. Callahan. Are you carrying any firearms?"

"No."

"Good. The ladies are expecting you. Please park over there."

"Sure, thanks."

Gabe parked as instructed and opened his trunk to retrieve hanging bags and luggage. The Greg/Ken man watched every move he made, but made no effort to help him. *I'm not his job,* thought Gabe. Not wanting to stand around in the open, he briskly walked around to the back of the church property to the guest house. Diane came out both to embrace him and help him with the bags.

"The red shirt is a nice touch; shall I just paint a bull's eye on you?" she laughed nervously.

"My camouflage one was in the wash. Where's the blushing bride?"

"In the rectory with Liliana, who's helping her with her hair. She's got fierceness about her today, very un-bride like."

"She's not the only one," Gabe said, holding her close to him. "No heroics, you hear?"

Diane nodded. "Mom said the same thing, and the same goes for you, you hear?"

"Who me?"

"You, shark hunter." Then she said, "So, you met Greg and Ken?"

"One of them, I don't know which."

"I don't think they know either. Come on, let's take cover."

"Benny, how much longer?" Cho was weary of the heavy waves that assaulted the rickety boat they had chartered for the trip back to Maui. Options were limited for open water craft out of the sleepy village of Hawi. Benny said that he thought the guy who rented him the boat was a ghost.

"Maybe another hour to Kipahulu. We get gas there, and I call Luca."

Cho sighed with exasperation. This was taking too long. And the longer something took, the greater the risk that something could go wrong. If Luca was caught and made a deal with the cops, Ma'alaea would be a trap. Had Cho been wrong to entrust so much to Luca?

He mentally listed all the people who needed to be taken care of, today if at all possible. Duke, Edgar, Wally, HoHo and his wife, the lady pilot and her lover, Duke's girlfriend. Anyone around them would just be collateral damage, part of the cost of cleaning house. When you exterminate rats, sometimes birds and other innocent creatures die, too. It was the way things were, a cost of doing business.

Wedding guests at the church were met by either the Ken/Greg duo or Frank and Jason, who had just arrived to help their colleagues with security. Each person was asked for identification and was asked to vouch for someone else. By now, all guests knew one another. The photographer, florist, and caterer were asked to park up the street so that their comings and goings could be observed. They grumbled at the extra distance they would have to carry their equipment, but they were not given an option. Occupants of all cars driving anywhere near the church were stopped and asked for identification. For this, Thomas and Micah were enlisted to verify identities as well. Alec was charged with keeping watch over the puppies, while letting them lead him around the grounds in surveillance. Attack dogs they were not, but their keen senses and vocal alarm systems added a measure of protection and warning.

An unmarked police car with darkened windows arrived and was directed to pull into the driveway, close to the back door of the church. Owen and Malia quickly emerged and went up the stairs and into the church. All guests were shepherded into the church rather than being allowed to stroll around the grounds.

Sarah watched her guests arrive from the security of the guest house. Her bridesmaids attended to her needs and tried to sway her mood to that of a joyful bride.

Jeannie giggled, "You guys can have your pick as long as I get Greg…or is it Ken? The one with the dark hair."

Stephanie agreed, "If only I wasn't married…"

Diane teased, adding, "And living in Chicago."

Sarah asked, "Can you see Dan out there?"

Diane responded, "I hope not. Gabe was in charge of keeping him away. I think Dan and the rest of the guys are in the rectory."

Sarah shouted, "Look, there are the puppies. I love to watch them play."

Diane admonished her with mock seriousness, "Now is not the time for you to play with them. Here comes Mom, anyway, probably to give you your wedding night instructions. This ought to be good."

All the girls laughed, and Sarah blushed, a fact not missed by Diane. "At last we have a blushing bride! Too bad your bachelorette party hat has lost all its—uh, enhancements. You'll just have to find a substitute."

Jeannie said, "All of a sudden I'm feeling very warm."

"Shall I call Greg in here for some private guard duty?" asked Sarah.

"Oh, would you? Diane, she's not nearly the *prima donna* you said she has been."

Sarah put her hands on her hips and pouted in playful protest for the accusation. "I'm just storing all this away for your trip down the aisle, Diane."

"I'm more the Moloka'i Mule Ride type."

"We'll see, sis. Open the door and let Mom in."

"As you wish," said Diane.

Carolyn Donovan greeted Sarah's bridal party with gasps of admiration. "You all are gorgeous. I see what you mean about Diane's plunging neckline."

"Hey, Mom, at least I have something to plunge; it's your fault anyway. What would you have me do with it?"

Carolyn laughed and the girls broke out in hoots and hollers that got the attention of Gabe outside.

"You all OK?" he called lyrically. "It sounds like cat fight in there."

Diane called, "We're fine. They're just having a joke at my expense. It's always the poor maid of honor who bears the brunt of the teasing."

Carolyn said, "Well, it's almost time, Sarah. All the guests are here. Our cavalry is stationed at all the ambush points, and the pups are on guard. We've got flowers, a caterer, and, oh, the photographer. She wants to get a few shots of you all here. Come on over, Rose."

Rose the photographer gathered the girls into a few poses at the guest house and on the porch. Not to be denied their due attention, the puppies broke loose from Alec and ran over for some affection. The bridesmaids caught them and kept them from Sarah's ivory gown until Alec could corral them again. When he saw Sarah, he gasped.

"Wow, you look…great! I mean…wow!"

"Thank you, Alec. You do, too. And thanks for helping out with perimeter security."

"Oh, sure. No problem."

Sarah felt an inward glow with the first kind word she had heard from Alec in perhaps forever. His reaction was instinctive, which made it all the more special. Perhaps in time they could be friends. It could start today, and that would make the occasion even more memorable.

Carolyn gently called a halt to the photo shoot, announcing, "Here comes your father, ready to walk you down the aisle."

Will Donovan hugged his daughters warmly, asking, "Now, which one am I escorting today? It's clear you're both in love."

"My turn, Dad," said Sarah. "It's practice for Diane's."

"We did well, didn't we Carolyn?" asked Will of his wife. "All right, let's go. I think Brian has Dan at gunpoint, although that's probably not a very funny joke today. Say, who's that over there with Cousin Eddie? Oh, it's that Vanessa girl."

"Vanessa!" exclaimed Diane. "I'd forgotten about her. She and Cousin Eddie…are they holding hands?"

Sarah stopped in her tracks, aghast at the sight of Vanessa with her cousin. "What have they been up to, Diane? Or, should I say, what have you been up to?"

"Who, me? I'll tell you later. I just hope I haven't created a monster, or a cousin-in-law." She then called out to Jason, "It's OK; they're fam…it's OK!"

Sarah continued to stare at her with her mouth open. "This had better be good."

"Apparently it is, just not what I expected. But now that I think about it…" Diane started to giggle.

Carolyn and the bridesmaids met the groomsmen and paired off as assigned. Will and Sarah followed, the bride suddenly preoccupied and walking more slowly.

"You OK, honey?" asked Will.

"Something."

"Something, what?"

"Something's wrong. Something Mom said."

"Do you want me to get her?"

"She's already in; it's probably nothing. I can't put my finger on it."

The organist began to play Bach's *Sheep May Safely Graze,* the signal for Stephanie, Jeannie, and finally Diane to walk down the aisle with Cal, Dan's father, and finally Brian, Dan's Best Man.

But Sarah heard and saw none of it.

"I just remembered! Dad, she said we have a florist, a photographer, and a caterer."

"Yes, so?"

"We don't have a caterer! We're going to the hotel!"

Will felt himself grow faint, and Sarah took hold of his arm, as much for her own support as his. The altar guild woman tending to the logistics in the narthex came over to offer assistance, and Sarah said, "Tell Ken, Greg…tell them all: *there is no caterer!*"

Luca was amazed at how easy it was to gain admittance to the wedding location. A van with a magnetic sign reading "Island Romance Catering—When the Affair Lasts a Lifetime" was almost all he needed. That, together with a mocked up catering order and a real invitation, and he was welcomed with open arms. He parked as instructed, turning his van around so he was parked facing the guards. That way, he could tend to his "catering equipment" in the back of his van without being observed. In fact, there was nothing in his van except his library of magnetic signs for all occasions—pest control, plumber, cable guy, air conditioning repair—along with an assortment of license plates, all with current, albeit counterfeit, tags. The non-descript but well-maintained van would provide a good vantage point from where he could observe the events unfolding. He thought he would recognize Diane from photos at the condo, but he had no idea who the others were on his list. HoHo might be easy to identify because of his reported size, and his wife was probably with him, unless they were still in protective custody. He had to be careful to avoid being sighted by the two men from the condo; the blond guy was probably the groom, since all the photos of Diane were with the other one. Eventually it wouldn't matter who saw him. They wouldn't see him for long.

They're here for the taking. All that's missing is the silver platter. And I'm the caterer.

He removed the white caterer's jacket and checked the weapons tucked into his waistband and leg strap. He decided he might need a silencer on his main weapon in order to dispatch the cops. He watched as all the guests entered the church after being checked by the cops, some of whom were probably FBI or DEA. His pulse started to race when he saw one car pull up directly by the door to the church. Two people emerged and were whisked into the church. *HoHo and his wife.* He felt for the gun in his waistband but stopped himself. *Patience. They're all here. Wait until they're all in the church.*

He put on a thin stocking cap and gloves that would disguise all aspects of his identity except gender and size. White gloves and sunglasses would complete the head-to-toe disguise so that even his eyes would not give away racial features. *Get in, get out, leave nothing of yourself behind.*

Even the shoes he wore for special jobs like this were new, purchased from a discount store that catered to everyone. He put on brand new pair at each job site, so that nothing of his existence could be gleaned from even his footprints. He was a professional, with a reputation that made him a good living and kept him alive. He was more accustomed to having one target at a time, but this was more like having multiples of the same target.

The four cops continued to patrol the grounds, and he suspected that they were relieved once everyone had been ushered inside. Their casual island attire helped them blend into the crowd and put everyone at ease, but Luca knew better than to underestimate their capabilities or what might be hidden under their loose shirts.

Luca watched as the four cops naturally slipped into a standard patrol routine that made it easy to predict where each of them would be at any given time. All he needed to do was to time his movements so that he encountered them one at a time, quietly taking out each one in turn before proceeding to the next. He smiled at the knowledge of how good he was at calculating human behavior and responding as needed.

With a soft pop from his silenced revolver, he brought down the first cop. Quickly he moved the body behind some bushes, surprised at the lack of blood on the man's chest. *Bullet-proof vest. He's simply stunned. No problem.* Luca took easy aim directly at the man's head and fired, but a flash of white from the side startled him and caused the bullet to fly sideways into the bushes. Paco and Lucy dashed at him, tripping him to the ground where they pawed, licked, and chewed their way through Luca's protective clothing. Luca tried to take aim at each of the dogs but couldn't get a shot off while they were chewing on his mask, licking his sunglasses, and stomping on his chest. One of them sniffed his crotch and proceeded to try to claw and chew its way in deeper. He thought he would go deaf at the incessant high-pitched yapping that was a fraction of an inch from his ear. He screamed in pain when sharp puppy teeth impaled the sensitive flesh in his groin.

"If I were you, I'd lie very still." A stern voice ordered him onto his stomach with his hands behind him, but Luca couldn't make out the man because his sunglasses were coated with drool.

"Perhaps you didn't hear me, or don't understand English."

"No, I understand English. Call off the dogs."

"Maybe I will, and maybe I won't. First, on your stomach, hands straight out at your side. My friend here will be searching you, although not in the same way as good old Paco, here. Good boy, Paco. Lucy, could I have that mask, please? Good girl. Although he really is a lot better looking with it on. Oh, look, you scratched the bad man's sunglasses. Tsk tsk, you naughty girl."

Luca cursed silently when the man found not only his primary weapon but the one in his leg strap. He groaned when his arms were brought behind him and cuffed.

Jason informed Luca that he was under arrest and read him his rights. He also told him that he was lucky that he had not killed Greg, because "we have a special plank guys like that get to walk, right over the volcano on the Big Island."

Frank helped Greg to his feet, helping him shake off the shot to his chest and remove his vest. Ken kept his gun on the handcuffed Luca while Jason arranged for transport.

Alec ran around from the other side of the church to see where the dogs he was supposed to have on leash had escaped. Instinctively, Frank started to retrieve his own weapon, but stopped when he saw it was Alec. By then the entire congregation was peering out of the windows and doors to see what had happened.

Not taking his eyes or gun off his prisoner, Ken shouted, "Puppies: One, Asshole: Zero."

Jeannie noticed that it was Greg who had been shot, and she rushed to his side. Frank let her tend to him, knowing he needed no tending at all.

Gabe joined the men, saying, "Yup, that's the guy that broke down my door. Better double up on those cuffs. He's pretty strong. Or maybe we'll just let Paco and Lucy guard him. Owen, Diane, have you ever seen this guy?"

Owen came out to take a good look at him, but said he had never seen him before. Likewise, Diane shook her head, wishing she had. There were still two of them out there.

Frank studied Luca's driver's license, comparing the picture it to the man sitting on the ground. "Luca Corazon, address in Kahului. Well, Mr. Corazon, it looks like your 'Luca' has run out! Who hired you?"

Luca shook his head, saying, "No one, man."

Frank replied, "No surprise there. No one's going to hire someone who gets tripped up by a couple of cute cuddly puppies. Oh, it looks like one of them pee'd on you. Don't you hate it when that happens?"

"I've got his cell phone, Frank!" called out Jason. "And it's still got his recent call log."

Frank said, "Oh Luca, your résumé is getting better all the time. You may turn out to be the best man on our team!"

Diane burst in, slugged him across the face before anyone could stop her. She shouted, "Tell us where Cho is, you jerk! Frank, make him tell us."

Luca glared at her, sizing up her figure from head to toe. He gave her an evil smile and licked his lips.

Frank said, "I suspect that his cell phone log will prove to be very revealing. Here comes the paddy wagon. I'll go with him and see what we can find out. I may come back for the puppies if we need some help. Now, I suggest that you all get back to the happy occasion that brought you here. The other guys will stick around, and we'll get this low life out of the way for you."

George had been standing inside the church with Dan, Sarah, and their parents. He asked them, "Are you ready to try this again?"

Sarah shook her head, "There's no trying; let's do it!"

Dan raised his fist in the air, shouting, "Amen!"

George laughed, saying, "We don't get too much of that in this church. But I have to say, I agree with you! Amen! Everyone, let's gather again for the service…fifteen minutes for us all to collect ourselves."

Sarah said, "I've just appointed one more bridesmaid. Lucy! Come on girl!"

Dan said, "Alec, would you bring Paco over here and hold him? We need all our heroes up here with us."

Upon landing in Kipahulu, Cho debated whether he wanted to take the long road back through Hana or reboard the boat for the trip to Ma'alaea. He knew there was only one answer. The latter would take an hour or two, the former four or more.

Benny said, "Mr. Cho, I got message from Luca. He say 'job done.' He said call him with next order."

"Did he say what he meant by 'job done?'"

"No, Mr. Cho."

Cho recalled his mental list of who comprised 'the job.' Surely Luca couldn't have taken care of all of them. But hopefully HoHo, his wife, Diane, Duke, Duke's girlfriend, Wally, Edgar. Even that was a lot to accomplish unless he just blew up Wailuku.

"Tell him to meet us in Ma'alaea, and to watch for us on the…what's the name of this garbage scow?"

"*Ghost Lady*. Sure thing, Mr. Cho."

Cho picked up his own cell phone and called Swan to let him know where he was and when they could expect to meet in Ma'alaea. Having had no problem taking a flight from Kona to Kahului, Swan was already on Maui, and had gotten over his anger at the change of plans.

Benny said, "Luca say everyone at wedding. Easy like. Hard to hear him, he was near airport, go see Edgar, Duke, and Wally now. Then Ma'alaea."

"Good."

"Mr. Cho, Edgar good brah."

"I know, Benny. I'm sure if Luca can get Edgar out, he will." *No, he won't if he wants to keep his job and his life. Benny had to know this. So did Edgar.*

"Very good, Mr. Corazon. You're getting smarter by the minute," said Frank condescendingly. As a reward, we're going to outfit you with a new set of clothes. Too bad; I'm not sure orange is your color. Officer, don't you have something in blue? No? Mr. Corazon, this officer will assist you. I know that you'll be happy to get out of those dirty things."

When Luca had changed into the prison attire, the officer brought out his old clothes and handed them to Detective Paolo Iglesias, a close physical match to Luca. Detective Iglesias asked Frank, "What made him cooperate?"

"His fingerprints matched those related to an unsolved murder on Moloka'i two years ago. When I pointed that out to him and his attorney, we had the makings of a deal. Don't get me wrong; Luca will never see daylight except through bars until he is well into his 90's. Fortunately for us, he wasn't always so careful about wearing gloves on the job."

"Never underestimate the value of pure luck."

"Are you feeling lucky, today, Paolo?"

"Triple sevens."

"Good. It's a nice day for a visit to Ma'alaea. Go catch up with the rest of the meet-and-greet party. I'll meet you shortly; I have to make a phone call."

Frank dialed the number on his cell phone that he hoped would be answered immediately. He started breathing once he heard the simple "Lawrence."

"Officer Lawrence? This is Agent Frank Browning from the FBI on Maui. I understand you're keeping our lady company."

"Yes, Agent Browning. What's the situation there?"

"Some good news, we think. We have a man in custody who we believe was assigned to your charge, Ms. North, is it?"

"That's her."

"Is she OK?"

"Upset, understandably, but fine. She's here. Do you want to talk to her?"

"Sure."

Ian handed the phone to Erin, who said shakily, "This is Erin."

"Erin, this is Agent Browning from the FBI. You are OK, I hear?"

"Oh, just fine. Never better."

"I'm glad you are safe, and I want you to know that we believe the threat has been eliminated."

"You *believe*...?" said Erin, with a tinge of anger in her voice.

"Yes, the person who had targeted you is in custody. I'd like you to remain on Moloka'i for another day under Officer Lawrence's protection. Is that OK?"

"But what about who hired him? Won't he still be after me? You can't protect me forever!"

"That's why I want you to stay where you are. I will contact you later through Officer Lawrence."

"I don't really have a choice, do I?"

"No ma'am. I won't try to kid you."

"What about Duke?"

"He remains in custody."

Erin was quiet, and Frank asked, "Erin, you still there?"

"Yes. Do you want to talk to Ian?"

"Yes. You take care, OK?"

"Sure, no problem," she said with a touch of sarcasm.

In the narthex at the back of the church, Sarah took her sister aside. "So what's the story with Vanessa and Cousin Eddie?"

Diane winced and said meekly, "Are you sure you want to know? It was sort of wicked. Brilliant, yes. But wicked."

"You're not the one who has to share a town with her."

"Well... I sort of kidnapped them."

"You *what?*"

"Are you sure you don't want to wait to hear this until later?"

"Out with it."

"I sort of left a note in each of their rooms, inviting them to go to Moloka'i..."

"You invited them to go to Moloka'i."

"Well, not me exactly. You sort of invited Cousin Eddie, and Dan sort of invited Vanessa. I even re-wrapped the black nightgown for Eddie to take with him."

"*I* sort of...?"

"And my boss flew them over. Remember how he owed me for making me fly Cho over to Hawai'i, after I said the guy gave me the creeps?"

"Yes, and this is what you came up with."

"And it sort of..."

"Will you quit with the 'sort of'?"

"They apparently made the best of it. Look at them. They're in love. Well, lust anyway. I think your problems with them are over. That is, unless they get married, and then we get to have them both as cousins."

Sarah laughed, "And we get to be aunties to their children. One more vote for a move to Maui! OK, you were right; it was wicked. And brilliant. You still have to be on guard when George asks the thing about 'speak now or forever hold your peace.'"

"Got it covered; I have the gag ready. Now, would you please get married before I fall out of this dress any more than I already have."

"I think you look great! You can do no wrong today, baby sister. Dad, let's go!"

"Better do it, Dad," laughed Diane. "She's the Queen of Hearts, you know."

Will said, "Anything else you remembered you want to tell your mother, Your Majesty?"

"She forgot to tell me about the wedding night!"

"Sorry, daughter, you and Dan will just have to feel your way around."

"Dad!"

"I hear my cue. The sheep are grazing again. I'm heading down the aisle," said Diane, trying to control her giggles.

Alone with her father, Sarah said softly, "I'm glad you're here with me, Dad."

"We're happy for you, sweetie. We hope you'll have a nice boring marriage. You've had enough drama for one lifetime."

She giggled and kissed him, saying, "I love you Dad," and they stepped into the doorway, pausing briefly while the organist switched to Clarke's *Trumpet Voluntary*. George invited the guests to stand. Beaming with happiness, they walked arm in arm down to where Dan reached out to take her hand, relieved to have the woman he had loved almost from the moment they met, next to him as they embarked on their lifelong journey together.

Both turned to face George and Malia, smiling in their most festive of priestly vestments befitting a joyous occasion. George was in a beautiful floral embroidered chasuble, the flowing poncho-like garment worn to celebrate Holy Communion. A similar embroidery theme was extended to Malia's deacon stole, worn over her left shoulder and fastened at her hip on the right side.

George said softly, "I've never seen a happier or more relieved couple." Any butterflies that Sarah had felt subsided when she realized she was among those she loved most in the world.

George began the ceremony, "Dearly beloved: We have come together in the presence of God to witness and bless the joining together of this man and this woman in Holy Matrimony..."

At the point where George called out to the congregation, "If any of you can show just cause why they may not lawfully be married, speak now; or else for ever hold your peace," Sarah glanced over at Diane, who had a white handkerchief discreetly tucked within her bouquet, as well as a determined smile on her face. Sarah glanced back at Dan with a knowing smile, and George continued.

George took the leather bound New Testament and moved into the midst of the congregation for the gospel reading from Matthew.

[Jesus said] *everyone then who hears these words of mine and acts on them will be like a wise man who built his house on rock. The rain fell, the floods came, and the winds blew and beat on that house, but it did not fall, because it had been founded on rock. And everyone who hears these words of mine and does not act on them will be like a foolish man who built his house on sand. The rain fell, and the floods came, and the winds blew and beat against that house, and it fell—and great was its fall!*

Sarah looked at Dan, realizing that their chosen gospel reading had taken on a special meaning today. George then addressed the couple.

"Sarah, Dan, you've done well. Your house is built on a solid foundation. Look around you; you have everything that you need. Your family, your friends, the love of God, and the love of each other. Perfect weather, perfect flowers, perfect hair, the FBI, puppies…" George paused to let everyone enjoy the joke. "And when it rains, the flowers dry up, the hair—well, Dan, sorry, but I've seen your father—remember the foundation that is present here today. It's not going away. There's no such thing as a perfect wedding, although I'd say we're already aware of that. But everything that is important to the marriage is as permanent as can be. Your house is built on a solid foundation. Keep the paint fresh, the lawn mowed, and the roof intact. The rest of it is secure. It's God's gift to you today as you celebrate your partnership."

George continued through the exchange of marriage vows, the exchange of rings, the blessing, and the exchange of the peace between the newly married couple and with their friends and family. He and Malia then moved to the altar to preside at Communion, inviting all present to share in the bread and wine that Sarah and Dan had carried forward to the altar for blessing.

Upon the conclusion of Communion, George gave the final blessing, and the organist launched into Widor's lively *Toccata.* Dan and Sarah turned to the smiling congregation and began their recessional to the applause of their family and friends. The puppies barked joyfully, finally allowed to run freely down the aisle and out to the lawn where they romped on the spacious lawn, happy to be let loose in the sunshine.

Cho had never been so glad to see a place as he was to see Ma'alaea Harbor at last. The sound of *Lady Ghost's* old motor would rumble in his ears for days. With binoculars he scanned the harbor to make sure there was no unexpected welcome party. Satisfied with what he did not see— Coast Guard, Police, FBI, DEA, or even IRS—as much as what he did see—fishing boats, dive boats, sailboats, and party boats, he handed the binoculars to Benny.

"Do you see Luca?"

"I'll look, Mr. Cho. I see Swan. No Luca, tho'."

"Good. I'd like to be done with this in five minutes."

"Me, too, Mr. Cho. Oh, that be Luca over there. He hiding some. He wave."

"Is he alone?"

"He always alone."

"I like him already." Cho was glad to have Luca in reserve in case Swan tried to amend the terms of the deal again. "Let him stay in hiding unless we need him."

Benny and Cho checked to make sure their guns were concealed but accessible under their aloha shirts. It was important to look like they belonged at Ma'alaea Harbor.

"Smile, Benny. You're on Maui with the rest of the tourists."

"I smiling, Mr. Cho. Money make Benny smile."

Frank felt a rush of adrenaline when he saw the *Lady Ghost* approach Ma'alaea Harbor. He had no reason to expect it wouldn't arrive. An unmarked police helicopter had made two casual passes over the shoreline confirming the *Lady Ghost* was on its way. It was tempting to have the Coast Guard apprehend it at sea, but the drug cache was only half the booty. Luca hadn't known who Cho was meeting, so Frank had to wait until all parties were in place. A dozen police and agents in civilian attire moved about in ways befitting their undercover roles as tourists, fishermen, and guides. Frank would have liked to evacuate the harbor, but he didn't want to lose the opportunity to apprehend Cho's partner. He liked to tie up loose ends. His team was highly skilled in covert operations in populated areas. He wanted everyone alive if at all possible. There was no telling how deep the business went, and the dead can't talk.

Two of the "fishermen" carried an empty ice chest over to the dock where Cho would tie up, and boarded a boat where they quickly went below. Frank continued his surveillance of the harbor from his truck bed trying to identify Cho's partner. The Pacific Islander with three sons was a possibility, but they were occupied with cleaning large fish they had caught. A slippery business, it was unlikely they were involved. A shuttle bus arrived, and a uniformed driver emerged, lighting a cigarette. He appeared to be waiting for a group returning from a sailing or fishing excursion. Frank signaled two of the "tourists" to keep watch over him. A family with two small children drove up, and Frank cursed. He decided to risk breaking cover to get them to leave the area. One of the soft drink vendors saw them, too, and signaled Frank that she would take care of it.

She took two shave ices over to the family and instructed them to leave quietly. Frank held his breath in a silent prayer that the mother wouldn't scream, and he exhaled in relief when he saw them drive off.

Held together with duct tape, bumper stickers, and at least a decade of bird droppings, the classic Maui cruiser pulled into the parking lot. Twenty years earlier the car had been red, but there was little left of the paint, much less chrome. Its recycle value was worth more than its resale value and made it essentially theft proof. Its value today was in the oversized trunk that was typical of American cars of twenty and thirty years ago.

Two well-dressed tourists got out, one a Hispanic man, one an auburn haired woman. The woman loosened a thick rope holding the trunk closed, but did not open the lid. The Hispanic man brushed the dust off his trousers and straightened his shirt. He leaned over to his rearview mirror to check his hair and teeth. No words were exchanged. Neither smiled or gave any indication of an intimate relationship. The man walked to the dock while the woman stood outside the car. It was apparent to Frank that her job was to watch for any sign of the authorities. If she had to drive away to avoid getting caught, so be it. A backup rendezvous point had certainly been prearranged.

Frank caught the eyes of his team and all nodded slightly. Timing was critical to minimize physical risk to his team and innocent civilians, and loss of either the drugs or the money, not to mention the suspects.

I want them all, thought Frank. *Alive, preferably, but I'll take them any way I can get them.*

Continuing their assigned charades, the agents and the police nevertheless gave careful attention to their prey. Frank silently willed each agent not to assume that the man was in charge, although it seemed likely.

Swan liked public places, particularly those where there was a lot of activity and unknowing civilians. It was unlikely that the police were there; very few people had been involved in this deal, and all indications were that the next steps would be successful and routine.

He waved to Cho standing on the dock, and the two greeted one another with hugs and smiles like long lost friends. They embarked on an innocent conversation that would remove suspicion from any eavesdropping bystanders.

"Good trip, my friend?"

"A little choppy, but fine. Have you been waiting long?"

"Just got here."

"How's your wife?"

"She's fine—come meet her."

"Excellent, Alonzo. I don't think you've met my friend Pedro. Pedro, this is Alonzo."

Benny and Swan exchanged smiles and shook hands warmly.

Swan asked, "Do you need help with your golf clubs?"

"That would be very nice, Alonzo. We brought along quite a few."

"As I expected, old friend."

"If we each take two, then Ben—Pedro will just come back to get the other two."

"Eight golf bags, old friend! You think having more will improve your game?" teased Swan.

"You never know. I'm feeling lucky."

"So am I, old friend."

Benny brought out two bags at a time and handed them to Cho and Swan, and finally carried two bags himself. They walked over to Swan's car, and the woman greeted them with newfound charm. Swan introduced her, and she opened the trunk to pull out two satchels to make room for six of the golf bags. Swan hoped the other two would fit in the open back seat. Benny went back to the *Ghost Lady* to retrieve the last two bags.

Swan and Cho gave their attention to the contents of the satchels while the woman examined one of the golf bags to verify its contents. She nodded, as did Cho. Swan and Cho turned, expecting to see Benny approaching with the final two bags, but the big man was nowhere in sight.

Frank's team noticed their two "fishermen" standing on the boat, giving a "thumbs up" signal. Frank nodded to the rest of the team, who proceeded to expose their hanging badges with one hand and their weapons with the other. In an instant Cho, Swan, and the woman were approached and surrounded by agents.

Both Swan and Cho pulled out guns, but before they could get a shot off, they were felled by two well-placed but non-fatal shots by the soft drink vendor. Cho's right hand was bleeding, and Swan grabbed his shoulder in pain.

"Still feeling lucky?" challenged Frank, kicking Cho's and Swan's firearms towards the waiting hands of another agent, who promptly unloaded and secured them. "Nice shooting, Agent Dobber! Maybe you won't have to spend your entire FBI career selling soft drinks. Too bad your aim was off. Looks like it was not your day to die, Cho. So I'll ask again: are you still feeling lucky?"

Cho looked up from the ground over at the boat and felt his stomach sink when he saw two men standing on deck waving.

In a last hopeful attempt to salvage the deal, Swan protested, "You have no right to do this. We're just tourists out playing golf. How dare you shoot us! You are just a band of thugs who prey on innocent people."

The woman started screaming, "You shot my husband, you bitch! Ricardo, I'm here, sweetie. What were you thinking, standing up to these guys? Ricardo, don't die on me! Can't you see they need medical attention—call 911!"

"Lady, the act won't sell with us," said Frank dryly. "But keep screaming, we'll wait until you're done, and then maybe we'll call 911."

Benny was brought over to the gathering handcuffed and tightly controlled by the fishermen. 'Luca' appeared from his observation post, and Benny shouted, "Luca! Hey, you not Luca!"

Frank said, "You're right, Benny. This is Detective Iglesias. He's a 'Lucalike!' Pretty good, huh, Benny? I'm really a very funny guy. And I'm glad you're here with us, Benny, so I only have to say this once. You are *all* under arrest..."

"Do you remember what song was playing the first time we danced?" Sarah glided over the stone lanai in the arms of her husband.

"Let's see. It was on the riverboat at the costume party. 'Sweet Georgia Brown?'"

Sarah shook her head.

Dan frowned, saying, "I can name all 206 bones in the human body. I don't suppose that counts, Mrs. Weatherby. I know... 'When the Saints Go Marching In?'"

Sarah sighed and shook her head, "I guess the romance is gone already."

"Come on, give me another chance. I could use Gabe's stock answer for everything, humuhumu... Oh, give me a hint."

"Isn't it Chicago's official song? About a cow…and a fire…come on, that should be enough of a hint!"

"'A Hot Time in the Old Town Tonight!' How could I forget?"

Sarah giggled, "You remembered!"

"How could I forget? It's our song. So appropriate."

"Oh, look, Jeannie and Greg are dancing. They're coming over to us."

Greg said, "I just got a call from Frank. Everyone is safe, and they were able to catch Cho, Benny, and the guys they were meeting. They got the drugs and the money. So Ken, Jason, and I will be leaving you soon."

Jeannie exclaimed, "Oh, can't you stay for the rest of the reception?"

Sarah agreed, "Yes, please. We'd like you to stay if you can."

Greg looked over at Ken and Jason, who motioned for him to stay, while they waved good-bye. It was not their style to call attention to their comings and goings. He nodded, and Jeannie said, "Great!"

Diane and Gabe approached Sarah and heard the good news. Sarah asked Gabe, "Would you make an announcement to the guests? I'm sure that would be a relief for everyone. And then we have a musical request."

"Certainly, Mrs. Weatherby. Your wish is my…"

"Oh, brother!" said Sarah, rolling her eyes.

"Someday, Mrs. Weatherby."

After Gabe let the partygoers know that the FBI had everyone in custody, he and Diane danced over to Sarah and Dan. Diane said, "Check out Cousin Eddie and Vanessa. It's a match made in heaven…or something. I'm a genius. Oh, Mom is signaling that it's time to cut the cake. Then we have the bouquet, and the garter, and then I think we should all change into bathing suits and go for a swim."

Dan offered, "Great idea…we'll be on Lana'i. Come on over."

"Speaking of Lana'i, when is your boss coming to fly us off into the sunset?" asked Sarah.

"About 5:00. Come on, I want some cake! Then I want the bouquet."

"I think you're going to have some competition."

Diane spit into her hands and assumed a ball catching posture, adding, "Bring it on. I'm ready for you, Vanessa. I think you know by now that I'm nothing to mess with."

Epilogue
Sunday, July 12

Owen and Malia stared at the pathetic little man held behind bars at the jail.

"I should forgive Wally," said Malia.

"Why?" asked Owen, in disbelief. "He made his own choices. He was greedy and uncaring, and he almost killed us both, Principal Crockett, too."

"True. I just don't want his actions to change who I am. Or you either. I don't want to be angry anymore."

Owen brought his wife close to him and kissed the top of her head. He said softly, "Me neither."

Duke could hardly believe his eyes, and at first he thought he was having another one of his medication induced hallucinations. He awoke to see Erin standing next to his bed with Officer Rubio standing close behind. Handcuffs and leg straps still kept Duke from moving too much. He was a caged animal, wounded and at the mercy of those tending to him.

"Duke," called Erin without emotion.

"Erin," he replied hoarsely.

"Why?"

Duke shook his head weakly, finally turning back, saying, "I'm sorry."

"Uh-huh. Why? Was it the money?"

Duke nodded.

"You lied to me. Was anything you told me the truth?"

"Everything that was important."

"You almost got me killed. That Luca man had my name on a list."

"I hear they got him."

"No thanks to you."

Officer Rubio interrupted, "Actually it was thanks to him."

"How so?" asked Erin skeptically.

"I made a deal, so it's not like I'm a hero or anything. I told them about Cho and Edgar and Benny. I never said anything about you. I tried to protect you, but there's no protection from these guys."

"You're right. You're no hero."

"It's like the sand castles."

"What sand castles?"

"You said it yourself, about how people build sand castles in their lives, but when things get tough, the sand castles can't hold up. The more you try to keep it standing, the more it falls down around you. But if all you have is a sand castle, you're stuck. I tried to wash it off, but that made it worse. And it was starting to stick to you. I tried not to let that happen. Does any of this make sense? I'm through with sand castles. I hope you can forgive me someday. I'll understand if you can't."

"I didn't know you remembered… Officer Rubio, what's going to happen to him?"

"That depends on the District Attorney, the value he places on Duke's testimony."

"Do you have a lawyer, Duke?"

Duke nodded.

Silence filled the room for a minute. Erin finally said, "Maybe I'll come see you again. I hope your leg gets better."

"Thank you. I'm glad you're safe."

"Yes, I'm safe. Good bye, Duke."

"Has it been 30 minutes yet?" asked Dan. "You know I don't want to get burned."

"Are you anxious to go back inside?" teased Sarah, checking the sun's effects on her own skin as well as Dan's.

"Only if you are. I trust your judgment in all the most important matters."

"Could I get that in writing?"

"I think you did that yesterday."

"Perhaps I did." She was silent for a minute and then asked, "When do you think we'll get to come back to Hawai'i?"

"Not soon enough. Thanksgiving maybe. You can come back sooner if you want to see Diane."

"Trying to get rid of me already? I've been apart from you too long as it is." She paused before continuing, "I do feel at home here. I had never lived anywhere but St. Louis when I moved here in April. I can make Chicago my home just as easily; you're my home now. As long as I'm with you, that's really all that matters."

"I know it will be hard. You've already made so many friends here— the police, the FBI, an assassin or two, a drug addict…"

"Hey, that wasn't Owen's fault! And he's not an addict anymore!" Sarah flicked an ice chip at his chest, where it melted quickly. "OK, time's up. Let's take cover."

"The queen has spoken. Say, have I told you today how beautiful you are?"

"I don't think so. No, I'm pretty sure you haven't."

"Well, you are."

"You make me feel that way. I love you."

"Oh, good. That makes us even. I love you, too."

A blaze of pink and gold shot across the sky as the sun set on another day in Hawai'i. Dan and Sarah strolled lazily on the beach in no hurry to be anywhere.

Sarah said, "I love the way the sand feels between my toes when it starts to cool off at the end of the day."

"I'll get you a sand box for our deck at home. I'll put a little palm tree on it, and a pail and a shovel so you can build your own sand castle."

"You'd do that for me?"

"Of course. Just don't tell George. Not after his warning to us about sand castles!"

"Our secret," Sarah laughed, taking hold of Dan's arm when a wave caused her to lose her balance.

They continued to walk in silence, listening to the surf, the breeze, and the sound of their own breathing. Then Dan started singing, "There be a hot time in the old town tonight…"